A COURAGE UNDIMMED

Books by Stephanie Graves

OLIVE BRIGHT, PIGEONEER

A VALIANT DECEIT

A COURAGE UNDIMMED

Published by Kensington Publishing Corp.

A COURAGE UNDIMMED

Stephanie Graves

KENSINGTON
PUBLISHING CORP.

www.kensingtonbooks.com

KENSINGTON BOOKS are published by

Kensington Publishing Corp.
119 West 40th Street
New York, NY 10018

All Kensington titles, imprints and distributed lines are available at special quantity discounts for bulk purchases for sales promotion, premiums, fund-raising, educational or institutional use.

Special book excerpts or customized printings can also be created to fit specific needs. For details, write or phone the office of the Kensington Special Sales Manager: Kensington Publishing Corp., 119 West 40th Street, New York, NY, 10018. Attn. Special Sales Department. Phone: 1-800-221-2647.

The K with book logo Reg. U.S. Pat. & Tm. Off.

Library of Congress Card Catalogue Number: 2022945835

ISBN-13: 978-1-4967-3153-1

First Kensington Hardcover Edition: February 2023

ISBN-13: 978-1-4967-3159-3 (ebook)

10 9 8 7 6 5 4 3 2 1

Printed in the United States of America

To the victims of the reprisals triggered by Operation Anthropoid, particularly the villagers of Lidice and Ležáky, and to the families of the paratroopers involved.

and

To my grandfather, Thomas H. Gibbons, who served in the Philippines during World War II and shared a name (near enough) with the pigeon-focused SOE operation mentioned herein.

IT IS A BRAVE THING TO HAVE COURAGE TO BE AN INDIVIDUAL.
—Eleanor Roosevelt

YOU WHO HAVE MURDERED SLEEP SHALL SLEEP NO MORE,
AND SHALL, WHO WROUGHT BY TERROR, BE AFRAID.
—Mary Stewart, from "Lidice"

The chapter titles in this work are pulled from a special training school syllabus of the Special Operations Executive (code name: Baker Street).

4 November 1941
RAF Elsham Wolds
Lincolnshire

Dearest Olive,

 It's taken me far too long to write, and while I could, quite easily, blame this bloody war, that doesn't quite cover it. I realise it's a bit of the pot and kettle, but seeing you with your captain came over a bit of a shock, and I've just been taking it in. I daresay you might have felt the same, faced with Bridget. You and I have been thick as thieves for so long, anyone else seems rather a sore thumb. I could see the way you looked at him, though—all soft round the edges. I didn't know you had it in you, my girl, but I suppose it's merely been lying in wait. Best of luck reining in your bossy tendencies, because your captain didn't look the type to let you run herd on him. Though if he's smitten, all bets are off.

 As for me, operational training has been a bit of a mad rush, getting us ready for frontline duties. I've been assigned to Bomber Command, flying a Vickers Wellington, and I admit, after all these months, I'm spoiling for a fight. The rest of the boys in the crew feel just as I do. Besides me, there's Teddy, the romantic, Oscar, the hooligan, Sterling, the peacekeeper, Gerald, the mechanic, and Jack, the brains of our outfit. Then there's the favourite of the whole crew: Shackleton, the pigeon. He's an upstanding fellow—blue chequered, with a broad chest and strong wings—and we're glad to have him aboard. We hope never to have to depend on him, but the birds' track record thus far in this bloody war was enough to have Bomber Command insisting on a pigeon on every flight. (And I'm counting on the St Christopher medal you gave me as further backup.)

 I'll endeavour to be as careful as I can, but we're all chomping at the bit to get into the fray. I happen to know you feel the same, and while you may be frustrated, I'm relieved not to have to worry about you in the thick of it all.

Your devoted,
George

P.S. Don't go looking for dead bodies. You deserve a break from that sort of ghastly business, and Pipley is a small village. At the rate things are going, there'll be no one left to celebrate my home-coming.

Chapter 1
Observation

6 November 1941
Station XVII, Brickendonbury Manor

The flakes of snow melted the moment they struck the windscreen, and the wipers smeared the wetness into oily streaks. Olive groaned in frustration. The moon was bright and nearly full, but clouds scudded maddeningly across it. It was difficult enough to drive at night in good weather, the anaemic beam of the masked headlamps demanding she hunch over the steering wheel, squinting into the oncoming darkness. But in bad weather, it was an ordeal. Add to that the fact that she was shivering with cold, and the car noisy with the sounds of the wind in wild tumult, and the drive was bloody miserable.

"Ma mère était anglaise. Elle est morte avant la guerre."

She was getting better, she could tell, but French certainly didn't come naturally to her. Her schoolgirl lessons were long forgotten, apart from a motley collection of words that hung in her memory, like the bracket fungus that encircled the beech trees in Balls Wood. But repeating the same words over and over—all of it an imagined cover story culled from the truth—pulled her thoughts in a direction they preferred not to go. *My mother was English. She died before the war.* She wasn't even certain she'd ever need any of it. All the more reason to take a break from her self-imposed practicing.

It had been more than an hour since she'd left the Firs, the Baker Street facility in Whitchurch, Buckinghamshire, dedicated to the development of explosives. The drive over had been comparatively pleasant. The weak autumn sun had given the sky a pearly glow, and the Austin had seemed much cosier with two additional occupants, particularly given their chatty dispositions.

The commanding officer of Station XVII, Major Boom, had been due for a transfer. He'd fractured his leg back in July, the injury a result of a parachute jump standard for all agents enrolled in the special training school and recommended for all officers. Ever since, he'd struggled a bit with the day-to-day operations at Brickendonbury Manor. At the Firs, he could hole up in his office and get back to the work of designing clever—and quite devastating—devices to sabotage the Nazi war machine. Liz was going with him.

Her fellow FANY was eager to be making a fresh start, free of the stigma of a certain indiscretion. Liz was clever, efficient, and a hard worker, and while Olive was sad to see her go, Jamie, she was certain, would be much relieved.

The situation was rather confounded.

By the time Olive had arrived at the manor the previous spring, she'd discovered that Captain Jameson Aldridge was the object not only of her *own* contrived romantic cover story but of Liz's very real aspirations, as well. When Jamie had approached Olive on behalf of Baker Street to supply birds for ongoing missions into occupied Europe, he'd made it clear that her role as pigeoneer would be contingent on secrecy. Not even her family could know what she was doing, or who he really was. Off the cuff, a burgeoning romantic entanglement between the pair had seemed a perfect solution: it would justify Jamie's presence at Blackcap

Lodge and in the dovecote and quell village gossip. Unfortunately, things weren't quite as cut and dried as Olive had imagined. Whereas Liz had been infatuated with the man's Irish good looks, broad shoulders, and air of competence, Olive had been subjected to the full gamut of his more frustrating qualities, a fact that had, bafflingly, led to a twinge of jealousy in the other FANY.

Suffice it to say that it was best for everyone that Liz was going.

They'd said their goodbyes, and Olive, never one to miss an opportunity to dispatch her birds on a training mission, had released a pair of them into the sky on the lawn of the Firs. With a vigorous flapping, they'd launched themselves straight upwards into the sky and banked in widening circles, their bodies dark against the waning light. Once they'd got their bearings, they'd flown with single-minded intention, eager to reach home before dark.

Olive, in turn, had climbed into the car to trundle the Austin back over the ever-darkening lanes. At first, she'd been content to be out alone in the gloaming, watching birds swoop through the skies and rodents scurry into the hedgerows, collecting a few final titbits for dinner. She'd dutifully practiced her French for a time, peppering in plenty of curses when the grammar eluded her, but then the weather had turned, growing blustery and wet, requiring focused concentration. Visibility extended just beyond the bonnet of the car, and she spent the rest of the journey worried over hitting something—or someone—in the dark.

When, finally, she turned the car onto Morgan's Walk, she sat back and breathed a gusty sigh of relief. The long line of old-growth trees bordered her favourite approach to Brickendonbury Manor. She'd soon return the Austin, to face the unpleasant task of driving the Welbike home. As much as she loved the freedom afforded by the little motorbike, she'd come to dread the wet, chilly rides.

Perhaps I can get Jamie to drive me home.

Olive was smiling to herself, considering the prospect of con-vincing him, when something moved in the darkness ahead of her. As her pulse set to thrumming in her throat, she stamped hard on the brake pedal. Two shadows detached themselves from the wide swath of darkness just beyond the reach of the Austin's headlamps. Olive's eyes were wide as the car shuddered to a stop, but she tempered her instinctive panic. It was surely just a pair of red deer.

But as she squinted to see past the fog on the windscreen, and the unpleasant weather beyond, peering through the pale light, the truth hit her like a thump to the chest. These shadows were no deer; they were carrying Sten guns. Even amid the swirling flakes of snow, Olive could clearly make out the weapons and the silhouettes of the men who held them with deadly intent. Pointed directly at her.

Shock whipped through her, but quick on its heels came calm calculation. As a FANY working at Station XVII, she was, of ne-cessity, aware of nearly everything that went on, on the manor grounds. That was not to say that she was let in on highly classi-fied intelligence, but merely that it was her job—along with the rest of the FANYs—to ensure that the day-to-day running of things went off without a hitch. And yet she could think of no justifiable explanation for the situation that now confronted her. Particularly given that hers was a familiar face. Though, at the moment, she *was* bundled quite thoroughly in a knit hat and scarf. It simply didn't make any sense.

While trainees were schooled in silent killing and hand-to-hand combat, there was no formal weapons training at the manor, although Lieutenant Danny Tierney was known to give the agents a lesson in his own brand of knife fighting. Everything else in that vein was part of the syllabus of the paramilitary train-ing undertaken at Arisaig House in Scotland. Olive had only ever come into contact with guns when she was packing the crates for an upcoming mission.

She squinted into the darkness, trying to make out the men's features, desperate for a shared flicker of recognition that would calm her racing heart and lower their guns. But it was too dark, and they came on, unchecked.

Olive's hand hovered over the gearstick. Should she take her chances reversing the Austin back down the lane or go forward, toward the guns? Either way, they were bound to shoot. And then she remembered Major Boom's parting gift. When he'd tucked it carefully into her hand, she'd thought it sweet but rather absurd, but her feelings for the object changed in the flicker of a heartbeat, the brutishness of a moment. If there was ever a time to use it, it was right this moment.

She glanced at it, sitting innocently on the seat beside her, then snatched it up and levered open the offside door. Crouching behind it, she peered closely at the object in her hand. And then it was done. The quick twist of her fingers seemed to break the awful stillness as a shout hurtled out of the darkness.

"Olive . . . don't!"

She knew that exasperated voice, and even those words, quite well. It was Jamie. And while the sound warmed the tight twist of cold and fear that had spread through her insides, it was too late to undo what she'd done.

She could hear the ticking now, muffled and ominous, and her eyes squinted hard, a wrinkle of worry furrowing between her brows. She couldn't see Jamie, but the men stood on the lane before her, their guns lowered, their flat caps pulled low over their eyes as they glanced round in apparent confusion. They were talking rapidly in muted tones, but not in English. It was difficult to keep the jumble of languages straight. Station XVII had trained men from all over Europe—Poland, Czechoslovakia, Norway, France, Belgium.

Her arm, weighted with responsibility, hung heavy at her side, a foreign object.

Then, suddenly, there was a flurry of movement. Men were emerging from the trees all round her.

"You've armed it, haven't you?" Jamie yelled, sounding eerie in the dark.

Olive stared down at the little device in her hand. "A new invention," Major Boom had said. An easy-to-arm, compact device, packed with a powerful explosive. She glanced up again to see Jamie's solid bulk barrelling out of the darkness, coming into focus in the dim light of the headlamps, the length of him haloed with freezing mist. He must have seen the answer on her face.

"Get rid of it, damn it!" He'd almost reached her when she turned and lobbed the little handful straight into the sodden darkness that ran along the lane.

Two seconds ticked past. Long enough for Jamie to yell, "Take cover!" Long enough for Olive to trace the shadowy outline of the trees, stunned into immobility and silence. Long enough for Jamie to reach her, push her onto the Austin's front seat, and throw himself on top of her.

The sound was immense, crashing over them, coursing through their bodies with teeth-rattling vibrations. The heat was quick on its heels, a bonfire, taking flame like magic, and Olive cowered on a wave of shock. Five seconds more, and the damage was done, the moment fizzling in the darkness, little fires burning quite merrily in the aftermath.

She felt Jamie's deep sigh, his chest pressed against her side, just before he levered himself off her. With his arms propped on either side of her body, he stared down into her flushed face.

"Don't you dare lecture me, Jamie," she said quietly, conscious of the fact that just beyond the confines of the Austin, men were waiting, eager for an explanation. Well, she'd bloody well like one, too. "When Major Boom gave that thing to me, he said a moment would come when it would be the only option." She speared him with a glare. "I decided that having two strange men armed with Sten guns charge me in the dark was that moment." It was a bit difficult, but she managed to shift enough on the seat to cross her arms over her chest. "Now," she said sweetly, "perhaps you'd like to tell me what's going on here?"

"No," he said shortly. "I wouldn't." Before she could even muster her outrage, his gaze flicked toward the Austin's back window. It seemed a second car had approached and was idling some distance behind them. "Right on time," he muttered.

As she arched up to look back, someone barked an impatient "Aldridge." Together, they turned to peer out the front windscreen, no doubt presenting somewhat of a compromising position. When her eyes focused on the looming, overcoated presence of the new CO, she promptly slumped back onto the chilly seat and let her eyes shutter closed.

Scrambling up, Jamie said in an undertone, "Let me do the talking. He doesn't look at all pleased, and you're about to have to explain why there's now a pass-through in the trees lining the drive."

Olive had yet to cross paths with the CO; she had, in fact, been dreading it. It was clear from glimpses and snippets that he was nothing like Major Boom, and he seemed the sort of disapproving curmudgeon to clash with her more imaginative tendencies. Tall and lanky, he was serious to a fault and sparing with words, often to the point of rudeness. He was evidently a genius, with a sixth sense for machines, and thus precisely the man to take over the running of Station XVII, Baker Street's school for industrial sabotage.

His code name was Major Blighty. A bit grand, perhaps, as the latter bit had long been the nickname used for Britain itself. But the man was imperious, lording it over them all with a stern word and a tight jaw, and it was his job to lead the charge in blighting the Nazi war machine. She felt his blight in other ways, too. So, really, the code name was perfect.

Olive had yet to see him smile, and she'd heard that he disapproved of women working for the war effort, particularly the FANYs stationed at the manor, who had their "fingers in every pie."

Her jaw tightened merely thinking of it. Of course they did. Because if they bloody well didn't, the place would be in shambles, everything misplaced or shunted aside. The FANYs—like women everywhere—did the dirty work and dealt in the details. And the CO would find he didn't have a bit of choice in the matter.

Olive didn't like dealing with men of his ilk, but she didn't shy away from it. Even now, her heartbeat still racing, her lips chapped, her uniform wrinkled, and her pride somewhat chafed, she stiffened, pressed her lips together, and took a steadying breath.

Jamie helped her up and out of the car, so she was tugging at the hem of her tunic when the CO charged up beside the Austin. His gaze, flicking over her, while furious, still managed to be dismissive. Olive bristled. She *had* just crashed their little party and detonated an explosive, whose residual flames were licking along the branches of several trees, casting a warm glow over the whole awkward proceedings. Not that she'd meant to, but this was precisely the sort of thing that happened when women were deliberately kept in the dark. Jamie nudged her with his elbow, obviously sensing temper, and she focused on breathing the frigid night air in through her nose.

The CO's thatch-coloured hair glinted atop the deep wrinkles in his forehead, and his cold grey eyes zeroed in on Jamie.

"Don't tell me she's one of ours?" he demanded.

"This is Olive Bright, sir, FANY and pigeoneer." Olive glanced at Jamie, startled by the defensive respect in his voice.

"Hmph." Olive couldn't decide whether to take offence before he was speaking again. "What is she doing out here"—his gaze arrowed to the destruction just beyond the road—"meddling in a top-secret operation?" Olive sucked in her breath, ready to leap to her own defence, but once again Jamie's elbow connected, forestalling her response.

"She was assigned as the driver to take Major Boom to the Toyshop." Olive nearly snorted. Officially known as MD1, or Ministry of Defence 1, the Firs produced diabolically lethal weapons. Only a man would think to call them toys. "No doubt the road was a bit tricky in the dark with this weather." He made a show of checking his watch. "I'd assumed she'd returned long ago and gone home. I should have confirmed it."

"What sort of operation has armed men ambushing cars in the lane?" Olive demanded, before belatedly adding, "Sir."

"None of your concern," the CO said shortly. "You are support staff and haven't clearance for details." Olive was seething but knew better than to argue. "Where did you get your hands on that explosive device?" he accused.

"It was a gift," Olive said flatly.

"From?"

"The CO." If he was going to be rude and abrupt in their dealings, she would be happy to go along.

"I doubt," he said tightly, "he intended it to be used on his own men."

"He intended it," Olive countered blithely, "to be used at my discretion. And I'm afraid with no knowledge of the operation, I was forced to draw my own conclusion, that the men were here on nefarious and unauthorised business. It seemed entirely justified with the information I had. Sir."

She glanced away from him at the men standing in clusters just beyond the reach of the headlamps, feeling more confused than ever. The focus of training at Station XVII was the sabotage of industry and infrastructure: factories, railroads, canals—anything that might undermine the Germans. While the curriculum included plenty of opportunities for field testing, it was rarely carried out in the dark or on the edge of the grounds, and certainly not with guns. Then again, perhaps all sorts of things were going on without her knowledge.

"It is a skill of mine, Miss Bright, to find the flaw in any system and bring every possible pressure to bear against it." His unflinching gaze was clearly assessing her potential as such.

Olive was momentarily struck speechless. She had time only to blink at him in disbelief before he went on.

"Return the car. Go home. New day tomorrow." He turned then and stalked away, calling out, "We'll begin again."

Jamie glanced at her. "Run the car up, wait for me, and I'll drive you home," he said shortly.

As he hurried after the CO, back toward the shelter of trees, snowflakes melted on Olive's collar. She shivered, not entirely certain whether the reaction was due to the weather or the warning. She glanced at the sheepish men, who clearly felt responsible for her dressing-down. She smiled distractedly at the pair that held the Sten guns loosely at their sides; they tipped their caps and turned away. But in the dim light of the headlamps, the profile of the shorter, stockier one kindled a flicker of memory.

She knew him; she'd spoken to him. She had, in fact, walked him to the nurses' station and set his finger in a splint after his opponent had met his intended chin jab head-on. His name was Josef Gabč.ek. He was part of the 1st Czechoslovak Mixed Brigade, most of whom were stationed at Cholmondeley Castle. The injury had made him fiercely angry with himself, but it had all been flare and fizzle—he'd soon been laughing at his own clumsiness. But when Olive had questioned him further, his mouth had shut quite firmly. All she knew was that he was one of a select group of recruits whose members were kept separate and given more focused and intense training, including with explosives she'd never seen before.

Now, as she stared at Warrant Officer Josef Gabč.ek and several of his compatriots lurking amid the trees on the Brickendonbury grounds on a slick and blustery night, the lot of them prepared to ambush an approaching vehicle, one thing was clear. The upper echelons of Baker Street were holding this secret close. Olive glanced back at the second car, its driver now standing waiting just beside it. Waiting for her to clear out and then what? Curiosity teemed inside her.

What is *all this?*

Knowing she couldn't linger—and daren't burn any bridges by

stashing the Austin and skulking back to observe—Olive slid into the car, slammed the door, and drove slowly down the drive, the falling snow quickly obscuring any activity that had commenced on the lane behind her.

She was torn between wanting to nurse her pride, tearing over the lanes on the little motorcycle she had on loan from Baker Street, and wanting to hear what sort of explanations or platitudes Jamie would offer. Her curiosity won out. Knowing she'd have a bit of a wait, she went straight to the kitchen, where a single lamp threw a warm glow up to the ceiling. She put the kettle on to boil and, after a time, settled down at the long wooden table to drink her tea and ponder the evening's discoveries.

Jamie found her there, and she didn't mince words.

"They're training for an ambush, aren't they?"

"Is there tea left in the pot?" Without waiting for a response, he found a cup, poured out the now-lukewarm brew, and dropped into the chair across from her. He took a long swallow, then a deep breath, and finally met her eyes levelly.

"I've never yet agreed to Twenty Questions, Olive, and I won't do it tonight, either. It's more than my job is worth." He smiled self-deprecatingly. "You're determined to buck the system, but you'll never manage it with Major Blighty in charge. You can't be in on every secret—for good reason. The fewer people that know a secret, the better chance there is of keeping it." His hands circled the cup as he stared down into its contents. "There's not a single reason you need to know what went on out there tonight. If there was, I'd tell you. Trust me."

Olive slumped over onto the folded arm she'd propped on the table and watched him. She was tired, frazzled, and bloody curious, but he wasn't to blame for any of it. He looked as run down as she felt. His dark hair was wet and curling at the ends, the grey blue of his eyes looked bruised, and the shadowy stubble that covered the lower half of his face made him look vaguely piratical.

"I miss Major Boom already. I wonder if they need another FANY at the Firs," she grouched.

Jamie eyed her, his face expressionless, but after a moment, his lips curved smugly. "Too many things tying you here."

"Such as?"

"The pigeons. They don't need them at the Firs, and without you here to champion the Bright birds, we'd likely find another pigeoneer."

Olive grunted. "That's *one* thing."

"Proximity to home—to Jonathon, Harriet, and your father." He had a point. Dispatched from London to Blackcap Lodge so that his mother might take refuge in a Scottish sanatorium, Jonathon would be torn up if Olive left him behind. Her step-mother, Harriet, had mostly recovered from the sprained ankle that had laid her up in early autumn, but her multiple sclerosis was beginning to take a heavy toll. And her father couldn't handle everything, including his veterinary surgery and responsibilities in the Home Guard, all alone.

"Two," she grudgingly admitted.

Jamie set his cup down slowly and gazed at her. "But *I* just might be the biggest draw of all."

Olive made to sit up straight, but her hair got caught in the buttons on her sleeve and tumbled out of its pins. She ignored the mass of dark, wavy hair hanging to her shoulders, having no intention of putting it up again.

"What do you mean?"

He spread his hands to indicate the breadth of his argument.

"Feel free to start anywhere," she said tartly, pulling out the rest of her pins.

"Very few officers would be willing to tolerate the sort of insubordination you dish out on a daily basis. I coddle you."

Her hands stilled for a moment as she stared at him, but she didn't object and instead lifted a single eyebrow. He went on.

"You've come to depend on me for information. The sort for

which you wouldn't otherwise have clearance." He took a drink of tea, appearing entirely too self-righteous.

He was right, but she wasn't in the mood to admit it—not after he'd denied her any details of that evening's mysterious business. "Is that all?" she said archly.

He shook his head slowly, then leaned forward, smiling wickedly. "Don't forget, you're in love with me."

Olive stilled, blinking rapidly. *No husband, no boyfriend. Traveling alone.* The words, part of her cover story, murmured in French, were constantly on the edge of her consciousness.

But in the privacy of her bedroom, in the lonely hours before dawn, she'd occasionally wondered if her feelings for Jamie transcended their fictitious liaison. In the months since she'd met him, he'd inspired a gamut of emotions: fury, exasperation, worry, empathy, and something more. Some indefinable thing. But it surely wasn't love. She felt certain of it. So, what had prompted Jamie to suggest it? Had she been behaving differently?

So absorbed was she in this private assessment that she barely registered when he started speaking again.

"Think of the grief they'll give you in the village. To say nothing of Harriet, who has informed me that she approves of my steadying influence on you." Now he raised both brows and stood up from the table, his chair raking loudly across the floor.

Relief made her almost boneless. He was teasing her. He'd not managed to discern her feelings—whatever they might be— and she wasn't going to bother about Harriet's misplaced approval.

"I'll take you home," he said, urging her up and out of the kitchen.

It was a quarter of an hour later. He'd pulled through the gate of Blackcap Lodge and waited until she'd opened the nearside door before he'd added one more item to the list.

"If you've any chance of becoming an agent, the best place you can be is here."

She'd slipped into the darkness then, heading for the dove-cote, wanting to check that her birds' evening, unlike her own, had been uneventful. After pulling the torch off the hook beside the door, she fanned its beam over the nests where her birds rested with puffed chests and contented coos. Safe and sound. Despite the random peril of her own evening, that phrase seemed to accurately reflect her own role in this war. No matter how certain she was that she was making a difference, she couldn't help but long to do more, to be viewed as more than an eccentric hanger-on: useful, perhaps, but hardly indispensable. To risk as much as others were, as selflessly and courageously as she could manage.

The other FANYs all aspired to be agents, which meant if they completed the required training and passed the interviews, they'd be dropped by parachute into enemy territory, tasked with spying, sabotage, infiltration, or communication. Little more than a month ago, she'd discussed the matter with Jamie. Rather than quash her intentions, as she'd expected, he'd offered to help her test her mettle. And so began the little lessons, and the quiet creation of a backstory.

But her confidence was a fickle thing, and her conviction was wavering. And Jamie certainly didn't make it easy. Would she, when the time came, be willing to walk into certain danger? She had no ready answer.

Flicking the torch beam off again, she trudged to the house, through the kitchen, and up to her room. It was a very long time before she slept.

Chapter 2
Propaganda

2 December
Pipley, Hertfordshire

Olive's eyes ranged over her porcine charges: Finn, looking rather dapper with the monocle marking round his right eye, Eske, with her liquid eyes and freckled snout, and Swilly, who'd been nicknamed the polka-dotted pig. The latter was bound for the butcher in the coming days, but Olive had put off applying for a license. She wasn't overly sentimental, but Jonathon had got quite attached, and she suspected their Christmas ham was going to be a bit difficult for him to digest. The members of the pig club, however, were much looking forward to the extra rations. There'd be no money earned this year from their fledgling club, but Eske was pregnant by one of the Henrys' hogs, and some of her piglets would eventually be sold to the Ministry of Food. Olive would need to find a roomier pen before the little plot behind Forrester's Garage was overrun, but that could be postponed at least until after the holiday.

On the auspices of pigeon training—not strictly a lie—she'd escaped Station XVII for the day and buzzed into the village, intent on errands and a cosy tea at the vicarage. Margaret Truscott, the newly minted vicar's wife, was slowly but surely scandalising the village. Not only had her friend signed up and gone to work as a spotter for the Royal Observer Corps, or ROC, but she'd also set strict limits on visiting hours at the vicarage. Gossip among the village harridans was fiercely disapproving.

"Olive," called a familiar, frazzled voice. Turning to see Jonathon approaching at a run, she casually tucked her basket behind her back. The boy skidded to a stop beside her at the fence rail. "Have you seen Hen anywhere?" he said breathlessly. "I've been searching for ages." Henrietta Gibbons, Girl Guide, as she was wont to introduce herself, was Jonathon's best friend and constant companion.

"I haven't," Olive admitted. "But I'm sure she's about—probably doing a good deed. Or taking someone to task. I'd say it's fifty-fifty."

"We both need spending money for Christmas presents, so we'd planned to collect holly and mistletoe and offer it up for sale." His shoulders slumped. "But she didn't show."

"I've never met someone fonder of pocket money than Hen— I'm sure she'll turn up." Olive laid a gentle hand on his head, tousling the too-long nut-brown locks.

He hooked his hands over the rail and stared forlornly at the pigs. With a glance up at Olive, he said, "Perhaps I'll find a special treat for them—Swilly, in particular."

She nodded her understanding and gave his shoulder a squeeze.

"If you see Hen, will you let her know I'm looking for her?"

"Of course."

He'd barely waited for her response before hurrying off again.

Olive frowned, wondering where Hen might have got off to but fully expecting she'd shortly appear, ready to get on with things.

She set off for the village lending library, slipping her hands into the pockets of her jacket so that the basket encircling her wrist pressed snugly against her hip. She'd stopped in at the chemist earlier. A cake of lavender soap for Harriet and a twist of lemon drops for Jonathon now lay tucked under a tea towel in the basket. With goods so difficult to come by, she had decided to get a jump on her Christmas shopping and planned to squirrel away her finds over the coming days. She was having a devil of a time deciding on a gift for Jamie. The man was like a locked box, and while she could always fall back on something useful, like razor blades or even a new, more flattering cap, those things seemed too impersonal. As indefinable—and bloody frustrating—as it might be, there was a bond between them, and Christmas was a time to celebrate that.

She was smirking to herself, imagining a knitted balaclava with no opening for a mouth, when she came upon a little crowd gathered on the village green. It appeared as if the village's most recent arrival—a Mrs Velda Dunbar—was making some sort of announcement, her strident tones reaching Olive in a somewhat garbled fashion.

"What on earth is she doing?" Lady Revell had come up behind Olive, her eyes focused on the considerable figure holding court beside the noticeboard, in precisely the spot the village Christmas tree was erected every year. A newcomer to the village herself, Lady Revell had moved into Peregrine Hall in late summer, along with her nephew, former squadron leader Max Dunn. Now a member of the Women's Institute and chair of its holiday toy drive, she'd been welcomed by the whole village. Mrs Dunbar's reception, on the other hand, had thus far been decidedly chilly.

While she'd arrived with her husband in tow, moving into the old Cheswick cottage on the edge of the village, it had been clear from the beginning that she brooked little interference from

him. Even now, Mr Dunbar sat a little distance away from the
crowd, on the bench dedicated to honour the lost souls of the
Great War. Huddled into his jacket, with his arms crossed, his cap
pulled low, and his chin tipped down onto his chest, he seemed
to be settling in for a catnap. But as Olive watched him, a flask
suddenly appeared in his hand. With a practiced twist of his fingers, it was opened and tipped back for a warming swig. The
barest second later, it was gone again, but he'd caught her eye
and winked mischievously.

"No idea," Olive answered, a bit bemused. "But Harriet will
expect full details, so I'd better go hear what she has to say."
They shared a smile and moved closer.

"I could claim I'd be reporting to Max, but he couldn't care
less." Her nephew was a decommissioned RAF pilot whose
plane had gone down in the Channel. The burns on his body
were gradually healing, but his mental recovery had been the
bigger struggle. He had, however, recently started work at Station XVII and was engaged in a rather mysterious relationship
with the village's resident celebrity, author Violet Darling.

Olive felt quite certain Jamie would have rolled his eyes and
walked on, but she couldn't help but be intrigued. To live in a
village was to be immersed in its business, no matter how small.

In a moment, they'd joined the crowd surrounding Mrs Dunbar. Olive had heard plenty of gossip but had yet to encounter
the woman. This was her first opportunity to form her own im-
pressions. She was tall and several stone overweight, draped in
shapeless, well-worn garments that served only to make her look
larger. She wore rings on her pudgy fingers and large pendants
round her neck, displayed prominently on the shelf of her bosom.
Above them, her face was doughy; her eyes were like two cur-
rants, thrust in before baking; her cheeks stained with the telltale
flush of someone prone to over imbibe. But it was her mouth that
was holding everyone's attention.

Hen appeared in Olive's field of vision, with Jonathon in tow, his anxiety now supplanted by the focused calm she'd come to expect from him. The pair moved to the front of the crowd.

Mrs Dunbar's words carried over the green. "There are many among you who would scoff at the idea that I can speak to those souls who have passed beyond this world." Cue scoffing, exasperated muttering, and fidgety movement. "And why should you believe me? Even the followers of Christ wanted proof." Her eyes locked onto her audience, flicking from one person to the next, demanding attention, even as they murmured and gasped at the woman's nerve in comparing herself to such an individual. "I have come here today to offer that proof. So that you can believe. So that through me you can reforge the bonds that were broken in death."

She paused a moment to let this sink in. The villagers seemed to be considering, willing to let her say her piece, reserving judgment.

Olive was now thoroughly convinced the woman was a charlatan, but was curious enough to stay and hear the rest of the performance. Her gaze shifted to Mr Dunbar, who sat unmoved and unaffected, before moving on to dart curiously among the villagers. Lady Camilla Forrester, George's mother, was frowning; Mrs Spencer was rolling her eyes beneath the sprig of holly tucked into her hat; and tiny Freya Rodery, who stood on the very edge of the green, as if not daring to come any closer, was rigid, her eyes troubled and her mouth a tight line of disapproval.

Now that her critics were momentarily silenced, Mrs Dunbar's movements became deliberately intentional. Her chin tipped up, her eyelids fell closed, and her arms hung straight at her sides, her palms turned up to the sky, the pudgy fingers spread wide. Then she spoke.

"I call upon my spirit guide to assist me. He moves among the lost souls, as one of them, but he has reached through the ether and found in me a willing partner, a medium." It seemed to Olive as if the hint of a smile hovered at the edges of the woman's lips, but it quickly disappeared. "And together," she intoned portentously, "we have forged the link between this world and the next."

So saying, the spiritualist's head tipped forward, rolled from side to side, and then steadied, with her face now hidden from view. The pudgy fingers quivered, as if beyond her control, then rose slowly up her body until they reached her face. They swatted awkwardly at her cheeks but shortly stilled, hovering in fisted control against her mouth. And then, suddenly enough to have them all starting with the shock of it, her face lifted. Her eyes stared out at them, unseeing, and her fingers pulled away, drawing something in their grasp.

Olive stepped quizzically forward, puzzled by what she was seeing. A milky white substance was emerging from the woman's nose and mouth, being drawn like taffy. There was so much of it, it began to overflow her hands and spill down the front of her garments. The gathered crowd was agog, simultaneously repulsed and drawn in. Because what in heaven could be coming next? Olive felt certain that Margaret was going to very much regret missing this spectacle, not to mention the village's reaction.

"What *is* all that?"

"Is that the ectoplasm you read about in the papers?"

"Ecto . . . What did you say?"

"It's unsanitary, is what it is."

Schoolchildren were beginning to close in on the medium, and Olive knew for a fact that Tommy Prince wasn't above giving the mysterious substance a solid tug for curiosity's sake. Mr Dunbar launched himself from his perch on the bench and hustled them backwards, in the way one might herd some recalcitrant sheep. Jonathon stood solemnly, Hen beside him.

"Don't tell me you believe any of this claptrap," said a voice in her ear. Olive turned to see Dr Ware, the village chemist, paused beside her, clearly eager to be on his way.

"Don't worry, Dr Ware. I'm just here to observe." His responding harrumph made her smile. Some people didn't have the patience for chicanery, but Olive felt it gave her good insight into others' deceptions—and the manner in which they got away with them. If, in fact, they did.

"I'll leave you to it, then," he said before hurriedly striding away.

With a great shudder, Mrs Dunbar drew herself up, her eyes darting urgently, blindly. "Evelyn," she said crisply, "are you there?" The ectoplasm, if that was indeed what it was, had come loose from her mouth, allowing her to speak freely, but it was still awkwardly tethered at her nose. Olive shuddered. A chill wind whipped up the trees and tousled the hats of the assembled party, but the mysterious Evelyn did not appear. But curiosity had been well and truly piqued—the assembled villagers were all glancing round, eagerly awaiting his appearance. Lady Revell, Olive noticed, kept her gaze trained on the now motionless form of Mrs Dunbar. And then the unexpected happened.

"I am here, madam."

The voice was a deep drawl with the accent of an American Southerner. Olive pictured Rhett Butler and craned her head to deduce who might be speaking. She frowned, quickly realising that the voice hadn't come from a man. At least not a corporeal one. The only one in attendance at this display was Mr Dunbar, and he'd gone back to his bench, some distance from his wife. The gathered crowd couldn't contain their reactions.

"Has she actually summoned someone?"

"Is the ectoplasm speaking?"

"Surely not!"

"It looks like meringue that needs a good deal more whipping."

The tittering was cut off by the adamant shushing of Winifred Danes. She had long been a vocal devotee of Marcellus, the newspaper columnist-cum-astrologist, and was clearly open-minded with respect to all sorts of questionable activities and pronouncements.

"We've our work cut out for us, Evelyn," Mrs Dunbar said crisply.

Olive squinted, baffled. Could she possibly be addressing the substance now undulating in the breeze like an untwisted sausage? Olive scoffed. As if any self-respecting Southern gentleman would present himself in such a state!

"There are a number of unbelievers here," Mrs Dunbar went on, "but I've confidence we can convince them."

"Well, now," Evelyn allowed, "that seems to be the way of things no matter where we meet, but the truth will prevail."

"Is there someone there with you who wishes to speak, Evelyn?"

"There is." Evelyn cleared his throat rather hesitatingly, if such a thing was possible. "A member of His Majesty's Forces." There was a pause, and the audience held its collective breath. "A seaman stationed on board the HMS *Bartholomew*." Stunned silence gave way almost instantly to a flutter of lowered voices, all of which were promptly quelled by Evelyn, who'd clearly taken charge of the proceedings. "He's tentative, I'm afraid, and will come only a little way. You'll have to listen carefully. His voice will surely be faint." As one, they all craned forward.

Olive kept her eyes focused on Mrs Dunbar. The silence felt heavy, and a prickle worried along her arms as her mind filled with long and short beeps, as if the message was coming through via Morse code.

"Tell me," said the medium, her head up, her eyes focused, "for whom is the message intended?"

"Alfreda Rodery," came the dutiful but grim reply, but not in Evelyn's exaggerated drawl. This was a new voice, a Britisher—a Londoner, by the sound of it. And his words were utterly unexpected.

All eyes shifted curiously to the figure that stood motionless at the edge of the green. Since coming to the village as the young bride of Captain Rodery, she'd always been simply Freya. She tended to keep herself to herself, and judging by the tepid gossip batted about, none of the villagers really knew much about her. Puzzled but curious, Olive turned back to Mrs Dunbar and the limp and swaying ectoplasm. Was it possible that Freya was an accomplice? Her expression certainly didn't hint that she was at all willing. But that could be part of the ruse. . . .

Mrs Dunbar cut into her thoughts. "What is the message?"

After a brief silence that had them all fidgeting, the answer came. "We were hit off the coast of Egypt by German torpedoes. There was no warning, no time . . . Everything happened at once—the battleship listing, the whalers coming loose of their lashings, men sliding down the decking, going over. Then one of the magazines went up. The explosion ignited the main, and then the world was on fire. Smoke, black as pitch, and debris hurtling through the sky. Men jumping ship, but so many others caught, trapped, burning. The other battleships in our formation could do nothing but take cover themselves." Another pause. "Eight hundred sixty-two souls perished on the twenty-fifth of November, among them Captain David Rodery. I was beside him when he went."

The sudden silence was deafening under the bleak autumn sky. Every last witness to that display was so shocked, it was impossible for anyone to think what to say. In the midst of this silence, Hen moved, breaking from the crowd, and ran full tilt across the green, away toward the river, with Jonathon in hot pursuit. Olive stared after them.

She'd let herself get caught up in the narrative, and now her thoughts were in a muddle. She'd forgotten her contempt for "Evelyn" and Mrs Dunbar. So real had been the images in her mind that her stomach had plummeted and a chill had overtaken her. But when the voice had gone silent, it was as if a spell had broken. She blinked and took a deep, steadying breath, pressing a settling hand to her abdomen.

Her message delivered, Mrs Dunbar gave a great, shuddering breath, swayed slightly, and would have slumped to the ground if Mr Dunbar hadn't been on hand, having moved quickly, to catch her considerable figure. She was like the parachutes Olive had seen at RAF Ringway—one moment, full of hot air, and the next, frowzily collapsed.

"Extraordinary," Lady Revell murmured beside her.

Sparing one last, hard look at Mrs Dunbar, Olive glanced round at Freya Rodery. This had been a horrible trick to play, and if the poor woman wasn't up to confronting Mrs Dunbar, then Olive would do it herself. There were reports of sunken ships on the wireless every week, and she was quite sure there'd been no mention of the HMS *Bartholomew*. The self-proclaimed medium may as well have been caught out in a lie. What on earth could she be playing at?

As Olive looked on, Freya stared across the green at the collapsed Mrs Dunbar with a look of mingled misery and hatred. Eventually, a cluster of villagers hid her from view. Olive frowned, utterly baffled by the entire business, and found her attention newly diverted by Mrs Gibbons, who was wandering aimlessly, nodding absently to herself and saying, "He's fine, right enough."

A bit of an odd bird, flighty and prone to fancy, Mrs Gibbons—presumably with help from the now long-absent Mr Gibbons—had somehow managed to produce the most sensible of daughters. Hen would have known how to calm her mother, having likely been called upon to do so countless times before. Given her reputation as a Johnny-on-the-spot, Hen had made her escape rather prematurely.

"What is it, Mrs Gibbons?" Olive asked, moving swiftly to the woman's side and wrapping an arm round her quivering shoulders.

"He wasn't among them, I'm sure of it."

Holding on to her patience, Olive tried again, saying gently, "Who are you talking about? Sure of what?"

Mrs Gibbons turned to her, sea-green eyes widened appealingly. "Marcus wasn't one of those poor boys."

Gooseflesh cropped up on Olive's skin. She'd forgotten. Marcus Gibbons, Hen's freckled, copper-headed older brother, had signed up for the Royal Navy in the earliest days of the war. She must have heard many times over that he was aboard the HMS *Bartholomew*, but she'd forgotten.

Hen's abrupt departure suddenly made sense, and Olive felt a twist of worry in the pit of her stomach and was grateful that Jonathon had gone after her.

"Surely not, Mrs Gibbons. Besides, the . . . spirit guide"—her mouth felt sticky even uttering the words—"said it happened on the twenty-fifth of November. That was a full week ago. You would have had a telegram by now if it were true."

Mrs Gibbons met her eyes, stared hard into them, unblinking. She gripped Olive's forearms tightly, as if willing the truth of the statement to flood into her, crowding out all doubt. "I would, wouldn't I? Of course I would." Her own body seemed to wilt, and her breath feathered out. "I should have realised. The shock of it . . ."

Olive nodded reassuringly and watched as Lady Revell began to make her way through the crowd toward the spot where Mrs Dunbar was now being offered some sort of restorative beverage—probably gin—by her husband.

"Henrietta, the poor dear . . ."

"She's likely to realise," Olive said comfortingly. "But if I see her, I'll speak to her."

Mrs Gibbons nodded, and with effort, Olive disengaged herself from the woman's clutching hands with a few more placating words. Turning, she hurried along in Lady Revell's wake, eager for the chance to denounce the spiritualist's morbid proclamations.

"Mrs Dunbar," Lady Revell was saying, her hand placed delicately on her breastbone, "I find myself at somewhat of a loss. That was quite extraordinary. Horrible, I'm sure—those poor men—but to have that link, that connection with the afterlife is rather a miracle."

Olive's gaze shifted from Mrs Dunbar's self-possessed, placid smile to Lady Revell, whose pulse beat like a damselfly's wing at the base of her throat. She appeared all aflutter. Olive was taken aback.

Mrs Dunbar heaved a mighty sigh. "Sometimes I wish I could hold it all back, but I never know what's coming. I've no control, you see. The spirits overtake me, and I'm simply at their mercy." She worried at the folds of her robes. "Mrs Rodery was surely shocked by that poor seaman's words, but I hope she can take some comfort in knowing what happened."

Olive frowned. Was there even an inkling of a possibility that Mrs Dunbar's claims and abilities were legitimate? The very idea seemed preposterous, but she appeared so earnest and contrite, and the picture her words had conjured had been so vivid. But surely, it was impossible.

"That's it precisely," Lady Revell was saying. "My sister passed quite suddenly, under rather curious circumstances." She paused and appeared to be swallowing down her emotion. "I wondered if I could prevail upon you to attempt a summons, so that I can finally have closure—and say goodbye."

Mrs Dunbar's eyes looked suddenly avid. "A séance, do you mean? I am at your service, Lady Revell. Presuming, of course, you can arrange the sort of environment that will be conducive to channelling. Evelyn is an old hand at this sort of thing, but younger, more timid spirits do need a bit of coddling."

"Of course. I defer to you, absolutely. You have only to tell me what you require."

Mrs Dunbar cleared her throat, canted her head, and let her eyes slide sideways. "I do prefer payment in advance, so that when the time comes, I may focus my full concentration on other-worldly concerns." Her hands, inside the pockets of her robes, were churning like millstones.

"Yes, of course," Lady Revell said politely, laying her hand on the woman's arm. "I quite understand."

"Are you able to summon more than one spirit in the same sitting?" Olive blurted. A sudden yearning to speak to her mother had overtaken her common sense. Serena Bright had died much too young, her real self kept hidden from Olive until too late. And confronting a chilly gravestone about a lifetime's secrets and lies was frustratingly one sided.

"It can be done," Mrs Dunbar said carefully, "but all participants must be fully engaged. Even one doubting Thomas can be enough to squelch the entire proceedings."

Olive glanced at Lady Revell. "Would it be all right if I attend the séance? My mother—" She shook her head, unwilling to say more, and then another thought occurred to her. If, by some miracle, her mother's spirit *was* summoned, she might reveal private things. Awkward, embarrassing things. "Perhaps I shouldn't—"

But both Mrs Dunbar and Lady Revell cut her off before she finished.

The former insisted, "You must."

The latter urged, "Of course, my dear. I'm hoping I can convince Max to sit with us, as well. Shall we have eight round the table?" Lady Revell had settled seamlessly into the role of hostess for this unorthodox event. "So long as everyone agrees to be on their best behaviour," she added quickly.

"Crowd the table with as many as you wish. I will not join you there. There must be room for my manifestation cabinet—it is from there that I will summon the spirits," the medium said imperiously.

There was a beat of silence as Lady Revell digested this information.

"Well, eight is a nice, round number." There was a hint of steel in her smile. "Perhaps I should invite Mrs Rodery and Mrs Gibbons to attend," Lady Revell said tentatively. "I would hope it might bring them a bit of comfort." Her voice sounded hollow on the last word, and Olive glanced at her with sympathy. She couldn't imagine losing someone suddenly, like a candle snuffed out. Her own mother, at least, had been drifting away for a long time before the end. But the longer war raged across the world, the better chance there was that she would lose someone dear quite abruptly.

Olive could understand the lure of a séance, despite her relative certainty that it was all a hoax, but to invite Mrs Gibbons and Freya Rodery after today's events seemed in very poor taste. Then again, it was likely neither would accept, so she needn't worry overmuch.

A subtle nod indicated that Mrs Dunbar was agreeable.

"I suspect Harriet would love to attend," Olive ventured, willing to bet her stepmother's curiosity would far outweigh her scepticism.

"That leaves three places." Lady Revell glanced at Mrs Dunbar. "Unless Evelyn requires a seat?"

"No, of course not," the medium said shortly. "Ectoplasm never requires a chair."

"Of course not," murmured Lady Revell.

Olive felt a presence beside her and realised with a start that Winifred Danes was hovering at her right elbow, her cheeks flushed.

"I couldn't help but overhear and wondered if I might impose upon you, Lady Revell?" she asked, smiling ingratiatingly, as she tugged her cardigan snug across her bosom. "I'm utterly devoted to Marcellus, but I confess that today's demonstration has quite sent my heart into palpitations. The chance to be present when a door to the spirit world is opened is positively—" Miss Danes shook her head, finally at a loss for words.

Ever gracious, Lady Revell said, "Please do attend, Miss Danes." She turned then, tentatively gesturing to the park bench. "What about your husband, Mrs Dunbar? Will he attend?"

"Oh, yes, he must," the spiritualist asserted, her head jutting pugnaciously.

"I suppose he will require a chair?" A look from Mrs Dunbar had her barrelling on. "Yes, well, then, we've only to find one more." Lady Revell glanced at Olive. "Would you like to take care of that, my dear?"

"Leave it to me." Olive would dearly love to invite Margaret, but she wondered if her friend's dual role as vicar's wife and displaced, cynical Londoner would put a damper on the proceedings. She'd have to give it a thought. She would dearly love to drag Jamie. His frowning disapproval prompted a wrinkle in his chin, which she'd seen so often she'd nicknamed it Horace, and lately there'd been a distracting new addition: a jumping vein near his right eye. But unfortunately, he was indisposed indefinitely.

"Shall we say the sixth?" Lady Revell was saying. "It will give me a few days to make the necessary preparations." Her eyes widened with expectation as she looked to Mrs Dunbar for confirmation.

"I am available to the spirits at all times," came the haughty reply. But the lines on either side of the spiritualist's mouth pulled down in apparent disapproval at such a delay.

"Wonderful." Lady Revell was clearly immune to such tactics. "Shall we say seven o'clock?"

Olive would have to make certain she had no after-hours responsibilities at Brickendonbury—or farther afield—on that day. Because she certainly didn't intend to miss a séance.

Lady Revell's gaze tipped downward, and her fingers curled

into her palms. "I'd offer to serve a light supper, but I confess I'm not sure how I'd manage a meal for so many with the rationing."

"Not at all, madam," Mrs Dunbar assured her stiffly, and not wholly convincingly.

"Supper or not, this promises to be a riveting evening. I hope Marcellus's weekly column will give some hint of what's to come." Olive thought Miss Danes's eagerness rather endearingly giddy; Margaret would only roll her eyes.

Either way, Olive had no doubt the evening was going to be memorable. In truth, she was eager to hear Evelyn's drawl again—and catch the infinitesimal movements of Mrs Dunbar's lips, which no doubt produced it.

All at once, with a speed and agility that startled Olive, the spiritualist sprang forward with the excuse "I must speak with Mrs Rodery." Then she was hustling toward the lone figure who'd turned to walk away. The three women she'd left behind stood looking on at the developing tableau. Within seconds, furious words drifted toward them in snatches on the breeze.

"Let go of me . . . impossible . . . no choice . . . won't be a party . . ."

Having delivered a furious rebuff, Freya Rodery spun on her heel and stalked off, while Mrs Dunbar, shoulders rigid, turned to expose her beet-red, tight-lipped countenance, her eyes searching the green. It was only a moment before they settled on the retreating form of her husband, his hand cupping the elbow of Eileen Heatherton, Pipley's loose-lipped switchboard operator.

"I'd say Freya Rodery declined the invitation," Olive said wryly, choosing not to comment on the rest. Miss Danes and Lady Revell stared back at her, momentarily mute. The gossip would go round, though. Of that, Olive had no doubt.

"If you ladies will excuse me, I require a word with Lady Camilla . . ." And then Lady Revell was off, leaving Olive standing alone with Winifred Danes.

"So much can be gleaned from beyond the veil," Miss Danes confided, "but it takes a gifted individual . . . a connected spirit—"

"I really must be off," Olive interrupted, squeezing the woman's arm. "See you Friday—it should be great fun."

"I do hope you're taking it seriously," the bosomy figure called after her disapprovingly. The rest of the lecture, Olive squelched with distance, but she was unable to avoid the turn of her own thoughts and found herself pondering the recent tableau and warily anticipating the event to come.

Chapter 3
Operational Orders

5 December
Station XVII and Blackcap Lodge

"So, did it sink or not?" asked the newest FANY, a frown crinkling her brows as she looked quizzically at Olive.

The pair was standing under the manor's porte-cochère, having a break from the frantic hubbub of Station XVII. There'd been an influx of agents recently, and the women were run off their feet. Olive had just relayed the tale of the mendacious medium, and naturally, there were questions.

"I can't imagine so," was her distracted reply as her gaze ranged over the tiny icicles hanging from the bumper of the black Austin that shared the space with them. "If the HMS *Bartholomew* truly had sunk, both Mrs Rodery and Mrs Gibbons would have received telegrams by now. To say nothing of its being mentioned on the wireless." Neither explanation had been enough to stifle the gossip: the whole village was atwitter. As far as Olive could tell, opinion was split between the wildly impressed and the contemptuous nonbelievers. Hopefully, Mrs Gibbons had shaken off the shock of Mrs Dunbar's pronouncement.

Then again, Hen might very well have her hands full. Olive hadn't seen the girl in days—an unprecedented situation.

"It always surprises me," her companion was saying, "that people can behave so shoddily when we're all trying so hard to bear up and get through this war." Her fingers curled in on themselves, and after a moment, she threw up her hands. "I wish I had the wherewithal to take up cigarettes. I think they endow a girl with a certain sophistication—and they're rather a boon in uncomfortable silences." She sighed heavily. "But I can't do it."

Olive's lips curled up at the edges. She'd taken to the girl from the moment she'd introduced herself—as Hell.

"It's what everyone ends up calling me," she'd admitted. "May as well start off as we're likely to go on."

A few moments' conversation had revealed her as the only daughter of the Hellberns, a clan who—from Hell's perspective—graced the society pages with embarrassing regularity, and for all the worst reasons. Her three brothers had thus far managed to shirk their responsibilities with regards to the war effort and been congratulated by both parents for their efforts. Fed up with all of them, Hell had walked out of the house, taken a train to Overthorpe Hall, and foisted herself on the FANY establishment. While there, she'd knocked a girl down the stairs, nearly set fire to the house, and run a car into a sycamore tree during her driving lessons. It was apparently incidents such as these that had inspired her nickname.

Possibly, the decision to send her to the special training school that specialised in explosive trials was a trifle foolhardy, but Olive, for one, was happy to have her on board. She was dauntless, unafraid to speak up for herself and others, and an utter brick.

Her appearance, however, was a study in contrasts. She was even taller than Olive's five feet eight and wore her uniform like a career military man, with nary a spot or wrinkle, keeping her reading spectacles on a chain round her neck. She wasn't above donning them merely to look down her nose at a truculent male, a practice Olive adored witnessing. Her hair, however, while pinned tightly in the morning, tended to come untethered by midday; her nails were bitten to the quick; and her eyes, without the spectacles, were a lovely chestnut brown and luxuriously fringed.

"But, golly, a séance . . ." She whistled. "How I'd love to be a fly on the wall." Suppressing a shiver, she stared out over the grounds, lost in thought.

"You can come with, if you want. I'm meant to be finding another person to round out the numbers. I rather think you'll do nicely." Looking her over, Olive had a momentary premonition of disaster but forcibly quelled it.

There was a sudden gasp of delight as Hell swung her wide-eyed gaze back to Olive. "Oh, how exciting! I'll be on my best behaviour." She wavered, as if wanting to go on.

"But?" Olive inquired.

"Could you possibly introduce me as Nancy?" Slightly crooked teeth flashed a wince of uncertainty. "I'm not sure the other would go over well in the circumstances."

"Naturally. As I understand it, Hell is your code name," Olive said with a grin.

For a few moments, the only sound was that of muffled explosions somewhere on the grounds. The two FANYs were lost to their own private thoughts. Finally, Olive spoke up.

"Do you think you have what it takes to be an agent?"

The other girl didn't respond immediately, but eventually, she said, "Mentally, I suspect so. I'm not sure the rest of me would cooperate, though. If I were dropped by parachute, they'd probably find me hanging from a church spire, with my knickers on display, or fried up like an egg across a power wire."

"I've been thinking about whether I want to try for it. They're going to need women—men are too noticeable, not to mention predictable. And I've loads of experience talking my way out of sticky situations."

"Pure quicksand, as far as I'm concerned," Hell said wryly, slumping against one of the porte-cochère's supporting pillars and scuffing her shoe over a glossy patch of ice slicking the gravel beside it. "The more I struggle, the deeper the hole."

"I've been learning French and fighting techniques, and whenever I have a spare minute, I listen in on the training courses. And besides that—"

"We're not looking for any women agents, Miss Bright," said a voice behind them.

Hell nearly jumped to attention at the sudden appearance of their commanding officer, but Olive merely gritted her teeth and turned slowly round.

"Maybe not yet, sir," Olive replied, attempting to keep her voice polite.

"If I have anything to say about it, not ever." His grey eyes held a storm of disapproval as he stared down at her. "If men weren't in such short supply, we wouldn't even have need of the FANYs. War is the purview of men. They're simply better equipped."

Jamie had tried to impress on Olive the need to steer clear of Blighty; a clash between the two of them, he'd asserted, could mean her dismissal. Olive had agreed with him and had thus far done her best, but in the face of such blatant chauvinism, she really had no choice but to defend herself—and women in general.

"Perhaps in some ways," she conceded politely. "Certainly not all."

He frowned heavily, great ridges appearing on his forehead, as his jaw shifted ominously. "You're not indispensable, Miss Bright. It's likely the position of pigeoneer will shortly be eliminated."

"What?" Olive spluttered, abandoning all pretence of subordination. "But that's absurd! Just recently one of my birds carried home a map of—"

He ruthlessly cut her off. "I'm aware of the intelligence, Miss Bright. But strategy is a matter of weighing risks versus rewards. I'm sceptical that your pigeons measure up."

"Captain Aldridge fully supports—"

"An officer in the Royal Navy is arriving tomorrow," he snapped, clearly fed up with the argument. Olive pressed her lips together in an effort to hold her tongue as he went on. "You are hereby assigned to escort him." Rather than the pride these words might have inspired, they instead instilled a sense of dread.

"Why is he coming to Station XVII?" Olive queried, curious in spite of herself.

He stared down at her, his eyes cold. Olive returned his gaze, hoping hers was colder. "Your concern in the matter is limited to insuring he's given a thorough tour of Station XVII, with emphasis on our training syllabus and procedures."

With those parting words, he stalked out into the gloomy morning, headed in the direction of the explosions, his shoes crunching over the icy gravel, his hat pulled low against the wind.

"He's quite the ogre, isn't he?" Hell said at her ear.

"I can think of all sorts of words I'd use instead," Olive said tightly. "He's the sort of man," she went on, her eyes trained on the stiff set of his shoulders beneath the overcoat that whipped round his long legs, "that requires a rather brutal comeuppance. Even then it's unlikely he'll change his ways, but defeat will nag at him, nonetheless, and sometimes that has to be enough."

"Sad, but true." Hell tsked. "Perhaps one of those explosions will singe off his eyebrows."

On that sentiment, they turned their backs on him, ready to get back to work.

Any other day, Olive would have stalked directly to Jamie's office and vented a blue streak about the insuperability of the new CO. That done, she would have quizzed him about the officer she was meant to be ushering about. But today she couldn't.

Jamie was away. His debilitating headaches—an indelible reminder of the early days of the war, when he'd served in Belgium
with the British Expeditionary Force—had become more fre-
quent of late, prompting him to request a leave of absence. He'd
gone home to Ireland for a time, and honestly, it rather startled
her how much she missed him. She'd got used to his wry smiles,
forbidding tone, and stormy eyes. Not to mention the long walks,
quiet conversations, and shiver-inducing kisses they sometimes
engaged in to further the fiction of their romance. On occasion,
in the quiet dark of her bedroom, she let herself wonder if he
missed her with the same sort of bittersweet yearning.

He'd sent only a single letter, and he may as well not have
bothered. It said only, *Nary a murderer nor an amateur sleuth in
sight. Headaches have abated. Surely not a coincidence. And yet I find
myself missing your invasive presence. Hoping to be back on the 7th. —J*

Olive had kept it, tucked between the pages of the book at her
bedside—a training manual for Baker Street agents she had on
loan from the manor. She reread the brief message every night
before bed, conflicted in her feelings and his intent.

"Coming?" Hell called. In her distraction, Olive had slowed
her steps, and now Hell was waiting patiently several feet on.
"We'd best get organised, or his nibs will subject us to another
lecture."

With a growl and a dramatic roll of her eyes, Olive hurried on.

Olive managed to escape the manor just after lunch, her thoughts
in a tizzy. Was her stint as pigeoneer truly coming to an end? It
didn't bear thinking about, particularly as her own disappointment was the least of her worries. If the CO made good on his
threat, her birds would be left high and dry. The Bright pigeons
were unwanted by the National Pigeon Service, thanks to her father's uncompromising standards and abrasive manner, and so
their service would be at an end. So, too, their supply of feed.

As she straddled the Welbike and started its engine, her eyes shuttered closed on the realisation that she might soon be making this journey on a bicycle. At the onset of her involvement with Jameson Aldridge and Station XVII, she'd wheedled the loan of the compact little motorbike for pigeon-related purposes. Now she quite depended on it and considered it the greatest perk of her secret arrangement with Baker Street—Jamie, notwithstanding.

Then again, if Blighty had his way, even the bicycle wouldn't be necessary.

She was in a blue funk as she drove past the red-bricked gatehouse, and only belatedly realised that a woman was standing behind the wall, waving a tea towel, seemingly intent on getting her attention.

Olive coasted to a stop and idled the engine, curious as to who this mystery woman might be. Her hair was tucked up in a messy bun, and her face was livened by a wide smile and pinked cheeks. Behind her in the little garden, there was a clothesline strung up, with pegged washing whipping about in the crisp breeze. Olive's brows drew together; when she'd stormed the manor gates in the spring, she'd been quite certain no one was living in the gatehouse. Comprehension dawned. This was surely Mrs Blighty. Olive deflated a bit.

"Good morning," the woman said brightly. "I'm Scarlet Chambers—my husband is newly in charge up at the manor." She looked at Olive expectantly, as if her visitor might possibly be unaware of the oppressive new commanding officer of Station XVII. *If only* . . . "He said we mustn't use our real names—top secret and all that—and he let me choose my new one."

"Well done," Olive said, smiling. She was having trouble imagining Blighty married, let alone to this spirited woman.

"Yes, I quite like it."

"I'm Olive Bright. I work as a FANY up at the manor."

"I can tell by your uniform," she said, her eyes flashing admiringly over every inch of it. They stood silently for a long moment as Mrs Chambers ran the tea towel through her hands. When it stilled, it seemed she'd made up her mind. Stepping closer, she glanced round, then said, "Would you care to come in for tea?"

"That's sweet of you to offer, but I'm on manor business, I'm afraid, and haven't time."

"Well, I really must talk to someone." She'd glanced down, and her words were barely audible over the engine. Olive had the sense that she was talking to herself. All at once, the woman seemed to come to a decision and, leaning over the wall, said, "Can I confide in you?"

Olive blinked, startled at the question, and then a frisson of wariness skated up her spine. Could she? Should she? Were there rules about this sort of thing? There were certainly rules about everything else. Olive was considering how best to form her reply when the matter was taken out of her hands.

"I'm going to sign up," said Scarlet Chambers, her eyes sparking with triumph. It was short-lived, however, her next words being, "Well, not precisely."

Olive realised she'd been holding her breath, waiting for the rest, but it seemed that was to be the sum total of Mrs Chambers's confidence. With a relieved exhale, she said encouragingly, "Good for you, then." While a second National Service Act had recently determined that single women between the ages of twenty and thirty were eligible for call-up to one of the auxiliary services or a production facility, married women remained, for now at least, exempt.

"I just don't know how I'll manage to keep it from . . . Gregory." When Olive frowned in confusion, she clarified, "My husband."

Gregory? As code names went, Major Blighty suited the man much better.

Olive, who was having enough trouble keeping secrets without worrying about a husband, blinked at her. With sudden realisation, she frowned and rolled the motorbike closer to the garden wall. "He doesn't approve?" she guessed.

Scarlet worried at the frayed edges of the towel. "Gregory is an utter dear, but he's loads too protective."

Olive blinked again, struggling to reconcile the stern, taciturn figure of the CO with the "utter dear" who had clearly captured the heart of this personable woman. "So, what will you do?" If she intended to pull off a deception under the nose of the man whose job it was to ferret out weakness, Olive fully intended to pay attention.

Scarlet sighed. "I would love to train as a FANY and work alongside my husband at the manor, but naturally, that would never work. And I can't go away, to be stationed on a base somewhere, so I thought perhaps the Land Army might have me in a voluntary capacity." She seemed to be appealing to Olive to flesh out the details of this plan.

Since arriving at Peregrine Hall, Lady Revell had encouraged the use of its extensive grounds for food production and had requested the occasional loan of a couple of Land Girls to help with the work. Perhaps Scarlet Chambers could put herself to use there.

"I could introduce you to Lady Revell up at Peregrine Hall, if you like. She often has need of such help."

"*Could* you?" Her hand reached out to clutch at Olive's forearm. "The moment I saw you on the drive, I hoped we might be friends. But partners in crime is much more fun." She caught Olive's eye, her own imploring. "You won't tell Gregory, will you?"

"My lips are sealed," Olive said with a conspiratorial wink.

The man's opinions on women doing war work—to say nothing of pigeons—were archaic. She'd be delighted to have a hand in thwarting them.

They spent the next several minutes making plans, and when Olive set off once again, her frown had been replaced by a contented grin.

* * *

The moment Olive walked into the dovecote, her eyes zero-ing in on the squeakers, now fully fledged at six weeks and ready to begin their training, her good mood promptly gave way to fresh worry. She wanted to curse Major Blighty and his bloody-minded decisions. With Jamie's encouragement, she'd proceeded with a second round of breeding in September. Ten breeding pairs incubating two eggs apiece had bulked up the Bright loft's numbers and ensured that there would be plenty of birds for Baker Street operations in the months ahead.

Now, it seemed, every one of them was at risk of furlough.

In the typical, paradoxical way of this war, things were rolling right along, while at any moment they had the potential to come crashing to a halt. And then detonate.

The timing was hardly auspicious. While the spring and sum-mer months had seen her birds return time and again with critical intelligence in tow, now the weather had turned bitterly cold, and fewer pigeons were being dropped into the wintry landscape of Belgium, Holland, and France. Baker Street was, with a few exceptions, getting along more or less without them for the time being, an argument in the CO's favour.

Olive shook her head sharply, refusing to dwell on the man's utter lack of imagination. But as she shelved one concern, an-other cropped up in its place. With Blighty at the helm of Station XVII, were her chances of becoming an agent effectively dashed? While her role as a FANY was certainly rewarding—the rugged, courageous men who came to train at the manor were, in many ways, as helpless as newborn kittens, and she enjoyed whipping them into shape—working as a Baker Street agent would be her only opportunity to be in the thick of it all, to test her resilience and abilities in a more immediate way.

Is that what I really want?

She had no time to consider the answers to these questions, as

Jonathon pushed through the door of the loft, just home from school. Olive didn't often feel sorry for herself, and clearly, she wasn't particularly skilled at hiding the emotion. He sat beside her on the bench and glanced at her apprehensively.

"Everything all right?"

Olive sighed. "It will be. Eventually. I need Jamie to haul himself home from the back of beyond"—she smiled—"but yes." She glanced at him, suddenly remembering the recent spectacle on the village green. "How's Hen doing?" she asked quietly.

He tipped his head down, and Olive rubbed her hand over his hunched shoulders. "She's all right," he said glumly, not meeting her eyes.

"You've told her it can't be true, haven't you? The War Office would have notified them by now. There would have been a report."

"Uh-huh," he mumbled.

"I suspect Mrs Dunbar has already got quite an earful," she said briskly as she stood. "And the pair of you will be all the richer for her bad manners. Your holiday greenery business is bound to go off like a house afire. Pity opens pockets, my boy."

He peered up at her, the seriousness in his face edged out by a watery smile. "Hen's probably already thought of that."

"No doubt," she agreed. As she moved toward the array of nesting boxes cut into the wall, her eyes ranged over the birds. There were so many of them she'd worried about keeping them straight, so in naming the hatchlings, she'd decided to take a cue from their parents.

She peered in at the offspring of Aramis and Roberta. She'd chosen Porthos and Athos as names for the pair, having concluded that a d'Artagnan might be inclined to excessive swashbuckling tendencies. She reached for the stockier of the two—Porthos—marvelling, as ever, at the anatomy of the birds. They felt as if they were full of air, held together by the barest framework of bone and tendon. Her finger brushed the ring on its leg, slipped on just recently over its still-bendable left foot, the official mark of a racing pigeon, or in this case, a war pigeon. The bird could now be traced back to the Bright loft and identified incontrovertibly, whether she forgot its name or not.

Olive turned toward Jonathon. "Want to come along on their first training mission?"

He sat up straighter, seeming to come out of himself at the thought of some bona fide war work.

For a couple of weeks now, Olive had been shooing the youngsters out of the loft just before twilight, knowing their desire to be home before dark, and their hunger for dinner, would keep them close. She loved watching them test their wings, first swooping and dipping in wide swaths in the sky above Blackcap Lodge, then going a bit farther afield, over the hedgerows and fallow farmland along the river. They hadn't yet ventured far from home, but for the past few days, they'd stayed out over an hour, returning only when she'd shaken the coffee can full of feed, which they'd come to associate with home and comfort.

By now they should have imprinted on the Bright loft and would have little trouble returning home from a liberation point one mile distant, which was, coincidentally, on the Pipley high street.

So, she and Jonathon collected a kit of them: six youngsters to be released en masse so that they could learn from and guide each other, and protect each other from predators, such as sparrow hawks and peregrine falcons. After tucking the birds into a wicker basket, and themselves more deeply into their woolens, Olive and Jonathon set off on bicycles down the much-travelled lane.

Jonathon's reserve gradually gave way to high spirits as he chattered on about one topic after another. What sort of Christmas present he might devise for Hen, how he missed his father and worried over his mother, his fervent wish to be in two places at once—liberating the birds and welcoming them home again—and even his recent discoveries in the hedgerows.

Olive was only half listening, her own thoughts distracted with the happy news that in two days' time, Jamie would be home.

* * *

1 December 1941

Dearest George,

I can tell by your description that you've landed yourself with a topping crew, so I'm merely going to say, "Be careful," and leave it at that. If I think about it anymore, my worry for you all will consume my thoughts, and that won't do any of us any good. Besides, if he's anything like his namesake, Shackleton will see you through in a pinch. I'm depending on it.

You needn't worry about me—I've no time for murder, excepting the sort devised by Mrs Christie and resolved by M. Poirot. (Although, I might give Lord Peter Wimsey a go for a change.) I've come up with an altogether different sort of scheme, and not the sort the WI gets up to, but something quite a bit more cloak and dagger. We've long chatted about wanting to be in the thick of it all, and now you've got your chance, so I'd say it's my turn. Nothing is yet certain, and there's every possibility I'll change my mind, but I like knowing that the opportunity is there for the taking.

Even Jamie seems to approve, which comes over rather a shock. The man can be quite frustrating at times—maddening, even—but I do adore him. In some ways we treat each other as we might a wild animal—with wariness and respect, ever circling—but neither of us, I suspect, has taming in mind. An odd way to put it, I know, but there it is. He makes my pulse race and my blood boil for all sorts of reasons. But you're not to tell him that—on pain of a punishment most unpleasant. Oh, how I wish I could talk to you. Letters aren't at all the same. So . . .

> *Fly home safe,*
> *Olive*

P.S. Please say hello to Bridget. Even if I hadn't seen the way you looked at her, I can tell by your letters that you are over the moon for the girl. Just don't let thoughts of her distract you when it matters.

Chapter 4

Ambushes

6 December
Blackcap Lodge and Station XVII

"I've never been to a séance. I really have no idea what to wear," Harriet confided, staring into the middle distance as she reclined on her chaise longue near the window in the parlour, her fountain pen held between her fingers, a replacement for the cigarette she was most likely craving. The white shock of hair that had run like a racing stripe along her temple for as long as Olive could remember had got wider in recent weeks. Less of a racing stripe, more of a Red Cross bandage.

Between her debilitating multiple sclerosis and a tumble that had sprained her ankle and consigned her to a wheelchair for several weeks, her stepmother found herself more and more often holding court from the parlour, which had become the domain of WI meetings, knitting circles, and impromptu gossips. Olive suspected Harriet was much looking forward to the change of scenery a séance at Peregrine Hall would provide.

Harriet said, "I rang up Lady Revell to ask if I could bring Violet. She's working on another novel, you know, and this could be quite useful. 'The more the merrier,' she said." Violet Darling had returned to the village that spring, after a long absence and a fascinating life, the acclaimed author of a number of Gothic thrillers. She and Harriet had quickly become fast friends, one needing a spark of adventure, the other yearning for a comforting maternal presence. It was the perfect symbiotic relationship.

"It's going to be quite a crowd," Olive said wryly. "And honestly, I can't decide whether to feel guilty about attending or not. It's not as if I *believe* . . ." She trailed off, uncertain what to say or even how she felt.

"I understand your feelings, dear, but village life necessitates a full measure of awkward situations. Better to keep Mrs Dunbar's particular skills contained than to have them unleashed indiscriminately." Olive was certain Harriet had heard the details from more than one witness to the shocking display on the village green. "We certainly don't want to have another murder on our hands." She huffed, tossed her pen down on the lap desk arranged before her, and reached for the enamelled jade box that held her cigarettes.

Olive frowned at her, a subtle reminder that she was meant to be giving them up. When Harriet ignored her, she said, "Well, I'm bringing one of the new crop of FANYs. Her name is Nancy Hellbern, but they call her Hell."

Harriet's eyes widened over her busy thumb on the lighter. A second later, the flame appeared, drawing her focus until the tip of the cigarette began to burn. She took a deep drag, letting her eyes fall shut in pleasure. "Hell, did you say? She sounds rather fun. I do worry that it might all be too much. I'm glad Mrs Rodery won't be coming, and I was really hoping Mrs Gibbons would refuse, as well. It's fine for the rest of us to treat the whole thing like an evening's entertainment, but we weren't singled out by a morbid, and surely quite worrying, prediction. If Mrs Dunbar had tried that on me . . ." She shook her head, clearly imagining such a nerve. "I wouldn't have been able to forgive her. Then again, perhaps it was a . . . miscommunication of some sort." Her face said quite clearly that she didn't understand any of it, not one bit. Olive couldn't help but wonder what she'd make of the ectoplasm, presuming it made a second appearance.

"And Hen there to hear it, as well," Olive added with a shake of her head. "She's a stalwart girl, but quite sensitive. Hopefully, she'll have a letter from her brother soon to smooth everything over."

"Hmm." Harriet was distracted again, perhaps musing on revenge.

Olive smiled and glanced down at the dregs of her tea. She had finished her toast long ago but had got a second cup to fortify her for the day ahead at the manor. She wasn't at all looking forward to being saddled with a pompous individual who likely felt as Blighty did about the FANY.

It suddenly occurred to her that this assignment could serve as an audition of sorts. If she *were* to become an agent, she'd need to work in close proximity with unfamiliar individuals—many of them the enemy. Blighty's visitor knew nothing about her, except possibly what the CO had seen fit to tell him. Well, little did *he* know. She could be clever and charming. She could behave as if men had hung the moon and she was content to fawn on their accomplishments and abilities. She didn't have a lot of practice with such rot, but she could certainly pull it off for a single afternoon. After all, it could play to her advantage.

"Ah, monsieur, vous devez être quelqu'un d'important."

"I'm glad to see you're practicing your French, dear." Olive startled out of her reverie to see Harriet looking at her expectantly. "Do you have time for a lesson this morning?"

"Afraid not," she said, getting to her feet, straightening her khaki-brown skirt and tunic, and settling her cap on her head. "I have to go meet a man."

"A rather important one, I gather." Her stepmother's smile

was altogether too knowing. "Well, wear a little lipstick. They all like that, and I'm sure Jamie won't mind."

Olive snorted. She rather hoped he would.

Olive was in the FANY carrel, sorting and filing personnel information on the various agents enrolled at the manor, when the phone rang. Kate Atherton picked it up, called to Olive that Blighty wanted to see her, then promptly went back to work, seemingly not the slightest bit curious.

Now that Olive was privy to the girl's secrets, she wondered how they'd ever eluded her. The fresh-from-the-farm, wide-eyed ingenue persona Kate projected was only a gloss. Behind the curtain of long lashes, the girl's eyes were steely and direct. Her movements were sure and efficient, and the subtle curve of her lips, which Olive had mistaken for shyness, was, in fact, self-possession. The truth of it had come out when Olive had questioned her about the murder of one of their own: it was simply the means to an end. Kate had been determined from the first to become an agent, to use her savvy to Allied advantage in occupied Europe, and having started off as she'd meant to go on—with a deception—she'd managed to fool them all, tucking her true self carefully away.

Olive had been utterly gobsmacked by the discovery. And also rather inspired. Not yet entirely certain that when push came to shove, she'd muster the courage to climb into an aeroplane that would drop her from the sky into Nazi territory, she'd decided, nonetheless, to put herself through the paces, to train, as best she could, alongside the agents. When her mettle caught up with her aspirations, she wanted to be thoroughly prepared for such an imperative undertaking.

So, with one last glance at her fellow FANY, she tipped her chin up and turned to walk briskly down the hall, flashing everyone she passed an Auxiliary Red smile.

Blighty's "Come" was issued the moment she knocked on his door. With a steadying breath, Olive pushed it open and stepped into the room, her gaze settling fleetingly on the CO before swinging to assess the man gazing out the window. He was very tall and athletic looking, his hands linked behind his back, fingers fidgeting. His dark blue uniform was a nice change from the khaki brown of Baker Street, and the wavy gold stripes circling his cuffs—a loop in the top one—looked quite prestigious.

Olive stood smartly before the desk, her features arranged in the expression she'd practiced in front of the mirror that morning: competent but deferential. "You wanted to see me, sir," she said with sprightly inflection.

The visitor turned slowly from the window. His shirt was almost blindingly white, and his black tie impeccably knotted. His eyes, under heavy lids, raked over her, and she allowed herself the same liberty, hoping her own face remained impassive. In truth, he was attractive but definitely not her type. With an aristocratic nose, made tougher by the evidence of a break, and impeccable grooming, his sort had crossed her path many times over at the Royal Veterinary College. But it was his eyes that caught her—there was a weakness there. It was impossible to know how it might manifest itself, but she recognised it, nonetheless.

"Miss Bright, this is Lieutenant Commander Ian Fleming of Royal Navy Intelligence," Blighty informed her, his voice dry. "He's the personal assistant to the director himself." Olive had no doubt the addition was meant to impress upon her the trouble she'd be in if she didn't handle the man with kid gloves. "This is one of our FANYs, Olive Bright."

"It's a pleasure, sir," she said, bobbing her head slightly in the direction of the lieutenant commander. By hook or by crook, she was determined to play to the man's ego.

"You've lipstick on your teeth, I'm afraid," the visitor said. "Not the sort of look I imagine you're going for."

Olive blinked, caught off guard, her smile dimming as she shielded her teeth. "No, sir," she agreed, refusing to look at Blighty. She kept her eyes trained on the map behind his desk as the visitor looked her over, no doubt finding fault at every turn. Finally, he walked toward her, his movements deliberate.

"Olive Bright. That's a very flat, quiet name," he said approvingly. "She'll do, but I intend to keep her very busy. It might be a late night." The comment, directed at Blighty, was heavy with suggestion.

"That's entirely up to her," the CO said flatly, but the warning in his voice was unmistakable. She had the impression that Fleming truly was someone very important, but that fact didn't seem to matter in the slightest to Blighty. Finally, a point in the man's favour.

Olive kept silent. Presumably the lieutenant commander would expect her to escort him over every inch of the grounds, but one way or another, she fully intended to be back at the manor by six o'clock. That would give her just enough time to get home and changed before hurrying along to Peregrine Hall for the séance.

"Let's be off, then, shall we?" said the lieutenant commander, retrieving his cap and overcoat from the coatrack by the door and laying the latter neatly over his arm. "I've brought my own car up from London, so I'll drive, shall I?" He placed a rather limp hand on the small of Olive's back to nudge her ahead of him out the door. "You need only aim me in the right direction."

They walked down the corridor in silence. Having run her tongue over her teeth, Olive smiled with a rictus of control. More than one FANY passed them, gazing appreciatively at Fleming before glancing askance at her.

Olive cleared her throat. "The CO said you wanted a tour of the training school and the manor grounds. A car won't be necessary. Everything interesting can be reached by an easy walk."

He looked down that long nose of his, seeming to channel a

schoolmaster. "Plenty of time for that . . . Miss Bright, is it?" She nodded. "Right now, I think I'd like to make a stopover in the village."

"Pipley?" Olive frowned, wondering if he was after a visit to the chemist. Or a drink at the pub. "Well, then, you don't need me tagging along." She came to an abrupt stop.

"I'm afraid I do, Miss Bright." His attitude was conspiratorial but not forthcoming, and Olive found herself wondering if he expected her to come along merely as a fawning admirer. Or a willing body. In that case, she'd be perfectly happy to practice Danny Tierney's number one rule for an encounter with the enemy: follow everything up with a knee to the testicles.

Olive shook herself in reminder. She was using him as surely as he was using her. Her goal was to ferret out his secrets without revealing her own. That meant she needed to put him at ease, play along, and convince him she was the type of girl who would be flattered by his smarmy attentions. Her knee would have to be a last resort.

"Why do you?" she asked sweetly. "Require my company, that is."

He gazed down at her with a self-satisfied smirk. "Because I expect having you there will grease the skids a bit, when the time comes." Olive frowned again, prompting him to add, "Come now, that's even worse than having lipstick on your teeth." He chucked her under the chin, and she fought down the urge to chop the side of her hand against his forearm. Or perhaps his neck. Unfortunately, he'd seen a flicker of something in her eyes, and it seemed to amuse him. "I can see I'll need to be careful round you."

"I've taken the same lessons in silent killing the men have," she informed him casually, stretching the truth only slightly. "Sometimes it's difficult to remember when training ends and real life begins." She didn't like the man—he was an absolute cad, if it came to that—but he was definitely up to something, and by the looks of things, Blighty hadn't a clue. Or else Blighty didn't care.

"You're a feisty one, aren't you?" he said approvingly.

She retrieved her coat from a long line of hooks beside the outer door, slipped her arms into the sleeves, and stepped out under the porte-cochère, where a snazzy red roadster had been pulled haphazardly under cover. The appreciative breath that feathered out of her drifted like a bit of white cloud on the frigid wind.

"It's a Graham-Paige," Fleming said, shrugging into his elegant overcoat. "I'd wager you've never had a ride in one of these." His words were innocent, if smug, but his eyebrows were engaged in an entirely inappropriate message of their own.

"But it's a convertible," she protested.

"You'll only feel the exhilaration. I promise."

Olive frowned. She'd felt plenty of exhilaration on the Welbike in the past few weeks and would have much preferred a bit of warmth.

She tried again. "Typically, the FANYs do the driving."

"I never let anyone drive my car," he said, walking round to open the nearside door for her. With the tiniest thrill, which she hoped wasn't writ on her face, she climbed in, noting that the car smelled strongly of cigarettes. He strode round the bonnet, opened his own door, and sent his cap spinning onto the seat beside her. He then folded his long length behind the wheel, cranked the engine, and they were off.

They roared down the manor drive, drawing startled and appreciative glances from agents and FANYs alike, and while Olive could admire the glossy, expensive fitment of the car, it was difficult to fully appreciate the experience, hunched as she was against the weather. Not to mention the fact that the space that separated her from her companion felt entirely too small. At the gatehouse, he turned toward the village, but a hundred yards on, he pulled into a lay-by and turned to look at her.

"From here on out, I'm afraid I'll need directions." He lifted his brows, but when she didn't comment, he pressed on. "We're going to pay a visit to Mrs Dunbar. I assume you know her whereabouts?"

Olive abandoned her silence and turned to him in surprise. "Mrs Dunbar? How do you know her?"

"I'm afraid I don't. I just need to have a little chat with her. So, if you don't mind . . . ?"

They drove on, with Olive speaking up whenever they needed to change course, unavoidably passing the village green, the grocer, with its queue of ladies waiting outside to collect the week's rations, the post office, and the lending library. In short, making certain to set every chin in the village wagging. And because everyone knew she couldn't discuss her work at Brickendonbury, they'd all craft wild tales of secrets, treachery, romance, and betrayal.

Olive sighed, knowing she'd have to come up with a more believable version to content Harriet.

"The third cottage on the left, at the end," she told him, staring curiously at its pale brick and slate-grey roof. In the spring, the wisteria bush beside the door draped the cottage with delicate lavender tracery, but it was barren now and oddly sinister. He pulled the car to a stop, the nearside wheels drawn up onto the verge. He stared out the window at the little overgrown cottage.

"What are you—"

He halted her inquiry with a finger laid flatly against her lips. Olive bristled at the nerve of the man but didn't shake free. "Stay here," he said sharply, with a lift of his brows and a grab for his cap. He was out of the car before a snap response might have got her into trouble.

She watched him nip through the gate and saunter up the

path, his gaze taking in the overgrown garden and the house's shabby state of disrepair. When he reached the door, he knocked sharply, then settled the Royal Navy peaked cap on his brilliantined hair. *The better to look official, my dear.* Olive shivered, rubbing rough hands over her bare legs and wishing for the umpteenth time that trousers were the preferred uniform for the FANYs.

As Olive had expected, Miss Pettifer answered the door in a pinny and headscarf. She was holding a wet rag in hands that were red raw from cleaning. Her exasperated frown turned on its head at the sight of the debonair Lieutenant Commander Fleming.

"Morning then. Can I help you?" she said.

Olive strained to hear his reply. "Yes, I'm looking for Mrs Velda Dunbar."

"Oh, she's not here, sir. Out running about—always things to do, she has, people to talk to. Her husband isn't here, neither." She leaned out the door, peered round. "Between you and me, he's got a hard row to sow, that one."

Fleming responded to this confidence with a sharp shake of his head and a dismissive flick of his hand. "That's unfortunate. Can you relay a message?"

"Certainly, sir." Miss Pettifer's eyes rounded with interest.

"Please tell Mrs Dunbar that a representative of the Royal Navy would like to have a little chat with her on the matter of the HMS *Bartholomew* . . ."

Olive, whose gaze had been caught by a pair of golden plovers winging overhead, promptly swung her attention back to the cottage door.

"You *heard* about that?" Miss Pettifer replied, her widened eyes locked on the visitor. "I didn't see it for myself, but there were plenty willing to tell me all about it. Most can't decide if she was conjuring real spirits or making fools of us—"

"Tell her," Fleming said, cutting across this chatty confidence, his voice low enough that Olive had to crane to make out even the occasional word, "investigation underway . . . fraudulent claims . . . utmost importance . . ."

Olive blinked, not at all certain she'd heard any of it correctly. Judging by Miss Pettifer's wide-eyed stare, she was similarly bemused. And that was when the housekeeper saw the roadster. Her eyes lit up at the treat of it, parked so casually in the lane, like a hot air balloon or a winged horse. She leaned forward, squinting, and called out in ringing tones, "Is that Miss Bright? How are you, dear?" Her hand went up in a jaunty wave.

Lieutenant Commander Fleming turned in time to see Olive waving jauntily back, a move that had him tipping his hat to the woman before walking briskly back down the path.

He climbed back into the car and laid his cap carefully on the seat between them. Curiosity burned the back of her throat, questions bubbling up unabated, but Olive was determined to remain cagey, even if it killed her.

With jerky movements, he shoved his hand into the inner pocket of his jacket and retrieved a cigarette case. Flicking it open with a well-practiced move, he selected one, then offered the case to her. When she refused, he tucked it away again and rummaged for a lighter. A moment later, he exhaled a stream of blue smoke into the space between them.

Olive swatted the air in irritation.

Fleming didn't react; he was staring into the middle distance, the fingers of his right hand occupied with the cigarette, while those of his left tapped a tattoo on the span of leather seat between them. Olive eyed those fingers until she was certain they had no ulterior motive, then turned to stare out the window at the comings and goings of the tits and chiffchaffs in the hedgerow. Finally, he said, "Did you hear any of that?"

"Only a word or two," she admitted.

"I don't suppose it was any of the important ones?" he probed.

She turned then to look at him with deliberately widened eyes. "Which ones were those?"

He didn't answer, merely propped his arm on the window frame and brought the cigarette to his mouth for another long drag. "What do you know about Mrs Dunbar? How long has she lived in the village?"

"Not much. Not long."

"How does she strike you? Just your average villager?" The latter was said with a deprecating smile.

"There's no such thing as an average villager," Olive said shortly and unhelpfully. Miss Husselbee would have had a field day with Fleming. Olive envisioned the woman's umbrella ferrule coming down smartly on his toe.

He flicked the ash from the tip of his cigarette, and Olive had a sense that he was keeping a tight hold on his temper. "Why don't you want to tell me about her?"

"I don't know what you mean."

"Don't you?" he said lazily. "Even if you didn't witness it yourself, I'm quite certain that the gossip's got round to you." He glared at her. "Or are you saying you're not aware of a recent spectacle put on by the lady in question?" He paused long enough to raise his brows. "There would have been wild predictions and amateur theatrics—all for show, of course."

"Oh, that. Well, yes, that was a bit out of the ordinary. But why does it concern you? Why would an officer of the Royal Navy drive his fancy Graham-Paige all the way from London to hear the details?" She blinked innocently.

He held the cigarette in front of his mouth, the haze of its smoke blurring his features. "Someone much more important than you, darling, has sent me, and I rather think they'd expect a member of the auxiliary services to assist in whatever way possible." *Auxiliary* may as well have been a slur in his mouth.

Olive balked at helping him without knowing precisely what

he was after. She felt quite certain this wasn't Baker Street business—Blighty probably had no clue that the pair of them were swanning round Pipley in Fleming's Graham-Paige. But Fleming clearly knew something about the HMS *Bartholomew*, and she could stand to know what. She certainly wasn't going to make it easy for him, though.

"All right," she said resignedly. "I was there."

"And?" he said, smugly encouraging.

"I really couldn't say." Seeing the tightening of his jaw, she quickly added, "If you must know, I'd no idea what to make of it. I still don't." She paused to wonder if she would come to regret her next words. "But I'm going to get another chance to decide."

"Meaning?" He had tossed his cigarette away and now stared out the windscreen.

Gritting her teeth at his tone, she went on. "She's holding a séance this evening, and I expect it'll be equally sensational."

He turned sharply to face her. "*Is* she? I'll admit, it's of rather critical importance that I observe Mrs Dunbar in her . . . spiritual state."

Olive frowned. "Invitation only, I'm afraid."

"I'll be your date. No one will bat an eye."

"Except," she said tightly, "that I'm already quite seriously involved with someone, a fact well known to everyone attending." *And*, she added silently, *if you even so much as touched me in an amorous fashion, I'd clock you.*

"Are you *really?*" He looked her over. "Well done, then." It obviously didn't occur to him that this might not be glowing praise, and he barrelled on. "Well, surely you can come up with a believable fib. I get the impression it's rather your stock in trade."

Damn the man. He'd managed to frazzle her right out of the gate, prompting an instant dislike, which she couldn't quite overcome. He was never going to believe she was a sweet, malleable girl, so she'd just as soon not waste time pretending. With Jamie still incommunicado, she needed to do her own reconnaissance. Changes were coming to Station XVII, and she wasn't at all keen on being caught unaware.

"My auxiliary responsibilities," she said carefully, "don't extend to village affairs. And I'm off the clock at five. If, however, I had a good *reason*, it's possible I could be convinced to let you tag along this evening." She brushed imaginary lint from her skirt before adding, "Take it or leave it."

He scoffed. "Tit for tat? Don't be ridiculous. We're at war—secrets abound. Every bloody thing is need to know."

"I'm afraid if I'm going to go out on a limb for you, then I do. Need to know, that is. At least part of it. Something."

He swore colourfully as she stared out the windscreen, seemingly unaffected. After a moment's rake of her profile, he demanded, "Are you *certain* you can get me in?"

She smiled thinly. "I suspect you'd be surprised what I can do when properly motivated, Lieutenant Commander Fleming."

His eyes held a flash of lascivious interest, quickly tamped down. And as he fumbled again in his jacket pocket, he sighed harshly and began to let her in on the secret. "The navy's had its eye on Mrs Dunbar for some months now—ever since her last séance purporting communication with a dead seaman." Having retrieved a second cigarette, he flicked his lighter to flame, then snapped it shut as he drew deeply. "While most of her claims are rubbish, there are some bits that are, shall we say, worth a closer look, so I've been sent up from London to investigate. Having the chance to witness one of her performances would be particularly useful."

Her pulse quickened, and questions burbled in Olive's mind, one rising quickly to the top. "How did you—"

"Further details aren't important. At least as far as you're concerned. I've given you quite enough to earn your trust and your willing assistance. In truth, considerably more than I should."

Olive ignored him, needing to know the truth. "So, it truly was sunk—the HMS *Bartholomew*?" His lips were mutinous, but Olive entreated him. "Please. There is a young girl, a friend of mine, who believes that her brother is dead . . ."

"It didn't sink," he said flatly. "But if I were you, I'd leave it for the families to find out on their own. My assurances are meaningless."

Her fingers might feel like icicles, but the warmth unfurling in her stomach trumped that little discomfort, obliterated it in the face of profound relief. Sweet, resilient Hen. She'd be so relieved—to say nothing of Mrs Gibbons and Freya Rodery. Perhaps Olive could think of a way to kindle a flicker of hope without coming right out with the truth. She'd have to consider very carefully.

Fingers were snapped before her eyes, rudely turning her thoughts back to her companion. "Focus, darling. What's your hook to get me in there?"

Olive reminded herself that the man had just compromised his standards at her request. He could be forgiven a lot, at least temporarily.

"Lady Revell tasked me with rounding out the numbers. I'll simply tell her you've come lately to the manor and don't have any friends." Raising her brows pointedly, she added, "I've already asked another of the FANYs, but I'll make excuses. She's a brick and won't bat an eye." Olive took in his white collar, gold buttons, and braid. "But if you've brought any civilian clothes, you might want to change into them so as not to give the game away before it even begins."

"Ah, yes, the good Miss Pettifer."

"Quite," she agreed.

"Fair enough. I'll use my mother's name and refrain from saluting anyone. Will that do?" he drawled.

"Shall we drive back, and I'll show you round the Brickendonbury grounds?" Olive said briskly. She was relieved to have reached a somewhat shaky truce but was feeling Jamie's absence even more keenly. It really was too bad that he'd miss the séance. He would have loved it—in the surly way of someone who took great pleasure in condemning the sort of thing he termed "utter bollocks."

Tomorrow. He'd be home tomorrow. It couldn't come soon enough.

Chapter 5

Communications

Their arrival at Peregrine Hall created a minor sensation. Even dressed in a pretty plaid skirt and sweater set, with her hair tamed and her complexion brightened with rouge and lipstick, Olive was under no illusions that she was the cause of it. Judging by the faces of the evening's other participants, Lieutenant Commander Fleming was a very welcome addition to their party.

Olive had to admit, in his well-cut jacket, open-collared shirt, and flannel trousers, he looked like a consummate playboy, perfectly at home at any evening's entertainment, whether staying in or going out. It was difficult to reconcile him with the uniformed individual she'd accompanied all afternoon.

He'd driven up to the lodge gates in the snazzy but impractical Graham-Paige, and she'd rushed out of the house in her warmest coat and a tightly cinched headscarf, eager to avoid a run-in with her father. They'd navigated the lanes in near silence, with only a word or two needed for direction. He hadn't commented further on his business with Mrs Dunbar and had only once glanced in her direction, to say that she looked quite approachable. While the words themselves hinted at flattery, the unspoken ones seemed to indicate otherwise.

But she got her own back when she introduced him to the gathered party in the drawing room of Peregrine Hall. Conscious of Harriet's sharp grey gaze and Violet Darling's deceptively cool demeanour, Olive endeavoured to keep her expression neutral. "I've brought along Mr Ian St Croix. He's recently arrived at the manor and"—a wry glance in his direction—"rather my responsibility, I'm afraid. Lucky for him, I'm constrained by the Official Secrets Act, or you'd all be getting an earful."

Half of the assembled company assumed this was only to the good, the other half knew her better, but everyone's brows rose curiously.

"Miss Bright is charming," he countered. "And quite a FANY." His lascivious smile was the sort to inspire a retaliatory slap, but Olive restrained herself as he went on. "I wouldn't have foisted myself on this intimate gathering, but in my spare time, I admit to being a student of phenomenology, with a particular fascination for the macabre."

Uncertain whether to be thoroughly exasperated with the man or grudgingly impressed, Olive merely shook her head.

"You're quite welcome, Mr St Croix," Lady Revell said graciously. "I don't begrudge you your interest. This is truly an opportunity not to be missed."

The drawing room was already decorated for the holidays, with festive swags of greenery draped over the mantelpiece and above the windows. A Christmas tree, decked with fragile glass ornaments and a scattering of tinsel, took pride of place in the corner.

The furniture had been shifted to make room for the evening's entertainment. A statuesque cabinet now dominated the space. It had been placed opposite the fireplace, with a circlet of dining chairs arranged to face it. The cabinet resembled a wardrobe but, in lieu of doors, it had been outfitted with a drape of thick, dark fabric. To its right, a marble-topped console held a wide silver salver and a vase of holly stems and white roses.

Mrs Dunbar had not yet made an appearance, so the rest of them stood about, chatting cosily while clutching cordial glasses topped up with sherry.

"When is Mrs Dunbar arriving?" Miss Danes finally inquired, her eyes darting and eager. "I'm quite looking forward to it, as Marcellus's column has predicted a dramatic appearance this week."

"Perhaps he was referring to a pimple," Violet murmured sotto voce.

Olive coughed to cover her snort of amusement.

"She's here at the hall," Lady Revell said. "I've offered her the use of the library for her mental preparations."

"Any moment now . . . ," Miss Danes said excitedly.

Olive's gaze, flitting about, settled on Mrs Gibbons. The poor woman looked as frazzled as she had following the medium's pronouncement on the village green. Olive crossed to stand beside her. "Everything all right, Mrs Gibbons? Are you sure you want to participate? We'd worked it out that she must have been wrong about Marcus, remember?"

The woman's pale eyes were wide as she turned to meet Olive's gaze. "Of course, dear. One can't be right all the time. I still find this business fascinating, and perhaps I'll even manage to speak to my mother. I might finally get a word in," she said with a twinkle before wandering toward the stage set for the evening's impending drama.

"Will we all have a chance to summon someone?" This from Miss Danes.

"Oh, I do hope so," Fleming answered lazily, his elbow propped on the mantelpiece. With the firelight flickering over the contours of his face, he looked like a fallen angel. Unfortunately, he seemed well aware of the fact and determined to play up the similarity.

"You mustn't touch that, dear," Lady Revell said abruptly, hurrying in the direction of Mrs Gibbons, who was standing beside the console table, her hand poised over the salver. "I'm afraid I'm a little nervous and want everything just so for Mrs Dunbar." She smiled self-consciously. She was dressed more formally than the rest of them, in a navy crêpe evening dress and gloves, a string of pearls at her throat. It was a far cry from the serviceable costumes she used for gardening and painting outdoors. Her silvered dark hair was pinned back from her face with a pearl clip, and she was pale. Olive worried that she had put entirely too much stock in the spiritualist's abilities and would be distressed at the likely outcome. Olive suddenly wished Max had come.

Newly aware of the guest of honour looming in the doorway, their hostess beamed and took a deep breath. "Ladies," she began, "and our singular gentleman." A shy smile. "Most of you, I believe, were on hand to witness the unique abilities of our very own Mrs Dunbar earlier this week. I'm sure you'll all agree it was quite extraordinary." Her hand fluttered up to rest against her bosom, and she paused a moment, letting them all harken back to those otherworldly moments on the village green.

Olive stole a glance at Fleming, but his face remained impassive, his cordial glass held with casual insouciance. Relieved he was behaving himself, she let her gaze travel over the evening's other participants.

Mrs Dunbar herself, looking rather imperious, swathed in yards of cheap black fabric, her pudgy hands splayed stiffly at her sides.

Mr Dunbar, hovering just behind her, his unnaturally dark hair combed thinly over his round pate, his walrus moustache looking rather droopier than usual.

Harriet, draped in a woolen shawl and tucked into the wheel-

chair Jonathon had fashioned out of a broken pram and other bits
and bobs, her grey eyes bright with interest.

Violet Darling, dressed for an evening of macabre phenomena
in slim black trousers and a dark hooded cloak, which she'd chosen not to push off her red-gold hair.

Miss Danes, sipping her sherry with great solemnity as her
eyes nearly bulged out of her head.

And finally, Mrs Gibbons, in her Sunday best, all fidgety fingers and quivering lips.

Olive was struck by the thought that they looked like a gathering of suspects facing the imminent deductions of Hercule
Poirot. And she was the ninth.

Lady Revell, meanwhile, had sallied on. "I approached our
guest of honour with the request for a private séance partly for
myself and partly in the hopes that my nephew, Max, would attend and could benefit from the chance to speak to those lost to
him in his young life." Sadness tinged her eyes and mouth, and
she paused, then nodded to herself to go on. "But," she said
briskly, with an apologetic smile at Mrs Dunbar, "he's not a believer in spiritualist endeavours and prefers to deal with the
losses in his own way."

"A pity," Mrs Dunbar said flatly.

"Yes," Lady Revell agreed distractedly before hurrying on. "I
think all of us here, however, are eager for the chance to speak to
someone who's gone before, to experience the solemnity of such
an opportunity at the hands of a skilled medium." She gestured
politely toward the woman who was now moving farther into the
room. "May I present Mrs Velda Dunbar."

A smattering of applause followed, led by the rather star-
struck Miss Danes.

Olive felt a tightness in her throat, caught between possibility
and uncertainty. What if it was truly possible for a departed soul
to return and communicate through a medium? Her mother had

been lost to them for more than ten years. Had too much time passed? Serena Bright had thrived on attention—appearing at a séance in Miss Husselbee's old drawing room would be difficult to resist. Olive bit her lip.

"Now then," their hostess continued rather awkwardly. "Before we begin, Mrs Dunbar has insisted that one of our little gathering examine her in her . . . erm, dishabille." Her hands gripped each other in embarrassment. "To ensure us of the integrity of her abilities."

It wouldn't have surprised Olive if Fleming had leaned close to murmur a crass comment in her ear, but he remained soberly attentive, and, in fact, appeared to be taking his role in the proceedings quite seriously.

Lady Revell smiled and gestured toward a Japanese folding screen standing at the edge of the room between the drawing room door and the cabinet. It was painted with snowy white cranes stepping sveltely through a forest of bamboo and clearly was intended to guard against an apparent exposé. "To ensure absolute discretion," she confirmed.

Miss Danes naturally couldn't resist such an offer. And while Olive's own sensibilities revolted at the thought of peering closely at the substantial figure that lay beneath all those yards of black fabric, Violet wasn't nearly so squeamish. Neither, it appeared, was Mrs Gibbons, who seemed to come abruptly to a decision, setting down her sherry and trailing off in the wake of the other two as Mrs Dunbar swept behind the screen.

"They're braver than I," murmured Fleming, only slightly behind schedule. Olive held her tongue with difficulty, not particularly proud to have been thinking the very same thing.

The irony was, the séance had yet to begin, and Olive could already sense the disapproving presence of Miss Husselbee. The huffs of disbelief and snorts of disapproval nearly vibrated through the room. Olive tucked back a smile. If the Sergeant Major—

Olive's favoured nickname for the regimented Miss Husselbee— *did* appear, it would be by her own devices, so that she might call the spiritualist out on rampant charlatanism.

In the midst of these musings, Mr Dunbar had pulled back the drapery of the manifestation cabinet. From its interior, he produced a rather medieval-looking lantern, its panes a gruesome shade of red. After rummaging in his pocket for a lighter, he nimbly swung open the cage of the lantern and put to flame the thick white candle tucked inside. With an efficiency born of much practice, he latched the cage shut and hung the lantern on a hook at the front of the cabinet. The process imbued the proceedings with an otherworldly, almost demonic quality.

"Behold," Lady Revell said rather grandiloquently from her position beside the console table, "the manifestation cabinet."

"May I?" Fleming queried, already moving forward to take a closer look at it. Lady Revell gestured grandly, if belatedly, for him to proceed. A similar gesture from Harriet found Olive dutifully rolling the wheelchair forward. Close enough to allow her stepmother to watch the self-professed phenomenologist at work as he rapped his knuckles and ran the pads of his fingers against the wood.

"It's beautifully made," Olive marvelled. Above their heads, the wood was carved with a Gothic-inspired tracery pattern, much like the screen of a chancel, but below, the solid oak planks and red satin interior, the seedy red glow of the lantern and the rigid straight-backed chair that took pride of place gave the whole thing the look of a rather risqué coffin. "It's quite large, though," she blurted. "However did you manage to get it in here?"

She hadn't expected a response, but at that moment, the medium reappeared from behind the screen, adjusting the swaths of fabric round her.

"I must be comfortable," Mrs Dunbar said shortly, prompting

a wince from Olive, who hadn't considered the woman's spatial requirements.

"Of course," she mumbled. "I didn't mean—"

"There must be space for the spirits to surround me, for the exchange of energy. Or else they will not come."

Harriet's wide-eyed glance was teasing and pointed, as if to say, "Didn't you know?"

Fleming, meanwhile, appeared utterly convinced, saying only, "Well, there it is, then."

"It was brought in through the French doors, dear," Lady Revell said delicately before inquiring of the returning entourage, "Are you all satisfied that Mrs Dunbar is hiding no accoutrements that might assist her in her communion with the spirit world?"

Miss Danes nodded, the light of a zealot in her eyes, and Violet shrugged noncommittally. Mrs Gibbons didn't answer. She was staring at the manifestation cabinet.

"Let's carry on, then," Lady Revell asserted.

They took their seats, with Harriet's wheelchair positioned on the edge of the arrangement.

"Thus far, it's not the sort of evening's entertainment I was promised," Violet muttered dryly.

"You deserve a good stiff drink, darling," Harriet assured her. "Unfortunately, I don't think there's one in the offing."

Fleming leaned forward to proffer his cigarette case.

"Thank you, no," Violet drawled. "I suspect this business will be quite stimulating enough." His hooded eyes raked over her as he lit his own cigarette, but he made no reply.

"I thought you were bringing Hell," Harriet murmured, nodding her head toward Fleming, who was now wreathed in a haze of blue smoke.

"In a manner of speaking, I did," Olive said tartly.

Mrs Dunbar, who'd been conferring quietly with Lady Revell, suddenly swept forward, the light from the lantern falling over her pale face with vampiric gruesomeness. She glared at Fleming. "Absolutely no smoking. Mr Dunbar should have informed you earlier."

"There'll be no smoking," called Mr Dunbar, grabbing an ashtray from a nearby table and hurrying forward to retrieve the remains of the cigarette.

Fleming's fingers clung on. "Surely it can't matter that much." Facing down the marked disapproval of both Mrs Dunbar and Miss Danes—not to mention the pained look on Lady Revell's face—he stabbed it out. "I suppose we're certain she's not a witch?" he murmured in an aside to no one in particular.

"Mrs Gibbons." Lady Revell spoke abruptly. "If you'd like to take your seat, I think we're ready to begin." As the medium waited in some impatience, Mrs Gibbons, who'd apparently been emboldened to step inside the cabinet, now stepped out into the glow of the lantern light. The faded red of her hair, having long ago begun its transition to grey, seemed for a moment to blaze with fire.

"This has been a night to remember already," Harriet said quietly as Mrs Gibbons settled into the remaining chair.

"It is now time," Mrs Dunbar said portentously, "for the lights to be snuffed out and the fire dampened. The lantern"—she looked solemnly into its glow—"will light the way for the spirits." She tipped her chin up and let her eyelids fall closed. "My spirit guides are dedicated souls and very skilled at convincing other, more resistant spirits to come forth."

As Mr Dunbar hopped up, poised to move about the room to turn off the electric lamps, Lady Revell spoke up. "I know we're all anxious to get started, Mrs Dunbar, but first, I've collected some photographs"—she gestured toward the salver on the table beside her—"and I hope you'll spare a few moments to look through them, in hopes that they'll assist you in forging a connection. I'm so very eager to see my sister again." There was a catch in her voice, and Olive felt a stab of pity and a twinge of guilt at her own scepticism and, even, duplicity at inviting Lieutenant Commander Fleming to attend.

Mrs Dunbar's frown, prompted by Fleming's cigarette and Mrs Gibbons's unpredictability, seemed to deepen, but she moved to stand beside her hostess. She lifted the photos from the salver, then made a show of looking at each of them in turn, shuffling through the lot.

Lady Revell smiled mistily. "My sister's name was Cornelia . . . Nellie. We were very close." Her face looked distraught.

Mrs Dunbar carefully placed the photographs back on the salver, tugged at her ear and, with one last glance at Lady Revell, stepped ponderously into the manifestation cabinet.

Harriet leaned toward Olive and whispered, "Is it all going to be as fraught as this?"

Olive shrugged helplessly, once again struck by the paradoxical feelings the evening had inspired.

"What if we don't have a photograph?" Miss Danes whined. "I could sketch a likeness, I s'pose, but I've never had much luck with noses . . ."

"It is up to the spirits now," Mrs Dunbar said quellingly, rubbing her fingers against her palms in apparent irritation, then running a frazzled hand across her brow as the light in the room dwindled to nothing more than a carmine glow.

"All right, my love?" Mr Dunbar inquired. He stood at the edge of the cabinet, peering in at her. "Ready to make a start?"

She glanced at him in exasperation, her answer a single, tight word, "Quite," which prompted his retreat into the audience.

Glaring at each of them in turn, daring them to interrupt or protest further, Mrs Dunbar sank back into the chair, tumbled her hands beneath her robes, closed her eyes, and said, "Let us begin."

Violet reached for Olive's hand and squeezed it gently, possibly thinking of her sister, Rose, and wondering if it was possible she might manifest herself. Olive squeezed back, suddenly quite desperately hoping there'd be no surprises, no apparent visits from anyone still meant to be alive.

The drawing room grew silent with anticipation as they all awaited what came next.

The silence lasted for several long moments, during which they all peered into the shadows of the manifestation cabinet, where Mrs Dunbar sat slumped in her chair, as if she had imbibed too much sherry and couldn't even summon a bit of decorum. Even Mr Dunbar, standing off to one side, kept his focus on her. But as the seconds ticked past, anticipation gave way to impatience, and everyone began shifting and sighing, surely wondering if the whole business was nothing more than an elaborate hoax. Olive's thoughts had drifted to Jamie's imminent return when Mrs Dunbar finally spoke.

"There is a charge in the air flowing through me," she said excitedly. "The spirits are eager to be heard." Another silence as her eyes tipped closed, her head twisting to and fro, as if she was searching through the darkness. "Evelyn, are you there?"

Olive perked up, leaning toward Harriet to whisper, "You'll like Evelyn."

"I expect so," her stepmother replied.

A glance down the line of chairs caught the stiffening of Fleming's shoulders. He'd leaned forward, and Olive could picture his narrowed eyes boring into the medium, eager to catch her out.

"I am, indeed, Miss Velda," came the answer, slowly parsed out in a molasses drawl.

"Oh, my," said Harriet.

Violet cut her eyes round at Olive, who said merely, "Just wait."

"For those of you who are unaware of it," Mrs Dunbar intoned gruffly, "Evelyn is my spirit guide, my connection to those lost souls it is our intention to find." She darted a quick glance at Lady Revell, whose countenance was full of hope and encouragement.

"I'm afraid there's a clamour of them this evenin', Miss Velda. All wantin' a chance to say their piece."

"I'd swear her lips aren't moving," Violet murmured. "And neither are the husband's."

Olive didn't have a chance to reply.

"Each of them will have an opportunity," the medium said. "Who is with you now, Evelyn?"

There was a rough clearing of the disembodied throat. "There's one lost to the Great War and one just after—one hero and one not."

Olive gasped as a shudder ran through her. *Is it possible . . . ? Can Evelyn be speaking of Mother?*

Harriet reached for her hand and tightened her long fingers round it as Evelyn went on. "One a murderess, one murdered." The breath shuddered out of Violet Darling. "There is one poor soul who succumbed to desperation and another who died in service to King and country."

Someone cried out—Olive thought it might have been Mrs Gibbons. Everyone else was stunned into silence. It seemed each of them had identified someone in Evelyn's pithy descriptions. And they didn't know quite what to make of it, or him. Not to mention Mrs Dunbar.

"You'll need to get them sorted, Evelyn," the medium said brusquely. "And remind them to focus their energies for passage through the portal. I'll open myself as a channel to receive them one at a time."

"Right you are, madam," Evelyn said accommodatingly.

Mrs Dunbar's head fell forward. She breathed a deep, rattling breath, then called, "Who is here with us? I can feel your energy tingling my fingers, running up my arms, filling me . . ." Her body convulsed violently, and everyone watching jerked in reaction. "Introduce yourself. Be welcome," she demanded.

"Fleming." This voice was male, brisk, and aristocratic, and Olive, utterly distracted by the spectacle, wondered if she'd mis-

heard. She glanced warily down the line of chairs, but the lieutenant commander seemed perfectly relaxed under the circumstances.

Someone here, either spiritual or corporeal, knew the man's true
identity, and Olive couldn't decide which was more shocking.

"Who have you come for?" Mrs Dunbar bossily inquired. The
moment the words were out, her arm rose as if of its own volition,
her finger extending to indicate the lieutenant commander. A
convulsion rolled over her, and her face contorted in a rictus of
effort.

"I think the ectoplasm might be coming," Olive warned.

Harriet sat up straighter. "I don't want to miss that."

"I'm listening," the corporeal Fleming said lazily. In the absence of his cigarette, he crossed his arms over his chest.

Mrs Dunbar leaned forward, beyond the confines of her cabinet, and peered closely at him. Her eyes were wide, and her face
looked positively puce in the light of the lantern.

The aristocratic voice spoke again into the silence. "You always were a black sheep. And it seems the inclination never
left you—"

This little speech was interrupted quite unceremoniously by
Mrs Dunbar, who now speared Fleming with a flat look of contempt. "He's gone beyond my reach."

Judging by the sudden silence, it seemed Evelyn had also gone
to ground.

No one spoke, each of them likely still reeling from the cha-
otic display. Olive found she was getting a headache.

Only seconds later, Mrs Dunbar's arm rose portentously, shaking now. It hovered, ranging over the assembled group, stopping
on first one and then another of them, as she squinted into the
dimly lit room. But it was her own voice that tumbled into the silence.

"It's so difficult to keep them all straight," she began, before
abruptly pausing, a fierce frown marring her brow. "Mothers, sis-

ters, wives, mistresses . . ." Her chest shrunk into itself before puffing up again. "To say nothing of the men." And then she abandoned all pretence. She ceased to be a medium engaged with the spirit world and was simply a petulant guest. "I'm so desperately thirsty. I must have something to drink. *Quickly.*"

Lady Revell, who'd been riveted like the rest of them, now jolted into action. "Oh dear, I do believe we've finished off the sherry. Shall I get you a glass of water from the kitchen?"

"Arthur," Mrs Dunbar yelled plaintively, her voice sounding slurred. "Where's that bottle?"

Lady Revell wavered, uncertain whether to stay or go.

"Well, this is anticlimactic," Violet said. "I was promised ectoplasm."

"Yes, I quite wanted to see that," Harriet agreed.

As Mr Dunbar hurried forward, pulling a glass bottle from his jacket pocket, Olive rolled her eyes, knowing it was very likely gin. Oblivious, Miss Danes leaned toward her. "I'm ever so eager to see honest-to-goodness ectoplasm. Do you suppose she'll let us touch it? *Can* one touch it?"

"Either way, I don't think it's a good idea, dear," Harriet told her.

"Is this an intermission?" queried Mrs Gibbons from Fleming's other side, glancing about her. "So much energy is expended to bring these poor souls back to us." She shook her head. "Lady Revell really should have served sandwiches. Perhaps I have something in my bag." She began rummaging.

In the cabinet, Mrs Dunbar tipped back her head along with the bottle, thumping it against the wood as she greedily guzzled, causing liquid to run down her chin. As if this spectacle wasn't grotesque enough, a pale, amorphous presence materialised above her head.

Miss Danes let out a shuddering "Ohhh."

"Is that the ectoplasm?" Harriet demanded, her voice an awed hush.

Olive leaned forward, peering into the cabinet's shadows. She thought she could make out the nuances of a face on the sinuous vagary now undulating within the confines of the chamber. Gooseflesh rose on her arms, and she blinked, then peered closer at Mrs Dunbar, feeling all at once uncertain. If this was a hoax, how on earth was the woman managing it in her current state? A quick glance at Mr Dunbar showed no mischief from that quarter. He was standing before the fireplace, gazing at the flames while warming his insides with the contents of his own silver flask.

A second later, her bottle empty, the medium opened her eyes. With a choking gasp of surprise, she seemed suddenly to become aware that she was not alone in the cabinet, and began thrashing at the spectral intrusion. For a moment, the audience held its collective breath. All except Fleming.

"Well, this is curious," he said in the dim and macabre confusion.

"Get away, you Judas," Mrs Dunbar demanded, one hand reaching up to grab at the nebulous thing as the other clawed at her own robes, rending the fabric of her bodice and exposing a swath of fleshy skin the colour of porridge. Pink porridge in the current lighting. Miraculously, she seemed to catch hold of the vagary, entwining her hand with it as it writhed away from her. Almost instantly, she let it go to grasp her throat with both hands, as if she was choking on something.

"It's much more melodramatic than I imagined," Violet mused, frowning, her gaze riveted.

Olive, who had witnessed Mrs Dunbar's earlier spectacle, was struck by how much less controlled it was this time round.

Miss Danes, it seemed, was of the same mind. "Perhaps the other was a good spirit, and this . . . this one is evil." She cringed into herself.

Not one to put any stock in the woman's spoutings on spiritualism, Olive nonetheless felt a shiver run through her. *If only Evelyn would come back . . .*

Mrs Dunbar was now thrashing about the cabinet, her body heaving and shuddering.

"Evelyn," she croaked, "protect me from their knives. They . . . are . . . murdering . . . me." The final words were torn out of her, each on its own desperate gasp. It broke the spell that had come over the party like a douse of cold water.

Olive bolted to her feet just as Harriet reached to grip her arm. Violet shot up next, and with a look of wary uncertainty, Fleming uncrossed his legs and stood. Lady Revell was peering intently through the dark, stepping closer to the cabinet.

"Don't touch her," Miss Danes screeched, stilling them all with an appealing hand. "You mustn't ever touch a medium while she's communing with the spirits. It's impossible to predict what might happen . . ."

"What the bloody hell is going on here?" Fleming responded. He propped his hands on his hips and looked round at them in turn, clearly expecting someone to know what to do.

Mrs Dunbar's rasping breaths permeated the room, and they all looked on, uncertain what was happening and how to proceed.

"Mr Dunbar," Olive called urgently. "Has this happened before? Is she all right?" When he didn't answer, she turned to the fireplace. But he was no longer there. "Mr Dunbar?" Now every head was swivelling in search of the man.

"Something's wrong," Harriet said sharply, her gaze trained on the flailing woman in the cabinet. "Go switch on the lights, Violet, and call the doctor." Certain of the young woman's compliance, she turned to Miss Danes. "Winifred, go and find Mr Dunbar—"

"You don't understand," Miss Danes interrupted, clearly planning to school them all on the nuances of spiritualism.

A long, guttural moan issued from the manifestation cabinet, followed by what sounded like desperate weeping. Olive's stomach seemed to bottom out.

"Unless you want this woman's death on your conscience, Winifred," Harriet barked, "you'll do it, and quickly." A glare sent Miss Danes scurrying out of the room. Olive's stepmother, a nurse in a burn hospital during the Great War, had taken brisk command of the situation. "Leticia, do you have any syrup of ipecac? Perhaps the contents of that bottle didn't agree with her."

"Certainly," Lady Revell said and quickly hurried to the door, no doubt eager to be away from the grotesque spectacle of Mrs Dunbar.

"Olive, Mr St Croix, see if you can make Mrs Dunbar any more comfortable. Perhaps a fan or a glass of water."

"I'll go for the water," Fleming said shortly, glancing briefly at the medium.

"The kitchen is at the end of the hall," Olive told him, hurrying toward the slumped figure in the cabinet. The woman was clearly overcome, but her hands, going limper by the moment, still reached for her throat. The lights came on, and Olive gasped at the sight of her. She'd thought the pink of her complexion due to the lantern, but in the glow of the illumined room, it was now clear the cause was something else entirely. A touch of her forehead confirmed she was flushed with feverish heat, yet she was not perspiring. Olive leaned over Mrs Dunbar, saying urgently, "Are you hurt? Ill? Overcome by the spirits?" She felt compelled to add the last.

The answer, when it came, was entirely unexpected. "Murdered."

"What does she mean, murdered?" Mrs Gibbons asked weakly.

Olive frowned, glancing at Harriet, who sat rigid in her chair, worrying her fingers. "She's red as a beetroot and blazingly hot," Olive said. "Quite possibly delirious, as well."

Harriet gasped, but before Olive could press her, Violet returned. "Dr Harrington is on his way," she said quietly, moving to stand behind the wheelchair, her cloak having fallen back to reveal a pale face and a jaw tight with concern.

"Thank God for that," Harriet answered.

A flurry in the doorway prefaced the return of both Fleming and Lady Revell from their respective errands. Somewhat brusquely, Harriet demanded, "Do either you or Max use eyedrops, Leticia? Pilocarpine?"

Lady Revell shook her head, her eyes darting to the medium. "But I've brought the ipecac."

"We'll have to risk it. No, wait on the water, Mr St Croix. We'll try the ipecac first. Violet, if you could push me a bit closer."

"Yes, the ipecac should do the trick," Mrs Gibbons said urgently, clutching at the arm of the only man in the room. To his credit, he didn't shake her off.

Lady Revell pushed the bottle into Olive's hands, then stepped back, wringing her own. Fleming waited, his solid bulk something of a comfort.

Olive glanced at Harriet, who nodded at her to proceed, then promptly unscrewed the cap. "Here, this will help," she told the medium calmly, praying that it would. She put the bottle directly against Mrs Dunbar's lips, but it was pushed roughly away as the woman gulped and sputtered, trying to speak.

"She's"—the word seemed ripped from her lips—"not here. She didn't come."

"You can tell me in a moment," Olive soothed, firmly returning the bottle to her lips and quickly tipping it up to pour some of the foul liquid down her throat.

Mrs Dunbar gasped, gurgled, then emitted a long moan.

"Now the water," Harriet barked.

The glass was thrust into Olive's hand, and she repeated the procedure, tipping back the woman's head, urging her to drink. As trickles of water seeped from the corners of the slack mouth, Olive stared into the piteous, dilated gaze of Mrs Dunbar, willing the medicine to work.

When the glass was empty, Olive handed it back, and knowing what was coming next, she tipped the woman forward in her chair. But as the moments ticked past, an agony of uncertainty and anticipation, and the situation remained unchanged, worry and fear began to overtake them all.

"Where is that bloody woman?" Harriet demanded, clearly beside herself. Miss Danes could prompt such a reaction at the best of times, but these were trying indeed.

"Don't forget she's looking for that bloody man," Mrs Gibbons chimed in. "Where did he get off to? And in the middle of a séance." She tsked.

It *was* curious. But Olive couldn't spare the time to consider it. Every ounce of her concentration was focused on waiting for Mrs Dunbar to expel whatever it was that had caused this debilitating reaction. She was under no misapprehension that a spirit had done this; this was horribly real.

Dry heaves shuddered through the slumped body, leaving it limp with the effort but no closer to relief.

"Try a bit more of the ipecac, Olive," Harriet insisted. Olive complied, her heart beginning to race anxiously.

But it was no use. Miss Danes eventually bustled in with a contrite-looking Mr Dunbar, just in time to see the last rattling breath issue forth from the collapsed figure of Mrs Dunbar.

Her husband stared in disbelieving horror. "Is she—?" He didn't finish the sentence. "I was having a walk round the garden. The red light gives me headaches. It was all business as usual when I stepped out. What's happened?"

A flutter of sound had Olive glancing swiftly down at the medium, but she remained still and lifeless. Olive felt a shiver creep over her as she stood amid the red haze of the cabinet, the empty eyes of a dead woman staring up at her. Her stomach churned uneasily.

"Her spirit is still here among us," Miss Danes said with certainty, glancing about, as if the woman's ghost might readily seep through the wainscoting if they didn't attempt to corral it.

But no one answered either of them. The entire party was quite overcome with shock. All except Lieutenant Commander Fleming. He wasted no time in producing his cigarette case and filling the air with cool blue smoke. He was, in fact, the one who spoke first. "I suppose we'll need to call round for the police."

Chapter 6
The Use and Care of Binoculars

6 December
Peregrine Hall

It hadn't needed to be done, after all. Violet Darling had confessed that she'd rung up the constabulary right after she'd got through to Dr Harrington. "Better safe than sorry," she'd said dryly, with a pointed look at Olive. And it seemed only moments passed before the officers had crowded into Lady Revell's drawing room and instructed them all to sit down again.

Mr Dunbar wouldn't leave the body, and only Miss Danes returned to the chair she'd occupied during the séance. Violet went to stand beside the Christmas tree, and everyone else arranged themselves round the fire.

To the supreme irritation of every woman in the room—villagers, one and all—the newcomers looked to Lieutenant Commander Fleming for a summary of the evening's events. Olive placated herself with the fact that he didn't tell it very well. He left out all sorts of curious and important bits.

Still, it came as no surprise when Dr Harrington voiced his verdict. "Naturally, it'll need to be confirmed by a post-mortem, but as of right now, there's no question in my mind that this woman has been poisoned. The symptoms are indicative of belladonna."

"Murdered?" Miss Danes demanded, glancing askance at Violet, who met her gaze unflinchingly.

"Now, I didn't say that," he said quellingly. "That'll be decided at the inquest. But the symptoms match. She would have been flushed and thirsty, convulsive, and quite possibly hallucinating and spouting absurdities."

Glances were exchanged, none of them wanting to admit that they'd all just assumed the latter was part of her usual trappings.

He draped a sheet over the body, having to twitch it into place across the girth of the woman. Miss Danes hurried forward to assist, but Dr Harrington waved her decidedly away. He then swept the cabinet's drapery into place to shield the woman from scrutiny—or unauthorised examination by overzealous individuals. He'd already slipped the bottle Mrs Dunbar had drained into his bag, along with the ipecac, no doubt intending to have the contents of both analysed.

"She drank nothing else?" he demanded of the room at large.

"I think she might have had a bit of sherry," Lady Revell croaked, "but we all had a glass. There's no more, I'm afraid, but the decanter is still on the drinks cart." Olive noted that the raised veins of her hands were showing blue against her skin as she wrung them in shock and chagrin.

Dr Harrington nodded and suddenly looked very tired. His hair was askew, and there were dark circles under his eyes.

Harriet gripped Olive's hand in hers as Detective Sergeant Burris made a gruff announcement.

"I'd be obliged if you'd all make yourselves comfortable. We're going to need to question each of you." He looked to Lady Revell. "If you have enough tea to go round, I think we could all use a cuppa." Lowering his voice, he added, "I'll do what I can to see it's replaced."

Eager to be useful, their hostess rose and hurried from the room.

"You knew, didn't you?" Olive asked her stepmother quietly.

Harriet nodded, her eyes already glossed with tears. "I suspected. The way you described her, it was close enough to a mnemonic I learned in nursing school—'blind as a bat, mad as a hatter, red as a beet, hot as hell, and dry as a bone.' " She paused, her eyes troubled. "The symptoms of an overdose of atropine."

"But Dr Harrington said—" Violet protested.

Harriet interrupted tiredly. "Belladonna? Yes. Commonly known as deadly nightshade. Atropine is derived from the plant. And pilocarpine drops can serve as an antidote."

"Deadly nightshade," Mrs Gibbons breathed. Her lashes fluttered at the seeming impossibility of it. Harriet nodded, prompting her to go on. "But that means anyone could have done it. It grows wild in most every garden . . ." Her voice had risen hysterically.

Violet wrapped an arm round her, rubbing briskly, and said calmly, "But it would have had to be administered here—by one of us—wouldn't it?"

"It depends. A high dose would have worked quite quickly, but a lower one could have taken some time," Harriet admitted bleakly. Her arm shook ever so slightly as she raised a hand to rub at her temple. "But no one's saying murder," she insisted. "It could just as well have been an accident."

"But that doesn't make sense," Olive objected. "Mrs Dunbar was acting strangely almost from the moment she climbed into the cabinet. All she'd had at that point was sherry, and we all partook."

This detail sent a jolt through Mrs Gibbons, and Violet tightened her grip.

"True," Harriet said, "but perhaps that was all part of her performance, so to speak."

Olive thought back over the evening, with all its baffling moments, and considered. "I'm curious as to what was in that little bottle of hers."

At that moment they became aware of a shadow looming over them. They glanced up to find DS Burris gazing down at them in a manner familiar to them all. "Now, now, you mustn't let your thoughts run away with you. I've no doubt you find this business distressing—we all do. But this here is a job for the police." He straightened his burly form importantly. "You've only to make a statement and answer a few questions, and you'll be off home again."

As one, the four women arranged on the sofas looked up at him, their features displaying no offense or irritation at having a man explain the obvious. This was a game they all played with aplomb when the occasion demanded it. DS Burris, for his part, felt rather bolstered by the four complacent and appreciative smiles, and even more so at the prospect of a cup of tea.

"Now then, here's Lady Revell," he added unnecessarily as their hostess swept in with a tray. A maid followed with a second, and they arranged the provisions on a nearby table: two steaming pots of tea, slices of thinly buttered bread, and a jar of honey, glowing gold in the firelight. Olive was suddenly ravenous.

"You may go, Martha," Lady Revell told the maid, who looked very much as if she wanted to stay. The girl did as she was told, and Lady Revell busied herself with one of the teapots. "I'm afraid I can't offer sugar—it's all been parceled out in preparation for Christmas—but I think honey is just as good. And certainly, we could all use a cup of hot, sweet tea right now."

She began handing round the cups, first to DS Burris and his constable, then Dr Harrington, Mr Dunbar, and finally the dodgy Mr St Croix. The ladies, she served last.

Accepting a slice of bread and a cup of honeyed tea, Olive thanked Lady Revell. "Don't worry," Olive said warmly. "This horrid business will be over soon."

"Oh, no, dear," she said, her usually sturdy voice quavering slightly. "This will linger on in all our memories." Resigned to the truth of her words, Olive set down her teacup to squeeze Lady Revell's pale fingers. They were cold as ice.

"Where is Max this evening?" she asked.

"I believe my nephew is biding his time at the Fox and Duck," she said, a doting look in her eye.

"Shall I call down to the pub, Lady Revell?" Violet asked. "I'm sure he'd come home in an instant."

"He'll be home soon enough. I'll manage until then."

Olive moved off to enjoy her tea beside the fire, noting that the men had clustered round the console table, darting glances at the aftermath of a séance gone horribly wrong. They spoke in a quiet murmur, determined to keep their secrets. Bloody-minded males.

A voice in her ear whispered, "I see no reason why we shouldn't read their lips."

Olive's mouth hitched up at Violet's suggestion. "Unfortunately, I'm not very good at it, although I could use the practice." It would be an invaluable skill for an agent.

"Oh, I'm almost criminally good."

And so they proceeded to eavesdrop on the conversation not intended for their innocent ears, all of it relayed via subtle murmuring round lifted teacups.

"Mr Dunbar is protesting," Violet began. "He says, 'I don't know where she got that bottle. She gave it to me beforehand, then demanded it back again. Do you s'pose that's what did her in?' "

Before DS Burris could inquire further, Fleming took up the questioning.

"My turn," Olive insisted, staring intently at the man's lips. And if her voice shifted into a self-important drawl, she could hardly be blamed. "I couldn't help but notice that you left the room shortly after giving it to her. Why was that?"

Violet, who'd been sipping her tea, cut her eyes round at Olive. "Are we doing voices, then?"

Olive shrugged. "Only if they're spot on."

Taking her cue, Violet lent a bit of churlishness to Mr Dunbar's response. "Needed a bit of air . . . not easy being married to such a . . . formidable woman." She promptly dropped the act as her voice hissed with irritation, "The whole lot of them stand there smirking, and the poor woman is dead."

But Dr Harrington, Olive noted, looked very serious indeed.

DS Burris took a large bite of bread, crumbs collecting at the corners of his mouth, then spoke round it, so that Violet was frowning in concentration. "Likely some sort of homemade brew." He swallowed. "Mrs Dunbar was in a right state on the village green—might be that her communion with the spirits is helped along by spirits of another sort." His gaze flicked pointedly to Mr Dunbar. "Heard tell you've been making beer in yer back garden from a bumper crop of potatoes."

Violet kept on, conveying Mr Dunbar's admission. "Aye. It's turned out all right, but Velda weren't keen. If that brew had been in the bottle, she would have stopped after the first sip. And griped plenty."

Olive couldn't make out the hushed whisperings of Lady Revell, Mrs Gibbons, and Harriet, each of whom clearly had her own opinion on the evening's events. If she wasn't certain she could get the gist from Harriet, she'd have switched to eavesdropping on them instead.

She couldn't help but notice that Miss Danes was glancing between the men and the manifestation cabinet with darting-rabbit eyes. And so, when Dr Harrington finally spoke up, Violet beat Olive to the punch.

"This is almost certainly a case of belladonna poisoning, and to my knowledge, Mrs Dunbar wasn't taking it under the guise of medical treatment."

Mr Dunbar shook his head in an emphatic negative. "She weren't one for doctors or drugs."

DS Burris set his cup and saucer down on the console table and then proceeded to speak at such a volume as to make lip-reading entirely unnecessary. "Quite. Well, I think with a bit of questioning, we'll get straight to the bottom of this matter. I suspect we'll find it's been an unfortunate accident—beggin' your pardon, Doctor."

Olive nearly groaned aloud. She couldn't decide if DS Burris was naively optimistic or crushingly incompetent. Any sort of misbehaviour—right down to murder—might be consigned to blameless coincidence on his watch. And he had the ear of the higher-ups. No wonder she was considered Pipley's very own Miss Marple. In fairness, she would have preferred a comparison to Hercule Poirot, but the villagers doing the comparing were keener on a village spinster solving crime than a foreign male detective.

"If I were you," Violet said coyly in her ear as the men crowded their empty cups onto the table, "I'd take this opportunity to question your suspects."

"It's not any of my business . . ."

"And when, my girl, has that stopped you?" She smiled. "Besides, I really don't care to be a murder suspect twice in one year." Seeing Olive's frown, she added, "Even if DS Burris doesn't believe it, every one of us here tonight suspects foul play. And all but one of us want to know what really happened."

These ominous words were still echoing in Olive's thoughts when Violet drifted away and Fleming appeared beside her, much too close for comfort. She tried shifting away from him, but he gripped her elbow. "We agreed that I wouldn't reveal the official nature of my visit, and I want to know why you went behind my back."

Olive yanked her arm free of him, anger sparking at his accusation.

"Seeing as I've signed the Official Secrets Act," she hissed, "*and* given you my word, perhaps you'd consider trusting my discretion."

His gaze, under those hooded lids, never wavered, but she sensed somehow that she'd surprised him, and Olive found that very curious indeed. A spirit—either real or contrived—had called him by name and spoken of his past. A family member? Had he lied about his real reason for meeting Mrs Dunbar? Was it, in fact, unrelated to his job at the Admiralty? She frowned slightly, considering the other side of the coin. Would the Royal Navy have reason to silence the bombast of a spiritualist medium? Could he have been tasked with the job? If she *were* drawing up a suspect list, he'd be right at the top of it.

"As long as we're accusing each other," she said haughtily, "I might as well ask. Did you have a reason to kill her?"

He wasn't offended; that much was obvious. In fact, it rather seemed as if he appreciated her candour. "No," he finally said. "But I won't deny that this evening's turn of events has tidily dispatched my problem. Though I may have robbed Peter to pay Paul. I suspect the ordeal of being questioned by the village idiot over there will be just as excruciating as dealing with Mrs Dunbar."

Olive bristled. Her own opinions were one thing, the censure of an outsider quite another. But she was interrupted in her intended defence of DS Burris by the man himself. "If I may have your attention." Conversation stuttered to a halt as the occupants of the room turned to look at him. "If it's all right with you, Lady Revell, I'll perform the interviews in the library, which I believe to be right next door." At her nod, he went on. "Dr Harrington, I expect you'll want to arrange for the removal of the body . . . quite so." This as the doctor moved past him with a tip of his hat. "My constable will be stationed at the door here, and I would ask you all to be patient. I know you're anxious to get home, but we mustn't leave any stone unturned. This is official police business," he said, looking pointedly at Olive. His voice was clipped, his shoulders were straight, and the buttons of his uniform gleamed in the light from the electric lamps. But there was butter smeared over his chin as he walked from the room.

Every gaze swung round to look at her, but it was Fleming's that made her neck prickle with heat.

"Don't tell me you fancy yourself something of an armchair detective, Miss Bright?" He glanced round in mild distaste. When she didn't answer, he surprised her by adding, "My tastes run on a bit more adrenaline, and if I had the time, I think I'd write a dashed good thriller."

Olive smiled thinly, certain that he envisioned himself in the role of hero, full of swagger and seduction, probably in evening dress. "Why don't I ask Lady Revell for a pen and paper, and you can get started? DS Burris is as chatty as a retired army colonel harkening back to the glory days on the subcontinent. It'll likely be a while."

Fleming merely glared at her and turned away, his hand going unerringly to his jacket pocket and its cache of cigarettes.

Glad to be rid of him, Olive felt some of the tension seep from her shoulders but couldn't shake it entirely. The unthinkable had happened in this cosy drawing room, only weeks before Christmas. As her gaze touched on those involved, she couldn't help but view them through the filter of suspicion. Intentionally or not, it seemed likely that one of them had fatally dosed Mrs Dunbar with atropine, and the local constabulary was quite likely out of its depth. Much like Hercule Poirot, she felt a personal affront at anyone perverting the course of justice, which left her little choice but to get involved. Because like Violet, she was very much afraid that Mrs Dunbar had been murdered.

Despite DS Burris's heavy-handed warnings, she was, rather conveniently, ideally placed to investigate. She was confined to the drawing room with all the other suspects, which would allow her to question each of them before the police, and if she could avoid the notice of the constable, she could freely examine the scene of the crime, including the manifestation cabinet itself.

Spurred into action, Olive pushed up the sleeves of her cardigan, fumbled in her bag for the little leather-bound notebook she'd taken to carrying à la Miss Husselbee, uncapped her pen, and made a start.

Chapter 7
Minor Tactics and Fieldwork

6 December
Peregrine Hall

Olive noted everyone present during the séance, other than herself and the unfortunate Mrs Dunbar: Harriet, Violet, Mrs Gibbons, Miss Danes, Lady Revell, Lieutenant Commander Fleming, and Mr Dunbar. One among them was almost certainly a murderer. She felt relatively safe in eliminating both Harriet and Violet from her suspect list. While both were inarguably clever and capable enough to stage a baffling murder, Harriet had come along only at Olive's request, and Violet, at Harriet's invitation. That was leaving rather a lot to chance. Besides, she couldn't imagine that either of them had murderous intentions toward Mrs Dunbar. However, she'd learned from first-hand experience never to underestimate a woman, so she couldn't let either of them completely off the hook. For now, though, she'd assume their innocence. That left her with only five suspects and a closed-room murder. Olive felt a prickle of confidence edging out the shock of the evening.

DS Burris reappeared in the doorway. "Mr St Croix, if you'd

be so good as to come along." The man rose with alacrity and strode toward the door. "Phenomenology, you say?" was the sergeant's opening gambit.

Olive smiled to herself. Burris hadn't been able to resist a newcomer—particularly one as cosmopolitan as he imagined Mr St Croix—which meant she had first dibs on Mr Dunbar.

He was sitting off by himself, staring at the tableau created by the manifestation cabinet and the now jumbled arrangement of chairs. Olive noted with a wince that the booted foot of his wife was exposed beneath the hem of the cabinet's drapery. Mr Dunbar's hand rested on his thigh, clutching a familiar flask. It seemed unlikely that it, too, had been poisoned, as he himself exhibited no ill effects, with the exception of a mild case of drunkenness.

Olive crossed the room to stand beside him, then laid her hand on his shoulder. He looked up at her bemusedly. Before she could utter a single word, he was off.

"She had a knack for it—a gift. She felt things, sensed others, and the rest of it could be ferreted out without too much trouble." His eyes were blind to the tragedy now as he thought back to the past. "I think maybe she had a glimpse of our future in those early days, and it convinced her that we could make a go of it. I was invalided out of the army and not much use to anyone, but I built that cabinet. It made all the difference, she said. Worked like a charm."

Olive stared at the cabinet, with its sturdy walls and filigreed border, now thoroughly impressed with the man, who still had more to say.

"So, we travelled round, the pair of 'em putting on the show, and me settin' up and clearin' away. I thought we was a jolly good team, but then she left." He glanced forlornly up at Olive, his eyes red-rimmed and his face prickled with stubble, and she tried to mask her frown of confusion. He clearly counted Evelyn as a partner in their spiritualist enterprise, but if Mrs Dunbar had left, surely her spirit guide had gone, as well . . . *hadn't he*? "It was rough for a while after that," he went on. "But we managed. But now . . ." There was a lost look in his eyes as he imagined the future. "We're finished. It's all done. She's really gone."

He hadn't mentioned love or fondness, and in truth, their marriage sounded more like the sort of arrangement she had with Aldridge. The thought of it made her unutterably sad, for all of them.

Olive frowned, unable to resolve the various bits of the man's monologue. No doubt the confusion could be attributed to a mix of grief and drink. She was attempting to form a tactful question when she noticed a stealthy movement at the edge of her vision. She turned to see Miss Danes approaching the manifestation cabinet with the sort of caution one might reserve for a skittish horse. Sensible in some ways, the woman was unpredictable when confronted with potential evidence of the truth of her mystical beliefs. Exasperated at the interruption but feeling she had no choice but to intervene, Olive offered a few words of sympathy to Mr Dunbar, hurriedly jotted a few words in her notebook, then pivoted on her heel to confront the woman.

"What are you doing?" she demanded, a bit louder than intended, prompting both of them to glance up at the officer who stood guard at the door. He seemed to be working diligently at a rather troublesome hangnail, completely oblivious to the pair of them hovering near Mrs Dunbar's body.

"Looking for proof," Miss Danes said, glancing pointedly at Olive's notebook before meeting her eyes defiantly.

This brought Olive up short. She straightened, surprised. "Proof that Mrs Dunbar was murdered?"

Miss Danes rolled her eyes heavenward. "Don't be such a ninny." She leaned in. "There is no murderer. Channelling spirits is a risky business. Mrs Dunbar, poor woman, was a martyr to the cause."

Olive frowned. "What cause?"

"Spiritualism, of course." Mild frustration quickly gave way to eagerness. Here, after all, was a chance to educate an unbeliever. "Mrs Dunbar was obviously a skilled medium. But as the portal through which the summoned spirits must emerge, her body was at the mercy of each and every one she channelled, some of whom were surely bent on mischief and evil." Her eyes rolled accusatorially toward the other occupants of the drawing room. "Don't mistake me. Someone here tonight is indelibly linked with her death, but the blame lies in the realm of the spirit world."

Olive closed her eyes for just a moment, determined not to voice her opinions on this theory, to say nothing of the utter foolishness of the woman herself. When she believed herself under control, she started again. "What exactly are you hoping to find?"

Miss Danes spread her hands wide with open-minded possibility. "The evidence of her sacrifice could manifest in any number of ways."

Which meant she had no idea. That was fine, because Olive was similarly hampered.

"Why don't we both search?" Olive suggested, figuring it was the best way to end the conversation. While Miss Danes prowled for nonexistent clues belonging to the ether, she would search for evidence against a murderer. "But we'll need to be discreet, so as not to attract the officer's attention."

Glancing past her, Miss Danes peered at the man, then met Olive's eye with a conspiratorial twinkle. "You're right, dear," she said, grasping Olive's upper arm and yanking her out of sight, round the side of the cabinet. While Miss Danes eagerly raked her gaze over its wooden panels, as if expecting ectoplasm to be seeping from the joins, Olive was considerably less optimistic and was now second-guessing her original intentions.

Mrs Dunbar had been deliberately poisoned—at least that was her working theory. It was unlikely that examining the odd scratch on her cabinet or scuff on the carpet was going to lead anywhere. She was poised to leave Miss Danes to it when she realised that the boards at the back of the cabinet weren't flush with the frame. She frowned, moving closer, running her fingers along an exposed vertical edge. It was just barely askew, and she would have consigned it to haphazard workmanship, but then she glanced up at the beautifully carved trim work. Impossible that the same man had been responsible for both. Levering her fingers against the wood, she applied pressure until she felt the give. And as she stood still with shock, the back of the cabinet swung open, giving onto a narrow hidey-hole directly behind the medium's chair.

Miss Danes was at her side in an instant, her mouth puckered and her cheeks rounded in consideration. She was clearly ruminating on the use of this additional chamber. "Perhaps it funnels the energy—" Now fidgety with excitement and wide eyed with discovery, the woman was blinking excessively.

"No doubt," Olive interrupted, relieved there was no question of Miss Danes climbing in. Olive would never manage to extricate her.

Heads close together, they peered into the tight opening.

"What's that?" Miss Danes hissed at the precise moment that Olive noticed the oddly luminous item on the floor in the corner.

Setting her notebook down, Olive crouched and extended her arm into the dim recess. Miss Danes hovered over her, blocking out the light. Olive's fingers brushed over the item—some sort of cloth—but it seemed to be caught on something, and even a sharp tug couldn't retrieve it. Her efforts were instead rewarded by a sharp thwack to her funny bone, which produced a hollow thump and prompted a hysterical laugh.

The whole business suddenly seemed utterly ridiculous. She was in league with Miss Danes, for heaven's sake, prowling the bowels of a manifestation cabinet with a dead woman on the other side of the wall.

They both started at DS Burris's voice calling into the room, "Mr Dunbar, if you'll come along now."

"Hurry then," Miss Danes urged.

Olive would have happily pinched her, but instead she kept

still, clutching her elbow, her ears pricked curiously. If Burris was ready for Mr Dunbar, then the obnoxious Mr St Croix must have already been thoroughly questioned and stashed back in the drawing room. She didn't relish having to deal with the man any more than was absolutely necessary, particularly in her current state.

"Right away, sir." Mr Dunbar's groggy response precipitated a flurry of activity. There was a thump and a crash, followed by a muffled curse.

Olive winced, waiting, wondering if she should abort. Miss Danes was clearly unfazed and was making full use of her eyes and hands to urge Olive to get on with it.

"Had a bit of the drink, I see," the sergeant said with a put-upon sigh. "Come along, then. We'll do the best we can, old boy."

After another long moment, during which no one came to look for either of them, Olive set herself once again to her dubious task. She stretched, reached, and contorted herself, until finally, with a growl of frustration, she sucked in a breath of air and slid herself sideways into the narrow space, her skirt rucking up round her thighs. If Fleming found her now . . . It simply didn't bear thinking about. Her fingers closed over a metal hook tangled up in the cloth, and she tugged. It gave a little but was still held fast by something. With her side aching from the awkward position and her exasperation at full tilt, Olive gave a final sharp, forceful tug, and it all came tumbling free, sending her elbow once again into the wood panel.

She wasted no time on curses. Eager to be presentable before anyone rounded the corner of the cabinet, she scuttled back out again and stood, shifting her skirt back into place. In one hand, she held her notebook, and in the other, the prize of her efforts.

"Well done," Miss Danes enthused, running the long pale length of the elusive piece of cloth through her fingers until she reached the bend of wire that was still entangled in it. "What do you suppose it is?"

Olive had been momentarily distracted in dusting herself off, but now she frowned, took hold of that distinctive metal hook, and examined it. "It appears to be a modified clothes hanger." She peered closer at the markings on the fabric, then rubbed her thumb over their rough contours. Paint. She quickly pulled the object from Miss Danes's grasp to spread it in her hands. It was obvious at once that they were looking at the ominous face of the spirit that had materialised behind Mrs Dunbar's writhing body. Now much relieved that she hadn't abandoned the search, Olive felt mildly triumphant. Here was proof that the séance had simply been theatrical nonsense. How exactly it had all been done eluded Olive, but this was a clue—she was certain of it.

She glanced at Miss Danes with a single raised brow, but the woman was staring at what a moment before had been solid wood. Now it was empty space. It seemed the hidey-hole that ran along the back of the cabinet had a pass-through to the other side, as well, and the inner panel now stood open before them, quite possibly by the work of her own elbow. The prone, shrouded figure of Mrs Dunbar sat before them, and all three of them were shielded from view of the drawing room by the heavy drapery that fronted the cabinet.

With a look that dared Olive to stop her, Miss Danes adjusted her cardigan over the expanse of her bosom, pushed the panel open wider, and slipped in behind the medium. Olive stared into the cramped, dark space. The black drapery shielded them not only from view but from the fire and electric lamps, as well—from warmth and company. She really wasn't keen on squeezing in alongside the current occupants, but what choice did she have? If she didn't go in, any clues could be compromised. Cringing, Olive resigned herself. *In for a penny, in for a pound.*

A moment later she was facing Miss Danes across the bulk of the dead woman, her leg pressed against a still-warm, fleshy thigh, with the red glow of the still-lit lantern seeping through the cracks in the drapery like a red mist.

"Sacrebleu," she muttered.

"You could have waited a moment," Miss Danes said tetchily. "There's hardly room for three in here."

"I didn't want to miss any discoveries," Olive said faintly, glancing round for anything that might prove useful in her investigation. There wasn't much to see—the shabby black drapery, the sturdy oak panels, and the opening through which they'd come. She was running her hands over the panels when Miss Danes's words stopped her cold.

"Perhaps we could just take a little peek." As Olive turned, Miss Danes was reaching for the sheet where it covered the woman's head.

"Stop that," Olive hissed. She'd been close enough during the medium's final moments to know that she'd seen quite enough. "It's bad enough we're prowling round in here. Let's leave the woman a bit of dignity." She had a flash of inspiration. "The spirits could be lingering—she did, after all, die a violent death. You wouldn't want their, erm . . . energy to redirect itself to you, would you?"

Miss Danes pulled back as if stung, her fingers curling into her palms. Even in heavy shadow, Olive could see the thoughts warring in her mind. She was clearly wondering whether she should have risked the cabinet at all.

"We'll be quick," Olive assured her. "Is there anything on the floor or the walls on your side?"

With a renewed sense of purpose, Miss Danes shifted and turned, her considerable figure at odds with the space. The friction of her wool skirt against the sheet caused it to shift ominously, and Olive lunged forward over the body to keep it from slipping down off the woman's face. But she must have pulled too hard, prompting Miss Danes to grapple with the opposite side. The ensuing frantic tugging had the whole thing shifting up over Mrs Dunbar's lap, exposing the folds of her robes and the pudgy, flaccid fingers that rested on top.

They both stopped moving and flicked a glance at each other.

Olive felt certain Miss Danes was bracing herself against the on-slaught of disturbed and vengeful spirits; she was merely regret-ting the necessity of this indignity.

"Let's fix this and leave the way we came," Olive insisted.

They both saw the scrap at once, a bit of it exposed beneath the medium's fingers. Two hands shot out, but Miss Danes's was quicker.

She lifted her prize so that it was hanging in the air between them. "It's quite sticky." Her fingers opened and closed over it as she peered closer. "It's cheesecloth." She frowned. "Do you suppose she'd just now made her Christmas pudding? Good heavens!"

She was gabbling now, utterly distracted, and happy to relin-quish the cheesecloth. Olive peered at it, bemused at how it seemed to glow in the hazy light. She was confident now that this unseemly search had, in fact, been quite productive. With the unlikely assistance of Miss Danes, she'd solved at least one little mystery.

Chapter 8

Informant Service

7 December
Blackcap Lodge and Station XVII

Olive's father had left early, bundled to the hilt against the inclement weather, to dose the cattle of the surrounding farms with his home recipe cure-all—even she had no clue what was in it. She'd heard him whistling for Kíli, his Welsh corgi, and the dog's staccato replies. By then she'd quite given up on sleeping, despite her tumultuous night and fuzzy head. She told herself her brain was busy with suspects and the baffling nature of Mrs Dunbar's shocking demise, but really, she was full of anticipation. Jamie was coming home today.

She was smiling to herself as she opened her notebook to reread the previous night's entries.

> *Mr Dunbar (given name?): Built cabinet, prone to drink. Question further on the particulars of life with Mrs D. Could he have tired of being under her thumb?*
> *Lady Revell: Distraught and shaky but bearing up. Had the séance been merely a ploy to lure Mrs Dunbar in? For what purpose??*

Mrs Gibbons: Much as usual. Fidgety, worried, overwhelmed. Had she literally killed the messenger who'd brought news of her son's death—no matter that it was false?

Miss Danes: Convinced Mrs D was killed by vengeful or aggressive spirits—or perhaps she's merely a bloody good actress?? Could she have harboured a grudge against Mrs Dunbar?

Manifestation cabinet: cheesecloth, painted face of a "spirit" draped on a hanger, hidey-hole—for what, exactly?

By the time she'd scrambled out of the manifestation cabinet, flush with her discoveries, and gone to join the group in front of the fire, with Miss Danes trailing after her, no one had been keen to talk of murder. No one but DS Burris. And even he had seemed more interested in the results of the séance than the details surrounding the woman's death.

Harriet had suggested a round of bridge, and soon she and Violet, Lady Revell and Miss Danes had moved to the table in the corner of the room. Mrs Gibbons remained slumped against the cushions, staring into the fire. One by one, they all traipsed down the hall to be formally questioned. Mr Dunbar was stashed in an armchair to sleep off his excess, and Lieutenant Commander Fleming was simply gone. The cad had evidently appealed to DS Burris, then gone haring back to the manor, leaving her to make her own way home. His mention in the notebook was telling.

Lt Cdr Ian Fleming (né St Croix): Arrogant, condescending, secretive. Investigating Mrs Dunbar for the Royal Navy. Definitely hiding something. What is he really doing here, and who else is aware of his true identity?

"You're scowling, dear," Harriet said from her chaise longue. Her knitting needles clicked along as quickly as she could manage as she tried to finish a navy-blue jumper in time for Christmas. Her eyesight wasn't what it once was, and that caused no end of frustrations.

Olive glanced up at her stepmother, haloed in the light of her reading lamp against the still-dark windows of the parlour. "I can't help it."

"A moment ago you were smiling." Her voice was light, teasing.

"One moment a gentleman, the next a bounder," Olive retorted.

"Mr St Croix is the bounder, I presume."

"Very astute."

"You really shouldn't take it personally," said her stepmother calmly. "It's not like he left you stranded."

"I invited him," Olive insisted. "Common courtesy demanded he at least keep me informed."

"If it comes to that, why *did* you invite him?" she asked.

It was a fair question, but one she couldn't answer truthfully.

Olive shrugged. "He was curious. I was being polite."

"Hmm." Harriet nodded, clearly not believing a word of it, probably because she was well aware that her stepdaughter wasn't often deterred from her intentions by a compulsion to be polite. "Well, it's probably better he made his escape. I don't think you would have welcomed the interference," she said knowingly.

Olive winced. "Was it obvious?"

"What you and Winifred were doing? I think to all of us except the sergeant—and possibly the officer on guard. Naturally we were in favour, none of us having more than a passing confidence in DS Burris."

"I'd just as soon not be lumped in with Miss Danes. I was looking for evidence of a killer. She was more interested in soaking up any residual spiritual energy." Olive rolled her eyes, remembering.

Now Harriet dropped her hands to her lap, her knitting forgotten, as she settled back against her cushion, brows raised with patent curiosity. "And did you find any? Evidence, I mean."

Olive took a deep breath and revealed the secrets of the manifestation cabinet.

"Well, it's the sort of thing I would have expected," Harriet admitted. "All sleight of hand, smoke and mirrors. It certainly looked real enough, but I wonder if it would have held up to more intense scrutiny." At Olive's quizzical frown, she elaborated. "There was no ectoplasm this time, and while her spirit guide made an appearance, he was gone much too quickly. He'd barely delivered his message before the poor woman was overcome. None of us had a chance to look too closely."

"True."

They were both reliving those terrible moments of helpless uncertainty.

"Let's not think about it," Olive said briskly. "Did *you* learn anything interesting? By the time I rejoined the group, everyone was holding their cards close to the vest, as it were."

"Not really. Lady Revell and Mrs Gibbons both took it very hard. I suspect because they had the most invested. The poor dears believed they'd have an opportunity to contact their loved ones, and when their hopes died—quite violently—with Mrs Dunbar, it was doubly shocking, I suspect."

"No one knew where Mrs Dunbar had got the bottle she drank from?"

"No one admitted it if they did."

Olive glanced askance at her stepmother. "I've eliminated you as a suspect."

"I'm flattered, of course."

Olive had expected the sarcasm. "And while I'm tempted to do the same with Violet, I wanted to get your opinion." She winced slightly at having to inquire, even in such a roundabout manner.

"Oh no," Harriet insisted. "She couldn't have done it. She's been much too close to murder already in her young life and is really quite sensitive, despite her worldly demeanour. Absolutely not." The nod of her stepmother's head seemed to put an end to the matter, and as she adjusted the pile of knitting on her lap, it seemed her thoughts had already drifted, a memory pulling at the corners of her lips. "Your father was in a devil of a mood this morning. 'What are the odds?' he bellowed, whilst cringing through his cup of coffee." When the tea ration had started, her father had switched to coffee, viewing the bitter brew as both a challenge and a patriotic duty. To this day, he forced down a cup every morning, smugly satisfied to be doing his bit. " 'Three bodies in seven months, and Olive right in the centre of the lot.' " Harriet made a good job of his bluster, and they grinned at each other.

"He's got a point," Olive admitted. "Although, only one of them was a true villager. These latest two were . . . different." She bit her lip, considering.

"What is it?"

"The Dunbars moved into the village some months ago, but has anyone discovered why they did?" She hurried to elaborate. "Given their livelihood, you'd think they'd want to settle somewhere more populous than Pipley. More people and less scurrilous gossip equals more opportunities, I should think."

Harriet frowned. "You know, I'm not sure I've ever heard an explanation. It does seem rather curious."

Glancing at the clock on the mantel, Olive hopped to her feet. "Crackers, I'd better be off."

"Don't forget your smile, dear," her stepmother teased.

Olive flashed Harriet a mouthful of teeth and crossed her eyes for good measure. Then she hurried to the door.

"Olive," her stepmother called after her. She turned. "His name isn't really Mr St Croix, is it?"

"Evidently I'm not the only sleuth in the family," she said, with a sardonic quirk of her lips. She was almost out the door when Harriet called again.

"Jamie's coming home today, isn't he? It's about time."

A delivery had come in from the Toyshop, and Olive had spent the past quarter of an hour restocking the inventory in one of the outbuildings on the manor grounds, shivering against the pervading chill while busily pondering various suspects, possible motives, and diabolical natures. She started when the door creaked open, even though she'd been expecting Hell.

"Sorry," the girl said, shutting the door behind her. "One of the men was asking for a plaster, but what he really needed was a row of stitches." She stepped round to where Olive was unpacking a crate of jumping bombs and propped herself against the shelving. "I certainly didn't mean to stab him with the needle, but he was ever so fidgety."

Olive smirked. "A victim from Lieutenant Tierney's class?"

Hell nodded, her eyes busily roving over the shelves, which were heavily laden with crates holding the various supplies needed by agents being dropped into occupied Europe. Explosives of all sorts, pistols, rifles, ammunition, torches, field dressings, rations—a veritable treasure trove of resistance. She then shifted her gaze to the boxes stacked by the door, all of them still to be inventoried.

"Well, this is my afternoon sorted, isn't it?" she said dryly before remembering Olive's question. "One of the last, apparently. It seems he's being transferred."

Olive frowned and stashed the crate she'd emptied in the corner. "The agent?"

Hell shook her head, tentatively reaching out to heft a grenade. She turned it carefully, marvelling at the bumpy little thing. "Lieutenant Tierney," she corrected.

Olive blinked at her. "Danny Tierney is leaving?" she blurted.

"Evidently. I don't think my patient was delusional."

"When?"

"I've no idea."

Hell was clearly unaffected by this news. It was likely she barely knew Station XVII's devil-may-care instructor of self-defence. But Olive felt blindsided. Danny Tierney was one of her favourite people. Jamie would know the details. Then she remembered he wasn't yet back, and in truth, she was beginning to worry that his arrival might not be today, after all.

She huffed out a breath, visible in the chill. "I'll leave you to it, then, and see you later for tea." Hell had pulled a knitted beret out of her jacket pocket and was settling it on her head as protection against the chill by the time Olive reached the door. "I'm sorry for reneging on my invitation to last night's séance. One of the officers found out about it and wanted to attend. And you know how they are."

Hell's soft brown gaze shifted to look at her. "Just as well. Honestly, I'd just as soon not encounter a few relatives in particular who've shuffled off their mortal coil. If you know what I mean."

The look she shot Olive simply begged for a good gossip, but it was too bloody cold, and Olive had too much to do. It was clear her friend hadn't yet heard about the murder, and she wasn't quite ready to talk about it. With a wave and a reminder to stamp her feet and rub her hands together every now and then to stave off numbness, Olive left Hell to it.

She ran Lieutenant Tierney to ground in the makeshift canteen, where he was frowning down into a weak cup of tea, his cheeks chapped red from the cold and his ginger hair threaded with bits of dried grass. Olive dropped into a chair beside him, laid her forearms on the table, and leaned in.

"I heard you're leaving, and I'm not at all happy about it."

He glanced up, and she watched the corner of his mouth hitch.

"They say the FANYs can't keep up with all the injuries I have a tendency to inflict."

"What utter nonsense," Olive said, pursing her lips in amusement.

He shrugged. "Restructuring."

"Don't tell me the CO has booted you out? I was already irritated with the man, but now—"

"Nah, it's come from Gubbins himself. A bit more compartmentalising." Brigadier Colin Gubbins was the top brass of Baker Street.

"What do you mean?"

"They're sending me to Arisaig. I'm to be an instructor at the paramilitary training school. It seems Station XVII is to be strictly a school for industrial sabotage." Olive's mind flashed back to that haunting night in early November: the men, the guns, the explosion. And her suspicion that they were planning an assassination.

"Danny," she said lightly, "I know that the men of the 1st Czechoslovak Mixed Brigade are being trained differently, more rigorously. I've seen it for myself." His head canted, and his shoulders dropped in a helpless posture, but she went on, undeterred. "Are you teaching them more than you've taught the others?"

"I cannot tell you that, Olive. You know that." His eyes were steely, boring into hers.

She sighed. "I suppose I didn't really expect you to. I'm just worried for them—even more than usual. I've chatted with Kubiš and Gabček and a few of the others. They're so serious, as if they're certain they won't come back. I know the mission they've been assigned isn't run of the mill. It's bigger, more audacious. I think they're planning—"

Tierney surged to his feet, looking round nervously. "Why don't you let me get you a cup of tea?"

Olive caught at his hand. "I don't want it."

Somewhat warily, he sat back down, and they stared at each other for a long moment. Just when Olive was ready to give up on shared confidences, he spoke.

"I've trained hundreds of men in street fighting, close combat, and silent killing. Those two are as good as I've ever seen. They know what they're up against, and they're as ready as we can make them. If it's to be done, they're the men to do it."

The admission was vaguely comforting, but the situation, nonetheless, felt bleak. Before she'd come to Baker Street she'd been a strong believer in the adage that knowledge was power, but lately, every bit of intelligence she could glean seemed to produce the opposite effect. And the prickly unease that clutched her insides never seemed to go away.

Never had Olive been more delighted to use her pigeons as an excuse to escape Station XVII than that afternoon. She'd spent much of her day in close proximity to Lieutenant Commander Ian Fleming, and it had been an ordeal. They'd continued their tour of the manor grounds, which were considerably more crowded than they'd been only a few months ago. Major Blighty had convinced the higher-ups that his trainees would be much better equipped if they were able to practice on full-scale equipment. Thus, the vast lawn of Brickendonbury Manor was dotted with various planes, a Churchill tank, and even a steam engine. The agents were instructed to pinpoint the vulnerabilities and then set dummy explosives to effectively sabotage the machinery.

They had also popped in on one of Danny Tierney's self-defence classes, where, much to Olive's irritation, the lieutenant commander had taken part and acquitted himself rather well. After that, he asked to peruse the packing lists for agents being dispatched on secret missions, and that prompted a visit to the storage shed, so that he might examine the equipment first-hand. While she was compelled by duty to answer any question he posed, the converse clearly did not apply: he parried every question with a look of amused superiority.

It hadn't been obvious from the first, but the man was really quite intelligent. Olive would have had a great deal of respect for him if not for the playboy manner he adopted with every female they encountered. He seemed unimpressed with her competency, knowledge, and efficiency, instead persisting in treating her like a cigarette girl. Honestly, if she'd had something sturdier than a hairpin in her pocket, she might have stabbed him.

Finally fed up, she smiled sweetly and informed him of her alternate responsibilities, ready to make her getaway. But it seemed that pigeons piqued his interest.

"Is a pigeon sent along on every mission?" he inquired.

"Usually several."

"And you've had success with them?"

"Of course," she replied coolly.

"I'd like to take a look at the loft. Is it on the manor grounds?"

"No. It's my family's loft, on our property." She wasn't going to give an inch.

"I see I'm in a position of having to ask you for another favour."

"It's equally uncomfortable for both of us."

"Perhaps we could arrange something . . . tit for tat, as it were."

"I was under the impression we were at war," she countered, harkening back to his earlier objection to sharing information.

"Touché, Miss Bright." His smile was false and flat. "I see I'm going to have to appeal to your sense of patriotic duty." He glanced round him, as if to assure himself that they were alone; then he tipped his head toward her. "I am spearheading a new project, and I think it's just possible that a pigeon could be an extraordinarily useful asset. But I won't know unless I learn more about them—their abilities and their weaknesses." He met her eyes unflinchingly. "I could make a formal request, but the fewer people who know at this stage, the better."

Damn the man! She was loath to extend their time together, but as a proponent of pigeons—and lover of clandestine activities of all sorts—what choice did she have?

"Fine, but it'll have to be another day." She really couldn't take another minute of his company right now. She didn't even bother to excuse herself, merely slipped away from him, revelling in the thrill of escape.

With any luck, the person she intended to question next would be a bit more forthcoming with his answers.

Three quarters of an hour later, she was puttering up and down the familiar lanes, her reduced speed a product of the wind's biting chill and her newly distracted frame of mind. But the sight of a familiar car in the drive at Blackcap Lodge sent an electric current running through her. Jamie was home. Her heart hammered in her throat, eager anticipation vying with unexpected nerves. She would have much preferred a bit of notice, so that she could have brushed the tangles from her hair and tamed the red chapping on her cheeks and lips. But there he was, looking so very tall and dark and handsome, standing beside the dovecote, waiting for her. Almost like a real sweetheart.

For once, he wasn't in uniform. Having travelled down from Ireland on the train, he looked very smart in his tailored trousers and dark overcoat. His unruly curls, beneath the familiar flat cap, had been shorn since she'd last seen him, and his grey-blue jumper was the very colour of his eyes. He needed a shave, but he looked healthy—less pale and drawn than when he'd left. And he stood unsupported, surely a good indication that his broken leg had nearly finished healing. All this she noticed in one flickeringly shy glance, and it prompted a grin to spread across her face.

She trudged forward, wheeling the bike over the rutted drive to prop it against the wall of the stable, which now served as her father's surgery. When she turned back, he'd crossed the yard to meet her.

Olive spoke first. "At the risk of inflating your ego, I'll admit that I missed your curmudgeonly presence." She flashed a glance up at him. "I would, in fact, hug you if you weren't so respectable looking."

"I suppose I should be used to it by now, but your curious manner of expressing yourself continues to baffle me." So saying, he caught her up in a hug, and after a moment's startled surprise, she wrapped her arms tightly round him and felt a bit of tension seep out of her.

Much too soon, he was setting her away from him and eyeing her sternly. "And now, perhaps, you'd like to tell me what you've been up to this afternoon?" When she frowned, he clarified. "I stopped at the manor first, naturally expecting you to be there, but I was told—by someone named Hell, no less—that you'd left on pigeon business." He raised a single eyebrow. "Yet somehow I managed to get here before you, and you have that look in your eye that always means trouble."

"Ooh la la." She cocked her hip and glanced at him from under lowered lids. "Like a femme fatale?"

"More like an incorrigible pigeoneer who fancies herself the village detective," he said flatly, the words puffing out of his mouth on a vapour cloud to hover between them in the cold twilight.

"Very well," she admitted, rather put out that he could read her so easily. "But it's a long story, and if you're going to hear it now, I need to be somewhere much warmer. A cup of tea would be nice, as well. I've a hole in my glove, and my fingers are freezing." Catching the aggrieved look in his eye, she added, "Suffice it to say, there's been another murder, and it happened during a séance, if you can believe it."

She searched his face for the gratifying reaction she'd expected, but it remained impassive as he guessed, "And you're just home from questioning someone, aren't you?"

"Now you're using the little grey cells, *mon ami*," she teased. "I see I shall have to call you Hastings from now on."

"No, you will not," he said stiffly before looking mildly chagrined. "There's not a lot of entertainment on a sheep farm, and Harriet loaned me one of your mystery novels to take with me. Hastings," he continued with raised brows, "is utterly useless."

Olive's delighted laughter spread across the chill winter landscape, all barren tree branches and sturdy hedges crusted with ice, like a church bell choir. It even prompted a faraway, token bark from Kíli, who was probably curled up at her stepmother's feet in the parlour.

"That's the spirit," she said. "Although we can't both be Hercule . . . Perhaps you could be Inspector Japp—rather stodgy and by the book." She hitched an eyebrow in suggestion.

"Not a chance," he said shortly. "So, who was it?"

"Who was whom?"

Jamie rolled his eyes. "Who were you visiting?"

"You could have been inquiring as to who was murdered," she insisted.

"I'm certain you'll tell me," he said dryly.

"For your information," she said, "I went to see Dr Harrington. And persuaded him to go over his post-mortem findings with me."

"You really do have this village wrapped round your finger, don't you?"

"Lucky too. They're unpredictable when unraveled," she whispered, with a wink.

He caught her arm, ready to escort her in. She wondered if he could feel the electric jolt that skittered up her arm at the touch. If he did, he made no reaction. "Anything you need to tell me before we go in?"

She swivelled her gaze to look up at him, suddenly worried she'd given herself away. "What do you mean?"

He looked at her curiously. "Baker Street business. Namely, anything you wouldn't be able to share in front of your family."

"Oh," she said, drawing the word out with some relief and earning a quizzical look from Jamie. "Only that another irritating male person has turned up at the manor. One Lieutenant Commander Fleming."

Jamie seemed to roll this information over in his mind. "I know the name."

"Well, the village knows him as Ian St Croix."

"The *village* knows him?" Given that the Station XVII protocol advised that the manor occupants shouldn't mix with the locals—bringing Hell to the séance wouldn't have been strictly allowed—he had reason to be startled by this revelation.

"He was at the séance," she admitted. "No, don't ask. It's another story, and I really need that cup of tea after what I've heard today. There's plenty of time to catch you up." Then she remembered, pulled him to a stop, and peered into his face, as if she could read the truth there. "Have your headaches stopped?" she asked, her voice soft. "Or at least improved?"

He looked down at her for a long moment, until her nerves began to crackle with awareness. "They've not gone entirely, but I've had fewer of them." He tucked his hands into the pockets of his coat, and Olive took the opportunity to give him another look-over.

"And the leg? It seems to be bearing up nicely."

She smiled to herself as his cheeks flushed with colour. "It's coming along."

She nodded smartly. "Excellent. I'm glad you're back." She tucked her arm through his to lead him up the path. Not wanting to seem too sentimental, she added cheekily, "And I hope you've brought me something nice for Christmas."

Chapter 9
How Much to Use

7 December
Blackcap Lodge

After supper, they all, excepting Jonathon, who'd escaped to his room with the excuse of working on Christmas presents, retired to the study. Jamie set a fire going with Jonathon's diligently scavenged branches, and it burned with a lovely, sweet smell and a festive, crackling glow that set the racing trophies sparkling. Her father insisted on switching the wireless on low, so as not to miss the pips of the BBC Home Service, and then the talk turned to murder. Olive quickly recounted Mrs Dunbar's exhibition on the village green in order to provide a bit of context. Then, with a solemn nod from her stepmother, she described the evening of the séance. Peppered with copious additions from Harriet, Olive's summary of events culminated in the arrival of the doctor and police on the scene. Jamie's countenance remained utterly unreadable.

"Her death came as a shock to all of us, and so naturally, I was curious—" Olive frowned as the word 'naturally' was echoed back to her by everyone in the room. "Thus inspired," she went on tartly, "I called round to see Dr Harrington this afternoon."

"And he just invited you in, did he?" her father demanded. "Answered all your questions?"

"More or less. It helped that Dotty came to the door." She grinned.

In the early days of the war, Dr Harrington's wife had, like so many other panicked Britishers, believed her beloved pet would be better off put down, that it would be a kinder alternative than expecting the dog to endure the coming hardships. Olive had convinced her otherwise, and the spirited little Jack Russell had proven her mettle many times over in the years since. Dr Harrington, rather conveniently, was forever grateful.

"He hinted," Olive went on, "that he suspected Mrs Dunbar might have been murdered." She glanced triumphantly at Jamie before revealing the rest. "*And* indicated that, should it prove necessary to bring a killer to justice, he had more confidence in me than in the local constabulary."

Her father harrumphed his feelings. "Some of that's to do with Burris—he's not the sharpest tack—but the war is to blame for the rest. If the initial investigation into a suspicious death leads to nowt conclusive, and the whole thing can be put down as accidental, then it's case closed. The poor chaps are busy enough with the rest of it—black-market schemes, looting, fifth columnists and the like. They're overrun."

"Yes, well, we're all busy, but some of us find murder rather objectionable. Even more so than the rest of it. And I think Dr Harrington agrees."

"Go on, dear," Harriet encouraged.

Jamie, on the sofa beside Olive, didn't say a word.

"Dr Harrington's initial examination had him convinced the death occurred as a result of belladonna poisoning."

"I'd suspected that, as well," Harriet confirmed. "The signs are quite distinctive."

"But," Olive said portentously, eyes wide, "it's not quite so cut and dried."

Rupert Bright grunted, eyeing his daughter dubiously.

"She *did* have scopolamine in her system," she informed her audience. "Like atropine, it's a compound derived from the belladonna plant"—she glanced at Jamie—"commonly known as deadly nightshade. It's most often prescribed for motion sick—"

Her father's hand smacked against the arm of his leather wingback chair. "This village has got entirely too familiar with poisonous plants," he interrupted, full of bluster. He was referring to the Women's Institute's involvement in the Oxford Medicinal Plants Scheme and Olive's first case as an amateur sleuth—another death by poisoning.

"Yes, well, there's more," Olive went on dramatically. "Mrs Dunbar's stomach contents were a mixed bag, so to speak." She was encouraged by the lift of Harriet's brows, not so much by the placidity in Jamie's expression. She opened to the bookmarked page in her notebook and read from her notes. "In addition to the meat pasty she'd evidently eaten before the séance, and of course, the ipecac, there was gin, sherry, some bits of cheesecloth and paper, sloe juice and . . ." She paused for effect before adding, "Traces of lords-and-ladies." She snapped the notebook closed again.

"What?" her father barked, clearly unable to resolve this medley of ingredients.

Harriet frowned, and Jamie, as expected, appeared completely befuddled.

"What in heaven's name is lords-and-ladies?" Harriet asked.

"It's a shade plant," Olive informed them, "commonly found in woods or hedgerows. I'm sure you've seen its arrow-shaped leaves. Its flower in spring looks like a cobra hood, and in autumn its cluster of berries turns lipstick red."

"Well, that's what killed her," Rupert Bright pronounced. "Those berries are full of tiny crystals that tear up your throat. If you don't get them out of your system quickly, they can wreak all sorts of havoc with your insides." He shuddered. "It's as likely to be called devils and angels."

Olive swept on. "Dr Harrington believes that it was the combination of scopolamine and the lords-and-ladies that was to blame for her death," she began, with a nod to her father. "Normally, the berries would have had little time to do much damage before her body expelled them in the form of vomit. But as Dr Harrington explained it, the belladonna worked as an antiemetic, suppressing her body's signals to keep her from doing the very thing that might have saved her."

Agatha Christie, Olive acknowledged, probably would have been well versed in the effects of both of these poisons, as well as the consequences of taking them together. No doubt she would have made a consummate murderess. Which reminded her . . .

"I called round to see Dr Ware on the way home, as well."

"The chemist, too? You *have* been busy," Jamie said dryly.

"Quite," she said coldly. "I inquired whether he'd recently filled a prescription for scopolamine." Harriet's face managed to convey both disapproval and curiosity all at once. "He hadn't. Dr Harrington had got there before me and made the same inquiry."

"That's very curious," Harriet said, tucking her afghan round her and absently rubbing a slightly shaking hand over her legs.

"Isn't it just?" Olive agreed.

"And the syrup of ipecac?" Harriet's grey eyes were intent. "What did Dr Harrington say about that?" Olive suspected her stepmother was feeling rather fraught. It hadn't been easy to stand by while Mrs Dunbar succumbed to a painful death.

"It was his opinion that it made no difference to the end result. The two poisons were already acting against her body and each other. Her organs were failing, and her heart, already a bit dicky, evidently, was overtaxed by the pain and the panic. Eventually, it simply gave out. There was nothing more we could have done."

Her father clasped his wife's hand in his, then gently squeezed it.

"The belladonna—or, I suppose to be strictly accurate, I

should say the scopolamine—could very well have been the reason there was no ectoplasm, either," Olive informed them.

"How do you mean?" Harriet said, forestalling her father's opinions on mediums and their chicanery.

"It would seem that Mrs Dunbar's ectoplasm was actually a concoction of cheesecloth, paper, and something to moisten and hold it together. Dr Harrington indicated that egg white is a likely candidate for the latter."

"And she swallowed it ahead of the séance?" This was Jamie's first comment, and she turned to look at him.

"As revolting as it sounds, it makes sense. She conjured some of it during the spectacle on the village green—quite a bit of it actually—dredging it up out of her nose and throat. There must have been thirty villagers watching. I suspect someone would have called foul if she'd pulled the limp, sticky mess from her pocket and tried to pawn it off as the spirit of a navy seaman."

"And I suppose coming from her nose, it was ironclad proof of her abilities, as far as they were concerned?" Jamie countered.

Rupert Bright let out a loud guffaw.

Olive ignored them both and carried on with her narrative. She wasn't about to mention how taken in she'd been by the whole performance. "I suspect she'd swallow down the ectoplasm before a séance and regurgitate it at a pivotal moment as evidence of successfully summoned spirits."

Her father scoffed.

"I'm not saying I believe it, Dad. I'm just hypothesising as to how it might have happened."

Jamie spoke up again. "Does the lords-and-ladies have hallucinogenic properties? Could a bit of it have been used intentionally to get her into a state for her séances?" His tone left little doubt as to his feelings on the woman's credentials as a medium.

"That seems rather horrific, given the side effects," Olive replied.

"She could have used the scopolamine for that purpose, though. A large enough dose would certainly produce hallucinations," Harriet countered. "Were there traces of it in the bottle Dr Harrington took away with him?" she asked.

"That's where it gets really interesting," Olive informed them. "There were no traces of scopolamine in her stomach. But there was a considerable quantity of it in . . . other bodily fluids."

This news seemed to either stun or baffle everyone in the room. No one spoke.

Olive went on. "The bottle, which Mrs Dunbar emptied in a few desperate swallows, contained only gin, caster sugar, sloe juice, and the traces of lords-and-ladies. And according to Mr Dunbar, whom I spoke to last night, before he'd drunk himself into a stupor, he hadn't the foggiest idea where she'd got it. That's assuming he's to be believed."

"Well, that makes it a very important clue, then," Harriet said.

"Agreed," Olive said. "According to Dr Ware, the scopolamine was likely introduced in the form of a liniment or salve and thus absorbed through her skin, which would explain its absence—"

A crackle and a familiar voice on the wireless had her father sitting bolt upright, interrupting her musings. "Quick now, turn it up. That's right." This as Jamie leaned over and tweaked the knob.

The sudden movement had woken Kíli, who'd been twitching in his sleep, and prompted a bark of objection even as Jonathon bounded into the room.

"Hush," bellowed her father, quieting in time to hear, "*Alvar Lidell, reading it.*"

The next words quelled them all into stunned silence.

"*Japan's long-threatened aggression in the Far East began tonight, with attacks on United States naval bases in the Pacific. Fresh reports are coming in every minute. The latest facts of the situation are these. Messages from Tokyo say that Japan has announced a formal declara-*"

tion of war against both the United States and Britain. Japan's attacks on American naval bases in the Pacific were announced by President Roosevelt straight from the White House tonight."

It was further announced that Manila, in the Philippines, had also been attacked and that Roosevelt had mobilised the United States Army and Navy.

Her father was first to react. "Evidently push came to shove at the hands of the Japanese," he said jovially. His face, long held in grim lines, now seemed to relax sufficiently to allow a relieved smile to dominate his features. "The loss is horrible, make no mistake, but it seems it was the goosing the Americans needed to step into the fray, thank the good Lord."

"Bless those poor souls," Harriet murmured, just as her husband leaned toward her to plant a smacking kiss on her lips. After a little squeak of surprise, she smiled fondly at her husband, and when he turned to the rest of them, with his lips now tinted the same colour as Harriet's, Olive couldn't help the surge of relief that swept through her. This was what they'd all been waiting for. Britain had stood alone against Germany for so long; finally, the United States would carry some of the burden. That such a tragedy had been necessary to impel its involvement was horribly unfortunate.

"Well, Olive?" her father pressed, widening his eyes in encouragement at her. "Aren't you going to kiss the man?"

She looked blankly at Jamie, who was gazing at her in some amusement. Eager not to arouse suspicion, she smiled and, with the whole family looking on, leaned toward him. He met her halfway.

Kissing him for the first time in a fortnight, she didn't relish the audience, but she made do. It wasn't the wolfish, hungry sort of kiss she demanded whenever her emotions were in a tizzy about war and helplessness and secrets and, quite honestly, *him*. It was sweet and hopeful, a mere meeting of lips. For posterity. But she could feel the little spark, snapping across the distance before their lips had even touched, and the thought that raced through her brain in that moment was simply, *He's home.*

It was late when she walked him out. They'd celebrated the bittersweet news from the wireless with slices of hot toast with apple butter and tiny swigs of brandy from a bottle her father unearthed from a hiding place he seemed inordinately proud of. Jonathon was grinning from ear to ear, and she was happy he'd been absent from their troubling discussion of poison and murder.

Olive was still clutching her notebook, her mind still turning over the details of the crime, when Jamie spoke.

"You realise that if you were to become an agent, you wouldn't be able to write anything down." His breath drifted away on the breeze, but his silhouette, standing over her, was perfectly still and solid. "Contacts, codes, instructions, cheats—any of it would get you killed."

She knew that. She thought often of all the ways she might not be cut out to be an agent. Of the risks she'd have to take and the things she stood to lose. She hadn't yet fully committed, but she hadn't backed down, either. She hoped when the time came, he would support whatever decision she made.

Olive nodded once, a bob of her head. "A certain captain once told me I was a resourceful girl. I'll manage."

He didn't answer for a moment, and she had an odd feeling that the time they'd spent apart had caused a rent in the delicate fabric of their relationship. He seemed even more mysterious than he always had. But his answer, when it came, was more revealing than was typical of him.

"Honestly, that's what worries me the most. You would work tirelessly, take every risk, certain you could get away with anything. It would be your undoing. No one is infallible. Remember that, Olive."

Moonlight fell over them as they walked down the drive, the only sounds the quick, darting movements of predator and prey.

Two glowing eyes peered from the hydrangea bush, and the wind skittered a few curled leaves across the gravel.

She was lost in the mire of her thoughts, but as they reached the Austin, Jamie decided to make up for his earlier silence.

"I suppose it occurs to you," he said, in that quiet, knowing way of his, "that this was a very personal murder."

"What do you mean?"

"Her death was only the grand finale. It was staged to occur during the séance, and it sounds as if the poison was chosen specifically to prevent her demonstrating her purported skill as a medium. It not only kept her from conjuring the ectoplasm, but it also kept her from playing a role—it silenced the voices from the spirit world." He looked down at her, his face in shadow but his eyes lit in the darkness. "It seems to me that someone was very keen to expose her as a fraud."

A shiver ran over Olive's skin. "But that's diabolical," she said, thinking back to the horrors of the previous evening and viewing them in the light of this new possibility.

"Murder is very seldom kind."

She kissed him goodnight. It was more than a peck, more careful and deliberate. It overwhelmed her, and as they stepped apart, she shivered. Soon, she hoped, they'd settle back into their comfortable routine, where everything was, at the very least, manageable.

Olive trudged up the stairs to her room, pondering Jamie's parting words. She lay awake, curled under the chilly sheets, shivering as she waited for her little cocoon to warm her enough for sleep. If Jamie was right, then someone had held a mean grudge against Mrs Dunbar.

Or perhaps it was bigger than that. Had the Royal Navy charged Lieutenant Commander Fleming with getting rid of whatever threat she posed to their efforts at winning the war? She'd have to ask Jamie if that was at all likely. Then again, perhaps she could ferret the information out of the man himself. If she allowed him a look at her pigeons, and kept his visit to the loft hush-hush, he was going to owe her a favour. One she fully intended to call in.

Her thoughts drifted, quite unexpectedly, to a morning almost a month ago now, when she'd been dispatched to the train station to meet another Czechoslovakian soldier from Cholmondeley Castle by the name of Jan Kubiš.

He was tough looking but soft spoken, his English careful, his movements neat. She'd tried to engage him in conversation, but he'd said little, sitting rigid beside her in the Austin, staring straight ahead, clearly eager to be getting on with things.

She still remembered little snippets—bits she'd thought odd.

"You're a bit late to the game to join the others from the 1st Czechoslovak Mixed Brigade already at Station XVII, aren't you? They've all been there for weeks already," she'd teased.

He'd turned to her then, and she'd looked away from the road to see that his eyes were bright, nervous. "It is true, yes. But I hope to learn quickly—to catch up."

"There was a trainee injured at Ringway during a parachute jump. Are you to be his replacement?"

She hadn't been trying to ferret out information. She was curious by nature, particularly when it seemed everyone was intent on keeping secrets. But he'd answered her. "I am, yes. It was an honour to be chosen."

"Once your mission is complete, will you stay in your country to work with the Resistance?"

He was quiet for a long moment before he spoke. "It is a dangerous mission, and I am proud to be asked. It is better that I do not think beyond that."

At the time, she'd merely thought he'd chosen to maintain a narrow focus on the task at hand, but later, she'd wondered if he'd been hinting at a darker meaning. Hinting that he didn't expect to return. It was a risk faced by every agent, but none of the others had ever seemed so fatalistic. It made her wonder yet

again about the secrets surrounding this particular group of
trainees. The extra hours of training, above and beyond the typical schedule at Station XVII, with an even greater variety of explosives, seemed to hint that their mission was different in some
respect from the ones that had come before. And then later, there
was the ambush on Morgan's Walk—the guns coming out of the
dark. And that feeling that they were planning an assassination.
A murder.

That it would be different from Mrs Dunbar's was a certainty.
Neither weapons nor explosive training had been required to dispatch the spiritualist. The deed had been done with poison in
the drawing room of Peregrine Hall. But while one murder would
make little impact, the other, as yet undone, must surely be of
imminent importance to the war effort—and to the world.

As sleep began to tug away her conscious thoughts, Olive worried over where her own death might fall on such a spectrum, and
whether its placement might be different if she chose to become
an agent.

Chapter 10
Personal Meetings

The following morning, the manor was atwitter with the news from the wireless that the United States had officially joined the fray. Mugs full of coffee met in celebration, at times with enough force to send chips of porcelain flaking to the floor. Grins and hearty backslaps abounded, and everyone's mood was buoyed above its usual sober intensity. Wanting to revel in it for as long as possible—and avoid being subjected to an entire day with Lieutenant Commander Fleming—Olive volunteered for laundry duty and let her thoughts resume the previous night's musings as she scrubbed and folded. She'd passed an indeterminate amount of time in perfect solitude when a sardonic voice spoke just behind her.

"You're hiding, aren't you?"

Olive whirled from the trousers whose stains she was doctoring with bicarbonate of soda and rubbed her forearm over her brow, dislodging the tendrils of hair that clung there in the steamy heat. She smiled at her fellow FANY.

"What makes you think that?" she asked archly.

Kate nearly snorted. "There are plenty of tasks we're asked to do that I don't particularly enjoy, but this might be the worst."

Olive twisted her lips. "At least it's warm in here," she said lightly.

"Your head looks like a blowball," Kate said harshly. "And that blowhard Fleming is looking for you. Not a good combination."

Frowning, Olive said, "I miss the old, innocent Kate, who had a fondness for pudding." She applied her brush to the watery paste and then scrubbed vigorously at a spot on the trousers. "What time is it, anyway?"

"Lunchtime. Come sit with me. If I have to pretend for everyone else, I might as well pretend for you."

"Just let me finish this," Olive said, starting in on a dark brown pullover spotted with even darker stains. With a glance up at Kate, she declared, "You know, it's not going to be easy to convince Blighty to let you train as an agent. He's quite against women playing any real role in this war."

"That may be," Kate said coyly. "But I have an ace in the hole."

Olive stopped scrubbing and looked at Kate with real interest. "Well, do tell."

"Don't tell me you've changed your mind?"

"No," Olive said hurriedly. "Not yet. I'm still thinking it over."

Kate eyed her interestedly, but upon catching sight of Olive's expectant gaze, she answered. "I've discovered that someone has already blazed this particular trail." She paused for effect, then added, "An American."

"Who?" Olive demanded, riveted by this new information.

"Do you *know* any Americans?"

"Well, no, but specifics tend to lend credibility."

"Would you be satisfied with a code name?"

"Not really. You could make up anything you liked."

"Let's just call her Eve, shall we?" With her arms crossed over her chest, Kate began to pace. "This past summer Eve finished her Baker Street training—at one of the other special training schools, obviously, or we'd know all about her—and was dropped into Vichy France. She's been there ever since."

Olive frowned. "Where did you hear this?"

She shrugged. "What does it matter? It's true."

Olive pondered this information and gave the stains one last going-over. "Did your spycraft yield any other information?"

"As a matter of fact, it did. Evidently, she has a prosthetic leg, and the men in charge in F Section are very impressed with her success thus far." As Olive tried to imagine landing a parachute jump with a prosthetic leg, Kate added, "I'm keener than ever to follow in her footsteps."

Finished with the pullover, Olive washed and dried her hands, shrugged her tunic back on over her damp chemise, and walked with Kate to the door. "It's going to be a battle," she said. "I suspect Blighty is every bit as stubborn as you, and he has the advantage, being your commanding officer and the man in charge of all trainees."

"Then I'll just need to find a way to shift his opinion, won't I?" Kate said slyly.

After a delicious lunch prepared by Tomás Harris, the manor's charming dogsbody-cum-cook, and a bit of Kate's scheming, Olive resigned herself to an afternoon spent in the company of Lieutenant Commander Fleming. But first, she wanted to speak to Jamie.

A short time later she was propping her fists on Jamie's desk, demanding, "Did you know that a woman agent has been parachuted into France?"

He looked up from the documents he'd been reviewing and sat back in his chair. "Good afternoon, Miss Bright. I see you haven't yet taken up the antiquated notion of knocking."

Ignoring him, she pressed her point. "*Did* you?"

"Actually," he said, "there have been two."

She blinked, straightened, a little hurt. "You could have told me."

"I could have, but I didn't see any reason to." Olive took a steadying breath, determined to tamp down her frustration, and was taken aback when he barrelled on. "Honestly, I hoped you would have abandoned the idea by now." He glanced down and away before adding the rest. "I'm not at all sure you're cut out for the job."

Stung, Olive dropped her arms from their twist over her chest. For a long moment she merely stared at him, a hollow feeling welling inside her, but he remained silent, refusing to meet her eyes, and eventually, she turned away. "Lieutenant Commander Fleming is waiting for me," she said as she slipped out the door.

Lieutenant Commander Fleming's pigeon handling was as laughable as Jamie's had been when he'd first shown up at the Bright loft, and after the latter's recent comments, Olive relished the feeling of competence as she introduced the visiting officer to her birds. It was chilly enough that they'd puffed up their feathers and tucked their heads in for warmth, but their curiosity remained undimmed.

Queenie was saved the indignity of a clumsy examination when Olive carefully removed the bird from Fleming's grasp to highlight a few key features that made pigeons the sort of workhorses the War Office was keen to have at their disposal. The compact, lightweight body and broad, powerful wings, which allowed them to maintain speeds in excess of sixty miles per hour over hundreds of miles. Their keen sensory abilities, which carried them home in darkness, over water, through inclement weather, even with no discernible landmarks in view. Their love of home and family, their loyalty and intelligence. She belatedly realised that her recent conversations with Blighty and Jamie had prompted her to take a defensive posture.

"And the canister?" said Fleming, his gaze travelling round the dovecote as he fidgeted with the unlit cigarette in his hand. Watching him, Olive smirked at this feeble attempt to reassert himself. She had, after all, yanked the previous one out of his mouth when he'd refused to put it out upon entering the dovecote. She'd flicked it down beside the droppings, ground it beneath her heel, and then turned to him, brow raised in reminder that he was on very thin ice.

She produced a spare Bakelite tube from her pocket, held it between finger and thumb, and he looked it over with narrowed eyes.

"May I?" When she relinquished the tube into his hands, he turned slightly away. "Yes, that should be plenty big enough, assuming we can requisition some miniature cameras," he murmured, his breath puffing out of him like smoke in the icy air. He put the cigarette to his lips and spoke round it, almost as if he'd forgotten she was there. "The ones from Latvia would be preferable, but it won't be easy getting our hands on those."

Olive waited, shivering in irritation.

He'd listened carefully to her explanations, his eyes roving but intent. He'd watched the birds eating, bathing, and engaged with their young, but he'd not offered even a hint of his plans. As far as Olive was concerned, she'd held up her end. Now it was his turn. "So the pigeons would be carrying photographs?" Olive prompted, brimming with curiosity in spite of herself.

He spun round to look at her, his nose and mouth haughty, and pulled the cigarette from his lips. "If I can work out the logistics, yes."

"What's the problem?"

He narrowed his eyes at her consideringly. Olive narrowed hers right back. " 'Keep mum—she's not so dumb.' That's the assertion of the propaganda posters. Though it's not been my particular experience." He handed back the tube, tipped his head down, clasped his hands behind his back, and began to pace.

"But I'll admit, you've demonstrated a rare capacity for secrets. For a woman." He flicked a glance at her before adding, "If only you had a switch and could be turned off on occasion."

Before Olive could respond to this insufferable speech, he barrelled on.

"It's all based on a pinch." He turned to look at her, his eyes suggestive, his lips mocking. "Not the sort you're familiar with, I'm afraid." If Olive hadn't been supremely curious about his secret plans, she would have stomped out of the dovecote to get the pitchfork her father kept in the barn. "The sort I'm referring to is the act of obtaining secret documents by covert methods." He carefully tucked his cigarette into his pocket, then unearthed a handkerchief and proceeded to wipe his nose. "I plan to propose a commando unit that will accompany forward troops when a port or other naval installation is attacked. The purview of this assault unit would be to confiscate important documents, maps, and other classified materials before they can be destroyed." He looked at her then, clearly expecting her fawning approval.

"And the pigeons?" Olive said politely, tucking her hands into her pockets.

Fleming frowned. "Would be a plan B. As a precaution against the commandos not making it out with the documents intact, photographs would be taken, and the film sent on by pigeon. The difficulty is that that information would need to go straight back to central command to give the officers a chance to adjust attack plans accordingly."

"You'd need a field loft," she said decisively. No matter that neither she nor her birds were involved, Olive couldn't help but be intrigued by a fresh opportunity for pigeons to benefit the war effort. "The mobile lofts had widespread use during the Great War, and I suspect HM Forces are using them to great effect in this one. But then, that's just me jabbering, is all."

Now he eyed her with mild interest, having apparently ignored that last bit. "And will they home to the field loft, even at sea, rather than returning to England?"

"They can be trained to do so, particularly young birds who've not yet imprinted on their breeder's loft. But it would take weeks to accomplish that."

He wiped his nose again, his eyes darting from the birds back to her as he considered this alternative. "Well, there it is. I think having some of them at our disposal can only be a boon." He began to pace once again. "You see, it's all about having the upper hand. The Nazis might have bested us with their technology, but so long as we're aware of it, we can, to some extent, control how the game is played. It's all very cloak and dagger, but quite necessary."

He seemed almost giddy at the thought of that game, being played out hundreds of miles away on foreign soil, by braver men than he. She recalled his focused concentration as he toured Station XVII and even participated in some of the training exercises.

"Your visit to the manor has all been about this, hasn't it?"

"You're forgetting my business with Mrs Dunbar."

"I don't think I'll ever forget the business with Mrs Dunbar," she countered. "But as far as I can tell, nothing you did at Station XVII aided you in your dealings with that poor woman."

"You're too clever by half." He didn't say, "For a woman," but at this point, it was implied. "But I suppose you know enough already. You may as well hear the rest." He retrieved the cigarette from his pocket, tucked it between his lips, then caught her eye and cursed savagely, before yanking it out again. "I wanted to see how Baker Street was training their agents, whether the syllabus was the sort I'd want our commandos to undertake. And from what I've seen, it is, everything from the fieldcraft to the hand-to-hand fighting. I daresay the men could run up against that type of thing on every mission." He shot the cuffs of his deep blue Royal Navy jacket.

"So, you might say you've got what you came for, all the way round." Her voice was clipped, but he surely didn't notice it.

"I daresay." He glanced at her, the barest flush in his cheeks. "Not, mind you, the way I'd intended or preferred, but this is war, which means you have to take a win when it comes. No matter how it comes."

Olive didn't know if she could ever manage that sort of coldness. It was necessary, she knew, but that didn't change the way she felt. Perhaps she really wasn't cut out to be an agent.

"Now, I believe we're about even? And remember, loose lips sink ships, and there's been far too much of that already." He looked simultaneously somber and harried, and Olive couldn't help but like him the better for it. Amidst all the bluster, swagger, and cigarette smoke, she'd got a sense of the man beneath. It was clear Fleming was clever and calculating, willing to go to great lengths on the path to victory.

"I'll remember," she assured him.

"Then I'll say goodbye, Miss Bright," he said, turning abruptly for the door. "I'm headed back to London to write up my report on Mrs Dunbar and to add a pigeon contingent to my proposal for that other, quite top-secret proposal," he said wryly. The cigarette was already tucked between his lips, and his lighter was hovering at the ready.

"You can't leave," Olive blurted, disconcerted. "What about the police investigation? You're a suspect."

"I've been cleared," he said, the tilt of his eyes and mouth quite irritatingly smug. "The police have determined—quite accurately, in fact—that I'd no reason to kill the woman. But don't fret, my girl. Our paths may cross again." A pause. "I don't suppose I could trouble you for a cup of tea?"

"I'm sorry," Olive said sweetly before proceeding with a little white lie. "We've run out, but I could make you some acorn coffee . . ."

He frowned, shuddered, and then the flame caught the tip of his cigarette, and he strode out the door of the dovecote.

Olive propped her hands on her hips and watched him go, much relieved to be rid of him. Then she looked round at her birds, perched throughout the dovecote. In a flurry of feathers,

Queenie launched herself up from the tray of water at her feet. She'd almost reached the cupola when her droppings tumbled to the floor below.

"Really?" Olive said in exasperation. "You couldn't have done that a little to the left while he was still standing there?" She sighed, but her thoughts had already dispatched Lieutenant Commander Fleming for another worry. Despite her efforts for Baker Street—and even, peripherally, with the Women's Institute—she still felt as if the war was going on beyond her reach, as if she wasn't doing enough. And if Major Blighty had his way, her role as pigeoneer could soon be obsolete. Well, she was working on the situation, wasn't she? She'd taken steps to train as an agent. She'd just have to make certain she could pass all the tests. A small voice inside her whispered the rest: *And muster the courage.* She felt suddenly very cold. And very alone.

A moment later, she shook free of her worries, stamped her feet to thwart her numbing toes, and reached for the broom, determined to think of absolutely anything else.

The good news was, one more suspect had been eliminated. Not that she trusted DS Burris's judgment—she didn't. But, in truth, she hadn't really suspected Fleming. The method of Mrs Dunbar's murder wasn't his style. Much too messy. And he probably hadn't a clue what lords-and-ladies even was, let alone how to get his hands on it. He would have found another way. And he probably wouldn't have been able to keep from bragging about it.

The dovecote benefited from quite a thorough cleaning, thanks to Olive's frustration with the man. And by the time she was finished, she was more than ready for tea and company.

But as she was pulling the door to the dovecote shut behind her, Jonathon hurried up with a wicker basket slung over her arm.

"Hullo," Olive called. "What have you got there?"

"More to add to my collection."

"What collection is that?" Olive leaned forward in an effort to peer into the basket, but Jonathon neatly shifted it round behind him. His cheeks were chapped pink, but his eyes were bright with secrets.

"You'll see," he said mysteriously. "Am I in time for tea?"

"I was just heading that way myself," she said, wrapping an arm round his shoulders as they walked to the kitchen door. "Everything all right?" He still seemed a bit subdued, and based on past experiences, she would have expected him to confide in her, but he hadn't.

He nodded, not quite meeting her eyes. She sighed. It seemed they all had their demons.

While Olive readied the tea, arranging a few broken bits of shortbread on a plate as she waited for the kettle to boil, Jonathon scrambled up to his room, having promised a quick return. When he eventually pushed through the door of the parlour, his arms were full, and several stalks of gloriously red-orange Chinese lanterns appeared to be sprouting from his wicker basket.

"What's all this?" Harriet said slowly, straining to see. Her eyesight had improved somewhat since she'd curtailed her smoking habits, but it still wasn't quite up to snuff.

"Christmas decorations," Jonathon said triumphantly, setting everything on the floor beside Harriet's chaise as the women stared at him wide eyed. "I always read the newsletter put out by the Land Girls," he said proudly. "And they've got lots of good ideas." He held up the Chinese lanterns. "I've been saving these for months." He tipped his head to rummage further in his basket. "And I've got pinecones and feathers and all sorts of things." He then produced a carefully pressed stack of shimmery aluminum toffee wrappers. "We've only got a few of these. Hen suggested we turn them into fairy skirts." He glanced shyly up at Olive. "You'd probably make a better job of it."

"I'm not so old I've forgotten how to dress a fairy," Harriet said teasingly. "This looks wonderful, Jonathon. Just perfect. Now Rupert just needs to remember to do his part, and we'll have a tree," she said with a twinkle. "Why don't you leave those things in the corner? Olive can get the other decorations from the hall closet, and this evening we'll set to work. With any luck, there'll be Christmas tunes playing on the wireless, and we'll get right into the spirit of the season."

Jonathon smiled, but his eyes still seemed troubled. Olive handed him the plate of shortbread.

With so much urgency and uncertainty—and fear and turmoil—in the world, it was difficult sometimes to remember that Christmas wasn't far off. But she didn't have long to get her shopping sorted, and Jamie was proving particularly tricky. Particularly now that matters had shifted somewhat between them. She would have to give it some concentrated thought.

*   *   *

To Olive Bright, Village Sleuth

There's something you should know. Mrs Dunbar's death was an accident. She was only meant to be punished, but something went horribly wrong. The devils and angels should have only made her violently ill. Her body should have rid itself of the poison. She didn't deserve to die that way. If you believe punishment should still be meted out, please do your best to convince the police that accidents warrant more lenient sentences. So, too, does remorse. But she wasn't blameless. She preyed on frazzled hearts and minds for the spectacle and for money. There is nothing good in that.

A Friend

Chapter 11

Innocent Text Letter

10 December
Station XVII

Olive had found the folded letter trapped by a rock against the seat of her motorbike where it stood propped against the stable wall, and she'd stood in the bitter cold for much too long as she read it over again and again, all its clues getting tangled up in her mind.

She had thought of Harriet, tucked in against the chill, holding court in the parlour, and Jonathon tucked up to the table for a breakfast of eggs and toast, and had wondered if she dared share the contents with either of them. With stinging cheeks and numb fingers, she'd decided it better to confide in an outsider.

She desperately wanted to talk to Jamie, but her steps faltered as she started down the hall toward his office, her thoughts replaying their last conversation. With his long-awaited return from Ireland, it had felt as if her world had been once again set to rights. But that feeling had been fleeting. With one short, doubting sentence, he had upended it all over again. He didn't believe in her, didn't think that she could rise to the challenges required of a Baker Street agent. Despite their rocky start, Olive had imagined they'd reached a comfortable understanding, based on mutual respect, admiration . . . and affection. They'd been partners in crime. And that made it hurt all the more.

A few feet from his doorway, she stood immobile and uncertain for a long moment. Then, pivoting on her heel, she strode away again. With her fingers gripping the crumpled edges of the letter in her pocket, she ran Hell to ground and dragged her into the FANY powder room for a quick confab. A cursory glance confirmed that they were the room's only two occupants, so Olive pulled her to the ottoman that sat in the centre of the room.

"I need to tell you what happened at the séance," Olive said carefully.

Hell nodded, then sat unblinking as Olive relayed the details leading up to the death of Mrs Dunbar.

"Golly," Hell said when she'd finished.

"There's more," Olive said abruptly, thrusting the letter in her direction.

After reading it over quickly, Hell carefully folded it up again and handed it back. "First things first," she said. "Do you know who wrote it?"

"No . . . ," Olive said, frowning. "No one comes immediately to mind."

"Will you tell the police about it?"

"I'm not sure. I'd really rather know who wrote it before I take the next step." Unable to resist another perusal of the confession, she unfolded the paper, the edges of which were already well worn.

"Very sensible," Hell allowed. "It could make a world of difference in how you proceed."

Olive was silent, her lips pressed together, as she read. Hell had moved to the vanity mirror hung beside the window. She was tucking back stray curls that had frizzed from their pins.

"Well, let's make a start, shall we?" she said, meeting Olive's eyes in the mirror. "It's obviously someone who believes you want to get to the truth, thinks you might be sympathetic, and supposes you have the ear of the police."

Olive smiled, happy to have chosen Hell to confide in. Finding the letter had been a shock: another mystery, another layer to an already baffling murder. But it was time to get to work.

"I had the same thought. And I do—want to get to the truth, that is." She glanced again at the paper in her hand. "Another clue . . . The author of the letter is apparently unaware of the second poison. Or else they're playing a very cagey game." She paused a moment to consider this before shrugging. "That remains to be seen, but it would appear that there were two separate poisoners."

Hell nodded her agreement.

"This particular one," Olive said, indicating the paper in her hand, "would have to be someone familiar with devils and angels—or lords-and-ladies, as I've called it for as long as I can remember. They'd need to know not only how to identify the plant but also the side effects of consuming it."

"That counts me out. I'm hopeless with botany. Though I do love these fancy names for a murder plant," Hell said. Then she spun, her eyes flashing. "*I* might have mistaken it for something else entirely and poisoned a whole canteen of people quite by accident." Olive met her eyes as Hell added, quite unnecessarily, "But this was malicious. Someone had a mean grudge against Mrs Dunbar."

Just as Jamie had said. *Murder is seldom kind.*

"Yes, but not big enough to kill, evidently. Only to punish," Olive murmured. "If this is to be believed." The paper fluttered in her hand.

"True, but why write the letter at all, otherwise?"

"I haven't any idea," Olive mused. But she wondered.

Hell squared her shoulders and peered down her nose at Olive. "As much as I'd love to hole up in here and solve this little mystery, we should probably get back to work. We've loads of new recruits coming in next week, and we're not at all ready."

"You're right," Olive said with a groan. She wasn't much looking forward to spending the next few hours arranging the schedules, sleeping arrangements, and general welfare of dozens of men. Then a thought struck her: Was it possible that one of the new recruits might be a woman? The very possibility excited her. With her own thoughts in a tizzy about the prospect of becoming an agent, paired with Kate's assured perspective and Aldridge's discouraging attitude, Olive was hopeful of a fresh point of view. But it would have to wait. "Let's get a coffee first," she suggested, following Hell from the room. "I suspect we're going to need it."

Hell poured herself a quick cup and hurried down the hall, but Olive lingered. Max Dunn was sitting at a table in the corner of the canteen, reading over a stack of reports. By the looks of things, he'd been there awhile. After his Vickers Wellington had been shot up over the Channel, he'd been treated for extensive burns and severe depression. Not only had all but two of his crew perished in the crash, but he also faced a future quite different than the one he'd expected. He had been persuaded to come to work at Brickendonbury as an adjutant and was now regularly consulted on matters relating to the RAF.

Olive pulled out the chair across from him, the crutches he now used in place of a wheelchair propped against the one beside him. "Do you mind?"

He looked up, but she was well used to his face now, its shiny new skin courtesy of multiple skin grafts. Despite his altered features, the most striking aspect of his face was his seemingly depthless dark eyes. Gesturing for her to sit, he nodded at her cup. "The Germans have got us right where they want us—short on tea and dependent on this bitter brew. It's diabolical."

She slid into the chair. "One cup makes a martyr," she joked before taking her first cringeworthy sip. "How are things?"

"Fair to middling if you don't count a murder taking place in our drawing room. I suppose that's not what you mean, though."

"Oh, that definitely counts," Olive insisted.

"Then I'd say rather gruesome but beginning to come round. I still don't quite believe it. I honestly wouldn't have thought Aunt Leticia would have gone in for that sort of thing. My mother was the sort to ponder the meaning of dreams, wonder at the afterlife, and dabble in myriad philosophies. She was entirely too suggestible—you could say it was the death of her." His brows rose in a helpless gesture, and he ran his fingers over the curve of his cup's handle. They shook slightly, and he dropped them to the table before looking up to meet her eyes. "I suppose this war has proved well enough that people change." His lips curved in a fatalistic smile, but his eyes were sad.

Olive cradled her cup in her hands. "And Lady Revell is managing all right?" She frowned, remembering. "It really was horrible. Shocking and brutal."

"Yes, Violet said," he said softly. "Did you know the woman?"

Olive shook her head. "Hardly at all. None of us did, really, other than her husband."

"And yet someone knew enough to murder her . . ." He let the words trail off, leaving her to draw her own conclusion.

Olive thought of the letter, tucked into her pocket, and sipped her coffee musingly. She glanced casually over at him as she said, "Violet didn't, by any chance, share any gossip going round, did she?"

He grinned at her. "Only that she suspected the husband of extramarital interests, being quite clear that she didn't blame the man."

"I suppose that detail *could* be helpful," Olive allowed with a wry smile.

"Makes him a suspect in my book," Max said stoutly, grimacing as he drained his cup. "But I'm not Pipley's resident sleuth."

"It's just a hobby," Olive insisted, before flashing him a mischievous smile. "But I'll keep that in mind." She stood. "For now, though, it's back to work." She paused, looking down at him. "You're coming to the Christmas party, aren't you? It's also to be a send-off. Friday, the week before the holiday . . . There'll be drinks and—"

"Dancing?" he said wryly. "I'm not sure I'm quite up to that yet. I'll let you know, shall I?"

She smiled, nodded, and left him to his work.

By late afternoon Olive was dragging. She had been on her feet for hours and still needed to make a trip into the village. She wasn't particularly looking forward to ten blustery minutes spent on the motorbike, nor was she keen to make arrangements for Swilly with the butcher. Tea at the vicarage, however, was much anticipated, even if she couldn't share her news. She'd discovered that not one but two of the recruits scheduled for training at Station XVII were women. The news had prompted the smile that creased her face as she drew on her coat. It slipped somewhat as Jamie approached, favouring his leg just slightly.

"Off for the day?" he inquired, brows raised.

"I am." She adjusted her collar and buttoned up the front.

"May I have a word?"

"Of course," she said politely, settling her beret on her head.

"I spoke out of turn yesterday." He seemed to be considering his next words carefully. "My opinion on the matter is irrelevant. If you're truly not cut out to be an agent, the process—the tests and interrogations—will weed you out without any interference from me."

Pressing her lips together, Olive nodded. Rather than talk to her and explain his reservations, he was leaving her to fend for herself—to make her way on her own. That was fair, but she'd expected—hoped for—more from him.

"I can, however," he went on, "prepare you for what's to come. I want to." He took a deep breath before adding awkwardly, "If that's what you want."

The heaviness that had settled over her at his first words instantly lightened, the change so discombobulating her that she nearly flung herself at him.

"Honestly, I don't know what I want," she admitted, biting her lip. "But I think I can only benefit from the rigours you would choose to impose on my training." She didn't know if she'd even manage the training, let alone pluck up the courage to use it, but at the moment, it didn't matter. More than anything else, she was content to have his support. It shouldn't have been so important, but it was.

His gaze was, as ever, impenetrable, but his words were predictable. "You joke, but I won't go easy on you."

She was so relieved to have things a bit back to normal, and he was so adorably stuffy that Olive could no longer hold herself aloof. She leaned in, cutting off the rest of his lecture, to plant a smacking kiss on his cheek. "When have you ever?" she teased.

He held himself utterly rigid, giving not the slightest little bit, so that she was tempted to inch her lips a little to the right and plant another kiss full on his mouth. But she didn't. It wasn't appropriate for the halls of Brickendonbury Manor, and Jamie would be more scandalised than a maiden aunt. Naturally, he carried on as if nothing had happened.

"Fair enough," he said, his words stilted. "We'll begin when you're ready, making certain this endeavour does not interfere with the rest of your work."

Vibrating with possibility, Olive was tempted to declare herself ready right that very moment, but then she remembered she was expected at the vicarage and instead nodded emphatically before turning toward the door.

But Jamie stayed her progress. "Is everything all right? You were noticeably absent from my office today."

She swung round, determined not to feel guilty for not showing him the letter. He'd made his feelings on her sleuthing habits quite clear, so she'd simply found another partner in crime. "Just busy," she said, with a shrug and a shake of her head. "Enjoy your respite. When training begins, I suspect you'll be cursing my name." Then, with a broad grin on her face, she stepped from the bustling warmth of the manor into the damp, misty grey of almost-winter in Hertfordshire.

Chapter 12
Double Transposition

10 December
Station XVII and Pipley

She was oblivious to the cold, fizzing with delight that Jamie had reconsidered and decided to keep an open mind on the matter of her training. She had pushed in the throttle and was flying down the drive under the bare branch canopy, revelling in the smell of evergreen and woodsmoke, happily bellowing "Good King Wenceslas" as the mist streamed over her. But this little bit of winter magic was short-lived, ending abruptly when she rounded the bend and came in sight of the gatehouse.

"Oh, murder," Olive blurted into the wind.

She'd completely forgotten her promise to take Mrs Blighty—Scarlet—round to meet the Land Army girls working on the gardens at Peregrine Hall. And now there she was, bundled up against the cold in a raggedy old cardigan that must belong to her husband, Wellies, and a winter-white cloche hat, pinned with a tartan ribbon. She looked like a jumble sale, but her eyes were bright and her smile was delighted.

Olive coasted to a stop beside the gate and cut the engine,

having decided to lead with the truth. "Hullo! I've just now remembered our pact. We were going to be thick as thieves, and it went quite out of my head." She wiped the moisture from her face and smiled sheepishly.

Scarlet tipped her head down before glancing shyly up again. "I really don't want to be a bother, but if I have to stay cooped up in there on my own for much longer, with nothing to do but cook and clean and knit, I think I shall go out of my mind." There was wild in her eyes, but she took a breath and collected herself, smiling.

"I quite understand. I'd be exactly the same."

"It's just that Gregory is very busy, up at the manor till all hours, and the village is off-limits." She shook her head. "He's warned me again and again about the necessity of keeping secrets, but I don't *know* any." She tucked her hands into the pockets of the cardigan, hugged it close against her, and began pacing, her dark hair swinging forward to shield her pinked cheeks. "I want to be useful—I'm not helpless."

"Of course you're not," Olive asserted angrily. "I'm quite run off my feet, but I very often feel that way myself. It's not enough to be busy when others are making such sacrifices."

"That's it exactly," she said with a deep sigh of relief.

The wind was whipping up, and Olive was eager for a cup of tea in the vicarage kitchen. But she was torn. She'd already agreed to help Scarlet find a way to do her bit for the war, and she certainly had no personal loyalty to *Gregory*, but having a bit of experience with the consequences of being caught out, she'd recently come to the conclusion that winning a person over—no matter how grudgingly—was much preferable to sneaking round behind their back.

She decided to broach an alternate idea. "Why don't you come to carolling practice on Sunday evening?" Before Scarlet could object, she barrelled on. "Lady Revell will be there, along with several of the ladies from the Women's Institute. It will be a perfect opportunity to meet them and let them prod and bully you into taking charge of one of their schemes."

Scarlet was already shaking her head. "But Gregory . . ."

"Tell *Gregory* you've been invited and you daren't say no, or else the whole village will be gossiping about why you never participate or assist with anything, making you *quite* the centre of attention." Olive raised her brows. "And *then*," she added pointedly, "tell him how much you want to."

Scarlet's facial muscles tightened into a grimace, but she seemed to be considering, marshalling the courage it would require for her to defy her husband's wishes.

Olive suppressed a shiver at the thought of facing down those flat grey eyes, flashed an encouraging smile, and lifted her brows expectantly. "Will you come?"

"What if I can't?" Scarlet said, her face stricken.

"If you mean because of Gregory," Olive said sourly, "then we'll do it your way—top secret, cloak and dagger. But it really will be easier all the way round if he's in your confidence." Now that Jamie's office had taken on the guise of a confessional, he'd become quite tolerant of her various plans.

"All right. I'll try," she vowed. "Shall I send you a note through Gregory, if he's agreeable?"

"No, no-no," Olive blurted. "That's not a good idea. You don't need to tell him who invited you. If he knows it's me, he might worry about excessive fraternisation between the village and the manor." *Or he might squash the whole idea, citing me as a bad influence.* She smiled innocently. "I've found that being deliberately vague lets men draw their own conclusions—and they're usually much happier with those."

"If you say so."

"Right then. I look forward to seeing you in the village hall on Sunday evening at seven o'clock." Olive started the engine and set off with a wave.

But as she turned onto the lane, and the hedgerows streamed

past, her earlier exuberance fled. Now a feeling of fraught urgency thrummed in her blood, as if each and every secret she was harbouring was revolting, churning inside her, eager to be let loose. She felt an imminent urge to shout them all out amid the roar of the motorbike so that they could spin away from her, into the raised ears of foxes and hares, into the full-on frosty wind, the pressure finally released.

She was still miles from Pipley, and she felt certain no one was about in such frigid weather, so she gave in; she did it. She shouted a secret into the wind.

"Je crois que je suis amoureuse de lui!"

But as the words were swallowed up by the ether, her mouth clapped shut, and a sound-dampening shock rocked through her as the words echoed in her mind.

I think I might be in love with him.

The handlebars swerved under her hands, and she barely got control of the motorbike before it veered off the road. A moment later she sat still, reeling from the shock of it. She'd had plenty of secrets to choose from—any one of them could have been shouted into the wind with no one the wiser. But she hadn't settled on any of those. Instead, her subconscious mind had chosen that opportunity to tip the world off balance, to let go its own secret.

Olive didn't move, but she felt the wisps of hair, caught by the wind, lashing against her neck and face. She ignored them as her thoughts worked slowly through the possibility of it. She squinted, scrunched up her face, shook her head to start again as she considered the implications from every angle.

In love? With Jamie? Captain Aldridge and the irrepressible Horace? It was ridiculous. Impossible. He was by turns frustrating, infuriating, unimaginative, and gruff. But then the frown that had taken hold of her brows relented, ever so slightly, as she conceded the rest: he could also be surprising, encouraging, protective, and sweet. Honestly, she had trouble imagining her life without him. A shiver ran over her. She did have a habit of imagining their romantic endeavours as a bit more . . . thorough.

She blinked. *Was she?* The evidence was pretty damning, and the realisation was overwhelming. She was. Her skin flushed, her heart quickened, and her stomach was suddenly at odds with the rest of her. She was in love with Jamie.

And she had no bloody idea what to do about it.

She deliberately didn't think about it. She focused instead on all the things she still had to do in the coming weeks: finish her Christmas preparations, get her young birds into good flying form, improve her French, prepare for the influx of new agents at Station XVII, begin Jamie's training regimen and, not to be left out, solve a murder. And then there were the pigs.

She was flustered, that was all. Overworked, living a double life, frazzled and uncertain.

At that point in her musings, she arrived at the butcher shop. With a little clutch of her heart, she climbed off the bike and went to speak to Mr Dervish.

As she stepped back onto the high street, the unhappy business done, her eyes caught on the retreating form of Mr Dunbar, arm in arm with Eileen Heatherton. Olive stared after them until they'd rounded the bend in the road, trying to reconcile this feckless behaviour from a man whose wife had just been gruesomely murdered. He was an outsider in the village and, thus, her choice for the killer, *and* he'd been in possession of a bottle laced with poison. Was it really as simple as that? Her little grey cells were protesting. She couldn't see him writing out a confession, particularly to her, and there was still the little matter of the scopolamine. It was unlikely the solution would be an easy one, and she couldn't think about it right now.

Her thoughts were in a tizzy, her shouted words echoing over and over in her mind, along with their English translation: *Je crois que je suis amoureuse de lui. I think I might be in love with him.*

She desperately wished she could confide in Margaret, but that was out of the question. Her friend didn't know her relationship with Jamie was strictly a cover story—a ruse. Telling her that she suspected she might be in love with the man would only garner a droll comment or a dramatic roll of her eyes. Or, worse still, it would lead to probing questions that Olive couldn't answer. Margaret couldn't possibly understand how momentous a revelation this was, and how utterly fraught.

Olive felt almost dizzy with the truth of it. Until now, she could, if she chose to, confide every one of her secrets to Jamie. But not this one. This one had the potential to ruin everything.

Dredging up every curse she'd learned from the French agents that had trained at Brickendonbury, Olive wheeled the bike to the vicarage. After a brisk knock at the door, she stepped through to the hallway and shrugged off her coat, letting out a deep, contented sigh. She had missed these cosy chats with her friend and was looking forward to their catching up. Not to mention the respite from her own frazzled thoughts.

Margaret called to her from the kitchen. "Hurry up, then, or your tea will be cold."

Olive straightened her tunic and walked through, saying, "I have had a doozy of a day."

Two faces stared back at her from their places at the oilcloth-covered table in the cramped little kitchen. One deliberately innocent, made up with deep red lipstick and kohl-black eyeliner, and one as white as a ghost, with chapped pink lips and pale blue veins showing at her temples. It seemed Margaret had invited Alfreda Rodery.

Olive schooled her features to avoid the shock of surprise showing on her face. "Oh, hello," she said politely. "Tea for three, then?"

Freya Rodery was the veritable white whale. Ever since her arrival in the village, she'd mostly kept herself to herself, and then the attention she'd garnered at the hands of Mrs Dunbar had seemed to spook her further, but here she was in the vicarage kitchen. Olive couldn't imagine how Margaret had managed it.

"We were just enjoying a little gossip about this and that. Utterly harmless and all in good fun, but duty calls," Margaret said briskly, looking pointedly at Olive. "I thought you could help me convince Freya." She smiled winningly at the woman. "You did say I could call you that? Good. I quite like saying it. It's like a fairy name."

Freya smiled. "Actually, the opposite is true. 'Freya' simply means *noble lady*. 'Alfreda,' on the other hand, is old English and means *elf counsel*." She shrugged. "Elves are certainly not fairies, but if you believe in one, you may as well believe in the other."

Margaret shrugged. "Oh, well, I still prefer Freya. Do please sit down, Olive, and stop gawping." Olive sat, frowning, and reached for the teapot. Margaret pressed on. "As I was saying, I've been trying to convince Freya," she said, smiling, "that we could use a bit of help round the church, particularly with Leo's leg on the fritz, not to mention his work at Merryweather House, and my turn on the ROC's weekly rota."

Leo had been considering a tour as chaplain on a navy submarine when he'd taken a nasty fall and dislocated his kneecap. After that, it was generally agreed that having him aboard would be more trouble than it was worth.

"I really don't think—"

Margaret cut ruthlessly across the woman, even as she squeezed her hand. "I refuse to take no for an answer until you've had time to think on the matter. You've lived in the village for a little while now, rattling round in that cottage all by yourself, not getting involved." Margaret's face softened as she probed teasingly. "You're not, by any chance, hiding any skeletons, are you?"

Olive had just taken a sip from the still-too-hot tea and now struggled to swallow as the liquid burned against the back of her throat. "Margaret," she gasped in reprimand. A glance at Freya showed that her smile had fractured slightly and her eyes looked concerned.

"Not *actual* skeletons," Margaret said archly before leaning forward to clarify. *"Secrets."* Margaret blinked, glancing between them, her eyes widening as she hurried on. "Don't get the wrong idea. I'm not asking for gossip's sake or to offer judgment." She sighed. "But having gone through that very thing myself," she went on carefully as colour suffused her cheeks, "and come out the other side, I would offer you a bit of advice. And it's simply this. What's past is past. Whatever it is cannot be reason enough to lock yourself away from the world. Particularly with your husband away so much."

Freya lifted her teacup and drank deeply, her eyes darting from Margaret to Olive over the rim of her cup. Olive smiled in what she hoped was a nonthreatening manner and reached for an oatcake, which she spread with black currant jam.

"Nothing so exciting as that," Freya finally said. "I was an only child, and when my parents died, I had to make my own way in the world. There wasn't time for anything other than work." Her smile was self-deprecating.

"Well, now you're a kept woman," Margaret said slyly. "With plenty of time to do as you like."

Freya's smile was brittle but friendly. "Perhaps you're right. I've never lived in a village before. It's very close-knit, isn't it?"

"So much so that at times it can feel smothering," Margaret said brightly. "On those days, you should feel free to dodge into the vicarage. I've got quite good at thwarting nosy busybodies."

Olive frowned at her friend and suggested, "Why don't you make a start by joining us for carolling practice on Sunday? Just for fun. I promise no one will press you into doing the altar flowers," she said, flicking a meaningful glance at Margaret.

Freya was quiet for a long moment, until, with slow deliberation, her arms unbent and she set her cup in the saucer. Something inside her seemed to uncoil. "I've always loved the holidays," she said, her eyes misting slightly. "Particularly those quiet, peaceful moments of utter clarity and calm."

Margaret and Olive exchanged a glance, both of them preferring the Christmas crackers, the frenzy of present opening, and the rousing chorus of carols.

"So you'll come?" Olive pressed.

Freya nodded, her lips curved into the barest hint of a smile. But her eyes were suspiciously glossy.

"And with your husband being away, I hope you'll consider having Christmas dinner at ours," Olive added, "if you're not already expected elsewhere." She crossed her fingers that Harriet and Mrs Battlesby could stretch the rations a bit further, particularly with Jamie already invited.

"Oh, well, that's very kind, but I wouldn't want to intrude."

"Nonsense," Olive said quickly. "This year has been an ordeal, and this past week . . ." Words failed her. After a beat of silence, she tried again. "Needless to say, we could all do with a joyful celebration."

"I don't suppose you've heard," Margaret said archly. "The results of the inquest have come back." She paused before adding, "Poison, twice over, if you can believe it. Devils and angels—whatever that might be. It sounds quite medieval, doesn't it? And scopul something or other."

"Scopolamine," Olive clarified, recalling her chat with Dr Harrington. "And what was the verdict?" Surely it was murder.

Margaret's smile was wry. "Open verdict."

Olive huffed out an irritated breath. "Meaning what, exactly?"

"It seems the police will continue to investigate in hopes of more conclusive evidence. But honestly, this whole business is quite out of DS Burris's league."

"They're not bringing in an inspector?"

"They evidently haven't one to spare. This war has brought the rot out of the woodwork." Margaret tsked, staring into her teacup.

Olive cursed. She should have expected it.

Margaret went on, "I daresay they'll be knocking on your door before long." She leaned toward Freya, who was sitting in rigid silence, adding conspiratorially, "Olive was at the séance, and, as it happens, she fancies herself as somewhat of an amateur detective."

Freya's gaze flicked to Olive, her face a mask of shock.

Margaret continued, "That woman may have been a menace, but she certainly didn't deserve to die like that. Olive will see to it—"

"Margaret," Olive said warningly, but her friend hadn't noticed the effect her words were having.

"It was such a dirty trick she played on you, and in front of everyone on the village green." Margaret shook her head at the scandal of it. "And none of it—thank heaven—even true." Olive winced, knowing Margaret was trying to help, but feeling that this was too intrusive. "She was the sort of woman who craved attention. But to wreak havoc on people's emotions, playing with life and death for her own ends . . . Well, it was quite unforgivable. I would have wanted to murder her myself, and I suspect you felt the very same—"

It was then that Freya Rodery stood, the legs of her chair scraping backwards across the floor. Her eyes were wild and wounded; her hands, wringing each other despondently. "I didn't . . . I couldn't have . . ."

Olive stood, too, wishing Margaret had let well enough alone. "Of course not. Don't mind Margaret. She might run her mouth to no end, but that's all it is, just talk. She hasn't quite got the role of vicar's wife down pat just yet. Please stay and have another cup of tea. We'll talk of something else—Christmas, if you want."

Margaret sat still, blinking dumbly at the pair of them.

"No, I'm sorry. I can't." Freya was already skirting the table, intent on making for the front door of the vicarage and escape. "But thank you for the tea. I do appreciate it."

"Will you come for carolling practice on Sunday?" Olive said quickly, hurrying to follow.

"I really don't . . ."

"Think about it," Olive insisted. "We'll be much better behaved, I promise. Seven o'clock."

Freya Rodery slipped hurriedly into her coat and donned her
gloves and hat. Then she stilled for a moment and met Olive's
gaze. "I'll try," she promised. "Please thank Mrs Truscott for the
tea. I'm sorry to run out like this." She shook her head, snatched
open the door, and was gone, hurrying down the walk toward the
churchyard.

With her expression grim, Olive stalked back to the kitchen,
where Margaret was sitting primly, poised to take another bite of
jammy oatcake. Olive crossed her arms and speared her friend
with a look of exasperation. "Why did you say all that to her?"
she demanded.

Her friend seemed stunned at her reaction and said huffily, "I
was trying to be supportive."

"You're the vicar's wife, Mags! You should not be admitting to
murderous instincts."

Margaret rolled her eyes. "I wouldn't really have done it. And
nor would she. It was just a harmless chat over tea."

"Except that someone *did* murder the woman," Olive insisted.

"Well, it wasn't any one of us," came the sharp retort.

Olive sat back down and downed the rest of her tea, trying to
regain her equilibrium. Everything simply felt off. With her eyes
closed, she said, "Why was she really here?"

"She's a lost lamb in the Pipley flock."

"And . . . ?" Olive blinked one eye open, waiting to hear the
rest.

Margaret's shoulders dropped. "She's new to the village and
doesn't have the luxury of holding me up to my predecessors—
only to find me wanting. I can use all the friends—and allies—I
can get."

Sighing, Olive turned to her friend. "I get that. But you could
have taken a more delicate approach. I adore you, but some people prefer their gossip a bit more subtle and sugarcoated."

"Well, thank goodness you're made of sturdier stuff," she said emphatically. "Now sit down and let me tell you where I saw Mr Dunbar this morning, not even a week after his wife's tragic murder. God, I could use a cigarette."

"Mags . . ." Olive knew she sounded like a skipping gramophone record, but Margaret really had a nerve.

"It's not blasphemy, darling, if I'm talking to the man himself." She pouted. "I've promised Leo I'll stop. I think he might be allergic to the smoke. But it's brutal, truly. Though, between you and me, I often smoke one or two in the hut, while I'm on duty. I really don't think that counts, do you?"

Olive sank back into her chair and poured herself a second cup of tea, suddenly exhausted. Though now, it seemed, there was one more thing added to her account. Mrs Dunbar's poisoners were going to go free if she didn't get busy. But the whole situation was perplexing. Certainly, Mrs Dunbar had behaved abominably, but bad taste hardly warranted murder, so who had had reason to kill her? She *must* be missing something. Perhaps it was time to have another chat with Mr Dunbar.

Olive went straight from the vicarage to the Fox and Duck and slipped into the darkened pub. It took the barest moment to pin down her quarry. He was there, in a quiet nook beside a window, with two pints on the table in front of him. One was already halfway down, the other as yet untouched. She sank into the seat opposite and beamed at him.

"How are you, Mr Dunbar?" she said soberly.

"What?" He blinked at her in confusion before his memory clicked on. "Oh, hullo, then." Bringing the pint to his lips, he drank deeply, then squinted at her. "Yer not with the police, are you?"

"Of course not," Olive said, smiling.

He sighed in relief. "I answered all their questions. I cooperated," he insisted. "I didn't kill her."

Olive thought fleetingly of Eileen Heatherton. "Did you, perhaps, want a divorce?"

"*What?*" he blustered, clearly outraged. "No, no. I didn't. I wouldn't. Everything was grand, just grand."

"Was it? Mrs Dunbar didn't mind you spending time with Miss Heatherton?"

"Who?" He frowned, and Olive raised her brows before clarifying.

"Eileen. The switchboard operator."

He looked mildly chagrined and took another drink. "Mrs Dunbar," he said haughtily, "left it to me to get the lay of the land, and Eileen took me right under her wing. We was both obliged to her, if you take my meaning."

Olive considered a moment how to parse this response but decided he wasn't hinting at anything untoward, but was, instead, hinting at his wife's underhanded methods as a purported medium. A sideshow magician. She simply couldn't imagine someone mustering the emotions necessary to kill such a person.

Leaning forward, she whispered urgently, "*Why* would someone have wanted to kill her? Was there something she'd done—something she was ashamed of?"

Now his eyes, which had been in earnest, looked shifty. "Nothing. Nothing. She weren't an easy woman, and 'twere some who took offense, but she never minded the hotheads. 'The truth will out,' was what she said. It were all harmless." He glanced behind her, his eyes searching, before he tipped his pint glass up to finish off its contents. Nervously, his eyes flicked to the pint in front of her.

"But it wasn't all truth, and it wasn't all harmless," Olive countered, a touch of vinegar in her voice. "Making a spectacle in front of the village, pretending men had died—husbands, sons, fathers—that was cruel. Thankfully, I don't think anyone truly believed her." Olive wasn't finished, but her words seemed to galvanise him.

"'*Tis* true," he insisted in a hiss, the intensity of his gaze hitting her squarely in the chest. "That ship went down, and those men died." He grabbed the glass in front of her and drained half of it as Olive blinked at him in confusion.

"It *can't* be. There's been no news on the wireless, and Mrs Gibbons, whose son was serving on that ship, has had no telegram."

Mr Dunbar's lips pressed together, so that his face screwed up. He swiped off his cap, revealing greasy, unkempt strands, and wiped the back of his hand over his brow. As he placed the cap back on his head, he leaned forward. "You're to keep this between us, mind."

Olive nodded, having, at the moment, no other choice. She needed to hear what he had to say.

Lowering his voice almost to a whisper, he went on. "The Admiralty don't want the blow to morale, so they've been keepin' it secret."

Olive stared at him in horror. "How could you know this? And how, in good conscience, could you use the information for your own selfish ends?" She thought of Hen and Mrs Gibbons and poor Freya Rodery. They'd already had the shock of Mrs Dunbar's spiritual revelation, and now the blow would have to come all over again.

He gulped some more from the pint, his expression a cross between defiance and disgust. "'Tweren't all selfish," he said, the words bitten off. "And you don't understand. When Velda gets an idea into her head . . ." He shook his own. "Usually, it's just a matter of finding out who's willing to gossip, but I have an in at the Admiralty."

She thought instantly of Lieutenant Commander Fleming. "Who is it?"

"Stepbrother." He wiped a rough hand over his face, letting his eyes stay closed for a long moment before tipping his head. "I should never have told her, but she was on at me to find something she could use."

Olive blinked. "Something big enough for a public spectacle? But why? What are you really doing in Pipley?"

But evidently, he'd said enough; she'd egged him too far. Without another word, he pushed back from the table and lumbered through the crowd to take the last seat at the end of the bar. He didn't look at her again.

Olive struggled with the shock of these revelations. Could this information point to a murderer? It seemed unlikely. Two men connected to Pipley were dead, but their families didn't yet know it . . . did they? And even if they did, how could they blame Mrs Dunbar for a tragedy that had happened hundreds of miles away, in the Mediterranean Sea?

Something else struck her suddenly. If Mr Dunbar was to be believed—and she thought he was—then Fleming had lied to her, the bastard. Why was she not surprised?

*   *   *

22 October 1941

Dear Dad, Harriet, and Olive,

I won't bother to tell you where I'm stationed, as I suspect the censors black out the best bits, but suffice it to say I can, on occasion, feel the breeze off the Mediterranean and catch a glimpse of its marvellous blue. Unfortunately, the view is dotted with warships, and the wind peppered with dust and smoke, but if I squint, I can almost imagine I'm here on my own terms.

When I do get home, you'll not recognise me, I'm afraid. The pale skin of my English ancestry has crisped right up in the blistering sun of these dry desert countries. You'll be further surprised to learn that I'm now both bearded and moustachioed, and I think the additions suit me rather well. Olive will likely disagree and be unrestrained in her mirth. I do miss her—and all of you. I'm certainly eager to meet her captain Aldridge. He and Jonathon are no doubt bearing the brunt of her boundless energy and enthusiasm in my absence. Poor chaps.

It's unlikely this letter will reach you much before Christmas, and so I am already feeling homesick as I consider my second holiday away from you. There is something so cosy about Pipley in winter. So cheery and warm. I don't doubt we'll be carolling and drinking toasts, celebrating in our way so far from home, but it won't be at all the same as donning paper Christmas hats and watching Kíli prance with excitement as Olive and I fence with umbrellas for the first chance at the Christmas pudding. I will be with you in spirit, praying for an end to this filthy war so that I may be home with you again.

Much love,
Lewis

P.S. Send any letters care of the British embassy in Egypt, and eventually they'll find their way to me.

Chapter 13

Opinion Sampling

11 December
Blackcap Lodge and Station XVII

The letter from Lewis had smoothed over her worry and frustration, at least for a time, and Olive was enjoying a quiet morning in the dovecote, checking on her birds. A few were regularly dispatched on late-night sorties flying out of RAF Stradishall, to be parachuted into Belgium as part of an ongoing operation. Columba had been devised as a way for ordinary citizens in occupied countries to supply the Allies with up-to-date information on the German war machine, and Baker Street had initiated its own targeted version, called Operation Conjugal, and it was working. But none of her birds had returned in recent weeks, forcing Olive to assume that they'd fallen victim to natural predators, weather conditions, Germans, or even starving citizens. This morning's quick perusal of the nests and perches had been enough to preclude a triumphant return, and so she'd got on with the business at hand, examining a host of eyes, feet, and feathers for illness or injury.

Training was coming along nicely, with the young birds going out for longer and longer stretches in the evenings and gradually proving themselves as they were liberated on training missions farther and farther afield. She'd lost a few to the sparrow hawks, but that was to be expected, and as much as it saddened her, it was best. The ones that returned from each successive training mission would be much better equipped, if chosen, to make the gruelling journey home across the Channel.

Soon it would be necessary to choose the birds that would accompany the Czechoslovak agents flying out at the end of December, and Olive knew the selection process would surely be as nerve racking as her very first effort. All because she'd interrupted a secret, and quite ominous, training exercise on the dark lane leading up to the manor. *And* the fact that no one wanted to talk about what was planned. Even the trainees themselves had been more stilted and reserved than the usual lot. Taken all together, it made Olive uneasy, which was silly, surely. Every one of the agents that passed through Station XVII was heading into danger; every one of them was fully aware that one misstep might mean the betrayal of an entire network, and death. How could this mission possibly be more intense than that?

She tried not to think of it and instead got on with the tasks at hand, glancing distractedly at the pigeon splashing about in the water tray. A moment later, she looked again, and her heart began to accelerate. The bird's feathers had looked blue beneath the water droplets shimmering on their surface, but it was now apparent that they were, in fact, grey, and the bird was more compact than she'd originally assumed. Olive stared as a swell of pride and relief and anticipation made her breathless. This was Wendy, a Conjugal pigeon. Olive started forward, then faltered as she realised there was no canister clipped to the bird's leg—she'd returned without a message. She was hurrying to investigate when the door to the dovecote creaked open. She turned almost distractedly, expecting Jonathon. But it was her father, in tatty Norfolk jacket and scruffy flat cap, who stood there in the pale rectangle of light. His booted feet were set apart, his arms rigid by his sides, and he wasn't smiling. A cold feeling of dread crept over her.

"Morning, Dad," she said lightly, swallowing down her nerves. "Late start today?"

"I was up early," he said gruffly, eyeing her from under bushy, grey-speckled brows. "Came out to look over the pigeons." There was a long pause, which Olive wasn't certain how to fill. "I wonder if you can guess what I found."

Olive shook her head. But she knew, and as dread slunk closer, she was urgently grappling for an explanation.

He pulled something from his pocket, then watched her eyes as he revealed it. It was the canister that had, presumably, been detached from Wendy's leg before Olive had discovered her basking in her bath. Olive fisted her hands, feeling cornered.

Hoping to pawn off further inquiries about her training regimen and the sudden appearance of feed even after their birds had been rejected by the National Pigeon Service, Olive had resorted to a white lie. Her father had been delighted by the news that the Bright birds had been selected to assist in diverting German birds, carrying details of British morale and defences, from their flight back across the Channel.

But a pigeon on such a mission would have no need of a canister.

Olive cleared her throat and decided to brave her way through it. "Was there a message?"

"There was."

"Did you . . . look at it?"

He blinked at her in surprise. "Well, surely you can understand my bafflement, my confusion. I understood my birds to be fraternising with German pigeons. And as well trained as those Jerry birds are, they don't send messages all on their own," Rupert Bright said, giving each of the final words a full stop. "And certainly not from Belgium."

Olive swallowed, braced for a tirade. "I'm sorry, Dad—"

"*Sorry?*" he bellowed. "You lied to me, and as if that weren't bad enough, you had me lying, too." She frowned, but before she could question him further, he'd wound up again. "I happened to mention down the pub that my birds were rounding up Jerry's birds before they had the chance to snitch on all of us."

"Dad," Olive bleated. "That was meant to be top secret."

"Well, I didn't give any details, now, did I? And not a one of us believes the whole truth of what the others are boasting about—" He caught himself, frowned, and started again. "But I wasn't lying to a man's face about the use of his very own birds."

Olive had dreaded this moment ever since she'd agreed to work for Baker Street and keep secrets from her father. She'd thought her little white lie would thwart his curiosity and buoy his sense of pride in his birds, which truly were making a difference. But she'd known all along that it was a tenuous predicament. There was always a chance that she or Jamie or Jonathon would let something slip or that her father would notice an inconsistency. It had only been a matter of time.

Olive stood before him, paralyzed, light-headed. Her mind had emptied, and she had no excuses, no ideas, no alternative explanations. But words were welling up inside of her—once again, quite bafflingly, in French—and she couldn't hold them in. They tumbled out, alternately stilted and rushed.

"Je suis désolée. Je ne peux pas te dire la vérité. Mais c'est mieux ainsi."

She didn't know if he'd understood or come to the truth of the matter on his own. Staring down at the little Bakelite canister in his hand, he said slowly, "You can't tell me, can you?" Olive met his eyes appealingly. "You can't tell me, because you've signed the Official Secrets Act and consigned the use of my birds without my permission." The words came flatly, with no inflection. It wasn't a question. Rupert Bright blustered out a heavy sigh and ran a hand over his jaw.

He peered at her for a long moment, wrinkles of worry and frustration crowding between his brows. "You could have just told me, Olive. While I might not understand the NPS's bloody-minded objection to using our birds"—he paused to collect himself—"I do understand your determination to put them to work for the war effort. I wish you hadn't felt that you needed to lie to me."

"But I couldn't tell you—"

Her father silenced her with raised brows and responded, "You could have told me they were doing their bit and to trust you to handle it." When he caught Olive's incredulous glance, he added, "Not forgetting to mention the Secrets Act and the risk of treason you'd be facing if you confided in me." He shrugged, allowing that the conversation would likely have been difficult.

"I hated every minute of it," she insisted. "The deceit and the worry and the guilt. I'm sorry. I tried to make the best of a difficult situation."

"Say no more," her father blustered, extending the hand that held the canister. "I'll leave this with you, shall I?" He laid it in her palm, covered it with his own. "I do have one question," he said quietly, as if worried they might be overheard.

"Dad, we just went over this. I can't tell you any—"

"I know, I know," he said, waving her protestations away. "It seems I'm going to have to trust you and that Aldridge fellow, because I have a strong suspicion he's in on it, too." He frowned at her and raised a single brow. "Just tell me this. Are the pair of you even sweethearts?"

Caught utterly off guard, Olive blinked at him. "Why would you ask that?" she said, stalling. Once upon a time the answer would have been ready on her tongue, but because she was done lying to him, now she hesitated, not entirely sure what to say. Her own blurted admission the day before had taken her quite by surprise, and she'd been grappling with the truth of it ever since.

Her father looked uncertain now but determined to have an answer, nonetheless. "Because I think it all started when he showed up. No, no, don't say anything. You can't admit it, and if you deny it, and it's true, then we're back in the same boat. I just can't help but think that he's not the right match for you."

Olive blinked at him in surprise. "What? Why not?" she demanded sharply.

"So you *are* in love with him?" her father pressed suspiciously.

Once again, Olive felt the trap closing round her.

After a moment, she nodded the truth of it, and harrumphing, he turned away. She was biting her lip as she stared after him, wondering how everything had got so tangled up and having no idea what to do about it.

After pausing to knock quietly at the door, Olive waited for the summons before slipping inside to sink into the chair opposite Jamie's desk. Extending her arm, she uncurled her fingers and tipped her hand down, letting the canister she held roll off her palm and onto his desk. When it reached the opposite edge, he plucked it up.

Jamie looked carefully at her, brows furrowed. "Not your usual reaction to a message delivered by one of your birds. Did you read it?"

"No."

"Curiouser and curiouser."

Olive's eyes shuttered closed as she admitted, "Dad got to it first."

"*What*? How did you let that happen?" His voice had sharpened, and he was leaning forward, already extracting the curl of rice paper from its canister. He glanced up at her, apology in his eyes. "I take that back. It's not your fault."

Olive tipped her head in acknowledgment. "I believe it's written in Flemish, which he can't read—and neither can I—but there's a map."

Jamie was staring down at the unfurled message. "Damn." Setting it aside, he added, "What did you tell him?"

"The truth," she said flatly. Jamie stilled, and she met his gaze. "He already knew it."

"What? How?"

"It was obvious that I'd lied to him, so he drew the obvious conclusion. I'd signed away the opportunity to tell him the truth."

"So he doesn't know about Baker Street?"

She shook her head.

"That's good. Did he ask about you and me?"

"He did," she admitted.

"And?"

"I told him our relationship was never part of the lie," she said matter-of-factly, watching his reaction carefully.

"Right." His eyes were unreadable, and his face was without expression, almost as if he hadn't a clue how to respond.

Olive's insides clenched uncomfortably, and then she curved her lips into a smile. "Shall we find someone who can read Flemish, then?"

"I might know enough," he said, surprising her. "I was stationed over there at the start of the war, if you remember. I picked up a few things."

It took barely five minutes, and in that time, Olive managed to shake off the funk that had settled over her with the recent onslaught of troubles as she hovered at Jamie's shoulder, eagerly awaiting each word of the penciled translation.

The author of the message had outlined the existence of a special instruction centre in Bruges for teaching German soldiers English so that they might be parachuted into England—in English uniforms—for infiltration as fifth columnists, their task to ready the country for an impending invasion. The centre was indicated on the map by an *X*; arrows indicating troop movements toward the coast were marked as well, along with a radar station and a munitions storehouse. It further specified where to send additional pigeons. The message closed with the words *Belgium and England forever. God save the King and us with him!*

A surge of excitement coursed through her. "Well, this should convince the CO that the pigeons are doing their bit and are not at all dispensable in the way he imagines."

"Well, it certainly can't hurt," Jamie agreed, paper-clipping the curl of rice paper to the inside of a blank folder, then marking the outer label OPERATION CONJUGAL. BELGIUM. BRIGHT LOFT. 11 DECEMBER 1941. "I'll have someone double-check the translation, but I think I did well enough."

But Olive wasn't really listening. She was staring down at his profile: the dark hair crisping at his ear, the scar running like a seam down to his jaw, the strong line of his neck. . . . She yanked her gaze away and moved back round to the other side of the desk.

I can't be in love with him. I won't.

If only it was that easy. But her heart was now pounding so hard that the pulse in her throat was nearly choking her. She gritted her teeth. All it needed was for him to bark at her, roll his eyes, and forbid her to do something, and she'd be over her silly crush.

"What else aren't you telling me?" he said.

So many things.

But this was not an answer, and besides, his interest lay strictly in the business of Station XVII. She wanted to share what she'd learned about the HMS *Bartholomew*—and Lieutenant Commander Fleming's outright deception—but she couldn't see the point of it. The same could be said of her arrangement with Mrs Blighty and her efforts at solving Mrs Dunbar's murder. And then she had it.

She looked across at him. He had propped his forearms on his desk and was staring intently at her, his brow knitted, his body tense, as if awaiting news of an imminent disaster. Smiling, she said, "I'm ready to go ahead with the agent training." If anything was likely to put them at odds with each other, it would be giving him further control over her.

His face gave nothing away as his eyes flicked over her steady gaze and blithe smile. "You're sure?"

"Utterly."

"All right, then. First things first. If you *do* pass your training, your final stop before going off on your first mission will be a finishing school. There you'll be outfitted with appropriate clothes and papers so as not to give the lie to your new identity." He paused, nudged a stack of folders on his desk into alignment, then went on. "The final touch will be two tablets. Benzedrine and cyanide. The former will boost your adrenaline, and the latter . . ." His eyes met hers. Focused. Darkened. It seemed as if he was willing her to cry wolf.

"Yes, I know," she said hurriedly.

"They'll ask if you're prepared to use them."

She didn't answer. She wouldn't admit her doubts—her fears—or that she didn't yet have the courage necessary to go through with the difficult bits. Because she was determined to overcome all that.

Olive squared her jaw and tipped her chin up. "I am," she told him, pleased that her voice sounded assured. "I will."

His gaze didn't waver, and she had the feeling he was still doubting her, but he let it go. "Then I'll give you your first challenge, shall I?"

At her nod, he elaborated.

"Seeing as you're so curious about the mission assigned to the 1st Czechoslovak Mixed Brigade—yes, Lieutenant Tierney mentioned you'd been asking questions—you're instructed to break into the CO's office, locate the file marked OPERATION ANTHROPOID, read it, and report back. Leave no trace and don't get caught. Because if you do, it's extraordinarily likely that your time at Baker Street will be finished."

Olive sat very still, wrestling with the implications of this. It was a legitimate test, paired with a very real risk—Major Blighty would surely jump at any chance to be rid of her—and she wondered as she stared across the desk at him if Jamie was setting her up. He'd been quick to change his tune about her decision to train as an agent, and honestly, she'd been a thorn in his side for the past seven months of their personal and professional association. Could he be trying to get rid of her?

A chill settled over her as the possibility of betrayal began to etch away at the long-held certainty that Jamie was on her side. But even as the pain of the cut staggered her, it began to scar over. Not only was she going to accept his challenge, she was also going to make a damn good job of it, which included not getting caught.

His face was the same—the intense, stormy eyes with their crowd of long lashes, the dark brows, the angular cheekbones and jaw—but looking at it now conjured very different emotions. It must not have been love she'd felt, after all, because that feeling was gone, replaced by a deep-set wariness. She was going to need to be on her best behaviour and play this very carefully.

"I'll do it," she said emphatically.

*   *   *

6 December 1941

RAF Elsham Wolds
Lincolnshire

Dearest Olive,

I'm glad to hear that you've decided to steer clear of murder. Excellent choice, I'd say, even if you do seem to have a knack for puzzling out the clues and the suspects, homing in on the culprit. Bloody dangerous all the same. Then again, this new business you seem to have got lined up sounds just as shady. What do you mean, you'll finally be doing your bit? You're doing plenty as it is, my girl, between pigeons and pigs and your job as a FANY. No one would dare say otherwise, except you. I suppose I'll just have to leave it to your captain to convince you.

I won't be home for Christmas, I'm afraid, but it's just as well. Better, I think, to get on with things and not get nostalgic for something that's no longer the same. We'll have Christmas dinner on the base—it'll probably be better than what I'd get at home, honestly—and there'll be dancing and carolling. They do their best to keep our spirits up, but having Bridget by my side is all I need.

I really wish I had some leave coming up, so that I could come home to tell you my news, but I don't, and it can't wait. I'm too chuffed. I've asked Bridget to marry me, and she's said yes. We haven't set a date yet, or really discussed any details at all. But I can't tell you how much comfort it gives me when I'm sitting in the dark of the cockpit, facing down the Jerries, to know that she's waiting for me. I swear, those German pilots are bloody fiends. I thought I was good, but it takes every bit of training, cunning, and luck for us to come out on top every time we engage. Because in the end, one of us gets blown out of the sky, and the chaps and I are agreed, better them than us.

I hope you're happy for me. I suppose for a quick minute I might be the talk of Pipley, but it won't last—not with your tendencies.

Looking forward to the end of this awful war,
George

Chapter 14
Selection and Appreciation of Targets

14 December
Pipley Village Hall

Glancing over at the chattering group of women crowded round the upright piano, Olive felt unutterably alone. Even amidst the festive swags of greenery hung with glittery stars and shiny baubles, the camaraderie of Christmas eluded her. Even the presence of Margaret, who was peppering the gathering with wry remarks, witty barbs, and copious eye rolls, wasn't enough to pull her out of herself.

It was what she'd worried over from the very beginning: being caught up in secrets and lies, with no one to share the burden. Her fellow FANYs were godsends, truly, but village gossip held little interest for them, seeing as Pipley was more or less off-limits, in keeping with Baker Street rules. For a time, Jamie had been her—albeit, often unwilling—confidant, but that was over now. She was quite alone in things.

Mrs Blighty had arrived right on time and been positively thrilled to be welcomed into the bosom of the village and, by default, the WI. Margaret, in particular, had taken a shine to the woman, no doubt feeling an affinity with the glamorous, vivacious newcomer, and they'd chatted animatedly for several moments on Margaret's work with the Royal Observer Corps.

"That's marvellous of you, truly," Scarlet had gushed. "I wish I had the sort of brain that would allow me to do that."

"Not to mention the sort of husband," Olive said archly.

Margaret raised her brows, but Scarlet winked gamely and said, "I'd be much better suited to something simpler, but I'm not one to shirk away from hard work."

"Hmm. Why don't we speak to Lady Revell? She can introduce you to the local Land Girls, who can always use more help," Margaret said, linking arms with the newcomer and urging her forward.

Olive smiled, relieved to be able to check one thing off her list. Just so long as Scarlet Chambers could keep a secret . . . Olive's relationship with Blighty was already tense enough without his blaming her for corrupting his wife with war work. She bit her lip, glancing round the room. Judging by the woman's absence, it seemed Freya Rodery was not yet ready to face the onslaught of village gossip. Things would only get worse when the news about her husband was made public, but Olive couldn't think about that right now. She needed to use this opportunity to investigate. With luck, she could home in on the murderer this very evening, and that would be one less thing she'd have to contend with.

As she stood at the refreshment table, nibbling at the vaguely grey shortbread cookies on offer, she let her eyes flit among the gathering. Dr Harrington had indicated that, with the amount of scopolamine in Mrs Dunbar's system, it was likely she'd been poisoned less than a quarter of an hour prior to her death, thereby narrowing the suspect list. Everyone on it, excepting Mr Dunbar and Lieutenant Commander Fleming, was present this evening. And while both men were inherently suspect, her instincts told her neither was the culprit here. Which left only five, not count-ing herself.

Given that Violet had been closeted away, working on her lat-est novel, in the days leading up to the séance, it was entirely possible she hadn't even met the woman before the evening of her murder. And Olive agreed with Harriet that it was likely she'd shy away from another violent death. So, she could be elim-inated. And Harriet was above suspicion. By simple subtraction, Lady Revell, Miss Danes, and Mrs Gibbons were the most likely candidates, which seemed utterly absurd.

As Lady Camilla began riffling through her music, ordering it according to Mrs Spencer's instruction, Olive ladled a scoop of watery punch into a cup and sipped pensively, considering the three.

Lady Revell had clearly not recovered from the tragedy. Usu-ally so effortlessly gracious, with a beaming smile for everyone, she now looked wan and distant. She had forgotten to remove her hat when she'd come in, and was running her gloves distract-edly through her fingers. If Max was to be believed, her sudden interest in spiritualism was curious, to say the least. But she had recently lost her sister, and grief was a strong motivator.

Miss Danes had foisted herself on the party, begging an invita-tion, and she was well known to have strong opinions on prog-nostications of all sorts. Could she have been hoping to unmask Mrs Dunbar as a charlatan? Had her eager examination of the manifestation cabinet been solely motivated by a desire to de-bunk the woman's claims? Was it possible she'd felt impelled by the spirit world, or even another channeller, to commit murder? Olive rolled her eyes at the mere suggestion.

Then there was Mrs Gibbons. The idea that she was the mur-derer fairly boggled Olive's mind. Her husband had been a brute of a man who'd eventually run off with a burlesque dancer he'd met in the city, but Mrs Gibbons had convinced herself that he'd taken his own life when the traumas of the Great War had simply got too much to bear. The idea that the woman could have marshalled her thoughts sufficiently not only to plan a murder but to actually carry it out was dubious at best. Then again, Mr Dunbar had insisted that the HMS *Bartholomew* had indeed been sunk. If Mrs Gibbons somehow discovered the truth, might she have blamed, and punished, the messenger for her son's perceived death?

No, that was ridiculous. But it left Olive in yet another moral conundrum: Should she reveal what she knew? After all, a son and a husband had died, and their relations deserved to know. But would her interference put lives at risk? She couldn't help but think that the Royal Navy was playing a very dodgy game, and her head was beginning to throb with the consequences of it.

Now the ladies were shuffling through their sheets of music and arranging themselves into sopranos and mezzo-sopranos. She had only another minute before someone would beckon her—the only contralto in the group—to take her place among them. She tapped her nail against her cup, thinking hard.

And what of the anonymous letter? Someone had admitted to the lords-and-ladies poisoning, denying any intent to kill, but that left her where, exactly? Should she reveal the information to the police or keep it to herself? Either way, there remained a second poisoner.

So, to sum up the current trend of her investigation, at least one out of three seemingly harmless women had attempted to poison a self-proclaimed medium, heretofore relatively unknown in the village? Frustrated with her lack of progress—and viable suspects—Olive set her cup down with a crack that had the carollers all turning in her direction.

"Hurry up now, Olive. We've a lot of songs to get through," Mrs Spencer chided.

Olive smiled, resigned to singing Christmas carols with a poisoner, and retrieved her music from the table beside the piano.

She grimly sang the verses of "The Holly and the Ivy," her thoughts on other, less festive flora. Then came a silvery, poignant rendition of "O Holy Night," led by Mrs Spencer, that left her eyes glossed with tears. But as the group progressed through the selected songs, Olive's spirits lifted little by little, and by the time they'd finished a rousing rendition of "God Rest Ye Merry Gentlemen," she was in a better mood entirely.

"Well, now, I think you've all earned your reward," Mrs Spencer teased, collecting the song sheets and shooing them all off to the refreshment table. Olive, who'd eaten her share earlier, refilled her glass of punch, checked that Scarlet was busy chatting away with Harriet and Violet, and approached her first quarry.

"How is everything, Mrs Gibbons?" she asked, laying a gentle hand on the woman's back.

"This was always my Marcus's favourite time of year, so it's difficult not having him here to celebrate with us."

Olive watched her face carefully, searching for any indication that she was hinting at her son's death rather than simply his absence due to the war. "I understand," she finally said. "But I suppose Hen is looking forward to the holiday festivities?"

"Oh, naturally. She's got us all squared away. Took charge of the decorating and helped me make the Christmas pudding and a few other goodies, so we'll have a nice celebration. I don't know how I'd manage without her."

"That must be why I haven't seen her round the lodge." It had been curious, to say the least.

"I expect." She nibbled her shortbread, and Olive decided to dive right in.

"Did you hear the results of the inquest?"

Her head popped up, and she looked at Olive in confusion. "The results of what?"

"The inquest?" Olive repeated. "The investigation of Mrs Dunbar's death—her murder. You do remember what happened at the séance last week."

"Oh, that was terrible," she agreed, shuddering delicately. "But it wasn't murder."

Olive stared worriedly at the woman. "I'm afraid it was, Mrs Gibbons."

The woman blinked owlishly at her. "These things happen, my dear, and while they're certainly gruesome, they're not criminal."

What sort of things? Olive wanted to demand. *Slow poisoning? Imposed dementia? Assisted heart failure?* Was she really confused by what had occurred at Peregrine Hall, or was this merely an effort to deflect suspicion?

For Hen's sake, Olive decided to presume on her innocence. Mrs Gibbons was carefully holding a cup of punch and a square of shortbread, but Olive took hold of her elbow and led her to a chair at a nearby table, then pressed her into it.

"I've spoken to the doctor," she said firmly. "Mrs Dunbar had two separate poisons in her system, extracted from belladonna and lords-and-ladies."

"You make them sound so fancy," Mrs Gibbons said. She leaned in to add conspiratorially, "But that's not what we called them. It was death cherries and devils and angels when I was small. We liked a bit of drama in those days, I'm afraid." A bite of shortbread sent a flurry of crumbs tumbling down her front.

"Well, drama is warranted," Olive said sharply. "Both are quite dangerous."

Mrs Gibbons looked at her quizzically. "But Lady Revell didn't serve anything—just the sherry, and we all drank that."

Olive clung to the shreds of her patience. She had no clue how the brisk and efficient Hen lived with the woman. "Yes, but remember, Mrs Dunbar drank from a bottle of her own. Dr Harrington took it away with him and discovered it had contained homemade sloe gin, dosed with lords-and-ladies." The results of the inquest would certainly have gone round by now.

"I remember, dear." Having finished her shortbread, she brushed the crumbs from her fingers. "But she was already in the throes of strange behaviour at that point. And devils and angels wasn't likely to have killed her." Olive frowned at her, prompting her to go on. "When Henrietta was small, she often trailed after her brother into the meadow and wood. When they got hungry, they foraged for mushrooms, nuts, and berries." Her gaze had taken on a faraway look as she remembered those long-ago days. "I suppose the cherry-red berries of devils and angels were irresistible. But she quickly learned her lesson and vomited up the toxin, none the worse for wear." She smiled, with raised brows, as if the matter had all been tidily dispatched.

"Except that Mrs Dunbar never ridded herself of the poison," Olive said quietly. This reminder prompted a flurry of birdlike movements from Mrs Gibbons. "And there was also the scopolamine—the belladonna."

"Well, I'm sure I don't know where that could have come from," she said, standing. "Now, I think I'll have another square of shortbread."

She left Olive staring after her, marvelling that they'd found something they could agree on: the belladonna was indeed a mystery. Perhaps she should have a little talk with Hen, if she could find the girl. Her mother alone was enough to bear, but soon there'd be a telegram, breaking the news about her brother.

A moment later, Miss Danes collapsed into the chair beside her and rested her bosom on the table as she leaned forward. "What would you say if I told you that Mrs Dunbar was not at all what she seemed?" she said, nudging Olive's elbow rather too forcefully.

"I'd say bravo." The sarcasm could have been laid on with a trowel for all the good it did.

"I've been chatting with Mr Dunbar. The poor, dear man—

he's quite beside himself. I did manage to perk up his spirits with some fresh-baked scones and a bit of doting attention. He's been quite neglected. We had a long chat, and if he's to be believed—and I do think he is—his late wife was *not* in touch with the spirit world." She paused to allow this shocking news to sink in. "Or if she was," Miss Danes allowed, "those particular communications were entirely separate from her public performances." She tsked. "The latter," she went on scornfully, "were undertaken merely to prey on true believers."

"You don't say."

"Our connections to the otherworld are tenuous at best, and the emotions they inspire are fraught with worry and uncertainty. It was horribly cruel of that woman to take advantage in that way." Her hands were fisting on the table as her cheeks flushed in anger.

"Do you suppose someone thought her deception reason enough to kill her?"

Miss Danes turned rounded eyes in her direction. "Oh, no. I think it's much more likely that the spirits themselves took matters into their own hands."

Olive pondered a moment whether to forge ahead with this batty conversation or make a quick escape. She'd already heard Miss Danes's thoughts on the purported villainy of the spirits, but what was there to lose? She herself had no other viable theories. "So, you're suggesting that the spirits summoned by Mrs Dunbar decided to turn on her," she said sceptically.

Delighted to have a willing audience, Miss Danes puffed up, ready to expound on her favourite topic. "On certain evenings—a full moon is preferable, but the days just before and after are quite sufficient—the door between the realms slides open. A potent spirit may then walk freely, without a summons, from the otherworld into our own."

Olive stared into her cup of punch, wishing suddenly that it had been spiked liberally with something very strong indeed.

She scratched her temple, then said carefully, "So, you think it was a ghost that poisoned her?"

"Of course not."

Blinking at the rebuff, Olive was, nevertheless, much relieved and opened her mouth to extract herself from this nonsensical conversation, only to be startled into silence all over again.

Miss Danes's voice was hushed, reverent. "The spirit world cannot wield the weapons of this one." Pausing, she was gratified to see Olive waiting for the rest with bated breath. "It deals with matters in its own ways, which we cannot possibly understand."

"Right." Olive wondered fleetingly how Hercule Poirot might respond to such a suggestion. If things went much further, she might have to look into it.

"There will forever be a mystery surrounding the death of Mrs Dunbar, which explains why the police can find no explanation for what happened. Though . . ." A portentous pause. "A true medium with profound connections to the otherworld could, perchance, make a start, attempt to summon the spirit who wreaked its havoc . . ."

Olive stood abruptly, laying a hand on the woman's arm. "Yes, well, I'm glad I spoke to you, Miss Danes. You offer a truly unique perspective."

She preened. "If only others kept their minds open. Oh, careful!" This as Olive collided with a nearby chair in her eagerness to get away and out into the bracingly crisp air.

Seconds later, Olive pressed her back to the icy brick of the village hall, closed her eyes, and drew in huge gulps of the dry, biting cold. Her head was pounding with the reality that she didn't have the wherewithal to deal with everything on her own—it was simply too much. And in lieu of a confidante or a partner in crime, she needed a break, an outlet, an enemy. Honestly, she needed to kick someone in the testicles. Hard. But she very much doubted she was going to get the chance, at least in the near term.

Olive opened her eyes and was startled to see the orange glow of a cigarette hovering not twenty feet away, the acrid smell of its smoke belatedly reaching her.

"All right, dear?" came the disembodied, slightly quavery voice.

Squinting into the dark, Olive stepped closer to find it belonged to Lady Revell. "I didn't know you smoked."

"I don't, not really. I find it gives me a fierce headache. I used to borrow them from my husband when we went to parties. They're very social, and they provide all sorts of excuses." She lifted it in demonstration. "It got me out of there for a few moments." She paused, staring at Olive. "Looks as if you could use one yourself."

"I never smoke them, and I already have a headache," Olive said wanly.

They stood in companionable silence for a time, and then Lady Revell said, "I can't stop thinking about that woman, Mrs Dunbar. What happened to her—I still don't quite understand it—was horrible. Just horrible." She tugged her jacket closer round her and propped her elbow on the arm hugging her middle. She inhaled deeply from the raised cigarette.

"I know the feeling. I was just talking to Miss Danes about it . . ."

"Oh, that woman," Lady Revell said with feeling, the smoke streaming out of her mouth like vitriol. "How she can possibly think—" Cutting herself off abruptly, she sighed. "I should never have asked her to come. It was for Max, really. After his accident I've been so worried about him. He has trouble sleeping and sometimes calls out, shouting or screaming." The tip of the cigarette was moving like a firefly in her shaking hand. "But he won't accept any help. He won't even go back to Merryweather House to speak to the doctors. The burns still pain him and the memories plague him, but the treatment makes him feel ill."

She sounded resigned, and Olive's thoughts flew to George and what he risked.

"And now my own dreams are haunted." The words escaped on a sob, which had Olive shifting closer to put her arm round the woman. "She'd only just begun when it all went so horribly wrong, and all of us in shock, not having any idea what to do for her. It took only moments for her to succumb, but how could it have been *murder*? Surely no one would have intended . . ."

But someone had. In fact, two someones had intended to do the poor woman harm. Olive didn't say it, but the words hung silently in the air between them.

"Not to worry," Olive said brightly. "The police are still investigating, and I'm doing what I can, as well."

"You?" she said in surprise. "Oh, that's right. Harriet did mention it." She peered at Olive. "Honorary village sleuth and all that."

"Quite," Olive said dryly.

She started violently. "I'm not a suspect, am I?"

Olive hadn't the heart to tell her that moments ago, she'd been a prime one. "I don't think you did it," she said quietly.

But then she never did—she never believed someone she knew could be a murderer. But she'd been proven wrong before.

Honestly, she was utterly stumped. She couldn't imagine any of the women she'd just interviewed murdering Mrs Dunbar in cold blood—or even choosing to punish her in such a cruel manner. Someone was playing their role to perfection, but she couldn't figure out who.

There was always the possibility that she'd eliminated the guilty party prematurely. Her thoughts flew to Lieutenant Commander Fleming but then grudgingly drifted to Mr Dunbar instead. He had, after all, been the keeper of the gin, with plenty of time to doctor it with poison. . . .

If something didn't occur to her soon, she'd have to resort to a more direct approach to her investigation. Perhaps a search of his cottage would produce a clue. Trouble was, Jamie hadn't got round to teaching her how to pick locks, and she wasn't at all in the mood to ask him just now.

* * *

16 December 1941

Dearest Lewis,

I don't know if I'll ever send this, but I needed to talk to some-one, and it's not so easy anymore. We're, all of us, divided by secrets, and it seems as if every topic of conversation is booby-trapped so thoroughly that I'm almost afraid to open my mouth for fear of what might come out.

I won't tell you what exactly it is I'm doing, but suffice it to say, I'm restless. I know it's important work—there's hardly a thing any of us is doing that isn't—but somehow it doesn't feel like enough. I'm tired of being kept on the fringes, in the background, safe and sound. At the same time, I don't know that I have your courage to meet a Nazi face-to-face, to bluff my way to safety, to fight, should the occasion demand it, knowing that at the end of it, one of us must, unavoidably, be dead. Worse still, if I freeze, if I fail, then it's not only my own life that's forfeit. I don't know if I can do it. Does that make me a coward? I can't decide. So, I'm going ahead with my plans, such as they are, hoping that a clear answer will present itself.

As always, there's plenty of distraction. A newcomer to the vil-lage, a rather beastly woman—a spiritualist medium, no less—was poisoned while giving a séance at Peregrine Hall. I saw the whole horrible thing and now find myself playing Poirot opposite DS Burris's bumbling Hastings.

And that's not nearly all. You've not met Jamie, which makes everything harder to explain, and I can only imagine what Har-riet's told you, but I've discovered there's a world of difference be-tween fancying a man and falling in love with him. Then again, it's entirely possible I could have imagined the whole thing. Every-

thing is in a tangle, and I'm not sure of my own mind anymore. I need your high-handed brotherly advice to set me to rights. I miss you, Lewis. It feels as if everything calm and normal in the world went away with you, and I so desperately want it all back.

Happy Christmas. I'll save your paper hat and Christmas cracker till you're home again.

Yours ever,
Olive

P.S. I've now been trained in close-combat fighting, so consider yourself fair warned.

Chapter 15
Tactics of Small Raiding Parties

17 December
Station XVII

She had officially left Station XVII more than an hour ago, puttering off down the lane on the motorbike, a recognisable figure to anyone who might chance to notice her. But midway between the last view of the manor and the gatehouse at the edge of the property, Olive had pulled onto the verge and rolled the Welbike out of sight among the trees. She had changed swiftly into a dark jumper and trousers and had then sat shivering, biding her time.

Now it was officially dark, and she could no longer feel her fingertips. She was also desperately tired of Christmas carols, having quietly worked her way through her entire repertoire. She'd watched the CO stride briskly past her a quarter of an hour before, on his way home for the evening. Even on his own, his expression was the same dour mask, and she'd cringed on Scarlet's behalf. Now she stood and slipped a dark wool balaclava over her head. It had been knitted by a member of the Pipley WI and was intended for a Royal Navy seaman, but she planned to make good use of it first. So adorned, she stepped out of the trees and began the long walk back to the manor.

No one—not even Jamie—knew where she was at that moment, or what she planned to do. She had, in fact, lied to him outright. She'd deliberately bemoaned the prospect of spending the evening knitting Christmas presents with Margaret. She didn't like to do it, but it was clear Jamie doubted her abilities, so from now on, she would keep her own counsel. He'd know soon enough if her evening's foray had been a success or a failure. If the latter, it was likely all of Station XVII would know it.

It wasn't long before the manor loomed ahead of her, enormous under a half-moon. With its windows darkened by blackout curtains, it looked decidedly forbidding. After scanning the lawns, the porte-cochère, and the drive to confirm that there was no one to catch her out, she broke cover and ran, crouched like an animal. She saw no one until she was flattened in the shadows, edging her way round the building, fingers clutching at the stone. Poised to turn the corner on the last stretch, she pulled herself up short, narrowly avoiding a collision with the person standing smoking in the dark.

The cigarette alone was proof enough it wasn't Jamie, but Olive would have been able to tell by the tilt of his head, the breadth of his shoulders, and the curve of his jaw. She shut her eyes against the images flooding through her mind as she waited for the cigarette to burn down and its owner to go back inside.

The moment she heard the door snick shut behind him, she was round the corner, all but running past the door into the shadows beyond. With no possibility of retaining a key to Major Blighty's always locked office, and no experience picking locks—she really must remedy that—Olive had quickly come to the conclusion that if she was going to complete her mission, she'd need to go in through the window.

To that end, she'd found a reason to infiltrate his office that morning, justifying her presence with a task she suspected he'd consider suitable to her skill set. She'd performed a thorough cleaning and emptied his trash, discreetly undoing the catch on the window as she gave the glass a good shine.

Now, as she stood before those darkened panes, the cold stinging her lungs and making her eyes water, she was painfully conscious that the evening's efforts hinged on this window having remained unlocked. She glanced round one final time. There was no one to witness her insubordination, and no one for moral support, either. But there wouldn't be if she was dropped into occupied Europe, either. A line was being crossed. With a deep, steadying breath that feathered out of her on a vapour cloud, she stepped closer, and girding her courage, she laid her fingers against the casement and gently pulled.

Olive nearly yelped with excitement. It was still open. Relief and adrenaline surged through her, and she forced her trembling fingers to steady, her breathing to calm. Then, nudging the window fully open, she pushed the blackout curtains aside, laid her hands on the sill, and levered her body through. Once inside, the hair on her neck and arms prickled in awareness, each one a sensory antenna, primed and vigilant. Each success was a new line crossed, with no going back. She listened carefully for any hint that Hamish the Scottish terrier, Station XVII's honorary mascot, might be wandering the halls, eager to send up the alarm, but it seemed that for now, at least, she was in the clear.

Her eyes were already acclimated to the dark, and they darted first to the major's desk. The CO wasn't nearly as tidy as Jamie, and while that might work to her advantage once she'd gone, it was bound to hinder her search. There was a large stack of files in the box on his desk, and Olive carefully lifted them out, squinting at them in the dark. Unable to distinguish the letters, she carried the lot to the window and tipped them toward the attendant moonlight. She rifled through files on power plants and steam turbines, individuals of all nationalities, Baker Street operations, and the various country sections and branches of the armed forces.

There really was no order to the madness, but she was careful not to shift so much as a page out of place. When she finished with the first stack, she returned to the desk to retrieve a second, then hurried back to the window, willing her heart rate to slow. And finally, there it was: a thick folder near the bottom. The cover read TOP SECRET: OPERATION ANTHROPOID, and scrawled in pencil beneath it, barely legible, were the names Gabček and Kubiš.

A tightness spread in her chest. Olive chalked it up to nerves and pride of accomplishment, overlaid with a gloss of fear. Finding the file was only the beginning, and honestly the easiest part. Poring through the pages would require her to hunker down for an extended stay in the office of a man who would relish any reason to be rid of her. If, after the recent burglary, someone had been assigned to make the rounds, checking offices after hours, there was little chance she'd escape unrecognised. And yet the consequences would be nothing compared to the ones she'd face if she qualified as an agent and was caught in such an act by a Nazi.

The thought flared like a lighter in the dark. *What am I doing here?* Olive stood very still, trying to remember and decide. Had she intended to prove something to herself—or to Jamie? It didn't matter, she realised. She was here now, and she needed to get on with things.

She carefully arranged the curtains over the window, then unwrapped the scarf from her neck and nudged it up against the base of the door to keep any chinks of light from showing in the hallway. Then she slowly lowered herself into the CO's chair, laid the file in front of her, flicked on the torch—thank heaven she'd remembered it—and got to work.

There was a handwritten note, paper clipped to the very first page. On it, the words *Best candidates*. Her curiosity well and truly piqued, she shifted it aside to read more.

The operation had been under discussion as early as October, with the Czechoslovak government-in-exile working closely with Baker Street. Director of the Gestapo and acting Reich protector of Bohemia and Moravia Reinhard Heydrich was to have been assassinated on 28 October, Czechoslovakian Independence Day. Warrant Officer Josef Gabček and Staff Sergeant Karel Svoboda had been hand-selected from among their compatriots to carry out the brazen and controversial mission.

Olive sucked in a long breath and slowly let it out again.

Pushed to the brink by the horrific brutality of Heydrich, nicknamed the Butcher of Prague, the Czechoslovak government-in-exile had decided that something must be done both to focus the attention of the world on the ongoing atrocities and inspire the Czechoslovak people to persevere. That something was to be the assassination of Heydrich. Opponents of the plan feared reprisals would be swift and unimaginable, but the Czechoslovak intelligence officers had the support of Brigadier Colin Gubbins, head of Baker Street, as this was precisely the sort of ungentlemanly warfare the organisation had been tasked with from the beginning. It was a daring mission, an enormous risk, and the element of surprise was absolutely critical. Which was why this latest round of trainees had been so tight lipped—more so even than usual—and why their training had been more rigorous than the Station XVII syllabus typically demanded.

Olive sat stunned as the words swam before her on the page. She'd been right. All along, they'd been planning an assassination. Her heart was thumping now, as if the immensity, the urgency, the secrecy of it all threatened to swamp her. Needing to know the rest, she kept reading.

It seemed that, like Major Boom, Svoboda did not make it through parachute training unscathed. As a setback, it was significant—a replacement needed to be chosen, documents produced, and training continued—but the entire mission seemed fraught with difficulty. The Germans had rounded up many members of the Czechoslovak Resistance, and communication with London was all but broken. So, the decision was made: Anthropoid would be delayed, and additional planning and operations would be undertaken to better orchestrate its success. Jan Kubiš was selected to replace Svoboda, and the men undertook an intensive and unprecedented training regimen, courtesy of Baker Street's special training schools, which included coursework on weapons handling, survivalist skills, explosive charges, specially made bombs, and fuses of all sorts.

There was a report signed by Lieutenant Danny Tierney, scoring them perfect in ju-jitsu and describing them as "deadly efficient in hand-to-hand combat." It was just as he'd told her. Page after page of instructor accolades lauded the men with such descriptors as "wholly reliable," "true patriots," and "fiercely determined."

Olive's memory flashed back to the snowy night several weeks past when men had appeared out of the dark of the manor grounds, aiming their guns at her. They'd been waiting for a different car, one that would prepare them for a moment hundreds of miles and weeks away. A moment that would demand their greatest courage and commitment: the ambush that would lead to a high-ranking Nazi official's violent death. She had recognised Gabček, had seen his face and the grim determination writ there. She had no doubt his thoughts had been trained on that future moment, which would be the culmination of months of preparation and training. She shivered, staring down at the pages in the file, reading the words while the reality of life as a Baker Street agent flooded her thoughts and preyed on her emotions.

Over an hour had passed when she quietly stood and tucked the file folder beneath a stack of others. She hadn't read every word, but she knew enough. She knew precisely what Gabček and Kubiš would face when they were dropped into the Protectorate of Bohemia and Moravia just after Christmas. A steely calm settled over her as she scanned the desk, looking for anything out of place, anything that might hint that there'd been an intruder. There was nothing. She'd been careful. She pocketed her torch, retrieved her scarf, and, with one final glance round, exited the window, twitched the curtains back into place, and pushed the casement shut.

Still wearing the balaclava, Olive moved like a shadow over the wide lawn, making for the trees, the Welbike, and home.

18 December

"The Butcher of Prague," Olive said simply. She'd settled herself in the chair opposite Jamie, his desk yawning between them, and kept her eyes trained on his now perpetually empty sweet jar.

She was pleased to see her words startled him. He had been poring over a report on his desk and hadn't even looked up after summoning her in. Now, his work forgotten, he sat back in his chair and looked carefully at her as he rolled his fingers over his palms. This little triumph gave her no joy; she would rather his expectations had been high and this meeting merely a formality.

"You've read the report, then?"

"I have."

"Last night?"

She nodded.

"And you didn't have any trouble?"

"No."

"Has the CO seen you? Spoken to you?"

"No, but neither is that surprising," she said dryly. "He doesn't exactly seek out my company. But I've no doubt if he knew I'd been in his office, I would have been summarily fetched and dispatched."

"Very likely," Jamie agreed. "Although he's rather a hard nut to crack. Only time will tell." He drummed his fingers on his desk. "I assume the report cleared up any questions you might have had?"

"More or less. Though I did wonder about code names."

"What about them?"

"It seems as if the agents in question are to be dispatched under their real names, not code names, as per Baker Street protocol."

"That's correct. They aren't our agents. We've offered to assist with training and equipment, but the men are acting at the behest of the Czechoslovakian government-in-exile. They've chosen to act under their real names."

Olive nodded, struck once again by their courage. Inspired. It was on the tip of her tongue to question him about his reasons for setting her such a risky task. Particularly given that it was the first she'd undertaken. But he spoke first.

"I'm not sure whether the information will assist with your pigeon selection, but given what you already know and your intentions going forward, I thought it best that you not be in the dark about this."

Olive frowned at him as the words settled in her mind. "Wait a moment." She canted her head to the side, as if she could thereby shuffle her thoughts into sensible order. "You expected me to succeed?"

His stare was incredulous. "You must be joking." When she didn't answer, his brows knit in frustrated anger, and he shot out of his chair and came round to her side. She stood to face him, unflinching. "Why on earth would I suggest such a scheme if I didn't think you would come away with the information intended? I told you before, Major Blighty would likely have you out on your ear if he knew."

"You did tell me that," she said pointedly.

"And you thought that's what I wanted?"

"I wondered," she tossed back. "You've not been particularly supportive since you got back. And in the spirit of efficiency, you could get rid of me and solve a great many of your problems."

After a second of stunned silence, in which his eyes bored into hers, he finally barked out a humourless laugh and stepped back. Running a hand through his hair and over his jaw, he paced the tight space. Olive's pride was a fragile thing at that moment, so she stood very still, with the sole hope of holding it together.

And then, suddenly, he was right in front of her, not laughing, not even smiling.

"You're right," he said in a voice that raised the hairs on her arms. "You are one of the most difficult parts of my job here. You're argumentative and frustrating and pushy to no end. You're reckless and rebellious, and you ate every last aniseed ball I had in the jar." He huffed an exasperated breath and shot her a warning look when she would have protested. "But despite all that—and quite possibly because of it—you've managed to succeed at every task I've set you. If you say you're going to do a thing, there isn't a question of it getting done, only whether your own recklessness might in some way undermine your efforts."

The chill that had settled over Olive at the first possibility of betrayal was warming—no, basking—in response to his words. He shoved his hands into the pockets of his trousers and went on.

"I suspect Blighty will never know what you've done, and the truth of it should both inspire and intimidate you. It won't always be that easy. No one here is expecting insubordination and certainly not thievery as an inside job. But if you go"—his eyes met hers, willed her to listen—"you'll be hunted from the moment the parachute lands. Quite honestly, you're a disgrace to the womanly ideal of the new Germany, which is focused strictly on husband, home, and family. The Nazis won't like you and your flippant mouth at all, particularly if you're outsmarting them."

Olive neglected to tell him precisely what she thought of those German ideals and ruthlessly tamped down a shiver of apprehension. She'd examine her thoughts on the matter later; right now she was entirely too distracted. For once, Jamie was staring at her flippant mouth with seeming approval. Her gaze shifted between his eyes and lips. Her emotions were fizzing and unsettled. She wasn't at all certain what she felt for him now, but even love, with its myriad nuances, felt overly simplified.

Her mouth hitched up on one side. "I suppose this means I'm ready for the next challenge."

For a moment Jamie didn't move or speak, his eyes scanning her face, but then he took a step back, tipping his head down in acknowledgment. "Clearly."

"Something a bit more difficult this time?" she said encouragingly.

He snorted.

Her grin broadened. "Excellent. I suppose I should get back to work," she said before turning to slip out the door.

She was going to have to get him a very nice Christmas present indeed. And make certain the opportunity for a very thorough kiss presented itself.

But as she walked down the hall, back to the FANY carrel, her thoughts weren't nearly as smug as her attitude. No matter how skilled she was at facing down Jamie's challenges, she wasn't entirely sure footed when it came to the idea of progressing to the real thing.

Olive suspected it came down to the difference between capacity and capability. She was confident in her abilities in familiar circumstances, but unconvinced that she could face the unknown with equal aplomb. She *wanted*, quite desperately, to be the sort of person ideally suited for the role of a Baker Street agent, but in refusing to sugarcoat the matter, Jamie had prompted her thoughts to spiral down a rabbit hole of uncertainty and fear. Quite simply, she didn't know if she could manage any of it.

To be an agent was to accept an assigned mission unflinchingly, with the unspoken understanding that you would use any means necessary to ensure its success. It meant a new identity, an alternate truth, and a much stickier web of lies. And failure meant hideous consequences.

So much was at stake, and a blossom of doubt pressed heavy

on her chest. It hadn't lifted since she'd read the chapters in the Baker Street training manual dedicated to the German police and intelligence services. Her dreams were plagued by a recurring nightmare. Caught in an act of subversion by an agent of the Gestapo, she garbled both her French and her cover story. He saw right through her, marking her as a spy, and was poised to haul her in for interrogation. She stood helplessly clutching a pencil, which could gouge his eyes out, and was jolted awake at the crack of a pistol.

Chapter 16
Surveillance

18 December
Pipley and Blackcap Lodge

To live in a village like Pipley meant going along with all manner of quirky and questionable activities, as well as some that were truly touching and inspiring. As far as Olive was concerned, today—the day Swilly the pig was bound for the butcher—could easily qualify as both. While everyone involved in the pig scheme was eager to see a return on their investment in the form of bacon, chops, roast, and trotters, their excitement was bittersweet. The WI might have given Olive charge of the creatures' well-being, but Jonathon had inspired all of Pipley to embrace the three pigs as village mascots. The boy's good manners, chipper attitude, and pig walks had prompted a constant supply of table scraps and visitors to the pen. And that included the curmudgeons.

When Hen and Jonathon had suggested a proper send-off for Swilly, Olive had been encouraging but not optimistic. The war had been going on for more than two years. Rationing was hard, and the traditional festive sparkle of Christmas had dimmed considerably. People were eager for the comfort of bacon. But she'd underestimated the pair.

Coasting round the bend in the lane that led to Forrester's Garage, and beyond it, the pig pen, she was forced to come to an abrupt stop just shy of the crowd of people gathered along the fencing. It seemed every child in the village had come out, and they were all wearing festive hats and carrying boughs of pine and holly. She spied Hen and Jonathon, standing a bit apart, a paper chain of red- and green-painted newsprint strung between them. After stashing her bike out of the way, Olive hurried over.

"What *is* all this?" she said in surprise. A glance into the pen showed that Finn and Eske were going about their day as usual, while Swilly had been brought out and feted with a red ribbon collar and a paper hat decorated with rowanberries. She was feasting on what looked like windfall apples mixed with general breakfast slop, all of it nearly gone. Olive's nose twitched.

"A parade," Hen said simply, as if that made all the sense in the world. "We invited the whole village to see her off."

"And it looks as if they've turned out en masse," Olive said, marvelling at the group.

While Hen was stalwart and matter of fact about the impending goodbye, Jonathon was another matter. His lips were pressed tightly together, and his eyes were suspiciously moist.

With a brisk nod and a single sniff meant to keep her own unexpected tears at bay, Olive said, "Are we ready, then?"

"We have to do it, Jonathon," Hen said quietly. "Don't be sad. It won't hurt her a bit."

Olive added, "I'll be at the end and will take her in to Mr Dervish. You needn't worry about that part."

He nodded sharply and took a deep, faltering breath before turning to the villagers and letting loose a single sharp whistle.

"Thank you, everyone, for joining in this bon voyage parade for our pig Swilly." He glanced sadly at the pig. "She's been a good friend to all, and I hope we'll all remember her fondly."

A cheer went up and seemed to go a long way toward boosting

Jonathon's spirits, and a moment later, he took hold of the lead he'd fashioned for the pig, hoisted his end of the paper chain, and led Swilly off.

As everyone fell in line, Olive was left to glance over at the pen and its two remaining occupants. She was startled to see Jamie leaning against the railing, his hands deep in the pockets of his trousers. Frowning, she hurried over to him.

"What are you doing here? Has something happened?"

"Jonathon invited me." At her dubious look, he went on, "I did name the old girl, you know."

"I remember," she said, smiling shyly.

"I'm surprised *you* didn't invite me."

She eyed him. "He didn't tell me there was going to be a parade, but even if I'd known . . ." Olive let the sentence trail off and shrugged her shoulders. Then she started again. "Would you like to join me in bringing up the rear?"

"Where else would I be?" He studied her beneath quirked brows, and while his expression didn't alter, she had the impression that he was amused. "It's important to keep up appearances. It's a big day, after all." And just like that, he took her hand, and they followed behind the procession.

With much ceremony, singing, and cheering, the group made a circuit of the village green, then marched down the high street, prompting claps and cheers from passersby. Olive was so enjoying herself, particularly the warm cradle of Jamie's hand, that she didn't want it to come to an end. But when the butcher stepped out of his shop, thankfully wearing an unstained white apron wrapped round his middle, she dutifully slipped away from Jamie, flashing him a thankful smile, and went to take the lead from Jonathon's hands.

Without a word, Jonathon removed the pig's ribbon collar and hat and made her a snack of its decorative berries. Then he draped his body over hers, one final hug. That done, Hen yanked at his arm, determined to draw him quickly away, and together they started up another rousing cheer as they led the procession back down the street.

Olive stared after her, a frown marring her brow as memories caromed through her consciousness. An idea occurred to her, a possibility, but her little grey cells objected mightily. *Surely not.*

"I can take it from here, Miss Bright," the butcher said tentatively as Swilly tugged at the lead, snuffling the ground for a snack.

"Yes, of course, Mr Dervish," she said, relinquishing the lead. With a single stroke down the pig's back, she leaned in to whisper, "You were the best of pigs, and we thank you." Then she smiled a bit bleakly and stepped back. Jamie had disappeared, no doubt back to the manor, but it would hardly have mattered. She hadn't confided in him, and he knew very little about her thus far inconclusive investigation. And he didn't know the players the way she did.

As she walked back the way she'd come, needing to fetch her bicycle, she replayed her recent conversation with Mrs Gibbons in her mind. Hen's ingestion of lords-and-ladies, her mother's baffled—and emphatic—objection that such an ingestion might result in death. The woman's admission that Hen had got them squared away, paired with the girl's efficient handling of matters this morning, stoically doing what needed to be done.

Perhaps it wasn't so far-fetched. . . .

But poison was a harsh punishment for Mrs Dunbar's admittedly cruel exhibition, particularly as the information had been widely accepted as false. But what if Hen had somehow discovered the truth? Could she have wanted to lash out at the woman without truly meaning to hurt her? The task would have been easy enough. The gin could no doubt have been sourced from her own mother's larder—Mrs Gibbons was known for her sloe gin, but she certainly wasn't the only one—and she could surely identify the berries that had long ago needled her own throat.

Olive didn't believe for one minute that Mrs Gibbons could

have managed the thing without giving herself away, but Hen was another matter entirely. And the anonymous letter was one more clue. Who but Henrietta Gibbons, Girl Guide, would have addressed the letter to "Olive Bright, Village Sleuth"?

The matter was far from conclusive, but Olive suspected that she'd identified the author of the anonymous letter. That person was an admitted, if unwitting, contributor to the death of Mrs Velda Dunbar. The shock of this development brought her up short in the street.

She needed, quite urgently, to find Hen.

Hen and Jonathon were standing at the edge of the green, leading a rousing chorus of "For She's a Jolly Good Fellow." When they'd finished and the revelers began to disperse, Olive approached.

"Well, I think that went smashingly," she said. "What about you two?"

Hen squared her shoulders and replied, "Yes, it was very nice," while Jonathon merely nodded, offering a watery smile.

"If you're not busy," Olive said quietly to Hen, "I'd like us to have a little chat." Olive's gaze flicked over the girl's clear green eyes, arched brows, and freckled cheeks chapped with cold, and she wondered if her suspicions were writ on her face.

"Just me, or Jonathon, too?"

"Jonathon can come if you'd like, but it's only to do with you." This cryptic little exchange had drawn Jonathon out of his sadness, and he now stood stalwart beside his friend, his eyes wide and wary as they looked at Olive. "But I'm too cold to do it standing here, so if you could come back to the lodge, I can make us some cocoa."

It would likely mean using the rest of the ration, but Olive had decided that there couldn't possibly be a more worthy situation. Honestly, she was going to be hard pressed not to break into her father's whiskey.

Barely a quarter of an hour later, she shut the door to her father's study. Hen and Jonathon were sitting side by side on the
edge of the sofa, so Olive set the tray down on the adjacent table
and handed them each a cup before sinking onto the ottoman to
face them with her own cup warming her hands.

"You've figured it out, haven't you?" Hen said, her tone hinting at both resignation and relief.

"That it was you who wrote me that letter? I suspected,"
Olive replied. "Does Jonathon know? All of it?"

"Yes, but he didn't. Not until later," she hurriedly admitted.
"Only after she was already dead." Hen's gaze fluttered up to
meet Olive's. It was imploring. "What I wrote in the letter was
the truth. I never thought she might die—I swear I didn't. And I
don't know what to do. I want to confess, but I'm afraid. How
will my mother manage without me?"

She was breathing quickly, the thrum of her pulse visible at
her temple. Jonathon took her free hand in his and squeezed it,
and Olive's heart broke a little as she looked at the pair of them,
wishing she had someone by her side through life's current travails. She thought of Jamie taking her hand earlier and was
painfully aware that it wasn't at all the same.

"Why don't you tell me what happened, and we'll decide what
should be done."

So, in between quick sips of cocoa, Hen admitted that she'd
witnessed the séance on the village green and heard the news of
the HMS *Bartholomew*, as related by Mrs Dunbar. She'd been
nervous but not overly so, seeing as there'd been no telegram.
But the next day, she and Jonathon had been making the rounds
with the holiday greenery they'd collected to sell, and she'd
overheard Lady Camilla informing Lady Revell that Marcus's
ship really *had* gone down. Lady Camilla's brother did important
work for the War Office, and he confirmed it. Hen admitted
she'd cried for hours, until there were simply no more tears left
in her, and after that she'd been furiously angry. "The sort of

angry," she said, "that comes from your brain turning the screws to plan revenge—an Edward Hyde sort of angry."

Olive sat back, stunned, as she imagined the heartbreaking reality of Hen hearing the truth and acting alone. And then a memory struck her like a poison dart: asking Lieutenant Commander Fleming for the truth and him lying outright. It stung, burned even, but she flicked it away. The man was a bastard, and she hoped their paths wouldn't cross again. Oh, but if they did . . .

That thought was chased away by another: What of Freya Rodery? Was she still in the dark? "Did Lady Revell and Lady Camilla tell anyone else?" Olive demanded. "Your mother or Mrs Rodery?"

Hen shrugged. "My mother doesn't know, but I'm not sure about Mrs Rodery. I should have realised she'd need to be told, too." She hung her head, ashamed.

"It wasn't your responsibility to tell her," Olive assured her, cursing Fleming, Mrs Dunbar, and the entire Royal Navy afresh. "But why on earth didn't you go to your mother—or anyone else?" Her gaze darted distractedly to the sensitive boy just beside Hen, knowing he must have been utterly torn by his desire to help his friend even after she'd turned down a worrisome path.

Hen merely shook her head. "I didn't want to talk about it or even say it out loud. Mother would have wailed and clung, and I wasn't ready to console her. I needed first to console myself, and the only way I could think to do that was by punishing that woman. If she knew the ship had gone down, she could simply have told us, but instead she decided to make a horrid spectacle of it all—a mockery of all those tragic deaths. I just wanted to stop her talking—I wanted her to understand what she'd done." She took a sip of her cocoa, staring down into its depths. Hen wasn't the sort for tears, but her eyes were red rimmed and disconsolate. But she scrabbled on.

"It shouldn't have happened like that. The gin should only have stung her throat." Her gaze flew up to lock appealingly on

Olive's. "It couldn't have killed her, it just couldn't," she insisted.

"Except," Olive quietly reminded her in the same way she had reminded the girl's mother, "for the belladonna."

Hen's brows knit, and she could only stare in confusion.

"I take it you've not heard the results of the inquest." A startled glance between Hen and Jonathon confirmed the truth of it, and Olive remembered suddenly that Jonathon had not been present when she'd revealed the results of her chat with Dr Harrington either. "Mrs Dunbar had two different poisons in her system. The lords-and-ladies was only one of them."

Hen's face transformed, her eyes brightening. "Then it must have been the other that killed her!"

Olive tipped her head down, knowing the truth of the matter would come as a devastating blow to this young girl with so much capacity for good. "Dr Harrington indicated that it's likely both would have contributed to her death."

Jonathon was sniffling, and his eyes were glossed with tears, but Hen held hers back. Still, her cheeks had flushed, and her lower lip was trembling. She leaned forward to set her cup on the tray, then stood. "It seems I need to speak with Detective Sergeant Burris."

Hen had bravely made the decision to confess, but Olive couldn't help but think that nothing good would come of the girl admitting she'd intended to punish a woman who now lay dead. She'd had time while biking home from the village to consider the matter and even mentally consult the annals of Hercule Poirot. The pernickety detective had, on occasion, decided that justice would not be served by the perpetrator's confession, and it was Olive's opinion that this was a case of precisely that sort.

She set down her cup and caught Hen's arm. "Wait a moment, will you?" she said sharply. The girl looked miserable, and Olive softened her voice. "While I admire your courage, I don't agree with your decision to go to the police. A woman died, and while that may not have been your intention, it was, unfortunately, the end result. DS Burris may be sympathetic—you were, after all, a victim of shock and grief—but he may not. And even if he's content to overlook your involvement, he's not liable to keep your secret." Olive squeezed the girl's hands. "You're only thirteen years old—I don't want this to define your future."

"Don't do it, Hen," Jonathon chimed in, sounding a little desperate.

Hen collapsed back onto the sofa beside Jonathon and, finally, burst into tears. Olive moved to sit on her other side, and as the sun crawled down the sky, the girl huddled between them, sobbing out her guilt, her worry, and her abject sadness to have lost her brother.

After a time, Olive's own thoughts focused on something entirely different: Hen may not have intended murder, but someone had, and whoever it was continued to elude her.

Chapter 17
Handling

As a consequence of a sleepless night, Olive was up with the pigeons long before the sun. But as she moved round the loft, with her breath steaming out in front of her, and ran a practiced eye over her birds, she wasn't thinking about Hen or the murder. There was little more than a week left before she and Jamie would make the moonlit drive to RAF Tangmere with a wicker basket of pigeons carefully selected to accompany the agents of Operations Silver and Anthropoid.

Olive knew very little about the former, only that the men of the 1st Czechoslovak Mixed Brigade had hoped to be selected for one of the missions that would drop them back into their homeland. Five had been selected for Silver A, and five for Silver B. Only two had been chosen for Anthropoid, and she couldn't help but feel tremendous respect and worry for the pair. The top-secret information she'd read at Jamie's urging still haunted her.

Rather than ask the question outright, Olive had found the answer she sought in the manor's library. Translated from the Greek, *anthropoid* meant "in the form of a human." Given the objective of the so-named mission, Olive could only assume the Czechs viewed Heydrich as the embodiment of evil. She considered herself a brave person—or, at least, she had until recently—but the idea of coming face-to-face with such a man prompted the rise of gooseflesh on her skin.

The dossiers included in the operation file had indicated that both men selected for the mission had been informed that it would likely result in their deaths. Both were willing to go forward nevertheless, Gabček saying he considered the task an act of war and the possibility of death natural, and Kubiš expressing his honour at having been entrusted with a mission of such importance.

Olive couldn't help but wonder if this caveat was presented to every agent on the eve of their first mission. She imagined herself being asked, but her answer always remained trapped inside her.

It was hardly encouraging, but she didn't like to think about it.

She understood Baker Street's desire to stay informed of the progress of this audacious mission, but she'd been careful to point out that the drop point near Pilsen was some six hundred miles from Pipley. To liberate a pigeon there in such weather would strain the capabilities of even her most rigorously trained prizewinning birds. Olive simultaneously didn't want to risk them and was willing to send her very best birds. This was to be a tremendous undertaking, and it required full support from all quarters.

It didn't take long to make her decision. She would send Poppins, Captain Hook, and Billy Bones. All had proven themselves over long distances, Poppins having acquitted herself well on a mission earlier that spring, Hook having crossed the Channel on a training exercise, and Billy having recently made the trip home from Yorkshire after riding the train up with Dr Ware. They would have a better chance of returning than most. All between three and four years old, they were at the peak of their physical and intellectual abilities, and for this journey, they'd need every weapon in their arsenal.

There was still time for a bit of practice—one final training flight—but she didn't relish the thought of carting the birds out on the Welbike. Her petrol ration wouldn't get them far, and the idea of barrelling down the lanes for hours in this raw weather was rather horrible to contemplate. And there was so much to do at the manor. But needs must . . .

Then she remembered. That evening was the send-off party for the men being dispatched on the very same flight. Tomorrow they'd head to Special Training School (STS) 2 in Dorking, south of London, for their final round of training before departure. It must be at least forty miles distant, and if she could convince one of the men to take the birds along, it might inspire a little camaraderie. She'd corner one of them tonight at the party and try her best to be convincing. And she'd have Jonathon collect a few winter greens from the garden—and perhaps a bit of porridge oats from the larder—to boost the birds' nutrition prior to their long flight home.

After a thorough inspection, which included extending their wings to examine their feathers for moulting or pinholes, checking their eyes for discharge and discolouration, and assessing them for any hint of strain or sickness, Olive was satisfied. Needing to get on with her day, she stood at the door of the dovecote, her gaze flicking between the chosen birds. The upcoming mission could very well end in their deaths, but unlike the agents involved, they weren't being offered an out. Like Gabčck and Kubiš, they would do what was asked of them selflessly, to the best of their ability. She truly hoped the joint sacrifice of men and birds would be appreciated and understood. She shut the door on the comforting sound of cooing and fluttering and walked back to the house.

After donning her FANY uniform and scarfing down the grey-looking egg substitute, paired with a grey slice of bread, and warming herself with a hot cup of weak tea—all while listening to Mrs Battlesby bang on about Christmas cooking without nearly enough butter or sugar or dried fruit or meat—she was ready to be on her way. But the blue haze of smoke seeping through the doorway to the parlour had her peering in worriedly.

With Hen's agreement, Olive had shared the girl's confession with Harriet and her father, and then the pair had accompanied the girl home, with the intention of breaking the news to Mrs Gibbons. Olive had fallen asleep before they'd returned, but it seemed it hadn't gone at all well.

"You know you shouldn't be smoking," Olive said softly. "You'll be quite irritated with yourself later."

Harriet had tipped her head back and expelled a stream of smoke like a dragon might breathe fire, but then she'd stabbed out the source of it and looked appealingly at Olive. "I know I shouldn't but, my dear, it was positively beastly. *Absolument horrible.*"

Olive ignored the last. She hadn't time for a French lesson and so spoke quite deliberately in English. "Was it the news of Marcus that did it? Or did you tell her about Hen?" She cringed, thinking about the double horror of it.

Harriet's eyes flared. "I thought your father was going to have to resuscitate Althea at one point, she was so overwrought. And we hadn't even got to the little matter of poisoning." She sighed. "Hearing the news of her son was simply too much. We couldn't tell her the rest. Maybe later, but not now." She shook her head. "I simply can't believe it. That Hen would—" She cut herself off and met her stepdaughter's eyes.

The look they shared was a stark reminder that everyone had a breaking point. Someone else had been just as broken as Hen—broken enough to want Mrs Dunbar dead. Olive smiled, not wanting to remind Harriet after the evening she'd had. It would only prompt a second cigarette. Or perhaps her stepmother was further along than she'd initially thought.

"I don't know what to do about Freya Rodery," Olive said carefully, biting her lip.

"Yes, there is that," Harriet said, smoothing her hand along the shock of white hair running from her right temple into the curve of her chignon. "It's an extraordinarily awkward situation and will have to be handled delicately." Her lovely grey eyes appealed to Olive. "Although it seems needlessly cruel to reveal the truth just before Christmas."

"I hope it's no trouble," Olive said slowly, "but I invited her for Christmas dinner. She doesn't seem to have any real friends in the village, and I didn't want her to be on her own."

"Quite right," Harriet said, with an emphatic nod. "We'll want to make sure it's particularly jolly."

"And avoid all mention of her husband," Olive said. "I'll speak to Jonathon," she promised.

"And I," Harriet said tightly, eyeing the little enamelled box beside her, which held her cigarettes, "will wish for the Royal Navy to come through with the requisite telegrams, taking the matter effectively out of our hands."

"You might wish for a little more willpower, as well," Olive teased, letting her gaze stray pointedly to the box. "Shall I ask Mrs Battlesby to make you a cup of tea instead?"

Harriet made a face at her stepdaughter and shooed her away. "No, no. I've wallowed enough. Time we both got on with things. Why don't you bring Jamie round for dinner? Seeing him always cheers me up."

Olive felt a little flutter of heat, thinking about Jamie, as he was away from the manor, away from his role as her superior officer, but she quickly tamped it down. "It'll have to be another time. They're throwing a holiday party at the manor tonight, so I'll need to have a quick dinner if I'm to get ready on time."

Harriet's eyes widened with interest, but then a frown marred her forehead. "I suppose you won't be able to tell me a thing about it."

"Afraid not," Olive said, "but if they're serving anything good, I'll try to smuggle a bit home in my bag. The cook is a miracle worker." With a glance at the clock on the mantel, she tossed off a wave and hurried out of the house.

There was nearly a morning casualty. Olive had just managed to swerve the motorbike to avoid Psyche darting across the drive with feline intent when DS Burris turned through the gate. Distracted by the progress of the cat, he walked straight into her path. With a startled oath from both parties, and some quick manoeuvring, disaster was averted.

"It's quite early," Olive said pointedly as her heart raced and the blood thrummed at her temples.

The sergeant straightened his tunic. "It is indeed. I didn't even spare the time for breakfast, knowing I'd have to be quick to catch you before you were off up to the manor." He leaned forward conspiratorially. "That lot doesn't take kindly to trespassers—even the constabulary."

Olive smiled and nodded. They certainly hadn't taken kindly to her trespass, but she'd managed to sweet-talk them, nonetheless, and now she was one of them.

She shook away the memory and blinked as her thoughts got round to considering the reason for his presence. "Has something happened? It's not Dad, is it?" Olive glanced back toward the lodge. She'd not seen him that morning and assumed he was either out on a call or, if he was lucky, still in bed.

"No, no. Nothing like that. There's been no trouble—at least none I'm aware of. I suppose the desk sergeant might have something to report, but that'll save for later. I've actually come to speak to you about Mrs Dunbar." He had linked his hands behind his back and now rocked back on his heels, raising his brows suggestively.

"You've already taken my statement," she reminded him, eager to be off.

"Yes, but you see, it's not your statement I'm after." He tipped forward onto the balls of his feet and tapped his temple, saying coyly, "It's your little grey cells."

Olive frowned.

DS Burris flicked a glance toward the lodge as he explained. "Had a nice little chat with Mrs Bright at the village hall the other morning, while the toys collected for the evacuees were being loaded into the police wagon." Olive tipped up her brows encouragingly, willing him to get on with things. "We've both been quite impressed with your efforts in regard to the recent rash of murders hereabouts."

Did two make a rash? Olive wasn't about to inquire, and she supposed it was technically now three, although she hadn't been particularly useful with the latest one.

"Well, thank you," she said politely. "But I really do need to get to the manor."

"Of course. If you could just give me a quick moment of your time." He rubbed his red hands together and glanced again up the drive toward the lodge. "Perhaps over a cup of tea . . . ?"

"I'm sure Harriet would love a visitor," Olive said, not sure at all. "But I'm already running late. I'm sorry."

She moved her hand to the throttle, and apparently desperate, he blurted, "I need your help." Olive stilled, and he went on. "Rather urgently, I'm afraid. My own grey cells, it seems, are not quite up to snuff."

Olive ignored the last bit and focused on a word she never thought might pass the sergeant's lips. "Why urgently? Mrs Dunbar has been dead nearly two weeks."

"Yes, but it was a rather . . . sensational . . . death, and villagers have talked. Somehow the matter has got back to the Admiralty, and they're"—he cleared his throat awkwardly—"quite keen to quash the rumours. It seems *inconclusive* is not a word they're at all fond of. They've given us till the New Year to resolve the matter. And if it's not done, they'll send their own investigators down from London, and that promises to be quite the sticky wicket, if you take my meaning."

She considered answering in the negative, but then thought better of it, instead saying gently, "If I knew who murdered Mrs Dunbar, I would have told you already."

Would you, though? You didn't tell him about Hen.

Olive shushed her conscience as DS Burris, his expression now somewhat defeated, tried again. "Miss Danes has volunteered her opinion on the matter, but I don't believe that Evelyn, that is, Mrs Dunbar's spirit guide, would be considered a viable witness, even if I could contact him."

Olive suppressed a laugh. "Don't listen to her. She means well, but . . ." Shaking her head, she started again. "Mrs Dunbar was poisoned with belladonna and lords-and-ladies. The latter was found in her drink, probably put there by accident." She hurried on before he noticed the flush that had no doubt crept into her cheeks at the lie. "But the former"—she raised her arms to punctuate the mystery—"no one knows. Find out how the poison got into her system, and you'll find the murderer."

Now she really did crank the throttle, yelling over it, "Go round to the kitchen for your tea, and good luck!" Then she roared off, fully aware that she was going to have to solve this murder on her own. And it would be worth every bit of effort if it meant she'd never have to lay eyes on Lieutenant Commander Fleming and his ilk again.

As had become her habit of late, Olive stepped into Jamie's office with a question already on her lips. "Why do you suppose the Admiralty is hiding the fact that the HMS *Bartholomew* sunk nearly a month ago, leaving eight hundred and sixty-two men dead?" As soon as the words were out, her shoulders dropped, and her chest heaved with the weight of it all. For a long moment she stared into Jamie's unreadable gaze, wondering how much he knew.

"Why do you ask?"

She crossed her arms over her chest and let her fingers pinch at the khaki serge of her uniform. "Because two men from Pipley were on board, and rather than learn the truth of it from the Royal Navy, their relations heard it from a ghost, seemingly conjured by our resident—and newly dead—spiritualist medium."

"I know about all that—you told me yourself. But you also indicated that no one believed her. Why do you now think she was telling the truth?"

"Because someone has a high-ranking connection in the War Office. All of what she said is true, but there's been no announcement." Olive began to pace. "I convinced these women that the prognostications of that despicable woman couldn't possibly be true, otherwise, surely, we would have heard." She turned to look at him beseechingly. "But I was lying to them all along." She could feel her face fall with the distressing knowledge.

"You couldn't have known," he said.

She wanted to ask if *he'd* known, but it didn't matter now, and honestly, she didn't want to know the answer.

Olive sucked in a breath before admitting, "I asked Fleming outright. He denied the tragedy." She was shaking her head now, back and forth, as she bit hard on her lower lip.

Certainly, she understood the need for secrets, but if Mr Dunbar and Lady Camilla could both get at the truth over the telephone, then perhaps keeping it from the families of the dead men was simply wrong.

"Olive—"

She whirled on him. "*Don't* remind me. I don't need to hear that there's *nothing* I can do. It's the refrain for every bit of everything that I don't agree with in this job." She took a steadying breath before she added the rest. "The worst of it is that the truth likely would have prevented a murder."

"Sit down," he said kindly, and she fell into the chair. She'd never liked feeling helpless, and lately it seemed she couldn't escape it.

After rubbing a hand over his jaw in apparent consideration, he finally reached into his trouser pocket before dropping a twist of paper in front of her.

The mysterious object lured an immediate smile of anticipation, which broadened into a grin as she crinkled it open. "You bought me sweets?" she said.

"Or," he countered, "I bought them for myself and now feel sorry for you."

She shrugged and plucked an aniseed ball from the package. "I suppose you want to share?" She handed the rest back and sucked contemplatively, considering whether she preferred the taste of liquorice on her own tongue or his. Glancing at him, she hoped he couldn't read her thoughts.

"I do have some news that might cheer you up."

Honestly, the liquorice was working wonders, but she raised her brows curiously.

"The CO has backed off on his veiled threats to discontinue your role as pigeoneer."

Startled, Olive inched forward on her chair to hear the rest.

"It seems there was a meeting of the Combined Intelligence Committee on the continued use of pigeons and the importance attached to that particular channel of communication. Apparently, it was a unanimous decision that the birds be put to whatever use we can find for them."

The liquorice momentarily forgotten amid this thrilling news, Olive said, "The CO told you this?"

Jamie scoffed. "Of course not. I don't think the man's ever said so many words at once on a topic that didn't interest him. He had me read the memo from Gubbins."

"Did it say anything else?"

Now Jamie's smile, typically so elusive, spread slowly over his face, popping out his dimple and making him look years younger. "As a matter of fact, it did. Given the importance of Belgium as a launch point for a possible German invasion of Britain, it's been decided that introducing a secret pigeon network in that country could prove imminently useful. Given that many of the agents being sent into Belgium are being trained at Station XVII, and the fact that we have access to not only birds but a pigeoneer, as well, we've been tasked with the run of what's to be Operation Gibbon."

Olive sat in stunned silence. A secret pigeon network, run out of Station XVII, with her birds? She had so many questions, and even concerns, but they could wait. She said only, "Will I be promoted?"

Chapter 18
Use of Premises

19 December
Station XVII

The answer had been an emphatic no, but Olive hadn't let it dampen her spirits. She'd circle round to the topic again later, perhaps once the pigeon network was up and running and he had no choice but to be impressed.

Now, as they stepped together into the manor's drawing room, she was determined not to let her thoughts drift toward unpleasant or divisive topics. It was a party, after all, and at the far end of the room a lofty evergreen tree lit up the gathering. She and Kate and Hell had spent the afternoon decorating it with fairy lights and homemade ornaments, and now, with a fire burning in the hearth, lit candles scattered about, and mistletoe hung in a few strategic locations, Olive had to admit the place looked charmingly festive. Particularly for a secret wartime school for silent killing and explosives training.

While she wasn't dressed for a party, having supposed her uniform would be expected, she'd taken a little time with her face and hair. But even a swipe of Auxiliary Red and a sweep of coal-black mascara were barely enough to counter the unflattering khaki of her official skirt and tunic. Not that it mattered much in the grand scheme of things. She glanced askance at Jamie and felt a bolt of disappointment down to her bones. An honest-to-goodness flirtation was out of the question, to say nothing of a legitimate romance. Still, she would have given quite a lot for a quarter of an hour alone with him on the library sofa. Imagining how Jamie might react to such an overture was both amusing and disheartening. Their embraces had become quite thrillingly believable of late, but that was down to her own moxie, rather than any apparent desire on his part.

But quite honestly, there was no time to imagine what-ifs involving her crusty superior officer with all that was going on. So tonight—and for the foreseeable future—he would merely be Captain Jameson Aldridge, and she a somewhat insubordinate FANY and pigeoneer. Though Harriet would likely expect a bit of demonstrable affection at Christmas. She'd have to nudge Jamie along when the time came. Right now, as she stared over the assembled company, she determined to leave her frustrations at the door.

The agents in training, used to wearing worn trousers and jumpers, had presented themselves in full uniform and were all smiles tonight, happy to pretend—for a few hours, at least—that there wasn't a war on, and that they weren't bound in the morning for the final step in their training before getting dropped into Nazi territory.

"Let's get a drink," she said abruptly, linking her arm with Jamie's and tugging him toward a sideboard where a prodigious number of bottles were set out in a sparkling, spirited display.

"Sure, and it's time for a toast," came the lilting voice of Danny Tierney, who was standing nearby, nursing a nearly empty glass and looking a little woebegone. "Seeing as this is to be my send-off, as well, I'll join you."

"I wish you weren't going, Danny," Olive said with feeling.

She wasn't going to bother with formalities tonight unless some-one complained. Major Blighty, of course, would be the exception.

"Arisaig will be a better fit, logistically speaking. No matter that it's bloody freezing up there."

"Well, I'm certainly glad I got here before they decided to boot you out," Olive said stoutly. "If nothing else, I've learned numerous methods for bringing a man to his knees."

Tierney smirked. "I suspect you knew more than a couple before our paths ever crossed."

"Perhaps," she agreed. "But now I'll always follow up with a knee to the testicles."

Jamie had poured the drinks and, turning to them now, winced.

Olive accepted her glass, smiling widely, then, with a pointed glance at the mistletoe hanging over the table, kissed Tierney's cheek. "I wish you the very best of luck in the wilds of Scotland. Try not to get too thoroughly bruised up, and do come visit us. Now, help Jamie loosen up, and I'll speak to you both later. Someone really must get the music going, or there'll be no dancing tonight, and I know the FANYs, at least, have been looking forward to it."

Feeling as if the party had already turned bittersweet before it had even got started, Olive took a swallow of her drink and strode across the room.

A group of freshly minted agents were clustered round the wireless, and she was poised to interrupt the now-recognisable flurry of Czech coming over the airwaves in order to encourage them all to join the party. Olive knew that the BBC broadcasted a segment every night from the Czechoslovak government-in-exile here in England. Occasionally her father let it play as they waited for the next bit of programming, but none of them knew what was being said. Judging by their focused expressions and canted heads, these men considered it critically important, so she bided her time.

The men shifted over for her, offering polite smiles, so thoroughly distracted it obviously didn't occur to them that she hadn't the foggiest idea what the broadcaster was saying. As the sober words droned on and her eyes darted among the men's faces, her nervousness increased, and she sipped her drink much too quickly.

She spoke quietly to the man next to her. "Has something happened?"

He looked at her then, his eyes shifting focus, as if coming back from a great distance—his homeland. "It is nothing new," he said grimly. "The Boche continue to round people up—members of the Resistance, dissidents, Jews. They'll kill them. We're going to stop it."

The words, said so matter-of-factly, sent a chill through her. As if it was a small matter to assassinate one of Hitler's top brass. Even if they got away with it, what then? They would be ruthlessly hunted, like foxes and rabbits. It could only end in death. She looked round at the men, who were straightening now that they'd heard the sign-off. They were clapping each other on the shoulders, tipping back their drinks, smiling, with the light of patriotism and camaraderie in their eyes.

Olive felt utterly sick. Only barely managing to hang on to her nearly empty glass, she spun away from them and walked quickly, wanting to reach the library, where she could shut the door and settle her thoughts.

It wasn't to be.

She'd barely crossed the threshold into the hall when she glimpsed the CO stalking in her direction. Olive considered an about-face, but the opposite direction offered no quarter—the hall was flanked with offices, all presumably locked. Feeling trapped, she snapped her mouth shut against what felt like impending sickness and drew a deep breath. Perhaps they could simply nod and smile at each other. Well, *she* could, but she'd be the only one. Blighty didn't smile.

Olive concentrated on breathing and walking and quickly came abreast of the CO. She went ahead with her plan, smiling, nodding, not breaking stride, but his words stopped her queasily in her tracks.

"I've been meaning to speak to you, Miss Bright."

She stared up at his impassive face, dragging air into her lungs through her nostrils. "Oh?" was all she could manage. Not even a "sir."

His eyebrow rose almost imperceptibly, but he didn't correct her. They stared at each other, his gaze hard, hers probably imploring. After what seemed an eternity, he went on.

"An individual broke into my office." Her eyes flared—she hadn't the wherewithal to control herself and hoped she wouldn't give herself away. "That person accessed certain top-secret files, one in particular." Olive's stomach churned as she waited for the rest. "I believe that individual was you, Miss Bright."

Olive wanted to curse like a sailor—she'd overheard Marcus Gibbons a time or two and was pretty sure every one of those words was warranted in this particular situation. *How can he possibly know that?* But she couldn't open her mouth. It wasn't the curses she feared might come pouring out but something else entirely. Conscious that such a reaction might send the wrong message, she tipped back the rest of her drink and let it burn a heated trail to her stomach.

When she didn't answer, he said quite grudgingly, "As far as unauthorised entry goes, it was well done, clean and efficient. Impressive." His steely grey eyes clapped onto hers, as if to will his next point across. "But let me be clear. Another break-in would not go unpunished."

Before Olive could respond, he moved past her, likely on his way to the drawing room. For once, his tendency toward terse replies had worked to her advantage. She wanted to collapse against the wall but didn't want to take the chance that anyone else might corner her for a chat. So, she walked to the library on jiggly legs, let the door snick shut behind her, and leaned back against it, sighing in relief.

"Had enough already?"

Her gaze swivelled in shock. Max Dunn was tucked up in an armchair beside the fireplace, his dark eyes stark against the blue jumper of the RAF, and a glass swirling with golden liquid in his hand.

Resigned to the fact that she was not going to get that quiet moment alone, she walked slowly toward him. Noticing her glass, he reached to the floor beside him and produced a half-empty bottle of whiskey. "You look like you could use another drink." Meeting her eyes, he added wryly, "Don't worry. I haven't drunk all of it. I certainly don't want Blighty cornering *me* in the hall." There was a flicker of amusement in his eyes, maybe a tinge of respect, but no curiosity.

Olive took the bottle and sat down across from him. She tipped a very small amount of the spirit into her glass before handing it back. Once they'd raised their glasses and swallowed, she let herself breathe and recover.

Several long moments later, she was relievedly pulled out of herself by the face of the man who sat across from her. "Looks like I convinced you to come to the party, at least," she said.

"And very festive it is, too," he said, glancing round.

"Well, it might be if you weren't sitting in here by yourself."

"It might," he conceded, then sighed. "It's difficult to celebrate amidst the pain, not to mention feeling rather the odd man out."

She leaned forward in her chair, propping her arms on her lap. "I had no idea it was still that bad."

He had the grace to look a little sheepish. "It likely wouldn't be if I'd finished the course of medicine as prescribed, but I didn't care for the side effects, so I've been trying to manage the pain on my own." He glanced at the spirit dwindling in his glass.

"I'm not as dependent on it as you might think. It's more about having the willpower *not* to drink it."

They talked for a little longer—about work at the manor, the quirks of the village, and Violet Darling, in particular—and before long, Olive could hear the strains of a foxtrot coming from the wireless down the hall. "Come back to the party with me?"

Before he could answer, the door flew open, and Hell crashed into the room. Seeing the pair of them already in occupance, she gabbled out, "Sorry to interrupt. I'll go out on the terrace." As she turned to leave again, Olive hurried forward.

"It's freezing outside—and you don't even smoke."

Hell came closer, looking very much put upon. Olive was startled to see that she was wearing powder and lipstick, and her hair had been curled and pinned into an elegant upsweep. "No, but I'm probably less likely to live up to my nickname out there."

"What happened?" Olive said worriedly as behind her Max chimed in with, "What nickname is that?"

Olive watched as her fellow FANY's chin tipped up. "Hell," she said, rather loudly.

Max's eyebrows rose with interest. "You're just in time to join this evening's private little club. We have whiskey, and here . . . ," he said, then finished his drink in one swallow and extended his arm. "Take my glass."

Hell glanced at Olive before striding forward, taking the proffered glass, and dropping into the chair she'd vacated. Max passed her the bottle, and she poured herself a considerable amount, then proceeded to gulp its contents. She put the whiskey on the floor between them, then inadvertently kicked the bottle with her foot. Max caught it up neatly and watched the newcomer with seeming admiration.

Catching him staring, Hell said, "If there's one useful skill my family managed to impart to me, it's how to hold my liquor."

Olive placed her hand on the girl's shoulder. "What happened out there?"

"Oh, the usual," Hell said, the words sharply sardonic. "Knocked Blighty clean over."

Olive and Max exchanged a stunned glance, and he said, "On purpose?"

"Don't be ridiculous. He would have frog-marched me to the door."

"What happened?" Olive echoed, desperately wishing she could have witnessed the toppling of the man. "Is he all right?"

"He's fine. He got right back up and wouldn't say a word to anyone," Hell said, frowning. "I suppose I'm no better—at least he stayed at the party. But what could I do? Those Czechs are rather exuberant, and I'm no featherweight."

"I don't dance for precisely those reasons," Max deadpanned.

Hell eyed him up and down, looking carefully at the state of his burns. "Well, you've heard my sordid tale. What's yours?"

Before they could get going, Olive interjected, "I should probably get back. Shall I leave my glass?" Hell reached for it, then paid her no more attention as she slipped out the door.

As she stood in the doorway of the drawing room, scanning the space for Jamie, determined to ask him to dance, the CO's wife bore down on her.

"Hullo," she said loudly from several feet away. "I'm Major Blighty's wife," she continued jovially. "Code name Scarlet Chambers." She was a bright spot of colour in a sea of khaki—the only one among them not in some sort of uniform. The deep green of her skirt and jacket was a perfect foil and in keeping with the season.

Olive smiled politely, shaking hands with the woman, playing along. "Olive Bright," she said.

They exchanged the usual pleasantries, within earshot of the CO, who was apparently recovering on a chair in the corner—and very likely eavesdropping. But after a few moments of their chatting, he went to join a group of instructors hovering near the buffet laid on by the Harrises.

Scarlet immediately clutched at her arm. "I've managed to keep our secret from him, and while I know it's wrong of me, I'm honestly rather thrilled to have my little deception."

Olive did not at all like the use of the word *our* in her confidence. "I hardly think *I'm* involved," she tried.

"Of course you are! If not for you, I'd still be puttering round the gatehouse, trying to find new ways with carrots and potatoes." Her lips twisted. "But now I feel as if I'm truly making a difference." She tipped her chin up and met Olive's gaze, then said in an undertone, "They've put me to work catching rats." Seeing Olive's widened eyes, she went on. "It's not what I expected, but I've got quite skilled at it, and seeing as the little beasts can eat some fifty kilograms of food in their lives, I don't feel a bit guilty about getting rid of them." Her jaw moved uncomfortably, and she smiled rather charmingly. "Well, maybe just a little. But war isn't easy for any of us, is it?"

"Not at all," Olive concurred. If she ever felt like grumbling over her own role in the war, she would do well to remind herself that at least she wasn't dispatching rats.

"It's been marvellous getting to know the girls, and Lady Revell is a wonder. She has us all into the kitchen for tea every afternoon." She frowned. "She's been so troubled by what happened at the hall . . . the séance." The last part was added in a whisper as the music ended on a flourish, and Scarlet paused as the next song was announced before leaning in to confide the rest. "She feels so guilty at having arranged it all, said it wasn't at all what she'd intended—the horrible death of that woman. It's given her nightmares, remembering. It seems her sister had been a big believer in that sort of thing, even went so far as to summon her late husband."

As if she'd intentionally summoned her own husband, who was now rapidly approaching, Scarlet turned to smile in his direction. Judging by his disgruntled expression, he clearly assumed

Olive had been filling his poor wife's head with headstrong notions. Olive took a rather perverse pleasure in the truth, smiling even as the pair walked away.

Finally with a moment to herself, she was about to find Jamie and drag him to the centre of the room for a dance when she saw Jan Kubiš striding purposefully toward the door, cigarette in hand. Not wanting to venture outside unless she absolutely had to, Olive moved to intercept him at the door.

The picture of politeness, he stopped instantly at her approach, nodding his head as he said, "Good evening." And then her brain stumbled, flashing back through the details of the mission that lay ahead of him—details she wasn't meant to know— and she could only gape at him. He was so very young.

She got hold of herself, smiling. "You are part of the mission scheduled to go out on the twenty-eighth?" she asked innocently.

"Yes." He nodded again. "The training, it has been difficult, but we are the better for it. We are ready."

Olive hurried on. "There will be pigeons dropped with you. They are my birds, and I want to make certain they are equally well prepared."

"Ah, yes. We will take care of them as best we can. It will be difficult for all of us. It is not a welcoming place there now." He nodded then and held up his cigarette. "If you will excuse me."

"Wait," she said quickly, pulling him up short. "I was wondering . . . hoping to ask a favour."

A frown puckered his forehead, but he waited.

"It's difficult, the way things are, to train the birds over long distances. Travel is limited, petrol rationed, and time is short. Could you possibly . . ." She started again. "Would you be willing to take the birds to Bellasis with you tomorrow and release them? It will help get them in flying shape for the long trip home from Czechoslovakia."

His eyes were dark and heavy with responsibility. She could almost sense him weighing this new responsibility, accepting it as necessary to the success of his mission. Soberly, he nodded. "You will bring them tomorrow morning?"

She beamed. "I will, and thank you!"

Another nod, and he turned to go out into the cold, dark night.

Olive went to find Jamie.

Chapter 19

Principles of Camouflage, Concealment and Disguise

25 December
Blackcap Lodge

Olive would never have admitted it aloud, but privately she'd worried that, despite the efforts of all involved, Christmas wouldn't be the joy of years past but merely a bittersweet celebration, overshadowed with worry and fear. But as her father carried the platter of pink roast pork in from the kitchen, and she looked round the festively decorated table to see the thankful smiles and faces flushed with happiness beneath their colourful paper crowns, she quietly conceded that she may well have been wrong. Everything was different, it was true, but somehow, it felt exactly right.

There'd been carolling the night before—quiet, peaceful moments of solidarity and hope—and then a bracingly cold moonlit ride home, with the North Star shining the way. Olive had gone straight upstairs to change into her robe and pajamas, then had hurried to her father's study, where the rest of the family was gathered beside the fire. One by one—first Jonathon, then Olive, Harriet, and finally her father—they'd stepped forward to relin-quish a letter to Father Christmas. As each folded missive burned down to ashes, they'd watched the smoke curl up the chimney, imagining the wishes enclosed would be visible against the night sky. Jonathon had no qualms about revealing the contents of his list and then made a game of guessing what the rest of them had wished for, but Olive kept wistfully silent. She'd asked for only one thing, and she wasn't about to admit the truth of it.

The morning had brought the delicious smell of bacon and a few trinkets in each of their stockings, then a walk to the village for the Christmas service. By late morning, Christmas dinner was well in hand, and Olive had curled into her father's wingback chair with the Agatha Christie mystery she had on loan from the library. She'd been quite determined not to think about anything more immediate than a country house party and a fastidious little man with magnificent moustaches, and anyone else's secrets but her own. When the door knocker sounded, heralding the arrival of one of their dinner guests, she hopped up, perversely hoping it was Jamie and wishing it wasn't so that she might spare a few moments to primp.

Jonathon's eager announcement provided the answer. "Happy Christmas, Captain Aldridge," he said smartly. And Olive stood shyly at the end of the hall, watching Jamie unload several wrapped parcels into the boy's outstretched hands so that he could remove his hat and scarf.

"I'll put these in with the others," Jonathon called, dodging into the parlour, where they'd placed the tree so that Harriet could best enjoy it.

Olive stepped toward him, and Jamie glanced up and down the hall. "No mistletoe?" he asked quietly, with brows raised. It was impossible to tell whether he was relieved or disappointed.

Her lip hitched. "Jonathon probably didn't want to be caught out under it."

At that precise moment, a long stick slowly inched out from

behind the parlour door. From its tip hung a red ribbon threaded through a tangled ball of the familiar rounded leaves and white berries of the kissing plant. As Olive and Jamie stood still, watching with amusement, the stick was shifted until it hung midway between the pair of them. With a final glance up at it, they each stepped dutifully forward to press their lips together.

Even as the mistletoe bobbled, momentarily brushing against Jamie's temple, Olive felt a frisson of urgency skitter over her skin. It was an ordeal of restraint to keep herself from drawing him closer as he started to pull away. Given that they were not alone—a cheer had already gone up from the parlour, with Harriet chiming in—and Olive wasn't at all certain of his feelings for her, it was probably best to let go.

As they stepped through the doorway, Jonathon was beaming and proceeded to pull a single white berry from the cluster still bobbing on his stick. "That's one used up," he said.

"What are you doing?" Olive said.

"One kiss per berry," he said stoutly. "When they're gone, they're gone." His cheeky grin was aimed squarely at Jamie.

Seeing Olive's frown of confusion, Harriet chimed in. "He learned all about the plant's history from Violet," she said. "Greek and Norse mythology, love and fertility, even evil spirits. But I wouldn't put it past her to have embellished."

"It's a parasite," Jonathon said simply. "And the berries are quite poisonous." He stopped abruptly, awkwardly, frowning down at the berry in his hand.

"Hurry and get rid of it, and be sure to wash your hands," Harriet said kindly. "Rupert will be back soon with Mrs Rodery, and it'll be time for dinner."

Head down, Jonathon slid past on his way to the kitchen. Jamie shot her a quizzical glance, but Olive merely shook her head. This wasn't the time to explain about Hen. Harriet attempted to shoo Olive off to check the dinner preparations, all quite capably arranged by Mrs Battlesby that morning, before she'd gone home for the day, but her stepmother's devious plan to have a cosy little chat with Jamie was thwarted by her father bellowing from the hall.

"One guest for Christmas dinner, safely delivered, and both of us quite famished. Please tell me it's time to eat." He pulled off his cap and jacket and stamped his feet on the rug.

Freya Rodery had stepped through the door behind him, rather dwarfed by his bulk, and seemed rather taken aback by his bluster.

"Nearly there, Dad," Olive assured him, smiling warmly at their guest. "Why don't you take Mrs Rodery's coat and go into the parlour with Jamie and Harriet."

Judging by his somewhat hangdog expression, her father had forgotten about their other guest, so it was with a sigh that he did as she'd suggested.

Olive turned back to Freya, who was carefully removing her hat and scarf, an effort that resulted in a staticky swirl of dark hair clouding round her pixie face. "Do call me Freya," she said, quickly taming the mass with a pair of combs.

Nodding, Olive said, "Happy Christmas, Freya. I'm glad you joined us. I just hope you weren't expecting a quiet dinner." With a twinkle in her eye, she drew the woman into the parlour.

Now, faced with a table groaning under the weight of some admittedly untraditional Christmas dishes, even her father was beaming. Besides the pork loin and gravy, there were mashed potatoes and parsnips, Yorkshire pudding, braised greens with leek and onions, stewed rhubarb, and carrot rolls with plum jam. Rupert Bright took his chair, glanced round the table, and said quietly, "For all those who cannot be with us for this celebration"—his gaze moved among them, and Olive knew that, like her, he was thinking of Lewis—"may they find peace today and victory tomorrow."

"Hear, hear," agreed Harriet, nodding.

The prayer said, her father smiled wickedly as he stood and

briskly rubbed his hands together. But as he prepared to carve the pork, Jonathon bolted from his chair.

"Wait a moment. *Please.*" The last was added respectfully, even as the boy's arm was flung out to stay the knife. Olive's father stared at him in shock and some little alarm, no doubt worried the loin might be snatched unceremoniously away from him. Jonathon glanced round the table, already seeming to regret his outburst but unwilling to back down. "I would just like us all to remember"—he tipped his head down—"Swilly. She was a lovely girl."

Her father met Olive's eyes in confusion.

"The pig," she mouthed, nodding at the loin.

At once, his eyes flared and flashed to Jonathon, before he respectfully lowered the knife. "A lovely sentiment. To all our animals," her father added gruffly, "working hard alongside us, some making the ultimate sacrifice. May they inspire us all." He glanced at Jonathon expectantly, and when the boy nodded, he breathed a sigh of relief and began to carve.

The conversation dipped and swirled through all manner of topics, many of them posed with the express intent of engaging Freya, who, while polite, was almost painfully reserved. Harriet talked up the WI and its upcoming schemes, while Jonathon offered to help their guest with her garden. He couldn't help but notice, he admitted shyly, that it was quite overgrown. It was Olive's father, surprisingly, who finally drew her out with an offer of the runt of a litter of kittens.

"Oh, I would love one," she said. "I've not had a pet since I was very young, and really, I suppose she wasn't a real pet. My . . . family wouldn't allow it. But I'd sneak her saucers of milk and bits of meat." Her face relaxed in memory. "She was the most beautiful marmalade cat."

"I daresay this one isn't nearly as beautiful, but it's a sweet little thing with unmatched eyes, one blue and one hazel," her father said.

"She sounds like the perfect companion." At that, Freya tipped her head down to focus on her plate, and it seemed the conversation was once again closed.

Olive met Harriet's eye, a silent message passing between them: *Are we doing the right thing, keeping the truth of her husband's death from her?* Neither had an answer, and for several long moments, there was only the sound of cutlery and the occasional groan of happiness from Rupert Bright.

It was Jamie, in the end, who brought up the séance—and the murder—an effort that prompted a minor Christmas miracle.

"How goes the investigation into Pipley's latest murder?" he said casually, letting his gaze slide in Olive's direction even as her father harrumphed in response.

She couldn't help but feel a little smug. Clearly, she'd whet his appetite with the bare bones of the case, and when further details hadn't been forthcoming, thanks to other priorities and mixed feelings, his curiosity had got the better of him. Little did he know that Harriet would thwart his attempt to discuss poisons and gruesome death at the dinner table.

"Are you a believer in spiritualism, Freya?" her stepmother asked politely. If Jamie was baffled by this misdirection, he didn't let on. "Winifred Danes has certainly endeavoured to instruct us all on the topic, and while I'm intrigued, I'm not at all certain what to make of it."

"I find it all quite ridiculous," their guest said emphatically.

"Really?" Harriet said politely. "I found some of it rather impressive, really—the things Mrs Dunbar seemed to know."

Freya smiled almost pityingly. "A medium always works with an accomplice. Someone whose task it is to unearth the little bits of information that can be used to make sweeping and portentous—but generally quite unspecific—statements and predictions." She sounded quite bitter, and her mouth was a hard line, yet she went on. "At times, even that isn't necessary, because the poor dears that engage the medium are so very eager to reach out to their departed loved ones. They don't even realise that they are giving the game away—sharing memories and photographs, which will be used with ruthless intention. The rest is all smoke and mirrors."

"The ambiance was certainly atmospheric," Harriet said, clearly hoping to lighten the mood.

"Of course," Freya allowed. "Eye-deceiving bloodred lighting, deep shadows, movement from an unexpected quarter, a second voice—or even a third—one that very obviously isn't coming from the medium. Perhaps even a face, appearing in the dark . . ."

The condemning words fell harshly, harkening Olive back to that fateful evening. She was instantly struck by the accuracy of the description and found herself trying to reconcile the hints at deception with the progress of the séance and the unexplained items found in the manifestation cabinet. At last, she couldn't help herself. "You were there," she said, her voice both marvelling and accusatory.

All eyes swivelled to stare at Freya Rodery. All except Rupert Bright's—his sole focus was helping himself to another slice of pork.

"Of course I wasn't," came the immediate, defensive reply. "I was invited, yes, but I refused. I didn't want anything to do with that woman."

Olive set down her fork and leaned forward, warming to the idea as puzzling bits snapped into place like a jigsaw finally shaping up.

She could feel Harriet and Jamie both staring at her, the former in confusion, the latter with wary curiosity. Jonathon sat across from her and beside Freya Rodery, his gaze darting between accuser and accused.

"Just after his wife died, Mr Dunbar said something that didn't make sense until now. He said, 'The pair of them put on the show, but then she left.' At the time, I merely thought him confused, mired in grief and drink, but now I think he revealed more than he'd meant to."

In between measured sips of water, Freya smiled tolerantly. "I didn't even know the woman."

"And yet, despite your admitted disdain for the movement, you seem to know a great deal about both the mystique and the method."

"There've been stories in the newspapers," Freya said, shrugging.

Olive ignored her. "An examination of the manifestation cabinet revealed a narrow compartment running behind Mrs Dunbar's chair. It would," she said carefully, "with difficulty, fit a small person, who could assist with the theatrical elements of the séance. Such as the voices of summoned spirits, or visible 'proof' of their presence."

"Bah." It was the first and only contribution from her father.

"I heard a sound in the manifestation cabinet, following the séance, that I couldn't account for—a movement or a gasp. I think, Mrs Rodery, that it was you who made that sound." Olive could almost imagine Hercule Poirot egging her on as she said this.

"You may think whatever you like, but that doesn't change the fact that you have no answer to the question that matters. Why? Why would I have helped her? I hated the woman for the spectacle she made on the village green." Freya's voice caught, just barely.

In that, at least, Freya Rodery wasn't lying. Even if Olive had missed the fierceness in her voice, she couldn't help but notice that her right arm was vibrating with some strong emotion.

Olive could clearly picture Mrs Dunbar standing on the green as the news of the HMS *Bartholomew* was relayed, ostensibly by a dead seaman. Freya Rodery had endured the exhibition in a red haze of fury.

Levelling the village newcomer with a steady stare, Olive said,

"But why single you out? And why concoct a tragedy that could be easily disproved? There'd been no announcement, no telegrams."

Olive's gaze flickered to Jamie. His eyes were boring into her with a familiar intensity, and while it was unclear to her what he thought of these accusations, he didn't intercede.

"Perhaps I seemed gullible, lonely, and sad," Freya allowed. "Perhaps she imagined I'd pay for the chance to contact my husband one final time."

"But she misjudged you. Rather than grief and wary hope, her words inspired only your hatred." Olive paused before adding, "Was it enough for you to want her dead?"

Freya blinked. Her mouth, a moment ago a mutinous line, was now a tiny O. "What? No! And how could I? There are witnesses . . . I wasn't even there that night."

"You've said," Olive said calmly. "But I think you're lying. And even if you weren't there, the source of one of the poisons hasn't yet been determined."

The accused pushed back her chair and stood, now on the verge of tears. "Is this why you invited me? To accuse me of murder? I didn't do it, I swear." She stared from one face to another, but none of them spoke. Even Harriet stayed silent, so Freya gabbled on. "I wouldn't have." She shook her head, disbelieving, denying, trapped, until finally she sighed. "You're not going to be satisfied until I unpick it all, are you?" Olive's expression didn't change, so, unprompted, the words came tumbling out. "She was my sister."

"Diabolical," Rupert Bright said, his voice awestruck, his fork released with a clatter.

"It isn't," Freya insisted. "Not anymore." Her shoulders slumped in defeat, and she sank, once again, onto her chair. Her eyes flicked up to meet Olive's. "For years I hid at the back of that cabinet, huddled in the darkness, waiting for her cues, while she sat out front, duping grieving, hopeful men and women with little guesses and half-truths. Our parents had died, and I had little choice but to go along with it. Where else could I have gone? But a year ago I met David. He was much older, but he was steady and kind and promised me a life far different—and far away—from the one of trickery and deception I'd grown to despise."

She took a sip of water, and Jonathon put a comforting hand on her other arm where it lay between them on the table. Smiling gratefully at him, Freya sniffed rather nobly and went on.

"I don't know how exactly, but she found me. More than likely she managed it through her husband's stepbrother, who works at the Admiralty. That would have been how she got the news before any of the rest of us that my husband's ship had gone down. That he hadn't been among the rescued."

Harriet sucked in her breath, and Olive stared wide eyed as she tried to grasp the intricacy of so many little deceits working in tandem. The mind boggled. *She's known all along.*

Freya Rodery's expression warred between rage and grief, but she mastered it so that it was, at once, resigned. "She wanted me back. Evidently, her performances were not quite up to snuff— too few revelations and unconvincing effects. She'd been re-ported and had a few run-ins with police, so she tracked me down and threatened to reveal my part in her controversial, and at times criminal, endeavours. News of the *Bartholomew* and the Admiralty's decision to keep it quiet was icing on the cake. It provided the means for the sort of public spectacle she adored, and it gave her the upper hand where I was concerned. With my husband dead, I was alone. There was nothing keeping me in Pipley, no reason that she could see for me not to come back."

"Oh, my dear," Harriet said. "I'm so very sorry."

"Even though David had gone," Freya said, her voice wobbly, "I'd decided to stay. I refused to go back into that too-tight, dis-mal hidey-hole to do her dirty work, and so I offered my sister a compromise—one final séance, and that would be the end. I even shared a few titbits of gossip I'd picked up in the village.

Then, on the night of the séance, I snuck in through the kitchen and hid in the cabinet. I was in position before the guests arrived and there for the entire performance. I stood there, trapped, even as her heart gave out on the other side of the panel."

"Why don't we get the pudding, Jonathon?" Rupert Bright said carefully, rising to his feet. "And put the kettle on." He glanced at Jamie, one eyebrow raised, giving him the choice. Jamie took it, with barely a look back at the three women, who remained at the table.

"I didn't kill her," Freya said stoutly. "She was a bully, I'll grant you. But she cared for me and even believed in her own abilities to a certain extent. I would have weathered the gossip. David had known about my past, and besides, he was dead. *Is* dead." Her voice broke on the last.

"What about Mr Dunbar? Do you believe he could have done it?" Olive asked.

"I really don't think so. He was harmless and content with his lot. They really were quite a pair. I don't know what he'll do now. Find another woman willing to lead him a merry dance, I suppose."

Olive groaned. "We're exactly no steps closer to finding the murderer."

"But," Harriet said emphatically, "we're going to enjoy our Christmas pudding, nonetheless."

They sat quietly waiting, each absorbed in her own thoughts, until a parade of men trooped in from the kitchen, led by Jonathon and his moveable mistletoe. And after four long weeks setting up in the larder, the pudding made its triumphant appearance, and thoughts of death and murder gave way, once again, to celebration.

Presents came later, once Freya Rodery had been driven home again, a new kitten cuddled in her lap. There were few surprises, with soap, knitted garments, and books gifted and given by all, but those few were standouts. Olive's father had got his hands on a ferret and made a gift of it to Jonathon; Harriet had sewn a scrap of parachute silk into a camisole for Olive. Jamie had brought presents from Ireland for everyone, including a tin whistle for Jonathon, woolen skeins and a single glorious orange for Harriet, and a bottle of whiskey for Olive's father. When it was Olive's turn, he handed over a little box wrapped in newsprint and tied with a tartan ribbon. He was sitting beside her on the sofa, close enough that she was leaning into him, appreciating his warm strength.

"Something sweet?" she teased.

"I suppose that depends."

"Cryptic even on Christmas." Peggy Lee's "Winter Weather" was playing on the wireless, and she was smiling cheekily as she opened the box and stared down at the contents, a sudden roaring in her ears.

"What is it?" Jonathon demanded eagerly from his spot beside the tree.

When she didn't move, Jamie took matters into his own hands, pulling his gift from the box. "It's a traditional Irish claddagh ring. A crowned heart held in two hands. The crown is for loyalty, the hands are for friendship, and the heart . . ." He paused. "Is for love." He took Olive's right hand and began to slide his gift slowly onto her ring finger. "If your heart's taken," he said, his voice lowered, "the ring is worn with it pointing toward your own."

"How romantic," Harriet murmured.

Olive watched the slow track of that point edging down her finger until it would go no more. She winced at the pinch of it, her gaze flashing nervously to Jamie's, and quickly tugged her hand away, took hold of the little crowned heart cradled in careful hands, and tried the ring finger of her left hand instead. When it settled into place, her breath hitched in relief, and she splayed her fingers, eyeing the point of the heart, arrowing back to her own.

"It's perfect," she said, flashing Jamie a brittle smile. But it wasn't. Perfect would have been an end to the secrets and lies. An understanding, a declaration, a future. This was simply window dressing. With her pulse thrumming at her throat and temples, Olive quashed her disappointment and glanced shyly up at him.

In the soft glow of firelight, his face was light and shadow, and his grey-blue eyes were gleaming, at once familiar and mysterious. He was looking at her curiously. If they were alone, she would demand an explanation, but with her family as witness, she just smiled, her thoughts in an uproar.

"Right," he said, staring down at the ring on her finger as he seemed to collect his thoughts. "It was my mother's." His voice, barely above a whisper, felt like a caress against her fragile psyche.

Her lashes fluttered wide at this information, and she couldn't help but wince at the extent of their deception.

"I love it," she said genuinely, curling her fingers. "I'm afraid my gift isn't nearly as good as this." With her ring finger twitching slightly, like a horse balking at the saddle, she stood and crossed to the tree, eager to cool the flush in her cheeks and slow the racing of her heart. Her gift to him was tucked into a biscuit tin, wrapped round with twine and embellished with a sprig of holly. With her stomach feeling utterly scooped out, she handed it over.

"I thought of getting you a kitten, as well, but I figured you wouldn't have time enough to devote to cuddling."

"Clever of you," he said wryly. Jamie's skittishness round cats was seemingly inexplicable, and Olive lost no chance in teasing him about it.

Jamie's smile, albeit rare, was a thing of beauty, and she basked in the transformation of his face, her gaze lingering on the dimple, which always took her by surprise, as he slowly unwound the twine. The biscuit tin popped open, and a tumble of wool overflowed onto his lap. Harriet had traded and bartered to gather a sufficient quantity of blue yarn so that Olive might knit him a scarf, and now that he held it up before him, she could see that its myriad hues set off his eyes rather beautifully. Her gaze caught on the lines of purl bumps, carefully placed at both ends, amid a sea of knit stitches, and her heart gave a nervous little flutter.

"It's perfect," he said simply, obliviously, wrapping it round his neck.

"Plenty of mistletoe berries left," Jonathon chimed in. "Shall I fetch the stick?"

A laugh bubbled out of Olive, and she tossed the wadded newsprint from her gift in his direction. "I think we can handle things on our own just fine." Glancing at Jamie, with a shy smile curving her lips, she realised how very ironic the statement really was.

"Olive's typical approach to knitting is rather devil may care," Harriet confided. "But she was extraordinarily careful with this project."

They sat up a little longer, listening to the carols on the wireless, watching Jonathon scramble after his very precocious ferret, which he'd named Bigglesworth, and sipping cups of apple cider. But soon it was time for Jamie to be off back to the manor. Eager that their goodbyes should be private, Olive walked him down the drive to where the Austin loomed in the dark.

"Thank you for the ring. I'll be sure to show it off all over the village." She glanced down at it, tilting her finger as it caught the moonlight. "And you needn't worry. I'll be very careful with it." Because there would come a time when he'd need it back.

"I'm not worried." And really, he didn't look worried. He looked as if he hadn't a care in the world, with the knitted scarf she'd made him hugging his neck, its telltale ends draped over his jacket. His arm snaked from behind his back, the mistletoe ball hanging from his middle finger. "Jonathon insisted I take it."

"Did he? Harriet probably put him up to it. Or else he just didn't want Bigglesworth getting into it."

"I think he knew I'd put it to the best use."

Olive had no ready quip. She stood still as he raised his arm above her head and leaned closer. "Happy Christmas, Olive." He was so close she could feel the words on his breath, and then his lips met hers. And silently, she wished a second time.

Chapter 20
Final Arrangements

28 December
Blackcap Lodge and Station XVII

Olive stared down at the ring on her finger, running her thumb across the back of it so that it shifted in the pale dawn light shining in through the pigeonholes in the roof of the dovecote. She hadn't removed it since it had first been slid onto her finger, and she was constantly aware of its presence. Shaking her thoughts free of the mire that always descended when she let herself consider all the possibilities, she swept her gaze round the dovecote. She had work to do and not a lot of time to do it. Today was the day. At ten o'clock that evening, Operations Silver A and Silver B and Operation Anthropoid would all officially commence. The agents, her pigeons alongside them, would climb into a Halifax bomber and fly out of RAF Tangmere, on their way home.

Envisioning the difficulties and, quite likely, the horrors they would face had her shivering with apprehension, but she forced herself not to think of it. Kubiš had been true to his word: he had departed for STS 2 with the birds she'd selected and had entrusted each of them with a message before liberating them for the journey home.

Billy Bones's message was succinct: *V. For victory.* Hook's read, *God save us all*, and Poppins's simply, *Merde alors*, the unofficial motto of Baker Street.

Content that they'd been prepared as well as possible for the journeys ahead of them, she proceeded to perform her final inspection. Poppins was first. Holding her in one hand, Olive once again examined her wings, palpated her chest, peered into her eyes, and cleaned her feet. Hook landed just beside her, willingly volunteering himself for inspection, and Billy Bones came last. She was relieved to confirm that all three birds looked fighting fit: they were ready. The final step in her routine was to rub a bit of oil on the bottoms of their feet to keep them unfettered by mud and droppings for the flight home. Olive whispered the same words to each of them: "You've trained for this—you're ready. You will make it home."

Jonathon had put together a hero's meal of winter greens, dried peas, and seeds collected from the hedgerow, and they ate quickly, in the cage used to trap returning birds, as if perfectly aware of the shortages ahead. As they slaked their thirst, Olive extended her hand to look again at the band of silver circling the ring finger of her left hand. The little heart seemed almost to be mocking her, but there was little she could do about it. Absorbed in the difficulties, she didn't hear the footsteps until they were just behind her, scuffing over the gravel, and she whirled, swinging her arm up behind her back.

"I thought I'd find you here," Margaret said, propping her hands on narrow hips clad in navy serge as she looked in at the birds, her ROC cap perched over a coil of golden-blond curls. "What's got you so fluttery? Pigeon troubles?"

"What? No. Just distracted. I thought these three could use some extra nutrients, that's all."

Margaret peered into the cage at Hook, who was splashing water up over himself, and Poppins, who was methodically picking out all the peas for herself. Billy Bones stared boldly back at her. "They look perfectly fine to me—even this cheeky bugger." She shrugged.

Olive merely smiled, relieved that her friend wasn't more curious about her birds. It saved her having to tell even more lies. Twisting sideways, she crossed her arms, tucking her hand out of sight.

"Well, look at the pair of us, smartly dressed in our uniforms, off for another day of war work. I don't have any idea what you'll be doing, but I'll be huddled in a shack, with my eyes and ears peeled, warming my hands at a hot plate and hoping Mrs Carden didn't serve her husband cabbage for breakfast." Her wide eyes perfectly conveyed her concern, but it passed quickly. "We barely get a chance to see each other anymore, and I've been dying to know."

Olive felt the wrinkle form between her brows as she tensed. "Dying to know what?"

"What your captain got you for Christmas, of course."

"Oh, right. Well, what did Leo get you?" she asked, stalling. She really wasn't at all sure what to say about the ring, simply because she couldn't decide what to make of it herself.

"I don't know how that man did it—there may have been a Canadian pilot involved—but he managed a brand-new pair of nylon stockings. And, even better, a promise that I can have one afternoon a week all to myself, where I don't have to answer the door to any comers. I'll make an exception for you, of course, but no one else."

Olive couldn't help but smile. "That's a lovely gift."

"But I bet Jamie got you something almost just as good," she teased. "Tell me."

With no other recourse and no explanation, she extended her arm, tipped her fingers down, and wiggled the one in question.

Margaret's eyes widened at the sight of the silver band with its trio of symbols, and she let out a delighted laugh. "I do believe you're wearing it wrong, my girl."

Olive glanced at it, frowning, wishing she could pull her arm back, but Margaret was holding her fingers in a viselike grip, and it was impossible.

"What do you mean?"

"Only that the way you've got it on now implies you're already married. You want to turn it round, so that the point of the heart faces out. *That* signifies you're engaged." Her eyes danced. "Your captain must have been distracted indeed not to notice."

A cold spill of dread washed over her, but her flusterment camouflaged it.

"Oh, right," Olive said, feeling her face flame as she slipped the ring off to turn it round. "You know an awful lot about it."

"I do, as a matter of fact. I also happen to know what it signifies if worn on the right hand."

Olive's heart thumped painfully. Jamie had tried to slide the ring onto her right hand, and she'd moved it to the left, unaware of the implications. He'd simply looked at her curiously and let the moment pass without a word.

"It's nothing so exciting," Margaret went on. "Point out means you're single. Point in means you're taken." She leaned in confidingly. "But once the ring is on your left hand, you're very definitely taken."

What now? She couldn't very well switch the ring back to her right hand now that Margaret had seen it on her left and drawn the expected conclusion. *Could she?* She took a chance, but Margaret forestalled her.

"Oh, no you don't. You'll get used to the idea, my girl. Never fear," her friend said with a grin.

Olive wanted to howl in frustration. The situation was impossible. What had Jamie been thinking to entrust her with such a perplexing gift? And now she was going to have to discuss the matter with him so that they could determine what to do. She didn't relish the thought of being subjected to his smugly amused smile, but what choice did she have?

That disheartening thought was interrupted by a near-violent hug that had Olive's chin rubbing roughly against scratchy navy serge.

"It's wonderful news!" Margaret said, her voice positively buoyant. "You, my girl, are a little rough round the edges, and rather too much for some men, but I've no doubt that Captain Jameson Aldridge will manage quite nicely." Her wink was more lascivious than teasing, and Olive barely resisted rolling her eyes. "And I quite like the sound of Olive Aldridge." She stood back, beaming. "Well, I'd say it was worth a couple extra miles on the bicycle for this news, but now I've got to book it, or else Carden will make a note in the rota book." She tipped her eyes heavenward appealingly, then turned, but swung back almost immediately. "I forgot to mention that I had an unexpected visitor to the vicarage yesterday."

"I hope you were nice about it," Olive said dryly, slipping her hands into the pockets of her jacket.

"I'm not as bad as all that." Faced with Olive's raised brows and pursed lips, she conceded, "All right, maybe I am, but I'm working on it. It was Freya Rodery."

"Was she ready to volunteer?"

"As a matter of fact, she was. And what's more, we had a very satisfying little chat. We talked about Leo and his work at Merryweather House, about poor Max Dunn and Lady Revell, and the gardens at Peregrine Hall and the Land Girls. It seems she's been thinking of signing up for the war effort, even though married women are exempt—at least for now. And the idea of staying in Pipley appeals to her."

"So, she's going to speak to Lady Revell?" First Scarlet Chambers and now Freya Rodery.

"Mmm," Margaret said, glancing distrustfully up at the sky, eyeing the mounding clouds to the west. "But it'll have to wait a day or two as Lady Revell has gone off to visit some relative or other. She's quite a tiny thing, though. Freya, I mean. I'm not sure how she'll manage. There's so much manual labor. Digging, hoeing, carting dirt and manure." She shuddered. "Better her than me."

Olive smiled. She was glad to see that Freya Rodery was no longer content in the role of shrinking violet. Though her interest in war work was no doubt partially driven by the reality that childless widows were not similarly exempt, although the Admiralty's decision to keep its secrets granted her a temporary reprieve. "I think she might surprise us all."

"No doubt of that. She's still as tight lipped as ever about herself, but she was quoting some poem or other by John Donne. 'It tolls for thee,' or some such. Miss Husselbee would have had a field day with her." Margaret raised her brows knowingly, then put up a hand to splay her index and middle fingers in the familiar V and spun on her heel to retrieve her bicycle.

"I can't wait for the news to go round the village," she called back. "Give the captain a congratulatory kiss from me."

Olive stared blindly after her, her thumb rubbing at the unfamiliar silver band on her ring finger as if it was a genie's lamp. If only she had three wishes ... Though it would be difficult to narrow things down. An end to the war ... a relationship based on honesty and true love ... a reversal of Harriet's MS ... everything back to the way it was ...

Olive groaned. Now she was being maudlin. Still, she couldn't help but remember an easier, happier time ... with Liam at university ... before all the secrets and the worry and the crushing uncertainty. She shook her head vigorously and pulled her hands from her pockets. She couldn't go back, and honestly, she wasn't at all certain she'd choose to. What she did know for certain was that she would very much like to solve the murder of Mrs Dunbar.

Ready to be off, she retrieved the motorbike from beside the barn and rolled it down the drive. Then, with a kick of the engine and a twist of the throttle, she turned into the lane, her thoughts already sifting back through her suspects.

Dr Harrington had indicated that, given the amount of scopolamine found in her system, Mrs Dunbar would have had to have been dosed with it shortly before her death. In other words, the murderer had been in the room during the séance. Olive frowned, trying to resolve that aspect of the case with the fact that she'd already questioned and eliminated everyone in attendance.

The raw chill in the air whipped against her face, stinging and eye opening.

It was probably more accurate to say that she'd sized everyone up—villagers and newcomers alike—assessing them through rose-coloured glasses. For heaven's sake, Hen had admitted to poisoning the woman, and Freya Rodery had stood silent and still as her sister had succumbed to a sudden violent death. The villagers of Pipley truly had hidden—and deceptively dark—depths.

Olive gripped the handlebars more tightly. She needed to get back to basics, to set aside her emotions and think carefully, critically about every last participant, which meant neither Harriet nor Violet Darling could be eliminated. Well, perhaps Harriet. That was quite impossible. . . .

She gritted her teeth. No exceptions. If anyone could get away with murder, it was her methodical, efficient, careful, and cagey stepmother. Not that Olive suspected her—not at all—but everyone had their secrets. She knew that better than most. And sometimes those secrets led to unforeseen consequences.

As she roared up Mangrove Lane, nearly to the manor, she vowed that starting tomorrow, she would take another look at *all* the suspects, including Violet and Harriet. But today she needed all her focus on the task at hand.

Tasked with packing equipment and supplies for Operations Silver A, Silver B, and Anthropoid ahead of that evening's flight,

Olive should have been in her element. She'd done this many times over the past few months, and it wasn't difficult. She was given a list that included everything from rations to weapons to utility gear, and it was her job to ensure its completeness and then proceed with packing each element into the crates and canisters that would be parachuted to the drop site alongside the agents and pigeons.

Jamie had suggested that this time, Hell should assist her. Going forward, he'd said pointedly, the job could very well fall to her. Assuming he was referring to the possibility of Olive's qualifying as an agent and thus giving up her current responsibilities, she'd merely nodded her agreement. But having endured Hell's near-constant chatter for the past quarter of an hour, Olive had nearly reached the frazzle point.

Hell had expounded on the Christmas Day celebration at the manor in excruciating detail, touching on Mr Harris's marvellous dinner, the toasts, the carolling, and the games. Then there had been a careful accounting of who kissed whom under the balls of mistletoe and whom she suspected of going even further. But Olive had barely listened.

While Hell was carefully sorting and packing the rations, Olive turned her attention to the weapons. There were so many of them—they'd planned for all eventualities, every possible situation. Two pistols, a .38 Colt, a Sten submachine gun, magazines, and two hundred bullets. And then there were the explosives. Working for months now at Station XVII, Olive had come to know quite a bit about the various types in use by agents trained in sabotage. Many of them had been designed and developed by Major Boom and the other clever men working in Churchill's Toyshop. But never before had her thoughts run to precisely the sort of damage they would wreak.

As Olive collected the items from the array of storage crates that supplied every mission, she couldn't help but think of these men, all of them from the 1st Czechoslovak Mixed Brigade, whose training at Brickendonbury had outlasted that of any previous agents. She thought of all of them hunched over the wireless, listening carefully for any news of their homeland. She remembered the dark loneliness of Blighty's office, the top-secret folder with every last collected detail, and the signed understanding of both Josef Gabčer and Jan Kubiš that the mission, Operation Anthropoid, would very likely be their last. And with a tangle of dread and fear, she pictured the Butcher of Prague: Reinhard Heydrich.

He was in the backseat of his green Mercedes convertible, being driven to Prague Castle from his home on the city's outskirts. But as the car approached the site of the planned ambush, it came to an abrupt stop. The driver and a second SS officer quickly climbed out, guns raised, shouting curses. And suddenly the road was swarming with Germans, all of them coming closer. A flurry of shots rang out just before the sky tipped and darkened and the scene before her disappeared.

"And do you believe he propositioned me after that?"

Olive's head swivelled toward the question, even as she slumped sideways from her crouch beside a crate of explosives. Hell, it seemed, had transitioned to long-ago stories of socialite holidays sparkling with champagne, diamonds, and swing bands, while Olive had slipped down the rabbit hole, imagining herself selected for Anthropoid, facing down death, torture, and retribution. And when the time had come to pull the trigger—to shoot the man responsible for so very many senseless, tragic deaths, she hadn't been able to do it. She'd escaped, rather than seeing it through, even in her own imagination. Feeling horribly ashamed, she let her eyes shutter closed and took a deep, steadying breath.

"Unbelievable," she muttered.

"Exactly what I thought. Naturally, I sent him packing." Hell looked more closely, her gaze flicking from Olive's face to her position on the floor. "Are you feeling all right?"

"A little warm is all." It was the truth, after all. She did feel flushed. Mostly with embarrassment.

Hell's eyes looked worried now. "Maybe I should take you to the nurses' station so you can lie down." She rubbed her hands briskly over her upper arms. "Because if you're warm in here, something's definitely the matter."

"It's nothing," Olive protested, righting herself with a smile. She daren't go in, anyway. If Jamie had any inkling that she wasn't shipshape, he'd refuse to take her along on the trip to Tangmere. "I just need to sit for a moment."

"You and Max Dunn," she said, double-checking her packing list with the canister in front of her. "He doesn't much like being a patient, either, and while I suppose I don't blame him, I think if I had his injuries, I'd be looking for relief wherever I could find it." She lifted the canister and carried it to the door of the outbuilding. "I'm done with this one. Shall I help you with yours?"

Olive nodded, handing over the list, relishing the feel of gooseflesh rising on her skin, crowding out the shame of her imagination. "It's mostly finished."

Hell took the paper, flicked it into crisp attention, and scanned the contents of the canister Olive had been carefully packing. She resumed her conversation. "But he's decided he's done dosing himself—from the sound of it, the side effects are quite horrible—so now it's down to his own fortitude. And time, poor man." She eyed Olive critically. "Feeling any better? You're still very pale."

"Don't worry. Another minute or two and I'll be good as new, and we'll be finished up in here." Olive watched as Hell's eyes roved over the crate labels, searching for the items remaining. "The Mills grenades are over there. No, to the left." Hell pulled two from the supply and handed them to Olive. Next came the timing pencils and fuse rope, and then all that was left were the six armour-piercing grenades loaded with plastic explosives.

After reading the markings on the relevant crate, Hell carefully extracted the required number, eyeing them askance. "I'm not sure I even want to know what they're going to do with these. But if anyone deserves the onslaught, it's the Nazis, the bastards."

Olive wholeheartedly agreed, but as she carefully sealed the canisters, she worried that even with all the careful preparation and supplies, Operation Anthropoid was doomed before it had even commenced.

Chapter 21
Individual and Collective Security

28 December
The Austin and RAF Tangmere

The drive to RAF Tangmere was long and dark and utterly freezing. Jamie had offered her a rug the moment she got into the car, but it wasn't nearly large enough—or warm enough—to stave off the wintry weather seeping through the cracks of the sturdy Austin. So she huddled in her woolens, her hands bundled up in mittens, hiding the obsession that Jamie's ring had become. They didn't talk, but the journey was, nonetheless, peppered with chatty coos from the pigeons, quite at their ease in the backseat. The fact that the birds were better equipped for both the cold and a mission into occupied Europe was, Olive thought, rather demoralising.

As the miles passed, her thoughts were heavy, distracted, and bleak. She didn't dare guess what might be going through Jamie's mind. It was a relief, finally, to drive onto the airfield, but seeing the four-engine Halifax looming large in the dark brought a clutch to her chest. And as they walked toward the half-lit figures of at least a dozen men, some of them clearly aircrew, she gripped the wicker carrier tighter.

It was Kubiš who came to meet her, his eyes on the carrier she held. "We meet again," he said lightly.

"Present and correct," she confirmed. "And ready to be loaded into their canisters."

Jamie organised a couple of men to retrieve the crates she and Hell had packed earlier, now stored in the Austin's boot, and Olive stripped off her mittens, studiously ignored the ring's silver flash in the moonlight, and set to work readying her birds. Each got the usual speech, but now she added a little more. "Tu es l'un de mes meilleurs oiseaux, et tu devras faire tout ce que tu peux. Pour la victoire." Men and birds, these were the crème de la crème. If this was going to work, every last one of them would need to pull out all the stops.

"*Pour la victoire*," Gabček said just behind her, having overheard her chat with Hook. "*Za vítě zství.*"

Olive assumed he'd voiced the equivalent in Czech, and repeated it back.

He then sent up a cheer. "*Za vítě zství!*" And the men answered as the birds were taken to be loaded in.

Olive smiled, tears shimmering in her eyes, and caught his arm. He turned to face her, his hair slicked neatly back, his gaze steady, his demeanour as solid as a rock. "Godspeed. We're all with you in spirit," she told him.

His lips curved then, the barest hint, and he nodded his understanding and his goodbye.

"*Merde alors*," Jamie added soberly, but Olive wasn't entirely certain anyone had heard but her.

They waited as the Halifax roared to life and the ground crew scrambled in readiness and finally retreated, leaving only the hulking beast, biding its time in the dark. A few moments more of finger-clinching nerves, and it shot down the runway, officially on its way to the Protectorate of Bohemia and Moravia.

"You shouldn't let yourself get so worked up."

Olive was suddenly aware that she'd been staring out the Austin's windscreen for some time. Flakes of snow were swirling down into the cavernous yawn of the countryside in front of them, lit only by slitted headlamps. She had little memory of leaving the airfield and no knowledge of their whereabouts. She'd been lost in a mire of her own troubles and the difficulties that the paratroopers would surely face every day until . . . what? Her jaw hardened, and though she knew he didn't deserve it, she couldn't stop the helpless fury pouring out of her.

"How can I not? *Why* would I not?" she demanded. "You sent me into Blighty's office for a single folder—Operation Anthropoid. I was meant to read it through, and I did. Those men are going to assassinate a butcher, a man who thinks it is his right, his *job*, to conform a population. To break their spirits and crush their rebellions, to eliminate those he considers unworthy, to lash out with hatred and violence. If he stood alone, they might have a chance, but he is supported, protected, surrounded by those mindless thugs, who are willing to carry out his every order. How . . . *how* can they possibly hope to come away from this in one piece?"

Jamie had pulled over by now, and the Austin was idling in a lay-by. Olive was shaking with tension, fear, and bloody cold, and as she speared him with a ferocious, challenging stare, she was one word from a tearing good cry.

Or, it seemed, one hug.

Silently, he gathered her close, blanket and all, folded her into his arms, and tightened them, as if to hold all the pieces of her together. And in the sheltered cradle of his shoulder, with her face pressed against the scratchy, liquorice-scented folds of his jacket, she let all the tears she'd been holding back run out. A long time later, as she pulled back from serge sodden with tears or worse, she took a deep breath and said the words he'd no doubt been waiting to hear.

"Well, you were right."

"Hold on a minute. I just want to bask in this moment. I've no idea what you might be referring to, but that admission is so unexpected, so utterly mind boggling, I'm rather at a loss."

"Clearly not for words," she said in some exasperation.

He grinned at her, and it was almost more than she could bear. Her thumb went unerringly to his ring as she considered all the difficulties between them.

"Now," he said firmly, "I'd appreciate if you'd clarify what prompted this clearly hard-fought admission."

Olive met his eyes and said flatly, "I'm not cut out to be an agent, and I'm officially done trying."

He frowned, which came as rather a surprise. "I won't pretend I'm not relieved, and I'm not about to convince you otherwise, but I am curious as to what changed your mind. From what I can tell, you've basically memorised the training manual, Tierney no longer wants to spar with you, and your mastery of French curse words is coming along rather vigorously."

She paused, her heartbeat ticking down the seconds until she'd admit the truth. Eventually, she just let it go. "I'm afraid."

His manner changed in an instant, and she thought he was going to hug her again, which would have been perfectly fine with her. But instead, he took her mittened hand and held it, saying, "Every one of us is afraid, Olive. What's at stake in this war is terrifying."

"Yes, but every one of the agents being parachuted into occupied Europe is able to push past that to selflessly do what must be done. And if it was just a job, I know I could do it, but it's the lurking terror that trips me up. If I met a Nazi in Balls Wood, I wouldn't blink, but getting dropped amid an army of them, with the ever-present threat of capture and torture and death hanging over me, I'd do all the wrong things." She stared bleakly into eyes that frowned in concern. "I don't want to be responsible for an operation's failure, an agent's betrayal, or any sort of German victory. I won't." Her lips curved self-deprecatingly. "Apparently, I'm all talk."

"Olive, you're making a tremendous impact just as you are. I'd wager that very few of the agents being trained at the manor could manage a loft and a pigsty in addition to a full-time role as a FANY. Most all of them are better suited to being inserted into an occupied country, because they belong there. They're going home to join the Resistance. You're doing your bit for Britain and its allies right here."

"I suppose that'll have to be enough," she said, feeling rather bleak.

"Believe me, it's enough. It takes another sort of courage entirely to stand down rather than forge ahead unprepared."

The vulnerability of her admission was one thing, but the urgent understanding in his words and the familiar grey-blue gaze, which seemed to effortlessly lay her completely bare, were more than she could stand. So she promptly jutted out her chin and blustered, "I would have aced all the tests you could have devised for me, and it would have irritated you to no end."

He didn't answer for a long moment, until finally he said, "Only because I would have been devastated if you'd failed the most important one of all."

Olive blinked. "Which is?"

"The one that means the difference between life and death."

She stared down at her mittened fingers, twisted tightly in her lap, marvelling at his ability to send her into a tizzy of emotion with a few well-chosen words.

He sighed, the warmth of his breath puffing into the air between them. "Now, we probably should get back. You're already going to have a devil of a time explaining to your father why you're out so late."

"If it comes to that, he's not above lecturing you, either," she said tartly.

After Jamie had pulled back onto the road and she'd allowed a nominal period to pass, she took an awkward breath and broached the second tricky subject of the evening.

"Everyone loved your Christmas presents," she started, "although Dad has privately threatened to hide Jonathon's tin whistle if he doesn't show improvement very soon."

"Feel free to extend my apologies." His voice was amused, but he didn't turn from the windscreen.

"I thought maybe we should clarify the situation with mine." The words had come out stilted and awkward, and now Olive cringed, wondering how he might respond.

He glanced at her, his eyes in shadow. "Meaning what, exactly?"

Her eyes flared in exasperation as she pulled off her mitten and stared down at the little twinkle of moonlight caught by the ring. "Well, it's just that you said it was your mother's . . ."

"It was."

Olive wanted to demonstrate some of the French curses she'd learned. The man was being deliberately obtuse.

"It's lovely, of course, but being a family heirloom . . ."

"You needn't worry. It's not valuable. It would have gone to Maeve, but now . . ." The muscles worked in his jaw, but he didn't finish.

His sister had died in the Blitz, and Olive now wished she'd never brought up the subject. She wasn't even certain how to parse his explanation. But in for a penny, in for a pound . . . "It's just that I'm wearing it on the ring finger of my left hand."

He turned momentarily to look at her, his face a familiar mask. "I remember."

The response left Olive at a loss for words, and for a time, the silence wore on. Olive was thankful he couldn't see her face or the pulse beat thrumming at her throat. *Murder, but this is awkward.*

Gritting her teeth, she tried again. "It's just that . . . it didn't fit on my right hand, and I didn't realise . . ." She looked again at the ring, then fisted her fingers so that the nails dug into her palm. "Margaret saw it and is now under the impression that we're . . . engaged," she finally blurted.

Her stomach lurched in objection as the car once again slowed and was steered onto the verge. He turned to look at her. "And you didn't correct her." It wasn't a question. It wasn't fair that she was so cut up about it all, and he seemed merely amused at her expense.

"I didn't know what to do. It wasn't the finger you originally chose, but you didn't object when I moved it. Of course, you might have just been being polite, or oblivious, but you're usually more—" She stopped.

"More what?"

"More circumspect. But it seems you're not at all concerned that this will start the Pipley gossip mill churning."

His eyebrow tipped up. "You led me to believe that I should be doing my darnedest to keep it churning."

"To a point, certainly," Olive allowed. "But it's quite a leap from dancing and kissing to getting engaged."

"It's not unheard of. These things happen."

She gaped at him. "That's all you have to say? We're effectively—and quite unintentionally—engaged, and that's just fine with you?" She tamped down her own hurt and frustration, refusing to utter the words that might clarify the jumble of her feelings.

"I don't see that it matters overmuch. If the gossips believe we're engaged, it can only work to our advantage. Neither of us is in any doubt as to the state of things between us."

Aren't we? Olive stifled a gasp, knowing she'd almost said the words aloud, which would have been a disaster. Instead, she said, "And what of Station XVII? You're my superior officer—"

"We've already been keeping the nature of our relationship a secret."

That was true, but this felt different. Drastically so. She let out a long breath. "It's my fault we're in this muddle. If you want to take the ring back, I can explain—or maybe I could try harder to cram it onto the original finger."

"What do *you* want?" His tone didn't quite match his words. It sounded, in fact, as if he already knew the answer. But surely not.

Pushed to the breaking point, Olive could contain herself no longer and fairly shouted, "I want to know precisely why you chose *this* particular ring—your mother's ring—as a Christmas gift. And why you didn't stop me from sliding it onto the wrong finger in full view of my entire family. Excepting Lewis." The last was added calmly as her whole body tensed, braced for disappointment.

He was quiet for a long moment, and she stared out the window, willing her mind to distraction. She thought of those paratroopers winging their way across the Channel, crossing over into occupied territory, braced for anti-aircraft guns, the Luftwaffe, bad weather, and mechanical difficulties. She took a breath, determined to put things into perspective. *Whatever his answer, it'll be fine. We'll manage.*

"I would have thought the engraving would have cleared that up."

Her eyes shot to his, perspective forgotten. "What engraving?"

"And therein lies the rub," he said, and she thought she heard amusement in his voice.

As he abruptly pulled back onto the road, Olive squinted down at the ring that had been the source of such angst and uncertainty ever since Christmas.

"It's much too dark. You'll have to wait." Now she was certain she heard smugness.

"It's not in Latin, is it? Because if it is, you should probably just tell me what it says. As you know, it wasn't my best subject."

"It's not in Latin."

"Can't you just tell me what it says?" Olive whined. She was nearly vibrating with the want of knowing.

"I'm not sure you'd believe me if I told you," he said dryly, flicking her a glance. "You have to admit, the whole thing is rather amusing. Here you are, the village sleuth, with your finger in every conceivable pie, and you've not managed to solve a tiny little mystery, despite the single, blatant clue that's been right in front of you for days."

She bristled at having the situation referred to as a mystery. Why must the man make everything so difficult? "I've had other things on my mind," she grumbled, shooting him a dark look as she rubbed her thumb over the ring.

As irritated as she was with the man, she couldn't help but be cautiously optimistic at the thought that engravings were meant to capture positive emotions, like pride and love. Surely he wouldn't have bothered to visit a jeweller, only to have him inscribe *Return at war's end*. Then again, he'd once sent a slap on the wrist via pigeon, so who really knew?

The final few miles were positively fraught with frustrated urgency, as she pondered the words he might have chosen for the inside of the band. At long last she glimpsed the dovecote, spearing up out of the darkness, its cupola sugared with snow. Jamie slowed the car to a crawl.

"I had no difficulty in finding—and interpreting—your message," he said casually.

"What?" she snapped, having been tempted to climb out of the car before they'd even reached the drive.

"The one you knitted into the scarf."

Olive could only stare at him in outright shock. She'd been rather certain that message would languish undiscovered for some time. Perhaps forever.

"I believe I decoded it correctly, although it was quite lengthy and rather indecisive. And I did have to make certain allowances for . . . inventive workmanship. But all in all, it was well done."

A moment before, she'd been shaking with the cold that had seeped through her layers of clothing, but now, suddenly, she felt the heat rising over her neck, seeping into her cheeks, and cresting her temples, even as the gooseflesh rose in warning on her arms.

He had understood the careful placement of purl stitches that encoded the words she couldn't bring herself to say and—if he was to be believed—had successfully decoded their Morse equivalent.

"You definitely have the mind of an agent," he went on. "There's a long history of women using their knitting and sewing to pass messages." He paused before conceding, "Probably not too many of this sort, though."

He'd found them—words she'd agonised over. Found them and decoded them, and that was that, business as usual. She'd grasped the nettle and encoded a momentous, if rather wishy-washy, declaration, and Jamie's only response was to compare her to other women. She had her answer then. He didn't feel as she did. The warmth of the flush fled as quickly as it had come, and now she felt simply cold. The breath feathered out of her, a mad, desperate hope trailing away.

She forced herself to look at him, chin up, defiant in her feelings now that they'd been revealed. "One less secret," she said stoutly.

"Beautifully rare." The quiet lilt of the words slipped over her bruised ego and, just for a moment, had Olive imagining the what-ifs. She almost missed Jamie's next words. "In the interest of fair play, I'll admit that the engraving is much the same sentiment."

The wind rocked against the Austin, sending snowflakes spinning across the windscreen to melt on the bonnet as the engine rumbled beneath, but inside, there was not a sound, only the frozen wisps of their breath as the implication of this latest brand of secrecy, now laid bare, took hold.

The same sentiment? When she'd finished the scarf, her own message had been rather unwieldy, but she remembered every word vividly: *I think I have fallen, entirely unintentionally, into the fantasy and now imagine myself a little bit in love.* And she wasn't about to admit that the words *a little bit in love* didn't do her feelings the slightest bit of justice.

It seemed utterly inconceivable that he might feel the same way. To look at him, to think back over all the frowning looks and exasperated sighs, the stern lectures and unreadable glances, it seemed entirely implausible. But he'd never been one to joke, much preferring brutal honesty instead.

Olive had no idea how to behave. She was, quite simply, numb. "But what about the ring?"

"What about it?"

"Even if you are a bit—" She stopped, tried again. "Well, you hadn't intended . . ."

"I confess I hadn't thought that far ahead," he said softly. "And at the time, I didn't know your feelings on the matter. But it serves our purposes quite nicely, I think, to leave it where it is."

"By all means, then," Olive said wryly, but a giddy feeling had quite overtaken her thoughts. "We're certainly an interesting pair."

"Very."

"So, what now?"

"I believe the mistletoe is still somewhere about."

The playful lilt in his voice sent a quiver of delight coursing through her, and the tension inside her began slowly to unfurl. "Going forward, I mean," she clarified. "It's likely the entire village knows you've given me a ring and which way it's pointing. Not to mention which finger it's gracing."

"So, they'll expect regular, gratuitous evidence of my devotion. I think I'll manage."

Olive worried her lower lip, envisioning a run-in with Blighty. Jamie read her mind.

"Don't worry about the manor just yet."

"What do you mean?" Her voice was sharp, edged with uncertainty.

"Only that comings and goings are quite regular. Baker Street likes a good shake-up now and then."

She opened her mouth to question him further, but he suddenly leaned toward her, the seat creaking slightly under his shifting weight. "Shall we save the rest of your worries for tomorrow? You need to get home, and we have, I believe, a bit of unfinished business."

She had only a moment to relish having him so close. Typically, their kisses were like quick, thirsty gulps, leaving her breathless before she'd even begun. But now she let her gaze linger on the long shadows cast by his lashes, the sharp lines of his cheeks and jaw, the subtle curve of his lips, usually so taciturn. . . .

Her perusal was cut thrillingly short.

It seemed they'd chosen the perfect night for their roundabout declarations and the resultant fervent response. Wary of the blistering chill and the certainty of snow seeping wetly into boots and collars, no one was abroad. No one who might take notice of a dark Austin idling in the lane outside Blackcap Lodge, its windows steamed to opacity.

Chapter 22

Interrogation

29 December
Blackcap Lodge and Pipley

It was impossible to dwell overlong on the revelations of the previous night, which was just as well, because Olive wasn't yet prepared to confront Jamie with her feelings on the ring's surprise engraving. And honestly, both of them were entirely too distracted to focus on such things, so she bided her time. Pigeons had returned from the protectorate. There'd been one attached to each operation, and an arrival meant intelligence on an otherwise potentially blind mission.

Olive had been waiting in the dovecote when the bell on the window cage jangled to announce the arrivals. Two birds had returned within an hour of each other, both looking rough but uninjured. Olive had quickly looked them over, removed the canisters attached to their legs, and then set them down beside the tray of water, where they'd got straight to the business of slaking their thirst and washing the travails of the journey from their feathers.

Poppins had been the first to arrive, and Olive had bolted into the lodge at the first opportunity to telephone Jamie with the news. He'd given her permission to decode the message the bird had carried, reminded her of the relevant poem codes, and indicated he'd be along as quick as he could. She, he'd ordered sharply, should stay where she was.

Until recently she might have offered a lippy reply—or even rolled her eyes—but now she had merely said softly, "Find me in the dovecote." Clearly unaffected by the shift in their relationship, Jamie had merely rung off. It was that response that had finally prompted her eye roll.

Olive slipped into her father's study to retrieve paper and pencil and hurried back to the dovecote, where she settled in with the curly bit of rice paper Poppins had carried home. She'd nearly finished her careful transposition when the bell jangled once again, sending her gaze swinging toward the window cage. Hook wasted no time and in seconds was drinking deeply at the water trough and splashing about with abandon. Moving quickly, Olive retrieved his canister and left him to his ablutions.

In the space of only a few moments, she had completed her efforts with the first message—from Silver A—and had set to work on the second, which had been sent by Kubiš, of Operation Anthropoid.

She was reading over the second decoded message, worry clutching at her heart, when Jamie stepped into the loft. Her eyes flashed up to look at him, and her body instinctively tensed, uncertain how to proceed amid the newness of their relationship and her latest suspicions. She was determined to take her cue from Jamie.

In the barest concession to the words—and other overtures—they'd exchanged, his lips curved into the hint of a smile before he crossed to the bench where she sat, and dropped down beside her, close enough that his thigh pressed against hers. He took in the pair of canisters on her other side and the shuffle of papers in her hands.

"Another returned?"

Olive nodded. "I didn't bother to telephone. You were already coming."

"Which teams did these birds get dropped with?"

"Anthropoid and Silver A."

"And? Is it good news?"

"Some," she allowed. "The agents are all accounted for. But neither team ended up where they were supposed to."

Jamie cursed. "Tell me."

"It would be easier just to read the messages. I can do it, if you prefer," she said, both of them aware that it would likely be faster.

He eyed her. "Go on, then."

Olive read the succinct message from Silver A first. "Plane off course. Dropped between Poděbrady and Městec Králové. No injuries and transmitter intact. We will be in touch when we can."

Jamie rubbed the back of his neck, thinking. No doubt having conjured an image of the map in his office, he said, "That's at least twenty miles from the intended target." After a pause he added, "And Anthropoid? Did they fare any better?"

Olive didn't answer and instead found the relevant page and began reading. "We landed some distance from our drop point due to snow and anti-aircraft guns—near to Nehvizdy, we are told. I was injured in the drop—my knee wrenched—and we could not go on without help. A farmer has hidden us, but we will go in the morning. The Wehrmacht will be looking for us. K."

Silent for a long moment, Jamie suddenly exploded with exasperation. "They're on the opposite side of Prague—at least seventy miles from their target—and dealing with a leg injury." His frown was ferocious. "This operation," he went on, with a violent shake of his head, "is utterly fraught with potential disaster. I'm not at all certain we should go ahead with it."

His gaze flicked from one pigeon to another while Olive considered what to say. As it happened, she agreed with him. It was impossible for her to think about the Anthropoid agents and their intended mission without worry gripping at her insides.

Suddenly, he was speaking again. "But it doesn't matter what I think. They have their orders, undertaken with a full understanding of the possible consequences. We can do nothing more than wait and see."

Shortly afterwards, he went back to Brickendonbury, and she stayed behind, awaiting the return of Billy Bones. There was a somewhat tentative kiss goodbye, initiated by Jamie, landing at the corner of her mouth. And while it was clear that what had risen up between them would be difficult to navigate, she relished that brief moment of tenderness.

She spent the next hour scrubbing down the loft, deliberately not thinking about Jamie or the ring and trying to reconcile the little bits of information she'd collected regarding the murder of Mrs Velda Dunbar. One poison was accounted for by Hen's confession, but the origin of the second remained a mystery. Dr Ware had said that scopolamine could be prescribed for oral or transdermal use. But given that it hadn't shown up in the woman's stomach contents, it must have got onto her skin. But how? Had Freya Rodery managed the task as she waited, a veritable ghost, in the secret compartment of the manifestation cabinet? Had something occurred behind the screen when Mrs Dunbar disrobed in front of Violet, Mrs Gibbons, and Miss Danes? What about the robes she'd worn? Could they have been doctored elsewhere, by another suspect entirely, to be slipped on after she'd arrived at Peregrine Hall? Would there have been a sufficient amount of exposed skin to result in her poisoning and death? Olive shuddered at the thought.

And just as curious was the question of where the scopolamine had come from. Between them, Dr Harrington and Dr Ware had indicated that they'd neither prescribed nor supplied the drug to anyone in the village recently. And the likelihood of anyone concocting a viable sample of their own accord from the belladonna plant was extremely unlikely, according to Dr Ware.

These considerations posed additional questions and generated further confusion, and Olive was forced to concede that she might be better off trying to determine who had the most compelling motive to want the woman dead. It would seem that Freya Rodery and Mrs Gibbons topped that list. Unless she counted Lieutenant Commander Fleming, and she really didn't want to think of him at all. She'd questioned both women and been convinced of their innocence, but she was, invariably, too trusting, and she'd been wrong before.

She glanced over at the window cage and the little brass bell, which had remained silent for too long. She didn't want to imagine that too much time had passed, that Billy wasn't coming back, but she was very much afraid that was the case. The journey would have been extraordinarily difficult, even more so with a blanket of snow on the ground. Fighting back tears, Olive stood, eager for a distraction, a change of scenery.

So, after conscripting Jonathon to listen for the bell, with directions to ring Jamie if it sounded, she was off down the drive, on her way to the village to visit Violet Darling.

"You've cut your hair," Olive said the moment the door was opened.

"You're a regular Sherlock Holmes," Violet drawled, stepping back to invite her in. Olive could only stare—Violet's glamourous red-gold locks had been lopped off in favour of a shorter cut with a soft sweep of fringe. With her wide eyes and unadorned lips, she looked deceptively like an ingenue, but her tongue was as sharp as ever. "I'm afraid I've no cocaine. Will tea suffice?"

"Lovely," Olive said archly.

"I don't suppose you want to sit in the kitchen," Violet said, her eyes rather sad and her lips tight.

"I'd prefer not, if it's all the same to you," Olive admitted. The kitchen held difficult memories.

"Go on into the parlour. I'll bring the tea."

As she waited, Olive once again set her thoughts to the question she'd been pondering since leaving the lodge, namely, how best to broach the topic of the pre-séance disrobing. As it turned out, she needn't have bothered, because as soon as Violet had settled across from her with a tray of tea and some thin buttered slices of the ubiquitous National Loaf, along with a small pot of jam, Olive blurted the first thing that came into her head.

"Did you notice anything out of the ordinary when you stepped behind the screen to watch Mrs Dunbar disrobe?"

Violet met her eyes for a long moment, canted her head to the side, and said, "I don't want to go down the wrong path here. Perhaps you could give me a little clue as to the sort of answer you're looking for."

Olive frowned, replayed her words in her head, and muttered an oath. "Perhaps you could just briefly describe what happened. You can refrain from any bodily description, unless it's relevant for some other reason."

Her eyes widened with curiosity, Violet proceeded to summarise the process. The trio—Violet, Miss Danes, and Mrs Gibbons—had followed Mrs Dunbar behind the screen, where the medium had proceeded, with no compunction whatsoever, to first remove her robes, then a voluminous tunic and floor-length skirt, all of it fashioned out of some inexpensive black fabric. Once she was standing before them in brassiere and underpants, she turned slowly to ensure they all got a good look at every nook and cranny. She offered to remove the remainder of her clothing, but her witnesses quickly demurred. With everyone apparently satisfied, she donned the flowing black garb all over again, and they stepped out from behind the screen.

"When she removed her clothing for the inspection, what did she do with it?"

Violet considered. "She tossed it at Winifred Danes, who, oddly enough, clung to it like a monkey with a banana."

They shared a look of distaste. "Just clung?" Olive pressed.

"I believe she sniffed at it at one point—not something I would have recommended—and she definitely rummaged about. She could have been searching for pockets, I suppose, but her attitude appeared to be one of awe, rather than scepticism."

Here was new information. Miss Danes had had access to the dead woman's clothes just before the séance. And she'd been quick to join Olive in the manifestation cabinet after the murder, as well. Could she have been searching for something in particular, with the intent to remove evidence? Very interesting indeed.

"That's helpful," Olive said. "Anything else?"

"That depends. Am I a suspect?"

"Should you be?"

"Well, I didn't know the woman, and I didn't care to, and apathy doesn't typically lead to murder."

Olive snorted. "No, you're not a suspect," she said honestly. "Harriet vouched for you, even though she didn't need to."

"Well, in that case, I thought all sorts of things were suspicious, but I suspect the bulk of them are merely tricks of the trade, smoke and mirrors, that sort of thing." Seeing Olive's raised brow, she went on. "The insistence on no lights except for that hideous red lantern, the drab black attire, the huge Gothic cabinet."

"Yes, I see what you mean."

Violet reached for her teacup and took a tentative sip. "Was this visit strictly meant as an interrogation?"

"Of course not," Olive objected. As the words died away and Violet Darling met her gaze with a wry lift of her brows, Olive squared her shoulders and changed tack. "How are things with you and Max?"

Violet stared down into her tea, her brows knit. "Not too long ago, I would have said, 'Very promising indeed.'" She smiled wistfully. "But lately . . ."

"What's happened?" Olive had noticed he'd been rather distant and occasionally brusque in recent weeks, but she'd been too busy to worry over it.

"He hasn't been particularly forthcoming. An odd comment here and there, a great deal of silent stoicism, and some rather creative cursing. But I think it's simply that he's taken on too much too soon."

"Is it the burns that trouble him or the memories?" Olive asked carefully, reaching for her own cup of tea.

Violet sighed. "Both, I think, but he's quite adamant he'll not return to Merryweather House." She raised a single brow. "He doesn't want to risk another examination, another optimistic assessment of how well he's doing. And I suspect he doesn't want to see the heartbreaking state of the other men."

Olive frowned and bit her lip. "Yes, I see." And she believed, finally, that she did.

Violet went on, "He's got it into his head that he's responsible for what happened to his men. He's not yet ready to accept that he did the best he could, that's he's a hero."

Olive nodded distractedly.

"I've spoken to Leo." Violet almost seemed ashamed to have done so. "In his experience, most of the men eventually come round and realise that life goes on and can be full and happy." She paused to look at Olive. "But occasionally there is one who cannot help but rail against the pain and the imagined betrayal. And that can result in a rather dangerous unpredictability."

Violet's eyes had glossed with the threat of tears, and Olive reached for her hand. "Surely not Max. He's managed wonderfully in the past few months—he's been feted by the village, taken on as an adjutant at the manor, and courted by a glamorous and rather famous author."

Violet sniffed and nodded, her lips twisting in an amused smile.

"I would like to speak to him, though," Olive added. There was a long pause, during which she sipped distractedly.

"Tell me you don't suspect him," Violet finally said. Her voice was amused but also protective.

"You really are very suspicious," Olive teased. "Don't worry. Just a chat between friends."

Violet eyed her shrewdly. "Oh, I think it's more than that, but I suspect I'll have an easier time getting the details out of Max."

Olive downed the rest of the tea in her cup. "I don't doubt it. And it'll probably be considerably more fun. Now, I really must run. Love the fringe!" And then she bolted.

A moment later, she stood in the village telephone box, waiting for Jamie to come on the line. When he did, he said abruptly, "Has the last pigeon come back?"

"I've no idea. I'm not at the lodge." She cut off his protestations. "I need to speak to Max."

"What?" Jamie's irritation was tempered by genuine confusion.

She tried again, enunciating carefully. "Is Squadron Leader Max Dunn at the manor today?"

"I haven't any—" He stopped, clearly flustered. "He was earlier. I'd forgotten I'd seen him in the library."

"Can you put him on the line?"

"What is this about, Olive?"

She paused and would have preferred not to tell him, but that way lay reprimands. "It's about the murder. I think I know who the killer is."

"It isn't . . . ?"

"Max? No. Now, if you could just—"

"I want your promise that you won't go haring off alone, because I don't have time . . ."

"I promise," she said with a deep sigh.

His own sigh heaved itself down the phone lines. "I will refrain from reminding you of your responsibilities if you can assure me that this inquiry will put an end to your investigation."

Knowing she couldn't possibly guarantee anything of the sort, Olive said politely, "I appreciate that."

"Your assurance, Olive," he said warningly.

Crackers. The man was a tyrant. How confident was she in her theory? Did she truly believe she'd reached the denouement— the grand unveiling? *Hmm.* Well, even if she hadn't, Jamie couldn't very well forbid her from sleuthing about on her own time. After a second's further consideration, she said briskly, "You have it. And don't worry. Jonathon is keeping an eye on the dovecote for me. If he has reason to ring you, he will." When Jamie's breathing could still be heard, she said pointedly, "You were going to fetch Max Dunn . . ."

He put the phone down, and she could hear a moment's grumbling, which included the words *utter cheek.* Olive waited while Jamie did her bidding, and soon the voice she was waiting for rumbled in her ear.

"You're going to ask for a favour, aren't you?"

"Not the sort you're worried over. I'm strictly interested in information, but it's rather personal in nature."

"I would expect nothing less of the famed village sleuth, Olive Bright," Max said dryly. "You're on the trail of a murderer, aren't you? The one responsible for that dreadful spiritualist woman?"

"I am."

"Hold a moment. Is this a formal questioning? Am I a suspect? Despite the fact that I spent the evening—quite uneventfully, I'm afraid—at the Fox and Duck?"

Was it to be like this going forward? Everyone wary of ulterior motives? Well, with any luck, there wouldn't be any more murders, so perhaps it was irrelevant.

For a brief moment she considered Leo's assessment, as relayed by Violet. But she felt confident Max Dunn wasn't the type to be ruled by dangerous unpredictability. "You hadn't any motive to kill her, had you?" Not that he was liable to answer truthfully if he had, but Olive suspected he wouldn't have been quite so forthcoming thus far if he was responsible for the woman's murder.

"None whatsoever. If my aunt chooses to entertain herself and her friends with a bit of sensationalism, I'm not the sort to inter-fere."

"I suppose you're in the clear, then."

"Just like that?"

"I presume you're busy," Olive said politely, trying not to grit her teeth. "Perhaps we could get on with it?"

She asked him exactly three questions. Two of the answers she'd been expecting. One came as somewhat of a surprise.

"I'm sorry, Olive," Max said, his voice flatter than it had been but a moment before, "but I've got to run. Not literally, but it sounds more immediate than *limp* or *hobble*. When it's all tied up, do come round and clue me in. I've discovered I've a certain cu-riosity regarding village shenanigans." And then he rang off.

Olive was left staring into the middle distance as her mind tried to rummage through the minutiae of village life to pinpoint the meaningful clues. She flashed back to that fateful evening; to a séance burgeoning with curiosity, scepticism, and . . . mal-ice; to subsequent interviews with a diverse cast of characters; and to the secret agenda of the Royal Navy.

And all at once she knew exactly how it had been done—and she had a strong suspicion as to why. In the end, a few seem-ingly innocent conversations, a little imagination, and a dose of determination had been all that was necessary to home in on a killer. That is, once she'd unravelled the diabolical twists of the case, courtesy of individuals not even present at the time of the murder.

She only had to hint and listen, gossip and inquire. Which begged the question, How could DS Burris, with his love of a cosy tea, not to mention his police training, not manage at least as well as she? She couldn't credit it. She certainly wasn't in Her-cule Poirot's league, but perhaps her recent successes would spread wariness and warning into the hearts of would-be murder-ers in the environs of Pipley. Then she could turn her attention to other important matters, whatever they might be.

A sharp rap near her left ear had her swinging round in shock.

"What are you doing in there?" It was Margaret, peering in through the glass, which was criss-crossed with tape.

Olive hurriedly replaced the receiver and folded the door open. How long had she been standing there daydreaming? "Just thinking," she said enigmatically. "But I really must dash." She moved to step out of the telephone box, but Margaret shifted into her path, eyeing her friend dubiously.

"I thought you might be interested to know that Mrs Rodery just popped round to the vicarage, wanting some advice. I don't suppose you know anything about that?" she said expectantly.

Olive frowned. "What sort of advice?"

Margaret's shoulders slumped dramatically. "I can't tell you."

"Why not?"

Tipping her chin up, she said primly, "Villagers expect their divulgences to be kept in confidence."

Olive raked up her brow. "I suppose you conveniently forgot that when you divulged that Mrs Spencer secretly fancies Mr Duerden? And when you shared Miss Featherington's catty comments about Lillian Crabbleton? Not to mention how Mr—"

"All *right*," Margaret interrupted. "I will admit, the expectations are taking a bit of getting used to."

"Which means you have the perfect excuse to tell me." She widened her eyes imploringly. "Please, Margaret," Olive urged. "It's important. What did she want?"

Margaret's lips pulled into a frown. "It was actually quite strange. She said that someone had done something horrible, something that she felt obliged to address. But she wouldn't say who it was or what they'd done."

"And?"

"And I suggested she go to the police." No longer skittish about sharing, Margaret went on, "But she said she didn't trust the police and preferred to deal with the matter herself, so I suggested they hash things out over a cuppa."

Olive blinked at her, remembering a similar hashing not so long ago that had turned deadly. "Oh, Margaret, you *didn't*." She sighed, then retorted, "My experience has been that a murder accusation doesn't pair at all well with tea."

"Murder?" Margaret blurted. "Are you referring to Mrs Dunbar? Wait a moment. Does Freya Rodery know who murdered her? Do *you* even know who murdered her?" Her eyes widened in sudden shock. "But she was poisoned! Bloody hell, I'd forgotten. You don't suppose she's in any danger, do you? From poisoned tea?" Her frenzied words were frazzling Olive's nerves, and she was clutching at Olive's shoulders.

"Margaret," Olive said sharply as she glanced round them, "keep your voice down and pull yourself together, or I'll have to slap you."

Her friend sobered instantly, dropping her arms. "You wouldn't dare."

Olive raised a single brow and held her gaze, coming to a decision. "I'm going to Peregrine Hall." She brushed past to retrieve the motorbike.

"Peregrine Hall?" Margaret said, trailing after her, with a baffled expression. "But why?" When Olive didn't answer, she added, "Perhaps I should go with you."

Olive considered the offer as she climbed onto the Welbike. "Yes, do," she said, remembering the promise Jamie had extracted. She was loath to disobey him and subject herself to a lecture that would tip the fragile balance they'd recently managed to negotiate, the engraving notwithstanding.

So, a moment later she was gunning the Welbike's engine, on her way to confront a murderer, with a loose cannon clinging to her back.

Chapter 23

Motives

Olive spent the journey to Peregrine Hall worrying over the answers to Margaret's manic questions. Had Freya Rodery truly discovered who'd murdered her sister? Olive herself had managed to work it out only minutes ago, after a bit of casual questioning had led, quite unexpectedly, to a pivotal clue. Had the widow been one step ahead of her all along? And was she, even now, taking matters into her own hands?

She opened the throttle, felt the motorbike lunge forward and Margaret's hands tug at her midsection even as her yelp was carried away by the wind. They were flying down the road now, bumping over stones, crackling over layers of ice, crowded onto the single seat of the Welbike. The icy wind was stinging her cheeks, and her heart beat an urgent tattoo.

At long last, the stately silhouette of Peregrine Hall hove into view, and moments later, they were whipping up the circle drive, spitting gravel behind them. The pair nearly tumbled the bike in their joint haste to stand, and when Olive finally straightened, someone was coming round the side of the house. The woman wore simple trousers and a tatty jumper—not the traditional uniform of a Land Girl, but the addition of muddy gloves and Wellies gave Olive the impression that that was precisely what she was. And then she realised it was Scarlet Chambers, looking very much in her element, with colour in her cheeks and lips, a glisten of perspiration on her nose, and a tam hat poised jauntily on her head.

She had removed her gloves as she approached, and now ran the back of her hand over her brow, flashing them a broad grin and letting out a gusty breath. "It's a busy day for visitors," she said by way of greeting. "Only a few moments ago, I stopped to chat with a Mrs Rodery. Seems she's another one looking for an opportunity to do her bit without officially joining up. So, I sent her into the hall to speak with Lady Revell."

"Oh, good," Olive said shortly, glancing nervously toward the hall. "We were hoping to catch her, as well." On impulse, she raked her gaze over Scarlet, sizing up the chances she'd be a help or a hindrance, and promptly decided to hedge her bets. The more the merrier—particularly if merrier meant that no one ended up dead.

"Seeing as we're partners in crime," Olive said quickly, her brows raised in reminder of their secret pact, "I wondered if you'd come along with us to speak to Lady Revell."

Scarlet smiled apologetically, glancing between the pair of them. "I would, but I need to be off. Gregory is coming home for tea. I'll need to change . . ."

Margaret leaned forward. "I don't think you'll want to miss this," she said portentously.

"Margaret," Olive snapped. "Stop that."

She needn't have bothered. Scarlet's eyes had widened with eager anticipation. "All right. As long as it doesn't take too long. Gregory—"

"The man can wait," Olive blurted. She forced a smile and added, "He'll be fine."

"Ready then," Scarlet said, doing her best to brush errant bits of dirt off her person.

With a deep, uncertain breath, Olive hurried toward the door, with the other women in hot pursuit, murmuring between themselves. "Let me do the talking," she instructed. "Just play along."

"It was you." The matter-of-fact words drifted into the hallway just as the little raiding party, trailing the housemaid, reached the drawing room door.

"Miss Bright, Mrs Truscott, and Mrs Chambers, madam," announced the maid.

The words echoed in the tense silence of the room, and Olive stepped round her, taking in the scene before her. Lady Revell and Freya Rodery had sprung up, each from opposite sofas, and both now stood rigid with indecipherable emotion. Accusation fairly hung in the air, and Olive sighed with the relief of having arrived in time.

The last time she'd been in this room, there'd been a murder done. Two of the women now present—herself included—had witnessed the horrible spectacle from the audience, and one, hidden in the dark depths of the manifestation cabinet, had been blind to the tragedy until it was too late. Now the ghost was accusing the host, and it was awkward in the extreme.

Lady Revell, wringing her hands, shot a nervous glance at Freya before her face cracked into a smile and she moved forward to greet her guests. Her gaze shifted bemusedly among the group. "I wasn't expecting visitors. Mrs Rodery quite took me by surprise." Sighing, she turned to the maid. "We'll have tea, I think, Martha."

The maid scurried out.

Olive smiled, including Freya Rodery in the look of warm camaraderie. There were bright spots of colour on the widow's cheeks and lines round the pinched edges of her mouth and between her brows. "I think we'll all benefit from a nice cosy chat."

Scarlet started to object, but a sharp elbow jab from Margaret kept her silent.

Resigned, Lady Revell beckoned Scarlet forward, gesturing to a seat beside the hearth. "Land Girls have it tougher than most. It's arduous work, day in and day out, and quite fatiguing. You must take care not to overtax yourself."

Olive took a spot on the sofa beside Freya, who now sat tense and silent, while Margaret remained standing.

"I understand Mrs Rodery was intending to join the effort, as well," Olive said, looking pointedly at the woman in question. "Is it all settled, then?"

"Not precisely," Lady Revell said, her typically composed face looking crumpled as she resumed her spot on the sofa.

"Not at all," snapped Freya.

"Perhaps I can help," Olive interjected. When no one objected, she went on, "I think it's time all the secrets are finally laid bare." Four pairs of eyes swivelled in her direction, all of them looking hunted, and she felt compelled to add, "Only as relates to the murder of Mrs Dunbar."

Scarlet and Margaret looked as if they might collapse with relief.

When no one spoke, Olive decided, once again, to take her lead from Hercule Poirot. This may not be a gathering of suspects, but it was a captive audience, and Jamie had given her the afternoon off. Smiling, she stood up, clasped her hands behind her back, and began, slowly, to pace.

"Why don't I start by telling you what I know and what I think happened on the evening of the séance that led to Mrs Dunbar's tragic and quite shocking death." She raised her brows, looking piercingly at each of them.

Scarlet had settled back in her chair and crossed her legs; she looked ready for a scintillating tale. Margaret was leaning over the back of the sofa with avid interest. Freya's expression was decidedly frosty, and Lady Revell was doing her level best to maintain her poise. But the cracks were already showing; no amount of social sangfroid could remain unperturbed in such a situation.

"Mrs Dunbar, a relative newcomer to the village and a practicing medium, died in the middle of a séance she was conducting in this very room. A séance commissioned by Lady Revell. According to Dr Harrington and the results of the autopsy, she died of heart failure, brought on by the poisons in her system. Two *separate* poisons administered by two separate individuals." Little gasps were expelled all round her, and eyes exhibited stunned surprise, but Olive pressed on. "But who might have wanted to kill her? And why?"

Scarlet was agog, and Margaret clearly riveted, but the other two seemed almost to be pretending that she wasn't there. She went on.

"The suspects, it seemed, were limited to the participants of the séance, as the poisons would have acted quickly. Those individuals included Lady Revell, Mrs Gibbons, Winifred Danes, Violet Darling, Harriet Bright, Ian St Croix"—seeing Margaret's abrupt movement, she held up a finger, postponing the explanation of his presence—"myself, and Mr Dunbar. Mr St Croix was a visitor to Brickendonbury at the time of the séance and a self-professed student of, erm, phenomenology. I agreed to bring him along, but my investigation has determined that he can safely be eliminated as a person of interest." *Despite the nefarious reason for his visit and his generally objectionable behaviour.*

"I assume you eliminated yourself, as well, not to mention Harriet," Margaret said, winking at her. "Oh, the benefits of living with the village sleuth . . ."

Olive shot her a quelling look. She was beginning to regret having decided to bring her along. Scarlet would have been a fine backup all by herself. "In the interest of moving this along, I don't plan on detailing each and every consideration and red herring. My intention is to present the case that leads—consummately, I believe—to the murderer. May I proceed?" The question was paired with a sardonic lift of her brow.

Margaret gestured grandly.

Olive proceeded. "So, it seemed very much a locked-room mystery, but motive was a puzzle."

"What about Mr Dunbar?" Scarlet suggested. "The husband is very often the guilty party. Perhaps he was seeing someone else and wanted to be rid of her."

"It's possible," Margaret allowed, then added, "Or Miss Danes might have been overcome by jealousy at the medium's supposed abilities. Perhaps Marcellus put her up to it. He's the astrologist with the column in the paper." The last was said in an aside for Scarlet's benefit and, judging by the latter's rounded mouth, was duly appreciated.

Olive was utterly exasperated. Dragging Margaret and Scarlet along, more or less at Jamie's insistence, was making the whole business more like a parlour guessing game than a grand reveal. She was surprised neither Freya nor Lady Revell had yet demanded what the other two were doing there. Then again, the pair had thus far sat rigid and silent through the whole proceeding. If she didn't get on with it, Olive very much feared one of them was going to snap. Though, if Scarlet and Margaret kept on as they were, she herself might be moved to violence.

"Wait a moment," Margaret asserted. "If Freya wasn't present at the séance, she can't be one of the poisoners—you said so yourself. I assume Lady Revell is the first, so who, then, is the second poisoner?"

This blithe statement was, quite naturally, met with reactions of all sorts. Olive's was to rub her fingers vigorously over her temples as she endeavoured not to lose her temper. "Perhaps," she tried when the room had quietened, "you could all pretend this is a lecture on murder investigation and refrain from interjections unless they are absolutely necessary." She shot a steely-eyed glance at Margaret, then swivelled it to include Scarlet. She couldn't remember if Poirot had ever had to deal with such indignities.

Margaret slid into a chair, temporarily chastened, and Olive continued, conscious that she was speaking faster than normal in an effort to get through her speech before anyone else managed to interrupt. That there would be further interruptions, she had no doubt.

"On to motive, then. Mrs Dunbar's exhibition on the village green a few days previous to the séance was not particularly well received. With every intention of making a public spectacle of herself—and Mrs Rodery, as well—she summoned her spirit guide, who, in turn, made a show of calling forth the ghost of a navy seaman who'd served on board the HMS *Bartholomew*. It was then revealed that the battleship and its crew, a crew that included Captain Rodery and Marcus Gibbons, son of Mrs Gibbons, had been lost in the Mediterranean Sea."

"Dear heaven," Scarlet murmured, her hand at her breast. "How tragic."

Olive ignored her. Her monologue was making her rather thirsty, and she was relieved when Martha hurried through the door with the tea things. Setting them down on the table, she inquired eagerly, "Shall I pour, madam?"

"No, thank you, Martha," Lady Revell said. "We'll manage. You may go, and please close the door behind you."

They all waited as she crossed the room and the door swung shut with a quiet tap. Then Margaret sprang up. "I'll pour, shall I? You carry on." The last was directed at Olive, who waited while she crossed to the tray before proceeding.

"Unfortunately for Mrs Dunbar, almost no one believed the apparent message from beyond to be true. While the sinking was purported to have occurred in late November, no mention of it had been made on the wireless, and no telegrams had been received by the families of the victims." Olive could see no reason at this point in the narrative to mention that the Royal Navy had, in fact, withheld news of the sinking for reasons of its own. And continued to do so. "But even so, it was cruel and shocking."

Margaret passed round the teacups, and Olive took a quick, scalding sip before setting hers down on a side table so that she could continue her pacing.

"As a consequence of that spectacle, there were now two women in the village who might have held a mean grudge against Mrs Dunbar. Namely, Mrs Rodery and Mrs Gibbons. But only Mrs Gibbons agreed to participate in the séance," she said, looking pointedly at Freya, whose face was pale and pinched.

"Oh, I can't see Mrs Gibbons as the murderer at all," Margaret protested, then quickly snapped her mouth shut as she caught Olive's look of exasperation.

"But now we come to a plot twist—a rather significant one." For a singular, beautiful moment, Olive had everyone's rapt attention. "Someone else was in attendance at the séance. In hiding."

"What do you mean?" demanded Lady Revell. "How is that possible?"

"This interloper was obliged to sneak in by way of the kitchen and insert herself in the hidden compartment at the back of the manifestation cabinet."

Scarlet's hand shot into the air, and her whole arm shook with urgency.

Olive eyed her quizzically. "What's the matter?"

"I've attended a number of lectures in London. It's appropriate to raise one's hand and be called upon to speak." She waggled her fingers and raised her brows. Olive smiled patiently and bade her go on. "Obliged by whom, exactly?"

"She would have got to it already if you hadn't raised your hand," Margaret said dryly.

"It was me," Freya blurted. "I was hiding in the cabinet. I'd done it a hundred times before but never by choice." She stared down into her teacup. "I married David Rodery and moved to Pipley to escape that life, but she found me and threatened to ruin it all."

"Who found you?" Scarlet demanded.

"My sister," Freya said flatly.

Suddenly, there was complete and utter silence. Olive rushed into it.

"Mrs Rodery was in place in the cabinet before any of the guests arrived and, in the confusion surrounding Mrs Dunbar's death, managed to slip away unseen before the police showed up, but she was there when her sister was murdered, and as she's just admitted, she had a motive to want her dead."

"I didn't—I didn't kill her," Freya insisted. "I told you that."

Scarlet's hand was inching up.

"Oh, just say it," Margaret bossed.

"This is all getting rather confusing. Perhaps if you could reveal the identities of both poisoners," Scarlet said expectantly.

Olive nearly growled in frustration but instead shook her head dismissively. "The other poisoner wasn't intending murder—"

"Neither was I," Lady Revell blurted. "It wasn't ever meant to go that far."

They all stared in shock at the elegant, dark-haired woman, who'd just confessed to being accidental poisoner number two.

Scarlet's tentative reply broke the silence. "So, the gist of it is that two separate people poisoned Mrs Dunbar, but neither with the intention of killing her?"

"That's diabolical," Margaret said.

The whole business was getting out of hand, with everyone talking at once, and even Olive was struggling to keep up. "Just wait a moment." Her voice might have been a bit louder and more assertive than necessary, but it did the trick. She moved to sit on Lady Revell's other side. "In the interest of minimising confusion, I'll continue, shall I? The pair of you can offer corrections or fill in any blanks." The last was directed to Freya Rodery and Lady Revell, and very deliberately *not* to Scarlet and Margaret.

Olive was poised to start again when Margaret decided to move closer, seating herself beside Freya. Anyone happening upon the group would imagine they were all cosied up for a good gossip. Which, Olive supposed, at this point they were.

She took a breath and plodded on. "While Lady Revell was not the intended target of Mrs Dunbar's very public display on the village green, she couldn't help but be affected. You see, Lady Revell recognised the medium—or at the very least, her name. Her own sister, after losing her husband, had visited such a person and taken her own life the following day." There was a hushed silence, and Olive went on carefully. "I suspect Lady Revell blamed that medium for the death of her sister." Olive reached for her hand. "It was Mrs Dunbar, wasn't it?"

The older woman's eyes were red rimmed and slick with un-shed tears. "She was very popular, and Cornelia would have heard of her exploits. When her husband died suddenly, Cornelia was away, visiting friends, and she was devastated. She wanted only the chance to speak to him one more time. So she hired Mrs Dun-bar. The woman had been in the papers, hailed as a charlatan, arrested, and yet she was in high demand, even more so after the war started and there were so many lost souls."

"It was all smoke and mirrors, it's true," Freya said quietly, "but why would you blame her for your sister's suicide?"

"Nellie had been a believer ever since she was a little girl. Fairies, monsters, magic, spirits. Nothing was too far-fetched. She simply wanted to imagine a world more ethereal than the one she lived in." She paused to dab at her eyes with the hand-kerchief she'd pulled from her sleeve. "So, when Mrs Dunbar pretended to summon the spirit of her husband and gave him voice, he spoke eagerly of the two of them being together again amid the peaceful beauty of the afterlife. Nellie took the experi-ence very much to heart and felt compelled to quicken their re-union. She left a note beside the bottle of laudanum, explaining precisely how she'd come to her decision."

Without a word, Margaret stood, walked to the little cart that held a single decanter and a collection of cordial glasses. She poured sherry into one of them and then hurried to press it into Lady Revell's hands.

After the woman had taken a few restorative sips, Olive prompted, "And when you saw her on the village green, manufacturing a tragedy to prey on people's fears and emotions, you had an idea to punish her . . . ?"

"I wanted only to expose her as a fraud," Lady Revell croaked. "The way the spirits manifested, the ectoplasm seeping grotesquely from her nose and mouth, the voices she summoned. I wanted people to see it all for what it was—the worst sort of trickery and betrayal. But Max didn't know about any of it."

Olive looked at Freya. "And you suspected what she'd done. You'd had the opportunity, while alone in the room before the séance, to glance at the photographs Lady Revell had set out for your sister."

Freya's look was wan. "I remembered her, and I remembered Velda reading about the tragedy in the paper the next day."

"You didn't touch the photographs?" Lady Revell blurted urgently.

Startled, Freya shook her head.

Lady Revell turned sad eyes to Olive, saying, "I thought I'd been so clever."

"Your method would have made Agatha Christie proud," Olive admitted.

"I doubt she would have approved of such failure. Not only did my efforts produce a devastating—and quite unintended—result, but you've found me out." Her voice was light, an indication of her relief at finally having her misdeeds revealed.

"It was rather a puzzle, but bits and pieces gradually slotted into place, finally making sense of a baffling case." Olive sat back, wishing her cup of tea was within reach.

"Well, get on with it, then, Detective Bright," Margaret urged. "Let the rest of us in on your deductions. Start with the photographs." She quirked her lips to temper the bossiness.

"Yes, please," Scarlet agreed.

Olive looked to Lady Revell, who nodded for her to proceed. "Lady Revell's nephew, Squadron Leader Max Dunn, had recently been recuperating at Merryweather House after his aeroplane went down in the Channel, claiming the lives of several of his crew. Beyond the extensive burns he sustained, he was also dealing with trauma-induced vomiting, pain, and depression. He'd been prescribed scopolamine liniment, and while it provided some relief, it subjected him to some troublesome side effects. The sort exhibited by Mrs Dunbar just before she died, although much less pronounced. Her symptoms matched the mnemonic—'blind as a bat, mad as a hatter, red as a beet, hot as hell, and dry as a bone'—so Dr Harrington suspected belladonna poisoning right off, and an examination of the body confirmed his suspicion. He found scopolamine, an extract of the plant, in her system."

Lady Revell chose that moment to chime in. "The doctors said it would help with the vomiting and subdue some of the memories but warned that too much of it could cause hallucinations. After a time, Max refused to use it, and it seemed the perfect foil for Mrs Dunbar's theatrical displays. She'd been in the paper, you see, investigated by the London Spiritualist Alliance. They'd exposed her as a fraud and detailed her methods. The woman was regurgitating bits of lavatory paper, mixed up with egg white and cheesecloth, and calling it ectoplasm." Her fists clenched in fury.

Olive glanced at Freya Rodery. The blue vein at her temple was prominent, and a troubled frown marred her brow.

"It was discovered," Lady Revell continued fiercely, "that the 'spirits' that materialised behind her, seen only in that horrible red light, were papier-mâché creations, hung on hangers. The woman purported a connection to the spirit world, claimed she could contact loved ones, but it was all a sham. She took Nellie's money, preyed on her grief, and made her believe that her husband was calling out to her from the beyond." A shuddering sigh escaped her, and her eyes stared sightless as she remembered. Then she lifted her chin. "I smeared the liniment on the photographs, knowing she'd pick them up, knowing she'd use whatever information was on offer to gain insights into her audience."

"It was only later that I remembered you'd been wearing gloves," Olive said quietly. "And that the photos had disappeared by the time the police had arrived."

"Yes, I tried to be very careful. My hope was that the medicine would not only keep her from producing the ectoplasm but would also have her hallucinating and spouting nonsense. I wanted to make a fool of her, to punish her for convincing my sister that she should leave this world and her son behind to join her husband." A single sob escaped her.

"It might have worked brilliantly," Freya said tentatively, staring into her teacup, "if not for the other poison."

Scarlet blurted, "What *was* the other poison?"

"Lords-and-ladies," Olive said resignedly. "Also known as devils and angels, it's a common enough plant, with temptingly attractive red berries. It's quite painful if ingested, but not lethal if vomited up quickly. Unfortunately, with a heavy dose of scopolamine in her system, Mrs Dunbar couldn't purge the lords-and-ladies. She died when her heart gave out, and according to Dr Harrington, it was the combination of poisons that resulted in her death."

It was a lot to take in, and no one spoke for a long time.

Finally, Lady Revell dabbed at her eyes and nose and straightened her shoulders. "It was wicked of me to have taken matters into my own hands. I didn't wish for Mrs Dunbar's death, but I took a hand in causing it and will confess to the police."

"No, don't," Freya protested. They all turned to her in surprise, but before she could go on, Margaret forestalled her.

"What about the other poisoner?" she demanded, belatedly realising the term was less than flattering. "The other *accidental* poisoner," she corrected.

"Yes, whoever it is really should have been invited to the discussion," Scarlet said.

The thought of Hen let loose in the conversation was mind boggling.

"We're not discussing—" Olive began, only to be cut off by Margaret.

"Really, Olive. If that individual is to be forgiven, and sins forgotten, doesn't Lady Revell deserve the same courtesy?"

Freya spoke up. "I'd prefer not to see either of them punished." She looked down at her hands, clutched in her lap, and then up at the faces that stared back at her. "My sister was not well liked, and that fact didn't matter to her in the slightest. She was determined to carry on despite the consequences—the police, the investigations, the notoriety." She took a deep breath. "Perhaps poison was a step too far, but one without the other would have likely produced a general unpleasantness and discomfort. Velda wouldn't have shied away from either. Her death was simply an accident."

"The lords-and-ladies was dispensed by a woman, wasn't it?" Margaret said softly.

After a moment, Olive offered a single nod, prompting her friend to go on.

"Mrs Dunbar's death was a horrible accident, brought on by women pushed to the breaking point. If the police haven't yet settled on a culprit, why don't we all simply agree that the matter has been put to rest and that none of us will reveal the truth?"

Olive frowned, considering, appreciating the simplicity of the idea. She hadn't intended to reveal Hen's part in the woman's death, and fairness compelled her to allow Lady Revell the same anonymity. She'd have to come up with something to satisfy Sergeant Burris, though, or the Royal Navy would likely descend on Pipley with an entire entourage of officers of Fleming's calibre. Talk about a misery. Then again, she'd very much like to see how they might handle the tricky matter of the HMS *Bartholomew*.

"Oh, I like that very much," said Scarlet. "It's as if we're a secret coven."

"Except that this will be our one and only meeting," Margaret said gently. "We must all promise never to breathe a word of the true nature of Mrs Dunbar's death." She glanced at Olive. "Perhaps you can pass the word to accidental poisoner number one?"

"I'm so very sorry," Lady Revell said, seeming to include everyone in her apology.

"I forgive you," Freya returned. "Truly. And I hope you can forgive my sister."

Which was how Olive, having intended a grand reveal and anticipated becoming something of a cause célèbre in the village, found herself toasting her intention, along with the other four women present, never to reveal the secrets behind the murder of Mrs Dunbar.

Riding the relative success of that confrontation, Olive made a beeline back to the manor in the gathering dark, her thoughts flashing back over the memory of the previous night.

Having hurried up to her room, flushed with optimism and the rosy glow of newfound love, Olive had eagerly tugged off Jamie's ring to read the promised inscription. And promptly been stunned into incomprehension. It had read simply, *Love, R.*

Quite naturally, her first reaction, blurted into the room, was, "Who on earth is R?" Following on its heels came the uncertainty, the hurt, and, eventually, bloody-minded pique. And all of it had festered. Well, no more. She fully intended to get to the bottom of things.

The manor halls were mostly deserted, and she cornered Jamie in one of the storerooms. She let the door snick shut behind her to stand in front of it, arms crossed. "Do you remember our conversation last night? The one about . . . us." She raised her brows encouragingly, but her voice was tight with restrained emotion.

He looked at her, and Olive supposed his frown could have been in response to her actions or tone. Or it could have been in realisation that he'd been caught out. "Of course I remember," he said, taking a careful step toward her.

"Then I suppose you remember there were certain . . . admissions on both sides."

Another step. "I do."

"You implied that your feelings were spelled out in the engraving on the ring you gave me."

"I remember."

"Well, that wasn't precisely true," she blustered. "Tu m'as trompé. Et d'une manière assez cruelle."

She couldn't hold back the French. Lately, whenever her emotions overcame her, she found herself blustering, cursing, and raging in that language. Almost no one understood her, and that felt more cathartic somehow.

Now *his* brows went up. "What were you expecting, then?" His voice had softened, gone Irish, and it felt almost like an ambush. She was suddenly flustered and self-conscious.

"You led me to believe that it was a message from . . . you."

"And it wasn't?"

He was too close now. She was having to look up at him, and it made the whole business even more awkward. She could feel the pulse at her throat, and judging by the glance he flicked in that direction, the thrum was sufficiently insistent as to be visible.

"I presume you know what it says?" she persisted.

"I do."

"Well, then, Jameson Aldridge, who is R?"

Something flashed in his eyes and seemed responsible for the barest tug at the corner of his mouth. He stepped closer still, so that Olive unconsciously backed herself against the door. "Do you remember when we talked about the importance of code names in this war, and I admitted that I wasn't using my real name?"

A bolt of some indefinable emotion shot through her—it could have been relief or triumph or lust or a combination of all three. "I do," she admitted, her voice hoarse.

"Does that clear up the matter, then?"

"Not exactly," she said falteringly.

"Go on."

"Seeing as you've never told me your real name, the matter remains inconclusive. R could be anyone."

"Is that right?"

"I suppose it could be you," she allowed, conscious of the absurdity of the situation.

He leaned forward, laid his hands flat against the door on either side of her head. "In future, perhaps you could just come to me for information rather than accusing me of . . . what, exactly?"

She blinked at him and swallowed hard, her mind buzzing with too many thoughts.

So, this was what it felt like to be a custard. She wasn't feeling cowardly, exactly. More like she was a quivering mess of being decidedly in the wrong. And feeling a rather urgent need for forgiveness. She ignored the question in the interest of getting on with the matter at hand. "Will you . . . tell me your real name?" she said, all politeness. "Please."

And then he leaned in and whispered it in her ear, the pure Irishness of it like a wisp of magic. When it was done, their eyes met for only a moment before his mouth settled heavily on hers.

By the time they'd resolved matters sufficiently between them— an effort that had required them to dip into the stash of condoms left over from the initial design of Major Boom's limpet mine— the hallway was dim and deserted. Lucky for Jamie, who, tousled and disheveled as he was, didn't look at all the part of brusque adjutant to the CO. Olive, meanwhile, felt as if she was floating, even invincible. While she might not have the sort of courage necessary to face down the Nazis, she was putting what she did have to good use much closer to home.

* * *

3 January 1942

Dearest George,

 Happy New Year! Perhaps 1942 will see the end of the war. Wouldn't that be wonderful! Though, so much has changed, I'm not at all certain what to expect when victory does come, now that our twosome has stretched to four with Bridget and Jamie. Congratulations, by the way, on coming up to scratch! I'm so pleased for you, and I look forward to long chats with Bridget one day in the future.

 We missed you at Christmas, and Lewis, as well. I hope you managed a slice of Christmas pudding, particularly now that dried fruits have joined the list of rationed goods. We've challenged Jonathon to make up the lack with a surplus of fresh fruit of all sorts, and the dear boy has taken our dietary adversity to heart. I've no doubt that as soon as the ground thaws sufficiently, he will be knee-deep in the garden, hard at work.

 It will no doubt relieve you to know that this letter does <u>not</u> carry news of another murder in Pipley; however, there <u>has</u> been a tragic death, particularly dramatic in its having taken place during a séance. I can picture the scepticism in your face even as I write the words, but it's true! A spiritualist medium had taken up residence in the village and been requested to do a summons. I happened to be in the audience and was, admittedly, rather caught up in the theatrics of it all when the evening took a rather gruesome turn. Moments later, the medium was dead and surrounded by a locked room of suspects, of which I was one! But I was also a witness and thus better positioned by far than Sergeant Burris to investigate. Which is how I discovered that it was a pilfered prescription and a bottle of carelessly made sloe gin that led to her death. Nothing nefarious, after all.

That's all the excitement round here, I'm afraid. Work carries on, as, it appears, does this grim weather. I'm eager for spring, for sun, and for you to be home again.

Much love,
Olive

P.S. Jamie has given me a ring. A traditional Irish claddagh, he says, meant to signify friendship, loyalty, and love. I'm not quite sure how it happened, but it seems we're engaged!
P.P.S. As ever, look after yourself and your crew. And Bridget.

Chapter 24
Objects and Methods of Irregular Warfare

January–June 1942

Billy Bones hadn't come back. It had been weeks since mission dispatch, and Olive had resigned herself to the inevitable. There'd been no further communications from Silver A or Anthropoid and nothing at all from Silver B. Olive desperately hoped that the agents' continued silence could be attributed to temporary difficulties. She didn't want to assume the worst, but it was what her mind conjured whenever her thoughts strayed to that fateful night at RAF Tangmere. And given what had happened on the drive home, they strayed often.

Operation Anthropoid had been intended as a swift and brutal assault, and Olive had expected they'd see news of its success— or failure—shortly after the men were dropped into the protectorate. But no news had come through the usual channels, and there'd been nothing on the BBC Czechoslovak service, according to the remaining Czechoslovak agents at the manor. Nothing to indicate that the operation had even been attempted.

Olive knew that Gabček and Kubiš were at the mercy of circumstances and had likely been thwarted by the grim state of affairs in the protectorate. The failure of a previous operation had led to the capture and execution of its agents and the roundup of several major players in the Czech Resistance network. Communication from inside the protectorate to the Secret Intelligence Service in London had been spotty, but they'd managed to get a message across: the Germans had known the paratroopers were coming, and patrols had been dispatched to search for them. The network had then gone dark. So, the Czechoslovak government-in-exile and their Baker Street cohorts were resigned to wait. And pray.

The news, when it finally came several months later, was shocking and heart-wrenching. Word went round through the remaining Resistance network and eventually got back to Britain.

On the morning of 27 May 1942, acting Reich Protector Reinhard Heydrich was on his way to Prague Castle to meet with Hitler. Gabček and Kubiš were waiting. When Heydrich's car—flagrantly open topped and unarmoured—slowed to navigate a turn, Gabček stepped into the street in front of it, armed with a modified Sten gun, prepared to spray it with bullets. But the gun jammed.

Kubiš then retrieved a specially designed grenade from the briefcase he carried, and lobbed it at the car. It missed its target and exploded just above the running board, barely injuring Heydrich. As Gabček and Kubiš made their escape, it seemed their mission, so long in the planning and preparation, was a failure, as Heydrich's Mercedes appeared to be the only significant casualty. But success had not yet eluded them.

As expected, the reprisals were brutal. In the ensuing manhunt, thousands were arrested, and many shot. A ten-million-koruna reward was offered for information leading to the capture of the perpetrators, but it seemed they had disappeared. In little more than a week, Heydrich was dead of septicemia, a complication of his injury. Days later, the Germans, working on information that the paratroopers had connections to the villages of Lidice and Ležáky, set about their utter destruction. Women and children were rounded up and sent to work camps, men were shot, buildings were decimated and burned, and cemeteries desecrated.

Station XVII was stunned by the atrocities. Olive was horrified, worried for the agents who remained in hiding, wondering when the Germans might close in. Her nightmares returned, and she spent her mornings with the pigeons, comforted by their steadfast presence. But it wasn't over. And the news, when it came over the wireless, prompted tears to fall unchecked down her cheeks.

The manhunt continued unceasingly, but sparked by a betrayal, the dominoes at last began to fall. Josef Gabček and Jan Kubiš had taken refuge, with several of the other paratroopers, in a church. It wasn't long before they were surrounded by the enemy. Outnumbered and outgunned, they fought to the bitter end, before choosing suicide over capture.

Heydrich was dead, but at tremendous cost. And Olive, feeling helpless, did the only thing she could. She named a pair of pigeons after the saints whose names graced the church that had sheltered the paratroopers in their last moments: Cyril and Methodius.

Life went on at Station XVII and in the village. The Royal Navy had closed the book on the matter of Mrs Dunbar and had finally put an end to their deception, sending telegrams to the families of the fallen heroes of HMS *Bartholomew*. The village had gathered round in support of Freya Rodery, Mrs Gibbons, and Hen. Lady Revell, in particular, had swept in like a mother hen, wanting to gather them all under her wing. It was to be, Olive believed, a family born of tragedy and hope.

Max was slowly but surely making progress—without any assistance from the belladonna plant—and a smitten Violet could regularly be found at his side. She'd confided that life in Pipley had actually been rather a boon to her writing, given all the murders and intrigue swirling about. Scarlet had come clean to her husband, although certainly not about everything, and was now a regular fixture in the village and at Peregrine Hall.

Danny Tierney had departed for Scotland, and in his absence, Olive had striven to form a closer friendship with Max Dunn. He had an irreverent sense of humour, which very much appealed to her in those fraught days. There were other changes, as well. Kate had been dispatched to begin her own training at Arisaig, and a pair of female agents-in-training had arrived at the manor. Olive occasionally found herself lingering at a window, watching their progress. Even Blighty seemed grudgingly impressed with them.

Jamie happened by one such afternoon. "Have you changed your mind?" he inquired, propping his shoulder on the wall beside her.

Olive shook her head. "There are too many things here that require my attention." Her aspirations of being an agent may have fizzled, but she'd convinced Jamie to carry on with the challenges. Just to keep her hand in. One day, she knew, those unorthodox skills would come in handy.

She inadvertently glanced down at the silver heart gracing her finger, winking in the sunlight. Despite their roundabout declarations and concerted efforts, there'd been a few tricky moments. But she hadn't uttered that secret whispered name even once since he'd taken her into his confidence. Though, at times, she'd been mightily tempted.

With heat rising to her cheeks, she smiled up at him. "I'd better get back to work."

He spoke offhandedly. "New orders have come down from Blighty."

Olive frowned. "You're not being transferred, are you?"

"Why would you guess that?"

"There've been so many comings and goings lately." And something he'd said had niggled at her.

"Well, I'm not one of them." But she knew there was something he wasn't saying.

"That's a relief," she said lightly, before adding, "Are these orders the good sort or the maddening sort?"

"Interestingly enough, they could be both."

"Tell me," she insisted, propping her fists on her hips. While Olive was quite fond of Scarlet Chambers, her husband was another matter entirely. And the feeling was mutual.

"The Americans will shortly be showing up in Hertfordshire with their pigeons, and Blighty wants you to engage with their pigeoneers."

Olive frowned. "For what purpose?"

Jamie kept his expression carefully neutral. "I suspect he wants a second opinion on the way we're handling things before we officially proceed with Operation Gibbon."

"You mean the way *I'm* handling things."

"Don't take it personally. We all just want to win the war. If we can do it faster the American way, do you really want to quibble?"

She looked at him, seeing a different man entirely from the one who had stepped into her dovecote all those months ago. He still infuriated her on occasion, but he was also a voice of reason and encouragement and even seduction, believe it or not.

Olive bit her lip, and Jamie must have recognised the mischief in her eyes. But judging by the manner in which his eyes darkened even as his frown lines appeared, his reaction was mixed. Which meant she had him precisely where she wanted him.

She linked arms with him, turning away from the agents-in-training to face whatever came next. "Fair point. But I fully intend to teach the Americans a thing or two."

Acknowledgments

If this were the end of a movie instead of a book, I would *beg* for the credits to be presented as an exuberant dance scene. It could be a lineup of contributors, like at the end of *Hitch*, or more of a free-for-all, like *When in Rome*. But everyone involved would get a well-deserved moment to strut their stuff.

I can just imagine my editor, John Scognamiglio, and agent, Rebecca Strauss, getting the party started, and then the whole Kensington crew, from design and marketing, to production and editorial, shimmying in to celebrate a job well done. Next would come the booksellers, reviewers, and librarians, who have shown Olive so much love, and finally, the screen would fade to black, with all those lovely book people dancing. Perfection.

As long as I'm imagining this book as a movie, why not go whole hog? When filming (on location in Hertfordshire) finally wrapped and my time across the pond (as consultant to the production) neared its end, I'd throw a little party in the garden of my rented cottage. I'd invite all the family and friends who have supported, assisted, and buoyed me through the writing of this novel (and every day). We'd have a lovely celebration amid Lady of Shalott roses and hollyhocks, under Chinese lanterns and fairy lights. There'd be epic charcuterie boards and gluten-free fairy cakes, and a gazillion Instagram posts.

But since this is a book and not a movie (at least for now)—and because things have gotten a little convoluted—let me be brief:

Thank you to everyone who has cheered for Olive and her pigeons. I'm so grateful to be writing her story.

And merci beaucoup to my nephew, Whitney Martin, for the French translations. Any errors are my own.

Author's Note

The Special Operations Executive (Baker Street) operations mentioned in this book were all actual missions carried out during the Second World War, and the men chosen to participate in Operations Anthropoid, Silver A, and Silver B were trained in part at Brickendonbury Manor. Training was rigorous—even more so than was typical for SOE agents. Jan Kubiš and Josef Gabček, the two soldiers chosen to carry out the assassination of acting Reich protector of the Protectorate of Bohemia and Moravia, Reinhard Heydrich, were accounted imminently qualified for the task. Their mission, while extraordinarily risky, was undertaken with the dual purpose of rousing the demoralised Czechoslovak citizenry and reasserting the country's commitment to the Allies. The Sudetenland was ceded to Germany in 1938, in accordance with the Munich Agreement, and the entirety of Czechoslovakia was subsequently occupied by the Germans in 1939. As the war went on, its people, living under the terror of Nazi rule, were not seen as putting up much resistance against the German war machine, and the Czechoslovak government-in-exile was determined to counter that impression. Heydrich, the Butcher of Prague, was the perfect target.

Gabček and Kubiš and their compatriots were parachuted into the protectorate at the end of December 1941. After months biding their time in hiding, they were able to carry out their mission successfully, despite a jammed Sten gun and somewhat faulty aim. The modified grenade thrown by Kubiš exploded beside the right rear fender of Heydrich's Mercedes, and on June 4, 1942, the Butcher of Prague died of septicemia, a bit of the car's upholstery having lodged itself in his spleen. But his assassins had gone to ground.

The Germans were indiscriminate in their reprisals, rounding up and killing members of the Resistance and families of the paratroopers, and tracking down every individual they imagined might have helped the men. In a grossly inhumane decree from Hitler himself, the village of Lidice was decimated, its men shot, its women dispatched to Ravensbrück concentration camp, its children murdered in an extermination camp in Chelmno, and every building razed to the ground. A smaller village, Ležáky, was also targeted, its buildings destroyed, its thirty-three men and women shot, and all but two of its children sent to Chelmno. The Nazis thought to warn others against similar treachery, but they succeeded only in convincing the world of their cruelty. In response to the reprisals, towns across the world renamed themselves Lidice in remembrance, and the Munich Agreement was deemed null and void by both Britain and France, a decision that would warrant the return of the Sudetenland to Czechoslovakia when Germany lost the war.

The paratroopers were eventually betrayed by one of their own, who led the Germans to various safehouses, where members of the Resistance were tortured for information. Eventually the Germans ran the perpetrators to ground in Prague's Church of Sts. Cyril and Methodius. Seven hundred fifty Schutzstaffel (SS) soldiers, armed with automatic rifles, grenades, water hoses, and tear gas, participated in the two-hour firefight. In the end, the remaining paratroopers chose suicide over capture. Operation Anthropoid was the only successful government-organised assassination attempt on a highly ranked German official during World War II. It took a heavy toll. I highly recommend the 2016 film *Anthropoid* if you want to know more.

While the Czechoslovak soldiers were preparing for their upcoming missions across the Channel, a threat to Britain's national security presented itself in the guise of a Mrs Helen Duncan, self-professed medium. The war years saw an uptick of interest in the spiritualist movement, with an estimated fifty thousand séance circles taking place across Britain, and Mrs Duncan's apparent abilities put her in high demand. Her methods were questioned by the London Spiritualist Alliance, a photographer, an acclaimed psychical researcher, and the police; all were convinced she was a charlatan. Her ectoplasm was nothing more mysterious than cheesecloth, egg whites, and paper; and her spirit guides had papier-mâché faces and bodies crafted of sheets and coat hangers. Still, she was considered relatively harmless until she "conjured" a sailor from the HMS *Barham* at a séance in Portsmouth.

The *Barham*'s sinking had been classified by the Admiralty in an effort to deceive the Germans and stave off a blow to British morale. Mrs Duncan's knowledge of the event instantly made her a person of interest, but her source was never determined, and she continued her séances under threat of police investigation. As D-Day approached, the authorities worried over what she might reveal and moved to silence her. She was arrested on a vagrancy charge but was later charged with obtaining money under false pretenses, purporting to have the powers of a witch, and engaging in public mischief. She was found guilty of "plain dishonesty" and given a jail sentence of nine months, but many believed her powers to be genuine. I've changed the names of both spiritualist (Mrs Dunbar) and ship (HMS *Bartholomew*) so that I could write in my own story details.

Given that Lieutenant Commander Ian Fleming (author of the James Bond thrillers) was at the very same time working as personal assistant to the director of Naval Intelligence—and might conceivably have been dispatched to report on the matter of the fictional Mrs Dunbar—I couldn't resist writing him in. His attitude toward women certainly didn't endear him to Olive, but she was able to see past that unflattering aspect of his character to appreciate his clever, crafty mind. He was the mastermind behind several operations undertaken by the Royal Navy during the war, as well as the architect of the 30 Assault Unit, which is referenced (though not identified outright) in the novel.

Operation Gibbon did, in fact, insert a Special Operations Executive–run pigeon information service into Belgium in February 1942, and while I've found few details of its operation or the people involved, Olive is naturally quite gung ho to be involved. She's reserving judgment on the American pigeoneers.